Ready to Slay

Adam D. Brown

authorHOUSE®

AuthorHouse™
1663 Liberty Drive
Bloomington, IN 47403
www.authorhouse.com
Phone: 1 (800) 839-8640

Published by AuthorHouse   05/29/2019

ISBN: 978-1-5246-1146-0 (sc)
ISBN: 978-1-5246-1144-6 (hc)
ISBN: 978-1-5246-1145-3 (e)

Library of Congress Control Number: 2016908913

Print information available on the last page.

"whereas you do not know what *will happen* tomorrow. For what *is* your life? It is even a vapor that appears for a little time and then vanishes away."

- James 4:14

Chapter 1

Clara thought she was lucky to have someone to attend prom with, even if it was her grandmother. Standing in her bedroom in front of a full-length mirror, the young woman wasn't at all in love with her complexion, nor was she in love with her breasts, which were nonexistent, even with her standing sideways. Sometimes, when she danced in her room and caught a glimpse of herself in the mirror, she would note how her breasts didn't even bounce, in fact they hardly jiggled. Clara wished they were bigger, but she knew such a desire was vain and sinful. Clara was petite with shoulder-length sandy blonde hair. Guys liked blondes best, wasn't that true? Guys liked girls who were virgins, she had heard that too. She looked at her face. Her skin was smooth, which she attributed to contraband skin cream she had smuggled in the house past Meem. (It was Meem's unshakable belief that girls should not be preoccupied with their appearance, "they should only be concerned with God.") She gazed into her eyes: her best feature, she thought, the color of seaweed, a deep green. She looked away from the mirror now, feeling a little embarrassed over how long she had been studying her features.

Rarely did Clara stand so long in front of a mirror, but lately she had felt the need to improve her appearance, or at least make herself more noticeable. How could she reach others for Christ if she didn't stand out somewhat from the crowd? Besides, she wanted to look good tonight. It was the night of her junior prom and she would be stopping by to see who was crowned king and queen. Would Jeremy be King?

Jeremy was her closest friend. They had known each other since 7th grade. He had the most adorable dirty blonde hair and blue eyes. He was so kind and gentle and she had loved him forever. Thinking of that certain irresistible twinkle in his eyes he got when he joked around with her now she felt herself grow wet. Thinking of the times he'd hugged her she felt herself grow wetter. As she put her arms around herself, she imagined they were Jeremy's arms, seeing those bulging

1

biceps as he briefly squeezed her. She felt her nipples – already they had grown taut and rigid. Her eyes widened and she felt a little alarmed over this mysterious heavy sensation between her legs. Her panties were saturated.

Clara lived with her grandmother, her Meem, from the time she was five. Her father had died and her mother, though alive, couldn't provide. Her mother was a severe alcoholic as her father had been before his death from liver failure after spending every night for 20 years on the same stool at the local tavern. Clara herself had never tasted alcohol, not even the wine they offered at church communion. If she had any interest in spirits, it was in the Holy One, the Spirit of Christ Jesus, who she had accepted into her heart at age 11. Accepting Him any younger, she reasoned, had little to no purpose, for how could someone much younger than 11 really understand the significance of accepting Jesus as their personal Lord and Savior?

Before she left for the dance with Meem, she wrote in her diary, a ritual she had observed since she was old enough to hold a crayon:

Lord, please come to me. Thank You for this day, Lord. Lord, You make me so happy!

Whenever I'm the least bit sad, I always remember that You are in my heart & You love me, then it seems as though everything is at least somewhat better. Lately I've come to fully see how nothing and no one can make me experience peace and joy like You Lord. With You I really feel like anything is possible. Lord, lately I've felt the need to reach out to others & help them. I know there are so many students at my school that don't know You, Lord, & I would ask that You please help me to reach some of them so that they might receive Your love & salvation. In Jesus's Name I pray, Amen.

Love,
Clara

Held at The Westman Inn, a local upscale hotel, the theme for the prom was Paradise Isle. Clara had helped decorate and now, standing in the crowd with Meem, she had a brief chance to admire her work. There was a large hand-painted mural along the wall with a beach scene on it. The water was blue, the sand white and there were very green palm trees which seemed to emerge, three-dimensionally, from the painting. Lookalikes were planted in barrels then placed at regular intervals throughout the ballroom. Sparkly streamers dangled down from the ceiling, winking and shining as they reflected light from the artificial tiki torches set in stands about the room's perimeter. Clara thought they had done a fine job transforming the place into an authentically gorgeous beach. A thrill passed through the crowded ballroom like a warm breeze. Clara glanced up at the clock and saw it was about time for the king and queen to be announced. She wanted Catherine and Johnny to win. Catherine was, as far as Clara knew, a nice girl, a virgin, and frequent visitor at the Genesis club meetings, which was far more than she could say about Stephanie.

A small Christian group, Genesis was the only school club Clara belonged to and the only one Meem would allow her to join. It was a place where she felt safe and loved, providing an atmosphere which encouraged its members and non-members to openly express Christian love, sharing testimonies and witnessing to newcomers and nonbelievers.

Clara secretly hoped to be president of Genesis one day, but for now she was wholly satisfied being club secretary and a devoted member. She often witnessed to others at school - telling them about her faith in enthusiastic detail and hoping they would have a positive response. She genuinely wanted to save people, introduce them to Christ's love, and have them join her one day in heaven. Clara knew there were a multitude of skeptics and nonbelievers she could never reach, but she thanked God for every person she was able to save.

If someone asked Clara why she never had a boyfriend, she would tell them she was saving her heart and body for the one – that right godly man she was certain existed somewhere out there waiting for her. Their paths hadn't crossed yet, that's all, and there was nothing wrong with that, as her Meem assured her almost daily. "Your body is an instrument of God, and someday you will share that instrument with a man. Just be sure it's the right man. Until then, let chastity be your watchword and purity your practice." Clara found it rather odd Meem referred to her body as an instrument, but she agreed with her anyway. "Once you do the deed," Meem continued, "You can never be pure again."

"Oh, I know, Meem."

"Do you?"

"Yes, I do. And I am saving myself."

"I love you, Clara."

"I love you too, Meem."

This is how it always was for Clara and Meem. They interacted like mother and daughter.

"Clara!"

Behind her she heard a rich baritone voice, then a hand on her shoulder. Somewhat startled, she turned around to find Jeremy, her good friend, crush, and Vice President of the Genesis Club. "Hi," Clara said, immediately smiling so widely she felt a little embarrassed, not wanting him to know just how happy it made her to see him.

"Did you see Stephanie up there?" It was only when Jeremy motioned toward the front of the ballroom that Clara noticed Stephanie standing near the makeshift stage and podium with a few other members of the prom court. The quintessence of female beauty, Clara thought Stephanie would have a career in modeling if she chose to pursue one, and if she could manage to lose a pound or two.

"No," Clara said curtly. "I didn't see her."

"Yep," Jeremy said. "My girl could be queen."

"Oh, joy."

"Is something wrong?" Jeremy asked.

"No, why?" Unaware her face was flushed and dour, Clara forced herself to smile, her teeth tightly clenched.

"You look sad, that's all."

Clara let her face relax and blew out a cleansing breath, "I don't know," she sighed. "It's just that..." About to explain her feelings, at least a little, Clara stopped herself short, not trusting to open up to him."

"What were you going to say?"

"Never mind."

"No," Jeremy said. "What?"

"Well," she said. "I was thinking we might do something afterward."

"Oh, yeah," Jeremy said, considering. "I'd really like to. Except there's this party I'm going to with Stephanie. I'm sorry."

"Oh, it's OK," she said. "It's pretty late anyway."

4

Jeremy felt bad for Clara, and this is exactly the type of reaction she elicited from many. She hated their pity, wanted to dismiss it, wondered why they felt that way toward her in the first place. Unfortunately, she knew she was a virtual pariah, she didn't fit in anywhere, with the possible exception of the Genesis Club. Her isolation was made worse because everybody who knew her also knew her family background. Closing her eyes, Clara thought: This too shall pass. She felt embarrassed, and wished Jeremy would go off to his trendy party with his chunky girlfriend and just do what popular kids do. She didn't want to talk to him. No longer did she care who was crowned King and Queen, she just wanted it to be over. Sometimes she wished her life would end so she could go home to God. She knew that's not what God wanted, though. God wanted her to endure. God wanted her to live her life to the fullest, but she often experienced days she wished she would go to sleep and never wake up. She didn't think death would be bliss, but sometimes she thought it would have to be better than living like this. On these occasions, she looked flirtatiously at her sleeping pills. No, she thought, that's sin. Sin!

Believing she would go to hell if she were to empty a bottle, she never went through with it. She believed she would miss the small things in life – long hot showers, baking cookies with Meem, taking walks downtown and reading. Sometimes she would just lay all day in her bed, curling up with a good book and gazing out her window as the snow fell. Waiting for the evening, dreaming of Jeremy or some other boy she had met, she wished she had a friend she might call.

Two girls from Genesis Club had given Clara their numbers, but Clara had never followed through. She didn't want to seem desperate, and she knew they had given her their name simply because they felt sorry for her. Tammy and Christina were both popular girls, and the only thing Clara could see she had in common with them was the fact they were both virgins who claimed to be waiting until marriage to have sex, both saving themselves for their one special man to come along.

At this rate, Clara would never find the one because no one took the time to get to know her. Tammy and Chris seemed inundated with requests – boys with blue balls begging them to cop a feel. But, no.

Tammy and Christina would only ever kiss (though Clara had heard a rumor – no, she did not seek out gossip, she simply overheard it in the locker room – one day after gym class, a couple girls were talking, and one said Chris had allowed a guy to "feel her up" and the other said Chris had "done things to make him happy.")

Clara often felt she was missing out on something, but she couldn't put a finger on it, couldn't quite identify what she might be missing out on. She missed boys that were only acquaintances: a boy here, a boy there, a boy from her gym class, a boy that sat close to her in Trigonometry. She longed for their brief and casual attention, and her heart sank with how pathetic that was. Certainly, they didn't miss her. Probably couldn't even pick her up out of a lineup. Sometimes Clara would write their names in her secret diary, a place where she memorialized boys that were nice to her, telling stories about how they had met, how long they were acquainted, brief conversations they had shared, and so on.

"Meem, can we go now?" Clara said, aware as she said it that would not work. The whole reason they had come to the prom was to see who was crowned king and queen. Meem looked at her, not having heard the question.

"What?" Jeremy turned toward her, apparently not hearing her either over the soft music and loud conversations.

"Never mind."

"They'll be announcing king and queen any minute now," Jeremy said.

Any minute now, Clara thought, *great, then I can go home and sleep.*

Chapter 2

Karen wasn't ready, as usual. Benjamin pulled up to her house and she wasn't ready. Again. Through the window he could see her — she fiddled with her hair, applied eyeliner, slipped on her black Doc Martens. She wasn't a girl to fool around with appearances, but she really liked Benjamin, and she knew he could replace her in a minute. Several times he had told her so. Often she wanted to get rid of him. Often she hated him. There were other times, though, when she felt nothing but potent love for him.

The first time she saw him she fell under his spell. Those blue eyes. The moment they locked with hers, she knew. It had been in the library. She had been working at the checkout desk and she remembered thinking what a surprise it was she would see a radical character like him in such a studious place as this.

Over the years, Karen had heard many things about him, a lot she didn't quite believe could be true. She had heard he belonged to a satanic cult, earning his membership by sacrificing eight different animals, including a number of cats which he had tortured and killed then allowed to decompose before taking the bones to make a necklace. When she first met him, it was one of the first things she checked. Seeing he wore no such necklace, Karen began to wonder how much else of what she had heard about him was nothing more than unfair rumors springing from a combination of student boredom and curiosity.

She heard his horn calling her from the driveway.

"I'm coming!" she shouted out the window, thinking how much she liked making him wait like this. She was usually the one who waited for him. He always took forever to get ready.

All that makeup he wore (the three standards: white face makeup, black eyeliner, black lipstick.) Before moving outside, she put on her favorite black jacket. Purchased at Hot Topic a few months ago, it had become her uniform once Benjamin had designed and sewn an intricate spider web pattern on the back of it. Karen could remember being quite impressed by the fact he could sew, almost as impressed as she had been over his tattoos, which covered over 15% of his body, or so he claimed.

Benjamin waited a couple minutes longer before throwing open the car door, rushing toward the house. Knowing her parents weren't home, he stormed inside. "Karen!" he shouted, climbing the stairs. "What the fuck are you doing?"

"Don't you knock?"

Benjamin moved into her bedroom and grabbed her wrists, pinning her against her open bedroom door. "You think you can make me wait like that, huh?"

"I didn't know you were –"

"Now you can wait on me."

"What?"

"Service me." He unzipped his jeans, his penis poking through his boxers - already he was hard. Without much hesitation, Karen dropped to her knees and began pleasing him.

Minutes later they were in Benjamin's car. "Where?" he asked.

"Huh?"

"Where do you want to go?"

"Wherever you wanna take me."

"I wanted to crash prom."

"That's tonight?"

He nodded.

"How?" Karen asked.

"I don't know," he said. This was just like him, coming up with ideas he would never follow up on. Like the time he said they would go on a vacation to an exotic island. Or the time he said they would destroy the life of Keith Samuels, the star quarterback who they loathed. He was so popular and hunky they had to listen to students and faculty alike sing his praises all the time.

"Let's just go back to your place," Karen said.

"Don't want to."

"Wanna go for ice cream?"

"What are we, ten years old? Ice cream?"

"Well, that place on Samson Avenue that has the best milkshakes just opened this week."

"I don't want ice cream."

"Hmm," Karen said. "We could go to Curt's Cliff and make out."

"Oh, so now we're fourteen. Fifteen? Jesus, K. If I'm going to screw you, I'm going to screw you. I don't need you to suggest it."

"All right. Christ," Karen then repeated Christ.

"I have a better idea."

"Yeah?"

"Do you trust me?"

"What?"

Benjamin turned around and grabbed a cooler from the backseat. Reaching inside he pulled out what appeared to be a large sewing needle. "Do you trust me?"

"Yeah." Karen sounded reluctant as she stared inside the cooler, seeing there was also a washcloth and some ice. "Yes."

He leaned toward her, needle in hand, touching her top lip and then her bottom lip.

"You wanna be forever? I pierce you, and then I pierce myself. When we bleed, we have to mix our blood together."

"I'd rather do it myself."

"Not a good idea."

"Why?"

"Fine." Benjamin handed her the needle. "Do it."

"Well, why'd you –"

"It'll hurt more if you do it."

Karen looked at him, giving him the needle back. "OK. Not in my driveway though. Let's go somewhere else and do it."

Benjamin grinned. "K, K." She found it unusual for him to agree with her so quickly. "And then we can really do it, OK."

"What?"

Benjamin shook his head as though she should forget what he had just said.

"Oh," Karen said, getting it. "Let's go back to your place and then maybe. Didn't you want to go to prom though?"

"Fuck that."

Benjamin peeled out of the driveway, and there was a squeal of brakes, the sound of teenagers anxious to start their evening.

Clara recognized him the moment he walked into the gymnasium. Where from, though?

That's right, last year he had been in her study hall, his name was Benjamin. Not that they had ever really spoken, but how could she forget him? The bizarre clothes he wore, all of his tattoos, the makeup, and those eyes. Yes, she had to admit: his eyes were gorgeous. They were so blue and intense. One time in study hall he had asked her for a pen, staring at her so directly that she had to look away, feeling a little disturbed by how attracted she was to a guy who could only be forbidden to her. Clara also saw the girl at his side that had a large ring through her lip. She didn't recognize her, though.

At the last minute Karen and Benjamin decided to go to prom, if for no other reason than to make people uncomfortable by their very presence. These preppy kids who thought prom was so important made them laugh. Benjamin thought the kids on prom court were the most amusing. He thought them all dumb animals, sheep who associated their own popularity and subsequent worth with the ability to fit in. He thought it would be funny to come to one of these popular school functions with a gun and start shooting, opening fire on all these preps and jocks. He would need to make sure he had enough ammo. After all, he wouldn't want to leave any witnesses. He grinned at Karen, as though to dismiss the gravity of his thoughts.

"What?" she said, for he was never one to smile so suddenly and for no apparent reason.

"Your lip ring," he said. "Looks good on you."

"Oh, I know, I love it!"

The whole process had been relatively quick and painless. He had numbed her lip with ice, so there had not been as much blood as she had expected.

"That girl's staring at you," Karen said.

By the time Benjamin turned to see, Clara had looked away, quickly averting her eyes in much the same way as she had last year in study hall.

"Do you know her?" Karen asked.

He shook his head.

"Well, she looks like she knows you."

The two had been lingering in the lobby for some time, standing beside a trophy display case and a large bulletin board displaying various and sundry announcements. One announcement in particular caught Benjamin's eye – *We would love to know you, so you can get to know Him – Genesis Club meeting Monday May 25 @ 10 A.M. in room 309.* He knew enough about Genesis Club to know it was a Christian organization and not much more. *Kill two birds with one stone,* he thought, knowing that if he attended this meeting he would not only have the opportunity to make trouble, but he would also get to miss class. He nudged Karen.

"Let's go to this club Monday," he said, pointing to the neon orange flyer on the bulletin board.

"What's Genesis Club?" She scanned the announcement and quickly rolled her eyes.

"Oh, that Christian club. Yeah, right."

"Don't you want to be saved?"

"Oh, you're an asshole."

"I'm serious about going."

"Fine," Karen said, not giving much thought to the whole idea. "We'll go."

That night in her diary Clara wrote:

Dear Heavenly Father,

    Lord, I long to be with You. I feel Your love surrounding me & inside of me & I always know I can come to You when I feel defeated in this world. I just feel so peaceful with You in my life Lord. Thank You so much for being in my life & for loving me even when I feel no one else really does. Lord, thank You for all you have blessed me w/! Thank You for my wonderful Meem. Thank You for showing me the right way in life, which leads me closer to You. Lord, please always be in my life & shine Your light through me. I love You so much Lord! I will always love You! Please help me to be closer to You Lord & please help my actions to show that I am a Christian. Lord, it just amazes me to know that You gave up your life for everyone on this earth so that we may live w/ You forever & so that our sins may be forgiven. Thank You so much Lord for my life.

Lord I must also say how I love finding out new things about myself w/ Your help & I look forward to getting to know You better. With You in my life Lord I feel like such a better person. I feel like I judge others a lot less & I put others' feelings before my own more often. I love people so much, Lord. I find myself trying to pick out the good in everyone because I know that is what Christ did, & Lord I want to serve You & only You & follow You in all I do. I pray that others can see Your love & kindness shining through me so they will know there is something different about me & that I then might have the chance to talk to them about Christ.

Love,
Clara

Chapter 3

On Monday during Genesis Club, Mrs. Henderson tried her best to ignore them. Attention is what they were after, and she wasn't going to give them what they wanted. Their obvious objective every day in dressing that way was to make people look at them, create controversy, thereby garnering attention. Genesis Club was open to everyone. As the faculty advisor she fully understood that, one of the club's goals being to welcome students of all different religious backgrounds. How else could they expect to reach nonbelievers, causing the club to grow? It was hard to ignore them, though — as they sat so nonchalantly in their seats, being defiant and making a mockery of God by their very presence. Multiple times she had to remind herself how Christ wouldn't have turned them away.

Clara herself tried to ignore them as well. She had no problem ignoring Karen. With Benjamin, well, that was different. He wasn't her type, to say the least. Still, she felt a strange magnetic attraction toward him. It wasn't only his eyes, it was the severe confidence he projected, and the fact he was attending Genesis Club made Clara believe she had a genuine opportunity to save his soul.

On that rather fateful dreary day, a Monday morning, when he had first walked into the classroom, Clara had felt intrigued by Benjamin and slightly afraid of him. Never had she talked to him before, not even when he had asked her for a pen in study hall. At the time she had only shook her head no.

Benjamin and Karen had been surprised they weren't asked to leave. As they sat there talking out of turn mostly, laughing during prayer, then describing how they didn't believe in God, they would admit to anyone they had stopped by to make trouble. In fact, their goal was to be asked to leave so they could protest and make a scene. No such luck that day.

"So what does God look like anyway? Is God even a man?" Benjamin had asked. "Is God old? Like with a long flowing white beard?"

Jeremy himself didn't have much of a problem ignoring them. He thought them both losers who dressed so outlandishly in an effort to be noticed or piss off their parents. He didn't mind their questions. They weren't asking foolish things, he thought their questions were worthwhile. Seldom did these Christian kids ask any questions at all. They blindly accepted their faith and surrendered to the will of Jesus Christ, humbly asking Him to remove all their shortcomings, humbly asking His forgiveness. For what, Jeremy sometimes wondered? The forty or so students who regularly attended never did anything he could see that would be recognized as sinful. Jeremy himself sinned quite often. As the Goth weirdos were acting out, Jeremy listed his sins in his head. Premarital sex was supposedly a sin, and Jeremy swore like a sailor. Sometimes he smoked, but a little nicotine now and then never hurt anyone, right? He had lustful thoughts, often undressing women with his eyes, like Mrs. Henderson. He could imagine her fat, pendulous breasts swinging their large tan nipples right in his face as she rode him like a crazed weasel. Fuck, he was a guy, he couldn't help that shit. Besides, those dresses she had been wearing lately had been so tight it was only human nature for him to imagine her naked. "Nature is sinful in itself," Clara had told him once. At the time, he hadn't disagreed, but he secretly thought she was wrong.

Seeing Clara again, Benjamin knew she looked familiar, though he couldn't quite place her. He thought she was very cute, and suddenly there was only one thing on his mind: how to get her in bed. He liked challenges, and this would be a challenge, he knew. Did she know what constituted oral sex?

Being here in a room surrounded by Christians didn't make Benjamin think he was a bad person. Not that he thought he was a good person either. It was a consideration of no consequence to him either way. He was what he was. If pressed, he'd say he was like everybody else, falling somewhere in the middle of the spectrum. Sure, he committed his share of what Christians would call sins, but wasn't that part of being human? If there was a God, Benjamin found it hard to believe He wouldn't expect us to enjoy being fully human. Perfection was unattainable, while sin could be found everywhere. It stood to reason, at least in Benjamin's mind, God must be sin's biggest fan, there was so much of it in the world He had created. So if Clara sinned in her thoughts, thinking negatively about another person and Benjamin smoked pot it didn't matter – all sin is equal in the eyes of the Lord. Not that Benjamin gave much thought to religion or God in general. Mostly, Benjamin thought of death metal music and drugs and tattoos and girls and guns. He seldom thought of Karen, truth be told. He'd had her so many times there was no challenge, no mystery. Shit, she gave herself up to him on a daily basis. Where was the fun in that? Poking Karen rarely made him feel like a real man anymore and he didn't think that was his problem. There was no adventure with her these days. Real men venture out and destroy and conquer. He was not destroying anything or anyone nor was he conquering. Sure, he still had sex with her, but for the most part Karen had slowly become undesirable to him. When the right time came he was fully prepared to cut her loose.

Clara didn't know what to say to her. Karen – leaning against Clara's locker after Genesis Club, arms folded across her chest appearing as though she had been waiting for her. Possibly, Clara thought she could start out by asking her what she was doing here. Instead she said nothing, hoping that silence would be effective in getting her to go away.

"I like your hair," Karen said.

Clara was surprised by that compliment. She herself had never liked her hair – it was too coarse.

"Look, is there something you want, Karen?" Clara asked, trying not to appear as uncomfortable as she felt. She still thought she sounded a bit harsh so she added: "If you want you can still come to Genesis. But otherwise please leave me alone."

"I don't really give a rat's ass about the club."

She felt a little offended, but Clara could appreciate Karen's bluntness and her honesty.

She did wonder why she was being honest now. Why not right up front? Why did she feign interest in a club that was entirely voluntary? For a moment, Clara thought Karen must care for her to a degree. Then, quickly, she dismissed this conclusion, thinking a more likely one was that Karen was just mocking her.

As the girls stared at each other Clara felt her heart race. "I - I have nothing more to say to you." Immediately she thought that sounded weak, certainly it had been unnecessary.

"Don't you?"

"If you want to hear more about Christ's love then come to the next meeting, OK?"

"No," Karen said. "I'd like to hang out sometime though. I think you have such potential."

"Potential?"

Karen nodded, and Clara couldn't help but to feel slightly excited over the fact that someone, who in her mind seemed to be one of the cool kids, was taking an active interest in her, wanting to spend time with her.

"Well, we should talk first," Clara said. "I mean before we hang out, we –"

"What's there to talk about?"

"Well, faith," Clara said. "I wanted to know if you believed in Jesus Christ. As a Christian, I feel it's important for me to –"

"I know who He is."

"Well," Clara said, searching for the right words. "Do you believe He is your personal Lord and Savior?"

Karen considered briefly. "No. That's why I think we should hang out. I want to know more about Christianity, you know?"

"You do?" Clara hesitated, thinking maybe it might be best to just walk away now – after all, Karen already said she didn't care about Genesis Club. Still, another part of Clara's consciousness nudged her in the direction of thinking that just because Karen had no interest in the club doesn't mean she had no interest in knowing God and being saved.

"I want to accept Christ into my heart," Karen said after a brief pause, "I do – you see, I just need to know more before I make a decision."

Clara thought Karen looked insincere. Her words were so carefully chosen she couldn't possibly mean them. "Please," Clara said finally. "Drop the act."

"Excuse me?"

Wait, Clara thought, was that rude? Should she be more patient with a nonbeliever, not so cynical? "If you really want to spend time with me, why don't you just ask?"

"I didn't know it would be so simple."

"What?"

"Do you want to hang out sometime?"

Clara grabbed one last book out of her locker as the bell rang. "Maybe."

"When will you know for sure?"

Clara scribbled down a number on a slip of paper and handed it to Karen. "Call me sometime if you want."

"I will." When Karen smiled Clara felt uneasy. "When do you think you –"

"I have to get to class," Clara said. "I don't want to be late."

Before Karen could say anything Clara turned around, looking worried as she hurried on down the hall.

The moment Clara got home in her bedroom she began dancing like no one was watching, which was alright, because no one was. She had heard somewhere that you were supposed to dance like that. She didn't get the chance to dance at prom, so she thought she might as well dance in her bedroom. Even if she was alone, Clara slipped on a white dress. She really liked the color white because she thought it represented purity. Meem had recently remarked the dress was too short, though it was barely above the knee. (Clara thought the dress being white made up for the fact that perhaps it was too short.)

Clara didn't know why she should wonder about her. Karen. Just what had she meant when she said she had *potential*? Was that a compliment? Was she being sarcastic? Was she sarcastic when she said she liked her hair?

Extracting her diary from the top drawer of her bureau, with her new ballpoint pen Clara began writing:

> For some reason, I just love to write real late at night, just before I crawl under my covers & fall asleep. I think I have a very open mind at nighttime. I always think the most before I fall asleep. Well, today was a pretty good day, mostly because we had a successful Genesis Club meeting with two new people who attended. Even if they are nonbelievers & even if they don't seem to be much interested in the club at this point, I was still happy to have them there. I feel confident I can witness to them. Lord, I am just so thankful that You have blessed me with Meem and Jeremy. I care for them both so much that I cannot even express how much. Lord, I am also very thankful as always that You are in my life and in my heart. Lord, please help me to be a better Christian & not judge nonbelievers. Help me to reach out to others who are hurting & help to ease their pain by telling them about You Lord.
>
> Love,
> Clara

Chapter 4

At the end of the week Karen and Benjamin attended Genesis Club again – it was the last meeting of the year and was being held to discuss the fundraiser.

"So let's get started here," Mrs. Henderson said. She waited for Benjamin and Karen to interrupt her, but they said nothing. They just sat there silently staring at her and Clara. Mrs. Henderson didn't like the way they were looking at Clara – she thought they might be making fun of her. "First order of business – the bake sale," Mrs. Henderson said. "Aaron, you want to take it from here?"

Aaron, president of Genesis Club, nodded and Mrs. Henderson stepped aside. He started talking about the fundraiser – a bake sale at Walgreens being held next week, the next to last week of school. As Aaron continued talking, Karen began composing two letters: one to Clara, and one to Jake, a prisoner at the county jail who she corresponded with weekly.

Benjamin didn't know she wrote Jake these letters. She thought he might have been jealous otherwise. Listening closely to Aaron, Benjamin thought it would be amusing to volunteer for the bake sale – he would make pot brownies and sell those. He had become so sick of high school and he had always wanted to be able to say he was in jail (he thought it would give him street credibility) so the punishment didn't deter him – getting expelled and arrested. Deterring him was the simple fact he didn't want to waste the pot on a bunch of random people he didn't know. He wanted to smoke the pot himself, with Clara preferably (he knew that was a long shot), and Karen if she insisted, which she most likely would. Benjamin was tired of this, terribly tired of the meeting, of school, the static narrow-minded students who seemed to populate this school. It no longer entertained him – making sport of these kids was just too easy. He wanted a real challenge. He looked at Clara, stared at her and, for a moment, he thought their eyes locked. She looked away then, as though she had seen a ghost, and that's when Benjamin knew he was right – their eyes had locked.

"We'll make something," Benjamin said. "Cookies."

"OK," Aaron said, sounding surprised though somewhat grateful. "How many did you want to make?"

"Three dozen or so," Benjamin said. "Karen will help me, won't you, babe?"

Karen looked up from her desk. Benjamin thought she had fallen asleep, but really she had been sketching a series of arbitrary vivid images she remembered from the last time she had tripped on shrooms with him. "What? Sure," Karen said finally.

A precarious situation, Mrs. Henderson thought, should she stop this now and say something? Or allow things to unravel as they inevitably would? It was clear to her that Benjamin and Karen had a definite interest in Clara, though she couldn't say exactly why, or how, their interest had developed very suddenly. When she had seen their names on the sign-up sheet for the club indicating that they wanted to become official members she thought really? Why? Mrs. Henderson didn't mind they were getting involved, but just what were they doing joining Genesis with only one week left in the school year?

Should she telephone the girl's grandmother? No, it had taken Mrs. Henderson a long time to earn Clara's trust. Any semblance of a relationship she thought would be over if she called Dorothy, who she had only met twice. Still, she worried. Just yesterday she saw Clara standing at Karen's locker, Karen laughing about something and Clara herself appearing somewhat pensive.

In her diary that evening Clara wrote:

> Lord, please be w/ me as I read Your comforting
> words & please help me to better understand Your ways.
> Lord, please draw me closer to You, so I may know You

better, Lord, & be a better Christian. Thank You Lord for bringing Karen & Benjamin into my life. I really pray for them, & hope that I can be a light & show them Christ's love and save them. Lord, I pray for guidance as the end of the school year is fast approaching & I really don't know what I'm going to do. Even though Meem has said nothing about me getting a job, I really think I'd like to have one. I have no idea where. But I think it would be good for me. Otherwise I don't know what I'm going to do w/ all my free time.

"For by grace you have been saved through faith, and this is not from you; it is the gift of God; it is not from works, so that no one may boast." – Ephesians 2:8-9

Love,
Clara

Minutes later, over a cup of tea, Clara shared a small amount of information about her day. Meem's ears seemed to perk up when Clara informed her of these "two new people" she had "kind of" met. Clara made it clear her intentions to save these classmates of hers who "didn't know God."

"Just because someone feels sorry for you doesn't mean they like you." Meem's comment, though possibly astute and insightful, did not apply to anything Clara had just said.

"I know, I know that," Clara said, eventually, feeling somewhat hurt. "But I just want to let you know that I think these are, or can be, friends. Real friends. More than just two people I witness to, you know? They've been waiting I think, just waiting for someone . . . to come along and show them."

"Show them what?"

"Christ's light."

Meem looked at her as though she had said something absurd. "Christ's light?"

Clara considered for a moment: "Yes."

"Oh, don't be so naïve, darling. They are using you. Make no mistake about it. Soon they'll get tired of you and then throw you away like trash." Always Meem had a rather harsh way of putting things, but Clara accepted this as Meem's way – she cared deeply for Clara, and that manifested by showing concern. Clara was certain she meant no harm, certain she meant to simply look out for her personal welfare and Clara loved her for it, but Clara couldn't help but feel that Meem was stifling her. If Karen and Benjamin were using her, whatever were they using her for? As far as Clara could see, they had nothing to gain from their friendship with her.

Perhaps, they really were looking to turn their lives around. The more Clara thought about it, the more she believed that was the case: *yes, and who better than me to try and help them? After all, Jesus helped sinners and outcasts.*

That night Clara could not sleep. At least three times a day she prayed – asking forgiveness for her sins, mostly. Thanking God for all the things in her life that were good and pure. Gratitude, she thought, was such an important thing. It was entirely too easy to become inundated with what's going wrong in one's life. She asked God to guide her, to give her some direction. The lights had been off for almost an hour when Clara gave up on sleep and decided to turn them back on. Saying another prayer did nothing. Often, reciting a rote prayer such as Hail Mary or Our Father did help her to drift off, but those prayers were meaningless, she thought. Like memorizing arbitrary facts and trivia and then regurgitating them on a test. Within a week, you forget.

Clara climbed out of bed and moved over to her bureau. Glancing at herself in the mirror, she wondered if she was pretty. Oh, how she hated this! How long she debated her looks! God did not want girls to be caught up with their appearance. She knew one's physical appearance was ephemeral, fleeting and unimportant, so why should it matter? Ugh, she wished she could just be certain of anything! If she knew she was beautiful, she wouldn't obsess over herself in the mirror so much. Pride was one of the seven deadly sins. But she didn't have any pride over her appearance, not at all. She just had one pressing question: Am I good enough? She didn't know. Meem had never complimented, or even commented on, her appearance. If she was honest she had many other questions, too, born out of a sense of self-doubt. These questions, most of them, had surfaced when she was a very young girl. Questions that revolved around whether she was good enough. Did she deserve happiness? Was she worthy of a boy's love? Her parents had abandoned her. Wasn't that an indication of her inferiority? Yes, she must have done something wrong, something sinful, what was it? Sometimes, she felt God had punished her with parents who were absent and unavailable. But, why? Desperately, she wanted to know, what had she done?

"Oh, stop navel-gazing." Clara could hear Meem in her mind. She had heard Meem say this many times before, "Waxing philosophical on matters solves nothing. Unless of course you're a philosopher. And even then it's dubious." Meem usually dispensed good advice and Clara invariably tried to take it. Now, standing naked in front of her mirror, she felt she was beginning a new chapter, one where she would decide things for herself, one where she would be in charge.

The next day Clara snuck out of the house without Meem knowing she had left.

"Clara," Meem called up the stairway. No answer. Meem assumed she had gone. Each day Clara left around the same time, normally having a short conversation with her before leaving, kissing her on the cheek and saying something like, "Have a good day. I'll see you after school."

Clara's car was gone. Why had she left without saying anything? Probably, Meem thought, she was just in a hurry, had to get to school for a meeting. Still, it irritated her, made her a little angry. After all she had done for that girl! How dare she fail to extend her the courtesy of a "Good morning" and kiss on the cheek? Well, she would have words with her as soon as she got home from school, that much was certain.

Chapter 5

Clara was afraid. She had ducked out the front door nearly ten minutes before her usual departure time for three reasons. Lipstick. Mascara. Eyeliner. (She didn't own any foundation, had only experimented with it once at the local mall when she had received a complimentary 'beauty assessment' at the Estee Lauder cosmetics counter.) Too, her hair was saturated with hairspray and styled with a wet, slick look. Never had she dared leave the house with makeup on, she was too afraid of Meem's reaction. She would deal with her later, maybe wash the makeup off before she went home.

Moving toward her locker that morning Clara noticed the hall was rather empty. She wondered briefly why, then realized she had arrived ten minutes earlier than usual. She felt so empty, standing in the echoing hallway, so lonely. With the possible exception of Mrs. Henderson, Clara had no real friends, no relationship with anyone that was deep and true. Sure, she had a great many acquaintances, mostly through her involvement with Genesis club. Not too long ago, she considered Meem her best friend. She used to tell Meem everything: her thoughts, feelings, desires. Slowly she grew out of this, feeling Meem did not understand. Mrs. Henderson said a generation gap was likely to be responsible for the sense of disconnect. Clara had to grudgingly agree.

Another obstacle to sharing with Meem was her incessant judging of everything. Never could Meem just listen. No, Meem insisted on burdening Clara with advice based wholly on scripture. After she confided in Meem, Clara invariably felt a strong, unshakable need to pray.

At night, then, she would pray until she fell asleep. Down on her knees, Clara would ask God for forgiveness, imploring Him to save her from her sinful ways. From the time she was born, she knew she was a sinner. All people, she knew, are born sinners. Christians call this 'original sin.'

When Clara was barely old enough to read, she remembered Meem talking about it. As she took her physics textbook from her locker, Clara thought: *yes, it is only through His love and grace that we are saved from our sins, only through Him that we can go to heaven.* She was saved already, though. The summer before she had entered middle school, Meem had sat her down and given her 'the talk'. Not the sex talk, the 'salvation' talk.

By sixth grade, the general consensus was everyone knew all about sex, anyway. Some had even had sex. Clara was unsure how to assess what constituted sex. As far as she knew, oral sex was sex, though it was not intercourse. Clara believed when a classmate whispered (if it was a girl) or proudly proclaimed (if it was a boy) they had done 'it', it indicated they had engaged in sexual intercourse and were therefore no longer virgins. Clara daydreamed about sex at times, wondering what it would be like, who it would be with, and whether or not she would still be considered a virgin if she sucked a guy's penis.

When she would come back to herself, she would quickly push these fantasies out of her mind and think of God and Him only. She would feel guilty for having those thoughts to begin with, ones she knew were impure and sinful. She wasn't always successful in switching subjects in her mind, but God knew how hard she tried, didn't he? Yes, He knew, He had to know.

Clara tried to keep her head down as she moved down the now filling hallway, not wanting to see the students she walked by, fearing she would be consumed with what they thought about her being all dolled up. Would they approve? Or would they be disgusted, casting slightly scornful glances her way? She didn't consider the other possibility: they might not care very much at all, being too caught up with their own day to care about her and how she looked. It was likely they wouldn't notice her transformation, and she *had* transformed herself, in a way that was subtle, and yet noteworthy. She wished she had the confidence to not care, to be blasé and project that 'as if' attitude so many of the pretty girls embodied. Mrs. Henderson had told her more than once she shouldn't be so insecure. She had plenty of reasons to feel confident and worthy. "What are those reasons?" Clara had asked her. Mrs. Henderson had looked at her and said, "Well, half the fun is finding out for yourself what those things are, honey. How about you start with this? When you wake up in the morning, look in the mirror and tell yourself positive things about you. What positive things you choose are up to you. You can say them aloud or silently to yourself, just make sure you say them. Pretty soon, I promise, you will believe them." For three weeks Clara had tried that last school year – when it hadn't seemed to work very well she stopped doing it.

Clara had almost reached homeroom when she heard her name and stopped. A hand on her shoulder made her spin around, startled.

"K-Karen."

"You look like you've seen a ghost."

"What, I –"

"Come on." Karen grabbed her by the hand. "You still have time before the bell rings. Let's get you fixed up."

Minutes later the girls stood in front of the mirror in the Girl's room. "You look like a ghost. I'm no makeup expert, but this isn't working." Clara tried to be as detached as possible as she stared at herself in the mirror with Karen assessing her at her side. "What I mean is your complexion is not right for this eyeliner. And this mascara!"

"What about it?"

"Too severe. Believe me, I know."

"Oh."

"Also you have on way too much lipstick. Do you want the guys to think you're easy?"

"Easy?"

"Oh, Clara…"

"I think I might know what you mean, I. You mean, like, slutty?"

"Uh-huh."

"I, I don't want them to, to think that."

"Of course you don't."

"What should I do?"

Karen considered. "There's not much you can do, not right now at least. Have you ever tanned?"

"At the beach once in Maine. I mean, when I was much younger. Sometimes I do over the summer, but not on purpose. When I go for walks I'll have on a tank-top and shorts and I get tan that way and –"

"Relax!"

"What?"

"Haven't you ever heard of a salon? Tanning beds. Cancer cribs?"

"Oh, I never –"

"Come with me sometime."

"I've never done that. I couldn't if I…how much does it cost? I don't have much money and –"

"It's inexpensive. I only started going because it was convenient."

"What do you mean?"

"For me and Benjamin. When we started dating. It was an easy place to go have sex."

"What?"

"You heard me."

"You have sex with him?"

"Oh, Clara…"

"I mean I thought maybe you did. I just never heard a girl –"

"Say fuck?"

"Well…"

"Say fuck."

"What?"

"Fuck. Say fuck. I mean you say it. Fuck."

"What?"

"Are you deaf?"

"No, I –"

"Look in the mirror with me." Clara was turned to the side at this point, facing the cold beige tiled bathroom walls. Karen grabbed her hand and squeezed it, as Clara seemed to be frozen, still, not moving, sinking into the tiles, her mind sifting through everything Karen had just said. Clara turned around, looking into the mirror with Karen.

"What do you want from me?" she whispered.

"For you to utter one simple expletive."

"I…"

"I guarantee you will never have any balls unless you can say fuck, and not feel bad about saying it. Forget all that Christian crap. Look, God doesn't care if you swear."

"He doesn't?" Clara asked, the whispered under her breath, "He does."

"Fuck fuck fuck." Karen laughed.

"I..."

Karen squeezed Clara's hand hard, crushing her tiny hand in her own much larger one.

"Ow, fuck," Clara said reflexively, more out of reaction to the sharp shot of pain than anything else.

Karen smiled, a little. "Feel better?"

"No, I..."

Karen squeezed her hand again, even harder. Clara held it in this time and said nothing, pulling away as she tried to escape Karen's deliberate firm grasp. Karen was much stronger than she.

"Fuck fuck fuck," Karen said, grinning, squeezing Clara's hand even harder. Clara thought she might break the bones in her hand. "Fuck," Clara said. "Fuck!"

Karen let go. Clara looked at her, shaking her hand as though she had a cramp in it. "I don't know what you want with me..." Clara backed away from Karen slowly, as though unsure whether she wanted to leave the bathroom and never see her again or stay and talk to her for hours.

"It's not me, Clara," Karen said. "It's you. It's what you want. God has led you to me. To Benjamin too. You have to believe that."

"I believe that God has -"

"You don't know what you fuckin' believe! You know it's the truth."

"Leave me alone!" Clara dashed out the bathroom door.

Karen opened her mouth to say something. She didn't know what, but, surely she might stop her, might try to explain something to her. Karen turned to leer at herself in the mirror.

She believed Clara would come back to her. Give her space, give her time, she will come back.

Clara arrived to her homeroom thirty seconds past the bell. She had not been late to homeroom all school year. Mr. Pratt looked at her as she entered, his raised eyebrows a judgment, but he did not say anything. Clara had a hard time holding back the tears that were welling up in her eyes. She didn't understand any of it, what had just happened, and she didn't know why she continued thinking about Karen, someone who clearly wanted to hurt her.

"Hey," said a smooth, deep voice behind her, one she did not acknowledge, her mind too occupied with Karen.

"Clara," Jeremy said, but she didn't turn to see him. "Are you OK?"

Clara peeked over her shoulder, her anxious, timid gaze meeting his calm, confident one. "I'm fine."

"You sure?"

"Yes!"

Clara faced forward in her seat now, listening to Mr. Pratt as he read off the announcements.

"Well, you look nice today. Wanted to tell you that."

Clara could feel the red rising on her cheeks. Maybe blushing would help with her pale complexion? She smiled slightly, thinking herself clever, at least a little. In this moment, she felt pretty. In this moment, she dismissed Karen and thought solely of Jeremy. Jeremy who was sitting behind her, Jeremy who rarely said anything beyond a nonchalant 'hey' when she arrived in homeroom. For a moment, Clara thought she might return the compliment. She reconsidered then, reasoning such a compliment would not be genuine, not quite, since Jeremy looked good every day. He gave the impression he had simply rolled out of bed and reached for the first clean shirt and pair of shorts he could find. Clara loved how laid back he was and wished she could be more relaxed like that. But Jeremy made up for his casual clothing with his hair. His hair was styled with gel or mousse. It always looked perfect.

"What are you doing this weekend?" he asked.

Never had Jeremy so clearly tried to start and sustain a conversation with her. Never had Clara been this reticent as a reaction to his attempts.

"Oh," Clara said. "Things."

Pause. Clara could imagine Jeremy was waiting for her to ask what he was doing.

"I'm playing in the district championships and then hosting a party at my house for the team. Thanks for asking."

Still facing Mr. Pratt as he rambled off the announcements, Clara whispered, "Well I didn't ask since I figured I know."

"What do you know?"

"That you'll be with Stephanie. Always with Stephanie."

"Not always."

"Most of the time."

Jeremy considered and then, "Fair enough."

Clara, at least a part of her, wished Jeremy would stop talking to her. Whenever he engaged her, these suppressed feelings she had for him were only exacerbated. What did he want with her? What were his motives? She often examined her own motives, just to make sure she wasn't self-seeking. It was OK to sometimes do things just for herself – like attend college or buy a new dress for church. As a rule, Clara believed you should do everything in your power to place other people's needs ahead of your own. As a Christian, she knew the ultimate goal in her life was to lead those who were not saved to Christ. It was her mission, and she thought it to be a divine one.

Jeremy was saved, but Clara sometimes wondered if his belief in God was authentic.

Clara had known him for years. Did Jeremy believe in anything besides Jeremy? She knew it was none of her business, but she couldn't avoid comparing her own faith with somebody else's. In the midst of such comparison, she would come away feeling her own faith was stronger or more genuine than that of others. She would then silently chastise herself for being self-righteous. Self-righteous Christians accomplished little next to their humble counterparts and such behavior was detrimental to one's spiritual growth. Jesus himself was not self-righteous.

He wouldn't have reached so many people if he had been!

Mr. Pratt was still rambling on his dull monotone. Clara caught herself wondering *when is he going to shut the fuck up!?*

That's when she thought of Karen. She didn't have any specific thoughts on her.

Thinking about her unearthed certain feelings in her – strong feelings that were contradictory and confusing. Jeremy had long since ceased paying her much attention. Never had she seemed so detached from him. Usually in homeroom, the two engaged in quiet banter during the announcements that was light and playful. Clara felt like a younger sister to him in those moments. Even though they were about the same age, Jeremy knew all about Clara's upbringing and felt an overwhelming need to look out for her, protect her.

He wondered what would happen when he graduated from high school and they were forced to go their separate ways. Who would look out for her then? Would they keep in touch?

How would she get through her senior year without him? Jeremy had been accepted to three different colleges and had already chosen the one he wanted to attend. He couldn't understand how ambivalent he felt about leaving high school. All through senior year, he felt excited, impatient, to get on with his life. Now less than two weeks away from his graduation, he felt anxious, almost depressed, over the fact he would be leaving his hometown, leaving all his friends, leaving Turner High School forever.

Karen had never gone to homeroom. Benjamin had texted her with his plan to stay home and get high. Karen asked if she might join him, and he replied: "Why do you think I told you? I want you to come over. I want to screw you till your eyes cross." Karen was slightly annoyed by his tone, but then she thought herself silly – one cannot be detected through a text message. Based only on his words, one might very well think Benjamin rather rude. Karen had long since learned to dismiss his abrupt, careless manner. It wasn't an indication that he loved her any less, or at least that's what she told herself.

Karen had almost arrived at Benjamin's trailer when she realized she had left her bong at home. Wrongly, she had assumed Benjamin was referring to pot as the substance they would be using to get high. Karen turned the wheel sharply – she had driven at least five miles out of her way. A car's horn blaring, as she proceeded to do her U-Turn she realized a car had been very close behind her. She wasn't scared to die, but certainly didn't want to die over something as silly as her abrupt decision to go home and retrieve her bong. Ignoring the horn as it continued to blare, she avoided looking at the driver, her thoughts solely on Benjamin now and how the last month or so, he hadn't made love to her. They'd had sex, but it was different.

Lately, he'd been so aggressive, very forceful! She felt no love. Rather, she felt instead he was releasing some deep pent-up anger. She felt she could've been anybody, simply a body to him.

The tiny plastic baggie contained methamphetamine. Benjamin had tried it five times before. Out of all the drugs he had tried, Benjamin liked meth the best. Even better than heroin, which he had done far more than the meth. Staying up for days wired with endless energy intoxicated him.

Benjamin was curious about injecting the stuff. He had only ever snorted and smoked it. Karen had never done any illicit drug besides pot and acid, she would be more open to trying it if Benjamin introduced it as a drug you snort. Once, he had been reduced to convincing Karen to do heroin with him by explaining to her that heroin, indeed any street drug, could be snorted or smoked. Karen had previously believed injecting was heroin's only method and Benjamin didn't hesitate to tell her how "ignorant" and "foolish" she was for such a belief. Karen had apologized for her naiveté – unnecessarily, Benjamin thought, and told her so. He detested her pathetic need to have his steadfast approval. Never would Karen apologize to anyone else besides him, especially over something so petty. Benjamin had already blown two substantial lines when Karen arrived.

"What's that shit?" she asked.

"The special stuff." He grinned.

"What…stuff?"

He pronounced the drug as five separate words: "Meth. Am. Phet. A. Mine."

"Is that like speed?

"Essentially."

"I've never –"

"Stronger though. More potent."

"Does it mess you up?"

"No. That's what alcohol does. And acid. Pot – well, that's debatable. Meth, though, meth enhances you. Here." Benjamin handed her a dollar bill, already rolled up so she couldn't tell what denomination it was. Had Benjamin asked first whether or not she was even interested in doing it, Karen thought she might have hesitated, or at least asked another couple questions. By handing her the bill and giving her a simple command, he was informing her that she had no choice. Afraid he might call her a name – a prude, perhaps (though didn't that particular put-down have strictly sexual connotations?) or, his favorite, coward. So, she accepted the bill reluctantly.

Benjamin motioned toward the dilapidated coffee-stained table – here, Karen saw nearly a dozen lines of methamphetamine, all with varying lengths and widths. Karen stared at the lines, gripping the bill.

"Waiting for something?" Benjamin asked.

"How many?"

Benjamin was impatient. He sighed and then lied: "To get high, at least five."

Karen tried to think of another relevant question to delay the inevitable – her doing precisely what he wanted her to do. If she wasn't slightly nervous, she might have stopped to think that five lines was quite a lot for someone who had never done the drug. If she wasn't so anxious to please Benjamin, she might have been able to accurately gauge how many lines to do based on how she felt after blowing each individual line.

Instead, in a hurry, Karen bent down, hovering over the table. "Do it very quickly,"

Benjamin said. So she did. In a matter of seconds, five lines gone. Excited, Benjamin took her hand and directed her toward his bedroom. He saw her eyes were glazed over – she looked simultaneously sleepy and alert.

"What are we, what are we going to do?" Karen rubbed her nostrils, crinkling her nose and then clearing her throat.

Benjamin looked at her gravely. "What do you think we're going to do?" Karen's smile vanished as soon as Benjamin had noted its presence. She thought it would be nice if he had at least asked how she felt. Instead, he slipped his hand inside her pants.

33

Chapter 6

As Mrs. Henderson taught Trigonometry to a class full of eleventh graders, she couldn't help but feel a little distracted, thinking about her husband Frank, and Clara. Several months ago Mrs. Henderson had begun sleeping in a different room than Frank. Sharing a house with a perfect stranger, this is what her life had come to. Should this have been depressing, or just a blessing? On long lonely nights she usually did not miss Frank. Nights when she read a book, took a hot bath, or called up a girlfriend to talk for an hour or so. Never could she talk to Frank in the way she talked to her girlfriends. She feared manipulation, feared that Frank would use anything personal she disclosed against her. That's what had happened in her first marriage.

She had not even been divorced a year before she met Frank. He had been so sweet and caring he had been at first, so attentive to her needs. Then, after they were married, he had changed entirely so that he had become a different person, seeming to put all of his time and energy into his job, always giving it top priority. At first, when Mrs. Henderson had begun sleeping in a different room, Frank ignored her. After a week had passed, though, he demanded that she offer some explanation, to which she had said, "If you don't know by now, you'll never know." Finally, she had explained to him that she felt the dynamic of their relationship had changed so much that she wasn't sure she was even in love with him anymore. Nothing he said could change her mind either, not "you're beautiful, Liz," or, "I miss you." Those nice things he said meant nothing though, Mrs. Henderson believed he only said them so she might have sex with him more often than she already felt required to. Believing she had made the right choice by sleeping in a different room, she wanted nothing more than for her husband to have to win her back, to earn her sleeping next to him again. Sure, they still got together once or twice a week for sex, but this wasn't Mrs. Henderson's wish, she did it simply to keep her marriage together, realizing she relied on Frank for a sense of security,

34

stability. If she withheld sex from him, she thought it very possible he would leave her.

Then there was this issue with Clara. Mrs. Henderson knew something was wrong, finding herself having to resist the urge to play mother or counselor. Clara's personal life was none of her business, and to inquire would be unprofessional. Still, as she continued teaching she kept wondering about her - what was she doing this summer? Did she have any real friends to spend time with? What made her decide to start wearing makeup? Was she dating someone now? Was she trying to attract the attention of a certain guy, guys in general, or both?

Pressing the marker onto the dry-erase board, much harder than necessary, for Mrs. Henderson still sometimes felt like she was writing on a chalkboard (the school had gotten rid of those years ago), she felt a sudden futility in her pursuit: most of the students in her classroom did not give a damn about Trigonometry - they were only taking it to fulfill an academic requirement. Never had Mrs. Henderson believed her teaching to be meaningless, most likely too satisfied with her paychecks (not that they were large by any measure, but they were more than enough to pay her college loans back, buy a new SUV, and help buy the house she lived in with Frank). As she approached middle-age now, she pondered philosophical matters with increasing frequency. What did it mean to earn a decent amount of money if you were not reaching any of your students? Was it even possible to reach students in any significant way while teaching advanced mathematical concepts? It was true Mrs. Henderson felt a certain need to connect with another human being, ideally a student - was this an indication of her own loneliness? Mrs. Henderson wondered if most teachers felt the need to connect with their students. Maybe it was because she had no children, so her students, in a way, were like her children.

Having no children had always been her husband's choice. Years ago when she had repeatedly expressed her wish to have a baby, Frank had been so steadfast and passionate in his desire to not have children that she thought it would be impossible to convince him. Now, with her 40th birthday next year, she wondered if she could change his mind, knowing she only had a few years left to safely have children. Over five years had passed since she had last discussed having kids with him.

If she was going to bring up this topic successfully, she would have to do it soon. All too well she knew him. Not an impulsive man, Frank would undoubtedly say he needed "time to think", and Mrs. Henderson thought years might pass before he made a decision. (Perhaps she could simply stop taking her birth control, as Frank generally ejaculated while still inside her. He would never know the difference and Mrs. Henderson, if impregnated, could very briefly explain to him that birth control, like condoms, was not 100% effective). "It's divine intervention," she might say. "Proof that God wants us to have this baby." As the period neared its conclusion, she could hear herself saying this. Such manipulation! Was tricking her husband really necessary to get pregnant? No, she liked to believe, of course not, that would be deceptive, definitely not the Christian thing to do. Still, she thought it sounded like a good idea.

Mrs. Henderson was still talking and writing on the board when the bell rang. Most of her students moved very quickly out of their seats, appearing so eager to escape this class and get on with their day. Mrs. Henderson wanted to say something to Clara, she didn't know what, but something, she thought, say something! What about the rumor she had heard? That Clara had spent time with Karen outside of school. Before she could think of a suitable subject to lead into asking such a question, Clara had gathered her books and was gone.

Clara felt invisible – always. The feeling was made worse because today, she was making an effort to be seen, noticed, by the guys primarily, but the popular girls also – those girls who participated almost invariably in a slew of extracurricular activities, were cheerleaders, or field hockey/basketball stars. There were so many cliques in high school. Clara herself was not in a clique – you could not say she was part of this group or that group, you could not label her. Beyond being a devoted Christian, she did not quite know who she was.

As she was walking down the hallway - "Who told you, dear, that life would be pleasant and nice? Just tell me who? Certainly not God, for His only Son died a miserable death: a glorious death, on the other hand, when you consider the implications of it, the symbolism I mean. We all have the chance to be saved if we only ask for His grace and mercy. Think of how most people die, the vast majority nowadays - asleep in a bed, at home or in a hospital, doesn't matter which, they die a peaceful, comfortable death. That's how you will die, Clara. Well, in all likelihood. Whenever you think your life is hard, just remember His suffering. Remember how Christ died - in absolute agony, forsaken by His Father, betrayed by His disciples. Yes, Clara, just think of those nails piercing His hands, His feet, just think about *that!*" It drove her a little crazy, made her very sad - hearing Meem's voice all the time. Often, when engaged in some demanding intellectual task, she could block it out, with moderate success at times, total success at others. Today, she could not filter Meem's voice, Meem's lectures, from her own voice which told her it was foolish to take everything that old woman said at face value. Meem was from the school of hard knocks, those old school Christians who felt mankind deserved to suffer through life because Jesus Himself suffered. Clara had been disobedient and disrespectful, that much she was sure of. Was she sinning? By sneaking out of the house so early, not even bothering to say anything to Meem for she knew Meem strongly disapproved of makeup as well as coloring your hair or using hairspray or wearing any clothing that accentuated your "figure" - "all that stuff is for harlots and vamps!" Clara didn't even know what a vamp meant. (Since the word 'harlot' was in the bible, she knew what that meant, so her best guess: a 'harlot' was rather synonymous with a 'vamp.')

"Clara." A deep, quietly commanding voice.

She spun around and dropped one of her books in the process. Benjamin immediately bent down to pick it up and Clara thought how nice of him! She felt like no one had ever been so kind to her, but how silly of her to feel so, over a simple spontaneous act like this! Others had of course extended her greater courtesies than this, but in this moment, she forgot all the others, deeming their kindnesses somehow perfunctory and Benjamin's genuine.

"How are you?" Benjamin took a step closer to her, almost breathing on her as he asked her this question. Yes, he blotted out the others wonderfully, and she felt suddenly very grateful for him. "How are you?" He asked again since she did not answer.

"I..." She looked down at the book she had dropped that he had placed on top of the two other books that rested against her chest. "Thank you, I'm fine."

"Yeah, only you're not. A girl who says she is fine is not fine. Girl says she's fine is anything but fine. Psychology of Women, it's a 100 level course, pretty easy, for a girl anyway, maybe you should take it."

Clara said nothing, too entranced with his every word to catch his small joke regarding the imaginary course.

"Where are you headed now?" he asked.

"What?"

"Did I stutter? No, I'm not you, so I wouldn't imagine I did."

Again, Clara seemed not to catch this either, too distracted by her own daydreaming.

"Physics."

"Oh. Smartypants."

"What?" Clara stopped at the water fountain, brushing her hair onto her shoulder as she bent down for a drink. "Don't you have Physics? Or haven't you had it, is what I mean. Since I know you're a senior."

"No," he said. "I say fuck that, fuck all of that. That's a college prep course. I am not a college prep. I will not stoop to that level."

Clara looked confused, not quite understanding.

He continued: "Do you really learn a single thing from all those advanced uber-academic courses? No. Least not anything of value, nothing you will ever use in real life."

Quietly she protested: "But it will help me do well in college I think."

"Might. Who cares though, right? Everything you learn from a classroom is superficial pretentious bullshit. Least most of it. Just someone's idea of what constitutes an education. They want you to be *well-rounded*. Yeah, well, that's a fuckin' crock of shit too."

"Could you please not use that word?"

He knew but asked: "What?"

"Fuck," Clara said, covering her mouth quickly. "I didn't mean to say that!"

Benjamin laughed loudly. "Obviously."

"I really didn't. It just -"

"Slipped out?"

Clara's eyes locked with his and she didn't respond, she couldn't: his eyes absorbed her again.

He put a finger to his lips: "I won't tell if you don't."

Clara smiled, very slightly, warily. "Well, I better go." She stepped away from him slowly. "I don't want to be late for class."

"So what if you were," he said, "You afraid of some reprisal?"

"What do you mean?"

"Retaliation, are you afraid? Afraid God might punish you?"

"What, I, no -"

"Then what?"

"I just don't want to be late is all! I don't want detention! I..." Clara stopped herself. Why was she explaining herself? She didn't owe an explanation to any boy, especially this one, someone who was so clearly a heathen. As a rule, she did not like to judge others (only God had the authority to judge others, she knew!) but he made his disdain for religion and God so very obvious.

Chapter 7

Karen: very high, she blew a few more lines, she had had sex with Benjamin twice and now he was gone, nowhere to be found. The whole time he had been aggressive and angry. She couldn't help feeling aroused – despite being fully aware that he was not making love to her, she couldn't help herself. Even though she had not reached an orgasm (Benjamin had come just as she felt herself on the brink of climax) she had been very into it, had not felt at all anxious as she sometimes felt with him. Perhaps, the meth had relaxed her? She considered, briefly, the paradoxical effect the drug had upon her: simultaneously, she felt relaxed and super energetic.

As he rolled off her, she found herself having to refrain from saying, "That's it?" She knew that would be an insult, but she was so close! How she hated his absolute selfishness. The world did not revolve around Benjamin, and she wanted to inform him of this simple truth.

"Benjamin!" Karen, after calling his name several more times, had gotten out of bed to look for him. Looking for him took very little time, as his trailer was so small the search was accomplished in less than a minute. Gazing out the front window, she saw his car was gone. The fucker! She called his cell phone twice and both times reached his voicemail. She texted him three times over the course of a half hour – no response. "That fucker," she whispered. Really, though, Karen got over his unexplained departure rather easily: she was too high to genuinely care.

Seeing there were two lines remaining on the coffee table, Karen extracted the rolled up dollar bill from her pocket and bent down over the table.

Benjamin had gotten annoyed with her, plain and simple. He knew how much she needed him. It was true he also knew how her feelings for him vacillated, frequently, between extreme infatuation and love to utter resentment and contempt. He thought it was cute: at times, when she became fed up with his games, she would try her hardest to be independent, pretending like she didn't need him, to disengage, detach. Despite her best efforts, she had no success in this endeavor.

One time, after only a single full day of not speaking to him, she had sent him a series of text messages, indicating that she was giving him the silent treatment, asking whether or not he had even noticed. Benjamin ignored all her texts and after another full day had passed, more texts: *you must not care for me, there's no way you love me, you probably never did, etc. etc.*

Benjamin had laughed and laughed and still he ignored her. That night, she had shown up at his doorstep. Wearing a trench coat and apologizing profusely, she described how she was just being childish, immature, "acting like a 7th grader in love." She begged for his forgiveness and he allowed her to beg for a good long while. Yes, he knew it was rather wicked of him - feeling such pleasure over her pain. Feigning contemplation, he scratched his chin and felt like God, listening to her continue, so desperate for his love, his attention.

He had ripped off her trench coat, and his suspicion was confirmed: she wore nothing underneath. How pathetic of her to initiate makeup sex when she had done nothing wrong. He introduced her to bondage that very night, and he had become aroused seeing how alarmed she was upon seeing the handcuffs, appearing quizzical, like she wanted to ask lots of questions but was afraid of the answers. Of course, she knew what he wanted to do, essentially, she was just afraid of relinquishing so much control, giving him so much power. "Do you trust me?"

Benjamin had asked and Karen had hesitated, not sure if in fact she did. Eventually, she nodded her head and he led her to his bed.

Benjamin had not planned on abandoning Karen after sex. It was a pretty abrupt decision. Shortly after he had fucked her for the first time, he realized it might have been a mistake: not having sex with her, but giving her methamphetamine. She became intensely giddy, giggling nonstop, acting like a "schoolgirl," he told her. Enjoying herself too much, she dismissed his comment completely, too fucked up or "enhanced" to recognize it as a reprimand, an insult, she continued to laugh, over nothing in particular. For a moment he wanted to strangle her (not to murder her but simply to silence her - moreover, he had always wanted to try erotic asphyxiation). Instead, he moved off the bed and walked out of the bedroom. She thought he was probably going to the bathroom or possibly getting a bite to eat, as it was almost lunchtime.

When she heard the front door slam shut, she thought he was going to retrieve something out of his car, more drugs perhaps? Minutes passed, and he had not returned. That's when she started her search.

Sitting in his sixth period Principles of Technology course (POT, some students called it) Benjamin deliberated how long he would play this little game. If he waited much longer, Karen would likely leave. Seldom did she cry, but he could see her driving home and crying. This mental image of Karen, tears running down her face, made him smile. Still quite high, he realized how horny he had become, which was one of his favorite side effects of meth. So, he decided to text her - not because he didn't want to torment her further, but because he wanted to have sex with her again.

Benjamin stood up from his desk and started walking out of the classroom.

The teacher: "Where are you -"

"Water fountain," Benjamin lied, cutting him off.

"Next time you ask, OK," the teacher said, not unkindly.

Benjamin mocked him with a half-assed salute and was gone. Walking down the hallway, Benjamin pictured Clara naked. It wasn't her beauty, or slight lack thereof, that intrigued him: it was her innocence, her absolute innocence.

Chapter 8

He made love to her. Once in awhile it was essential, he knew. To maintain, or reignite, Karen's feelings for him, at least once a month, never more than twice, Benjamin was sweet and gentle with her.

"Why did you leave like that?" Karen asked him this numerous times. Finally, in a tone that was both firm and gentle, he said: "Don't ask me again."

Slowly pumping himself inside her, in between his heavy breathing, he whispered, "I saw her today."

"Who?" Karen tilted her head back.

"Clara."

"Oh…" Karen moaned loader as his thrusts became faster, deeper.

He waited for her to ask him to elaborate. Surprisingly, it wasn't his intention to hurt her by revealing that: as is often the case when having sex, he just wasn't thinking, nothing more, nothing less. As soon as he had said it, he understood the implications. Karen might feel threatened, at the very least would feel hurt that he had left her to see some other girl. Instead, she laughed. Quickly, then, she muzzled her laughter, fearing what might happen if she were to become giddy again.

Dammit, though, she was still so high, in a state of bliss, heaven. As he continued making love to her, she thought about the bathroom incident. That poor girl, Karen thought her rather pathetic, in all her helpless naiveté. But she did not feel sorry for her, not even a little bit. She didn't know why she felt so devoid of empathy for Clara - after all, she knew most of the story, having received it piecemeal over the years from rumors: how Clara's parents were virtual indigents, abandoning her when she was barely out of diapers. And yet she felt this unexplainable undeniable attraction to her. She was physically attracted to her, was that it? Partly, though it wasn't as simple as that.

She wanted to get to know her. They seemed to be polar opposites, was that it? Opposites attract, Karen knew, but that was a weak theory, not an axiom.

Back at school, in study hall, the last period in the day, Clara wrote in her diary:

> Lord, please come to me. Lord, please always be with me & guide me in the right direction. Please help me to always be kind to others & to treat everyone the way I would want to be treated. Those two classmates of mine I mentioned before - Karen & Benjamin, well I am certain now that they have come into my life for a reason. They are not Christians, I don't think they even believe in God, based on the way they act & from the things they say. I'm not judging them, I'm only stating the facts. But I really feel like You have placed them in my life. I think You are giving me the chance to deliver the good news. (Good, I don't think that word does it justice. WONDERFUL might be better?) But Lord please guide me through this. I love You w/ all my heart, Lord! Thank You so much for being in my life & for shining down upon me, protecting & caring for me, & forgiving my sins. You are amazing Lord! Every day on this earth is a blessing from you, Lord. Please be w/ me always Lord, for as long as I live I will always praise & glorify Your name. I will try my best to reach out to others, Lord. And I know that w/ Your love & guidance I will be able to do this. Lord, please also help me to get to know myself better. So many times Lord I am confused of what to do in a situation. Please always help me to do the Christian thing. Lord, please help me

to always put my faith first, so that I am never persuaded by anyone. Please help me to stand up for what I believe in. I love You, Lord! In Jesus's Name I pray, Amen.

Clara

Closing her diary she glanced around the cafeteria: halfway full, as this was an enormous study hall, Clara guessed there were close to 100 students here - most of them were not doing work, it being the end of the school year, the likely reason why students seemed so apathetic.

Clara knew it would be prudent to work on her Trigonometry homework, she didn't have to do it all now (there wouldn't be enough time anyway) but she thought she should at least start it.

Some of the equations required 15 or even 20 minutes each. Since the homework involved a concept Mrs. Henderson had just finished teaching today, Clara knew she should set aside more time than usual to solve them. She couldn't concentrate, could not will herself to focus. It was likely she would have to read the entire chapter again, as her mind had been elsewhere as Mrs. Henderson taught.

Clara was alarmed to realize that what she had been doing during Trigonometry went well beyond daydreaming: she had been fantasizing, thinking lustful thoughts! Clara did not allow herself to have sexual fantasies, as she believed God did not approve. One day, she knew "sex thoughts," (as Meem called them) would be OK in God's eyes, as long as these thoughts involved her husband and her husband only. God wanted women to enjoy "carnal pleasures" (Clara was 14 before Meem had explained this to her, and she had googled "carnal pleasures", pretty sure of what it meant, given the context, but wanting to be certain.) Accidentally, she had clicked on one of the search results and was directed to a pornography website. Shocked, she reflexively clicked on the button closest to the cursor. Wrong button! Suddenly, she heard a woman moaning and saying, "hi, baby, you wanna play? I'm so wet and—" the speakers were turned up very loud too, as Meem, who was generally the one who used the computer, was hard of hearing. Maximizing the screen, Clara had covered her eyes and, peeking through her fingers at the upper right hand side of the computer, ended her accidental pornography session. A few days later, after reviewing the

45

search history, Meem confronted Clara, who explained everything to her. Meem hesitated, at first, not quite accepting what had happened was an accident. After grilling her for over a half hour, Meem acquiesced and believed what had happened was an accident. Nevertheless, two days later Meem had gotten a man to come to the house to install an internet filter. Meem's final question: "Dear, why didn't you simply ask me what carnal pleasures were?" Clara said, "I don't know, I guess, well, I guess I was embarrassed." Meem chuckled and walked out of the room.) "Yes, God wants you to experience those pleasures," Meem had assured Clara, "He wants you to wait until marriage, though. Did you hear me? God wants you to wait, wants you to be a virgin when you are married."

Ripping a page out of her diary Clara began drawing a flower with her pen, if for no other reason than to block out Meem's voice. In the midst of sketching petals that were large and exaggerated, Clara stopped: the drawing had not been effective in getting Meem to vanish. Her voice was still there.

Clara said "The Lord's Prayer" three times. But no. Meem was still present in her mind. Feeling defeated, Clara sighed and wanted to cry. Then she thought of Jeremy. If Stephanie was not in the picture she believed she would fall in love with him very easily. It would happen with or without her consent. True love, Clara believed, was not calculating, was not something you could control. But she had hardened her heart to Jeremy, for she knew that any romantic feelings she developed for him would be unrequited. Still, she really liked him, thought he was handsome with a good personality and was essentially a good person. Finally, Clara's mind drifted, pushing Jeremy out of her thoughts, perhaps subconsciously, and thinking of Benjamin and Benjamin only. Benjamin. Naked (!!). The image of him without any clothes on had popped into her "thought life" (as Meem called it) and she knew it was an impure thought. But she did not feel guilty over it. For the first time, she understood that, despite a person's best efforts, thoughts, especially sex thoughts, could not be entirely controlled. In fact, Clara believed the more she attempted to control these certain forbidden thoughts she had, the more they would surface.

So, Benjamin. She thought of Benjamin and only him. She smiled then, a bit, because she had achieved a calming blankness in her mind. And she felt no fear, no anxiety. Even if this blank clear state consumed her only temporarily, Clara thought it was wonderful. She liked to think he would be more muscular than he appeared with his clothes on. His clothes, always either extremely baggy or extremely tight, were consistently black, she didn't remember ever seeing him wear clothes that didn't feature black as the predominant color. She imagined he was lean, as opposed to skinny, which was the impression she got, when he had his clothes on, of course. Lean was preferable to Clara because lean meant he would be muscular but not too muscular. Lean meant he might have six-pack abs. Lean meant he might have biceps and triceps that were very pronounced and developed.

Meem confronted Clara as soon as she arrived home from school. The moment she walked in the door - "You have some explaining to do, young lady."

Clara stared at her blankly, not feeling, or not showing at least, the normal anxiety she experienced when Meem became angry with her. Meem's anger did not register in her tone, as it normally did when she lost her temper. Rather, her tone was pleasantly firm, detached from all emotion.

Seeing that Clara had decided to act clueless over the request for information, Meem, inspected Clara from head to toe, again, and a third time, then continued in a stern whisper: "I don't know what to say." And Meem had good reason to be uncertain of how to proceed. Her inspection had yielded nothing, as there was nothing out of the ordinary in Clara's appearance, since Clara had already washed all of her makeup off and forfeited her short skirt (which really was only short in her own eyes - not even two inches above her knees) for a pair of Capri pants.

"You left the house early - why?" Meem asked, after what felt like a good long while to Clara.

"I, I -"

"Oh, stop *that* nonsense, you know I *hate* it when you stutter! Hell, I should have *you* seen by a speech therapist." Meem's firm whisper had risen to a loud, angry tone. Almost shouting, annoyed even further that Clara had not responded with an apology, a customary one she offered over anything she did, however minute, even sometimes over things she was not responsible for, simply to avoid confrontation and to end the tension that inevitably resulted from a disagreement, or misunderstanding.

"I was in a hurry, Meem. I mean, I had to leave early so I could get there on time, that's all!"

"You don't have enough time to say goodbye to the one person, the *only* person, who has done *so* much for you? The one person who -"

"I had a Genesis club meeting! I had to leave early!" However, no such meeting was held that day. On one hand, Clara could count the number of times she had deliberately lied to Meem.

"I have cared for you, given you love and support *unconditionally*! Where would you be without me, huh? Clara, just tell me, hmm? Where!"

"Yeah, well, I thank you for all of that. But I think, well, I think it's time I have more freedom. I'll be out of high school in about a year and I -"

"You'll be OUT, if you continue this disrespect!"

"What disrespect?"

"Yes, you will be OUT!"

"Answer my question," Clara said, and then added: "Please," as though she was worried she sounded too bold, worried she sounded too much like she was making a demand.

"Yes, I see how it goes. You think that just because you are getting older you can slowly end our relationship. Well, just remember - pretty soon, I won't be here anymore, do you understand? Meem won't be *here* because the Lord! He will take *me*, yes, soon enough, the Lord will take me."

"Meem, I meant -"

"Yes, I see how it is. It starts small, with you leaving in the morning not saying -"

"MEEM! STOP!" Clara immediately covered her mouth, appearing as though her yelling at Meem was all a big mistake.

Meem raised her voice to match Clara's: "*DON'T* you raise your voice to *ME*! You understand? You don't ever do that again, understand!

"Yes," Clara said, lowering her head.

"You look at me when I'm speaking to you!"

Clara said nothing, only raised her head a bit. "I'm going up to my room now. She took several rapid steps past Meem. Meem, still quite spry for her age, reached out for Clara, grabbing onto her shirt.

Clara shouted, throwing Meem's hand off her and racing up the first set of stairs. Meem, eyes wide and angry, returned to her stern, quiet tone: "You know, don't expect any money from me, not anymore! Nope, not even a nickel. Not from this woman. Yes, if you want to stay here, you had better start chipping in. That means you *will* help with all household bills and buy *all* your school supplies yourself. Also, that car you drive - well it's *mine* and *I* want it back!"

Clara looked shocked, especially at this last stipulation. "How will I get to school?"

"You can walk," Meem said nastily.

"Walk? How do you expect -"

"I don't, DO NOT, want to hear it! When I was your age I walked five and a half miles to school, that's a total of 11 miles, missy! Case you didn't know!" Slightly winded, Meem stopped her ranting for several seconds.

"I am aware. You've told me many times before," Clara said, not disrespectfully.

Meem seemed not to hear Clara or, if she did, decided to skip it. "Uphill, no less. Yes sir, 11 miles uphill! Every single day!"

Clara dissented: "You mean five days a week. School is not every day." Clara was going to add that walking uphill both ways was rather impossible or, at the very least, unlikely.

"Better believe it! In the blistering cold, rain, snow, sleet, it didn't matter." Meem took several short sharp breaths. "And you better -"

"School is almost eight miles from here. So, I would be walking much further than you. Nearly 50% more, close to 16 miles every day. That's 160 miles in two weeks."

Meem opened her mouth, on the verge of speaking when suddenly she stopped, contemplating something, perhaps the calculations Clara had produced. "You can ride the BUS! Also, you are getting a JOB! And there are no if's, and's, or but's about it, young lady."

"Fine," Clara said, shrugging her shoulders, smiling slightly. "I'll get a ride to school. And I'll get a job. Problem solved."

Meem stared at her blankly, appearing confused.

"I'm going up to my room now," Clara said, "I have lots of homework."

Clara, in offering a reason as to why she wanted to go to her room, was extending a courtesy to Meem, who seemed not to catch it. Clara, secretly pleased with herself for taking the initiative to end the discussion on her terms, turned her back on Meem and ascended the rest of the stairs.

Chapter 9

Clara could not finish her homework. After reading the new chapter, she could not concentrate. She did work up enough focus to solve three equations, one of which required 15 minutes. Moving onto a fourth, she found her mind drifting, again. Benjamin. Benjamin - not sex thoughts, no, Clara was planning how she might ask him to hang out, and where, when? (Preferably, she hoped he would ask her!) Wait, what about Karen? She did not want Karen to be there, wanted to be with Benjamin, and only Benjamin. Clara imagined going on a date with him, dining at a fancy restaurant and then going to the movies. Then, they might take a walk around a lake or pond? Yes, holding hands and kissing - on the lips only, no tongue! Clara found the thought of spending time with him far more pleasant than the sex thoughts during study hall. Possibly, she found them to be so only because sex made her feel uncomfortable. Kissing, on the other hand, well, there was nothing wrong with kissing, so long as it didn't lead to anything else!

Clara felt undesirable and ugly when she considered the fact that she had never kissed a man on the lips. Well, yes, technically, she had: Clara didn't count that, though, how could she?

The kiss was in the script. Last year, Clara had worked up the confidence to audition for a play. Sponsored by Genesis club, this play delivered a message that contained Christian principles and, therefore, promoted Christianity by default. It was true Clara only had a minor part, appearing on stage five times, and then only briefly. She'd had a dozen or so lines, and the director could have selected anyone for the part she had been cast for.

Realizing any further attempts to complete her homework would be futile, Clara climbed out of bed and surveyed her room very briefly. That's right: she had left the cordless phone in the bathroom.

Jeremy didn't answer his phone when it rang, didn't even look to see who was calling. In the middle of making out with Stephanie, a session that quickly segued into Stephanie going down on him. Quite usually, he preferred oral sex, if only because it required no effort on his part. All he had to do was lean back, feet propped up sometimes, head tilted back always, and watch, watch her as she bobbed up and down on him.

"Your phone's ringing again," Stephanie said, glancing at the phone and looking up at Jeremy.

"Just...keep...going."

"You don't want to know who's calling?"

"Not really."

Evidently, Stephanie was curious herself. Picking up his phone, she saw the name and number and laughed. "Oh my God."

"What?"

"Your secret admirer."

"What?"

"Clara!" Stephanie began to laugh.

"You shouldn't laugh at her."

"Oh, I can't help it. She's just *such* -"

"A good person?"

"Oh, whatever, Jare," Stephanie said, standing up. "Why are you defending her?"

"She's my friend."

"And?"

"I think that's enough of a reason."

"Oh, you've got a crush on her!"

Jeremy shrugged his shoulders. "No, but if you want to think that, whatever."

"You've got a *huge* crush on her. You secretly want to do her all night. You -"

"Will you shut up?"

Stephanie gasped, and Jeremy realized he hadn't been too discerning with his request, if for no other reason than he wanted her to continue giving him pleasure. "I'm leaving," Stephanie said calmly, gathering her keys and purse and sunglasses off the floor.

Jeremy, about to apologize, decided against it - yes, his defense of Clara had been ill-timed (typically, he just ignored Stephanie, pretending he didn't hear her when she poked fun at Clara) but it had been genuine. Lately, Stephanie had been belittling her with increasing frequency, though. He suspected she was only doing it to feel superior, to feel better about herself, and that made him angry.

Staring at him, Stephanie fully expected him to say something to convince her to stay. He said nothing though - instead he grabbed the remote and turned on the TV. Still, she stared at him.

"Well, what?" Jeremy didn't even bother to look at her. Looking down at his penis, he saw he was still semi-erect. "Aren't you going to finish?"

Stephanie muttered something under her breath and stormed off. Before she slammed the door shut: "Jerk yourself off! Asshole!"

Shutting off the television, Jeremy grabbed his phone and called Clara.

Clara was sitting on the edge of her bed, and the large mirror, hanging above the bureau, cut off half of her face, so she could only see her face from the nose up. She frowned, not over her appearance, really, but over the fact that Jeremy had not answered her phone call. Twice she had called him. Also, she was very tired: it was not even 6:00. Obviously she couldn't go to bed yet. Besides, she had to complete her homework. Generally, Meem called her down for dinner around 5:30. Clara concluded that either Meem was mad, she had prepared dinner a bit later than the typical time, or both.

Why had she called him twice? It would have been OK, perhaps, if she had called him twice over the course of three or four hours. But no. She called him two times in a row, leaving a voicemail the first time, and then the second hanging up after it rang twice (at least then she could claim she had pocket-dialed him.) As she continued considering

Jeremy - what he was up to, how he presently perceived her, if they would ever be more than friends - her phone rang.

"Hello?" She hid most of the excitement she felt upon seeing his number, which she knew by heart. So concerned was Clara about seeming nonchalant over the fact that he was calling, she pretended she didn't know who was calling.

"Hello?" She cringed at the voice: it was Meem, on the other line (Clara did not own a cell phone).

"Meem, it's Jeremy!"

"Oh, Jeremy. Hi Jeremy!"

Before Jeremy could say hello, Meem hung up.

"Oh, Jeremy," Clara said. "What's up?"

"I saw you called." He thought that came across as rather unfriendly, but he was rather annoyed over Stephanie's abrupt departure, specifically over the fact Clara had interrupted his favorite sexual act.

"I left a voicemail."

"I didn't check it yet."

"Oh!"

"Something you need to talk about?"

No, there was nothing. She had really called him for comfort, just to hear his voice, to know he was there. Lately, when she came home, she felt so alone. On occasion, she called a couple girls from Genesis club, but she much preferred talking to Jeremy.

"Clara, you still there?"

"Yes," she said. "No, there is nothing."

Silence.

"OK, here it goes. I'm really depressed. And I don't know why. I don't know, I just feel like...there's this big void inside me. I know deep down you can't fill it too, even though sometimes I know I look to you to fill it. That does help, a little. Knowing you're there."

"I am here," Jeremy said. "But that hole is God-sized. No person will ever fill it."

Clara didn't know what to say - just what was he saying exactly? That she didn't have God in her life? She decided not to be defensive. "I pray a lot, Jeremy, you must know I do!"

"Yeah," Jeremy said. "I know."

"Up to this point, it helped, it always helped! Now, I don't feel anything. I mean, I pray everyday! Down on my knees half the time. And I do devotions every day! I don't know, I've been feeling sad. Like God is not there, I don't...I don't feel Him anymore."

"That happens sometimes, Clara. It's natural. I know it sucks but that happens with any Christian, no matter how strong his faith is."

"You think so?"

"How long have you felt this way?"

"I don't know."

"Try to think."

"Well, it started...I guess these feelings started this school year. The beginning of this school year."

"Why didn't you talk to me then?"

"Because I wanted to ignore it! I tried...to ignore it. Thought maybe I wasn't praying hard enough, or wasn't being a good enough Christian. Thought God was punishing me, only I didn't know what for!"

"You know that's not the case," Jeremy said. "How many times have I told you?"

"I know, I –"

"Our God loves you, He cares for you. Wants to see you happy."

"You think so?"

"I know so."

"I haven't told anyone, about how sad I get sometimes. I mean, sometimes I cry myself to sleep. I don't understand it! It feels so good to me though."

"What does?"

"Opening up to you. I haven't opened up to anyone before, not about my feelings, besides God, and even with Him I try to censor what I say, to stay positive."

"You shouldn't do that. God understands, you know."

"I used to open up to Meem. I don't anymore though, I don't wanna get into it either, I –"

"I'm glad you called."

"You are?"

"Of course. Let's talk about it tomorrow though, all right? It'll be better in person."

"When? When will I see you? We will only have a real short while in homeroom."

Jeremy hadn't considered this. "After school then. We'll go out somewhere."

And suddenly all the emptiness in Clara, the overwhelming sadness, was lifted. In this moment, she felt fulfilled and joyous. In this moment, she felt strong, confident even.

"Clara?"

"Yes?"

"Oh, you didn't say anything so -"

"Where do you want to go!"

"It'll be a surprise."

"OK!"

"I'll see you tomorrow then?"

"OK! Have a good night!"

"You too, Clara."

The next day Clara woke up over two hours before her regular time. Stretching her arms, she sat up in bed, thinking it wasn't even 5 A.M. Normally she required an alarm to wake up at 7 A.M. On this day, however, her alarm, though set, never went off. She was so excited. To talk to Jeremy, well, especially to hang out with him! What were they going to do? She obsessed over it, that morning, imagining where he might take her, what they might do. She came quite close to deluding herself with the idea that they would kiss - wasn't anything possible, after all? But she knew there was no chance of that happening. If he was interested in being more than her friend, he had had plenty of opportunities to make his move.

Jeremy and Clara had attended different elementary schools, so did not even know the other existed until seventh grade. Despite sharing two classes together, at first they were only acquaintances. In science class, the teacher had placed each student in a group of three. There were an uneven amount of students in the class, and it just so happened that Clara and Jeremy were assigned to work with each other. Clara remained reticent the entire time they worked together. Never did she initiate conversation, and when she responded to his questions, which were mostly related to the biology project, she replied with two or three words. At the beginning of the school year, Jeremy, who sat at the opposite end of the room as Clara (a similar seating arrangement in geometry prevented them from talking much that year as well) had overheard two girls, both cheerleaders, talking about Clara near the beginning of the year, calling her a "Jesus freak" and a "prude" who "probably [had] a vagina covered with cobwebs and dust."

Then, sophomore year, Jeremy was invited to a Genesis meeting by Mrs. Henderson. Far from enthusiastic about a Christian club, Mrs. Henderson urged him to go, citing no reason in particular, just saying that she wanted to see him meeting a "nice girl" and there were lots of "nice girls" who were very active in Genesis club. *Yeah,* Jeremy thought at the time, *but are they pretty? 'Cause if they are just nice and not pretty, what's the point?* So, initially, he said no, thanks for asking but I just can't, too busy with practice and – Fine, at the time, Mrs. Henderson put a hand up to signal she understood. Walking away briskly, he stopped her, "What time is it? And what day?" Smiling she informed him. Still very reluctant to attend a meeting that he would likely take shit from his friends for, Jeremy also felt indifferent toward the whole idea of religion. Up until his 8th grade year, when he had received confirmation, church had been mandatory. His father, a staunch Catholic, told his son that he could decide for himself. Jeremy took that freedom and ran with it. Never did he go to church after that, and if he was honest, he didn't miss it.

Standing in front of the mirror Clara brushed her hair, remembering what Karen's instructions were regarding how she should wear her makeup. On that morning, Clara felt daring. Gathering a secret cache of makeup she had stashed inside the pockets of her sweatpants, which were buried underneath a slew of sweaters she seldom wore, Clara stuffed all of the makeup into her purse.

Looking at herself in the mirror, still quite indifferent over her reflection, she decided she would leave fifteen minutes before her standard departure time. It would be easier this time, as she would not have to invent an excuse as to why she was leaving so early. Until she could find someone to pick her up on a daily basis, she would ride the bus. She didn't care, really: yes, the general consensus at Turner High School indicated that once someone was eligible to receive a driver's license, it was no longer acceptable to ride the bus. Clara didn't care about that, though. She was on her own path, and suddenly she found herself thinking about a poem she read in her 9th grade English course. She couldn't think of the author's name, but she still remembered some of the lines. The basic message of the poem, she knew: Always do your own thing, don't be a follower, take the road less traveled by and, in the long run, you will be a better person.

First, Clara thought she better check to see if Meem had really taken her keys. Often, in a rage that was rather unwarranted, Meem threatened to punish Clara. Then by the next day she had either forgotten about the punishment or decided not to enforce it.

Tip-toeing out into the hallway, Clara could hear Meem snoring, could see her bedroom door - it was shut. Clara kept her car keys downstairs in a bright ceramic dish. Always Meem directed her to put them there as soon as she arrived home. Last night Clara had placed them there right before she went to sleep. Still upset over the argument, Clara hadn't been thinking really, or else she would've kept the keys in her room.

The keys were not there. Clara looked in the other spot Meem sometimes put them, a hiding spot Meem used when she suspected Clara was "up to something", fearing she might sneak out in the middle of the night. (Clara stumbled upon the keys one night when she was searching for stamps). All of her suspicions were unfounded, for she never snuck out at night, not once. Opening the desk drawer, Clara slid all of the envelopes forward and peered inside the last envelope.

Empty.

She felt several more envelopes, checking for lumps, but they were all flat. She thought of Jeremy. Surely, he would take her to school. Only four or five times had he taken her to school, and those times only because her car was in the shop or the roads were icy and Meem insisted she not drive herself. Was it too early to call? Not even 6:00, Clara was sure he would still be sleeping.

After breakfast she called him. Without hesitation, he said he would pick her up around 7:30. Clara raced up the stairs, feeling a certain energy she had not felt in some time. She was excited to take a shower and she was excited to wear a blouse and skirt she had bought over a year ago. Never did she work up the chutzpah to wear either article of clothing. The blouse, pink and rather low-cut, aimed to showcase cleavage. Possessing A-cup breasts, Clara ended up wearing a push-up bra to acknowledge the blouse's intentions. Nearly three inches above the knee, the skirt would infuriate Meem, who would surely be awake to see it. So, that morning Clara wore Capri pants over the skirt and a baggy tee-shirt over the blouse. Once at school, she planned to take both off to reveal the real outfit. The only thing detracting from an entirely new look was the makeup. Applying any here in the house wasn't an option, and she wouldn't have enough time at school. If Jeremy picked her up at 7:30, they wouldn't arrive until almost 7:45.

The bell rang at 7:55, so by the time she got to her locker there would be no time. The makeup will be there tomorrow, Clara thought: yes, it will still be there.

Having said goodbye to Meem (whose mood had shifted from sour to stoic) Clara was waiting outside when Jeremy arrived. As he pulled into her driveway, she smiled very widely and started walking toward him, meeting him halfway. Unable to suppress her smile, which was bright and genuine, she opened the passenger's side door and hopped in.

"Smiley." Jeremy did not smile himself: he yawned twice instead, having just rolled out of bed.

"Still tired?"

"That snooze button will be my demise. I hit it three times."

Clara laughed.

"You seem happy today."

"I am," Clara said quickly, giving no thought to the question. "I really am."

"A good night's rest will do wonders."

"Yes," Clara said and then blurted out: "What are we doing? Later on I mean. After school?"

"Didn't I tell you?"

Quizzically, she shook her head *no.*

"Good," he said. "Cause it's a surprise."

Stephanie saw her man as soon as he walked to his locker. She noted Clara's presence, walking right beside Jeremy with a grin on her face. Ultimately, she dismissed Clara, not threatened by her at all, just annoyed, very annoyed. Stephanie liked driving to school herself.

On occasion she did ride with Jeremy. Most mornings, though, she drove herself, if only because she loved her car, a tiny red convertible.

"Hi Clara," Stephanie said and then, to amuse herself: "What the hell are you wearing?"

"What?" Clara asked, glancing down at her shirt, and her Capri pants, noticing there were -

"Lumps," Stephanie said. "There are lumps all over those pants. What do you have on underneath?"

Clara looked at Jeremy. "Let me know about." Clara stopped, seeing Stephanie, not wanting her to know. "After school. You know?"

Jeremy nodded and Clara dashed down the hall, escaping inside the nearest bathroom. Clara made it to homeroom just in time, and the first thing Jeremy saw was the skirt she wore: not the style, or the color, no, he noticed how short it was, and how nice her legs looked. For someone who stood 5'2", her legs appeared long. Responsible, at least partly, were the chunky heel sandals she wore. Elevating her four inches, these sandals were impulsively purchased in Macy's while shopping with Meem right before Christmas. Since the sections that held the appropriate clothing for Meem and Clara were at opposite of the store, Clara had suggested they shop separately. Meem had not been fond of the idea, but eventually relented, realizing the request was reasonable. During this brief separation Clara bought the sandals and planned how she might take them home. Never had Clara worn any footwear over two inches, and she knew Meem would not approve. The easy solution:

Clara, when Meem asked what was in the bag, said, "Oh, I can't tell you! Don't you want your gift to be a surprise?"

Up to this point, Clara had hid the sandals in her locker. Rather brazen she felt, exhilarated even, wearing them on this day with a skirt that seemed rather shorter than she remembered.

"What's wrong?" Clara asked. "Don't you like my outfit?"

"No," Jeremy said, looking away quickly. "I mean yes, I do like it." Jeremy realized he had been staring at her.

Clara nodded her thanks and Jeremy kept his gaze toward the front of the room, eyes on Mr. Pratt as the announcements began. No longer puzzled over the lumps in her pants, which he had seen first thing this morning, Jeremy presently wondered why she had not just worn the skirt first thing this morning? Jeremy knew Meem was strict and conservative and thought that might be the reason why she felt the need to sneak the skirt into school.

"Hey," Jeremy said softly, not knowing how to tell her. From experience, he had learned the best way to break bad news to someone was to be blunt and not try to soften the blow. "I can't hang out today." He waited for her reaction: she seemed to not quite understand. "Only if Stephanie is with us." Clara frowned, then smiled and frowned again. Was this some sort of trick?

"What do you mean?"

"Clara, I'm sorry. I really wanted to, and I thought we could. It's Stephanie though."

"Can't two friends spend time together?"

Jeremy lowered his voice then, as though about to reveal a secret. "She's a real insecure person. And I know she can be a bitch. She means well, though. She really does. And I think we have something real special together."

"You said we were going to hang out, Jeremy, you said you were going to…"

"I know. And I'm sorry for that."

"Save your apology." Clara's soft quiet tone had shifted and now she sounded angry.

"If you wouldn't have said that in the locker room. Stephanie picked up on that."

"So now it's my fault?"

Mr. Pratt, in the middle of the announcements, cleared his throat loudly, hoping this subtle gesture would be effective in getting Jeremy and Clara to be quiet.

"It's no one's fault," Jeremy whispered. "What can I say? I think she's the one."

With this, Clara wanted to cry, vomit, or both. Stone-faced, she faced forward, ending the conversation even as Jeremy tried to continue it. Truly, he felt bad, but after mumbling a few words, he was silent. Trying to pacify her would just make the situation worse, he seemed to understand that.

Clara completed her homework in study hall. Now, with time to meditate and pray, the negative feelings she had been experiencing for a good long while were all surfacing. She felt broken and disappointed with her life - not because of Jeremy, he was only the nail in the coffin. Everything, it was everything, and nothing in particular. She began writing about how she was truly feeling and then she stopped, crossing out those sentences. Since God was omnipotent, why should she tell Him how she felt today? *There are people much worse off than me*, she thought, *like people with terminal cancer or those starving children in Africa.* Yes, God certainly knew how she felt, and this was only a test, a brief trial, to see how strong her faith was. Clara did not think God wanted to hear people complain about every little thing. So, generally, she vented very sparingly. Today, though, she did not complain nor did she vent, not at all. On the contrary, she masked her feelings entirely, briefly pretending everything was hunky dory:

Lord, please be with me and help me to understand Your words & please help me to always live by them, Lord.

> Gal 5:5— "For through the Spirit, by faith, we await the hope of righteousness."

Gal 6:2— "Serve one another by love, and you will fulfill the law of Christ."

Lord, thank You so much for this wonderful day & all that You have blessed me with! I love You w/ all my heart Lord, now & forever! Please always be w/ me & guide me closer to You!

Love,
Clara

From her locker, following study hall, Clara saw an enormous banner the seniors had hung. In spray-painted bubble letters that were bright and bold: "SENIORS CLASS OF '15 - ONE WEEK!!!" It was true that the seniors had exactly one week until they graduated - only four days of school remained.

Clara was not jealous over the fact that the seniors would be graduating. She herself was apprehensive about going out into the so-called real world. What constitutes the 'real world', Clara wondered? Was it when you left home and went to college? When you got a full-time job? Or did you have to get married and have kids? At the same time, Clara looked forward to college, excited about getting away from Meem and starting her life anew.

So, she was ambivalent, unable to decide whether she was more tentative or excited about leaving high school. But thoughts were premature and irrelevant, at least right now, since Clara still had a full year left at Turner High. Opening her locker to retrieve her Trigonometry book, Clara saw a terse note on the floor of her locker. Bending down, she pondered why they created the lockers with those slight slits.

Did the three predominant items - books, folders, jackets - kept in these lockers need ventilation? Or did the manufacturers simply want to make it easier for students to pass notes? There were other reasons for the slits, but Clara didn't consider them, not now. Now, she read:

I am so fucking sorry if I offended you.

Love,
Karen

The warped humor and handwriting Clara recognized at once. A clear gamble: by using that particular expletive, Karen risked further offending Clara and alienating her for good. Benjamin had been the one to suggest Karen write the note. When she had said no, the suggestion became a demand. Already, Karen had begun to resent Clara and the attention she was receiving from *her* boyfriend. Why was Clara on his mind so much? Karen interpreted his initial interest in her as a simple sign of his sardonic sense of humor. When she realized Clara was not a joke she could dismiss, she began to slightly worry and wonder and resent. Nevertheless, to appease Benjamin, she wrote the note.

Clara ripped up the note, not because she didn't want to introduce them to Christ's light and ultimately save them - rather, she thought they were making fun of her, talking to her and attending Genesis meetings for kicks. Never would they listen to God's words with an open heart - no, their hearts were already hardened.

"Hey." Clara recognized the voice at once: Jeremy. Her hand deliberated on the locker handle, eventually decided to close it. "You need a ride home, right?" Still, she didn't turn to face him.

"No." She caught a glimpse of him as she turned to walk away.

In a lukewarm protest, he asked: "You sure? Come on, how are you going to get home?"

She picked up her pace, mostly to get rid of him, but also to see whether or not he would follow her.

His first instinct encouraged him to follow her. His second directed him not to. When Stephanie texted him with a sexual message, it was easy for Jeremy to ignore his initial instinct. Soon, Clara was out of his sight. Soon, Jeremy would seriously question his decision.

Clara saw Benjamin first. Was it a coincidence that he caught her at the end of a very long very bad day, a day where she was feeling even more vulnerable than usual? Was it a coincidence that today Karen had been issued three days of detention? So, Benjamin had to wait for her. Sometimes they drove separately to school, but not today - was it a coincidence?

Pulled up to the curb, waiting to leave, she saw him. Quickly, perhaps reflexively, she looked away. She would ride the bus, there was still time, none of the buses had closed their doors yet, students were still climbing inside.

"Clara!" She heard her name called out, and again. Even after the third time, she pretended not to hear. That voice, slightly familiar but she couldn't place it.

Finally, finding the appropriate bus (she had not taken the bus to school since sophomore year), she heard him again: "FIRE! FIRE! FIRE!"

He ceased shouting as soon as he had earned her attention. She looked at him. He looked at her. He grinned. She did not. "Excuse *me*," a student said to Clara - inadvertently, she had blocked the entrance to the bus. As she stepped aside, Benjamin moved closer toward her, asked where her car was.

"How do you know I have a car?"

"I'm omniscient."

She glared at him, the sun in her eyes. "I, I don't have a car."

Benjamin nodded and then grinned and attempted to flesh out his godlike quality claim:

"There are things I know about you, things you don't know I know because you don't know them."

She skipped over this. Raising a hand to her face to block out the sun, warily she said: "You, you can? Give me a ride home I mean?"

"Well, yes," Benjamin said and his grin was gone. "I wouldn't have offered otherwise."

The bus driver said something that Clara didn't bother to hear. Staring at Benjamin, she heard the door close beside her. "Where are you parked?" she asked him. "Is that your car? The black one?"

Benjamin nodded and started walking toward it. Slowly, then, she followed him.

Was it a coincidence?

In the car, Karen, after receiving a surreptitious text from Benjamin, allowed Clara to take the passenger's side seat.

As they pulled out of the school parking lot, Benjamin turned toward Clara and asked where she wanted to go.

"Oh, anywhere," Clara said. "Oh, wait! Meem expects me home in ten minutes! I mean, I eat dinner with her."

"Can't you call her?" Karen asked.

"I don't have a cell phone."

"Use mine." Karen extended her cell phone to Clara, who seemed overly grateful for the offer.

"Wait," Clara said. "What should I tell her?"

Benjamin shrugged. "Tell her the truth - you're hanging out with two friends for a few hours."

"Oh," Clara said, dialing Meem's number on the cell phone. "Oh, OK. That seems easy enough. I don't think she'll mind if - Meem? Meem, it's me. With two friends. You know Benjamin AND Karen? The ones I told you about the other week? Yes. By 9:00. I'm not! 8:30? Fine. We don't know. OK. OK bye!"

Clara was tired of this, terribly tired of living with that mean old woman. These negative feelings toward Meem were not new: they had, in fact, been building up for several years now. She was usually able to suppress them, push them out of her mind, at least for a decent amount of time. The thoughts, which included a recurrent mental image of Meem in a casket, made her feel guilty. After all, Meem had done a great many things for Clara over the years. It was true, at times, Clara felt overwhelmed by a sense of gratitude. On other days, though, she sincerely wished that Meem would go to heaven to be with the Lord.

As a Christian, Clara of course knew all about the importance of having a wholesome thought life. Sometimes, though, she believed completely controlling one's thoughts was next to impossible. Even pastors and ministers, who were supposed to be on a slightly higher spiritual plane, cannot control their every thought each and every day. Could they?

Chapter 10

Back at Benjamin's trailer, out of nowhere, Clara stated her belief that it was in God's plan for her to meet them. Karen laughed, and her laughter, not meant to be mean or rude, was simply a reflex.

"Why do you think so?" Benjamin asked, moving closer to her on the sofa then and, very suddenly, her countenance changed. No longer did she appear forlorn - quite the opposite.

"Well, I think God wants me to get to know you. There's a divine reason why, a reason not of this earth. I will -"

"Will you explain how we can be saved?" Benjamin asked, and he seemed so sincere in asking that Karen no longer thought he was just playing along.

Clara herself did not question his sincerity - she was too enamored with him to consider whether his interest was genuine. She looked at Benjamin now, looked only at him, as though wholly uninterested in Karen and her potential salvation.

"I will tell you how to get to heaven!" Clara started speaking in a rushed, manic manner. "I will tell you so one day, one day you can be sure you will enter God's Kingdom and live forever! I will even -"

Once Clara seemed to be at least somewhat comfortable, Karen, in an effort to be discreet and conceal her intention, which went well beyond getting Clara to stop talking about religion, stared at the television remote. "There it *is*! I've been looking for this for days now," Karen lied, standing up from the ratty loveseat and softly hitting Clara's rear a couple times. "Slide your ass up!" Karen reached in between the sofa's cushions.

"Oh!" Clara slid closer to Benjamin. Instead of moving over on the sofa to give her more space, he remained still. "I'm sorry," Clara said as Karen grabbed the remote.

Karen sat down beside Clara, briefly wondering if she would be uncomfortable being sandwiched between the two. Then, despite knowing the answer, Karen asked her if she smoked.

"Oh, no!" Clara replied rapidly, and then added: "I did take a few drags at my cousin's wedding last summer. I mean, just to see what it was like…"

When Clara's voice trailed off and she decided to say nothing further, Benjamin asked: "What was it like?"

"Well, I almost threw up! They said I inhaled too much at once, and I said, well, isn't that what you're *supposed* to do?"

Benjamin laughed, not at her but with her. Very surprisingly, Clara did not appear to be at all uneasy, even with them both sitting unnecessarily close to her.

"Give it another try?" Karen reached into her pocket and pulled out a cigarette. "Just don't inhale so much, you'll be fine."

"Oh, no," Clara said, putting her hand up for a moment. "I couldn't. I mean, what if I get addicted? I could never afford to buy. Besides, I'm only 17!"

"Clara, relax," Karen said. "You won't get addicted from smoking a single cigarette."

"Well," Clara said. "OK, if you −"

Thinking what a pushover she was, Benjamin stuck his lit cigarette into her open mouth. Her eyes widened then, as though she had seen something frightening. Slowly, then, she inhaled as he held the cigarette in her mouth. Squinting, Clara closed her eyes and started coughing, pulling away from Benjamin suddenly. He asked if she was OK and she nodded her head. "It's yours," he said, putting the cigarette between her two fingers. Reluctantly, she accepted.

"Don't worry," Karen said. "We won't tell anyone."

"Well, I'm not worried," Clara said. "I just don't want to smell like smoke when I go home."

"You still have a few hours before 8:30," Benjamin said.

"Oh, I guess you're right."

"I'll Febreze you before we drop you off," Karen said. "If that makes you feel better."

"OK, thanks!" Clara took a short drag off her cigarette and inhaled. "I really appreciate it!"

She followed with two long drags in quick succession. As she coughed, she slightly smiled and tried to talk. "I feel so dizzy," she said. "I mean, lightheaded. Same thing I guess."

"It'll pass." Benjamin laid his hand on Clara's. To his surprise, she seemed not to mind. She closed her eyes, her hand now inside of his. "I think I should go."

"Why?" Benjamin stared at Clara, and once her eyes had met his, she had a hard time offering an explanation.

"I...I don't know."

"Stay." Karen did not know quite why she said it, for truly she wished she would leave. "It's not even 5:00."

Clara considered, looking down at Benjamin's hand covering hers, caressing hers. She felt excited before, when he was simply sitting close to her, and now, now she felt something else.

"We could go somewhere else if you'd like," Benjamin said.

"Where?" Clara felt a certain subtle moistness between her legs. Having had experienced this wetness only a few times before, she mostly associated it with alarm and anxiety and Brad Pitt. (One night she had snuck an old movie by the name of *Thelma and Louise* into her house, having borrowed it from a girlfriend, knowing Meem would disapprove of its R rating).

"Where would we go?" Clara repeated her question, as though to distract herself from thinking about what had initiated this reaction in the first place.

"Where would you wanna go?" Benjamin asked.

"It...doesn't matter."

"So you want to stay now?" he asked.

Clara nodded her head and needlessly repeated that she didn't care where they went.

"I have a place in mind," Benjamin said. Clara, much more than Karen, waited eagerly for him to reveal where. Finally: "Where?!" Clara asked.

"It's a surprise," Benjamin whispered. "Let's go now, though. My step-mom's a stupid cunt."

Clara did not react to Benjamin's derogatory description of his step-mom. Looking at him curiously instead, she wondered what relevance the sudden mention of his step-mom had.

"She'll be home any minute."

"OK," Clara said, smiling. Secretly, she wished that wherever they were going, they could be alone together. Clara knew he had a girlfriend, but Karen didn't seem to care *so why*, Clara thought, *why should I?*

The unlikely trio ended up at Green's Grove, an amusement park that had reopened for the season about a week ago. Last year Clara had been here with Meem as a belated gift for her 16th birthday. At the time, Clara had playfully suggested to Meem that a car would've been a much better gift. Clara had not been serious about a gift of such magnitude, but Meem had scolded her nevertheless for being "greedy" and "ungrateful." Clara had then told Meem she was only kidding and Meem had said, "Of course, dear, so was I."

"Do you like roller coasters?" Clara presently asked Benjamin.

"I like haunted houses better."

"Except the one here isn't scary," Karen said.

"No haunted house is scary," Benjamin said. "The only one that has ever even remotely scared me wasn't a haunted house at all."

"What was it then?" Clara asked.

"Haunted hayride," Benjamin said. "And I might add that I was on acid at the time. So the hayride might not even be the cause."

"Acid?" Clara had heard about LSD from a mandatory drug and alcohol course she had taken her freshman year, but she had never heard the drug referred to by its more colloquial name.

Benjamin decided to skip over this. "Do you like roller coasters?" he asked.

"I do!" she exclaimed. "Well, I have to say it depends."

"On what?" Karen asked.

"On how high it is! And the ones that go upside down—no way! I get queasy on those!"

Later on, Benjamin did not have to persuade Clara to go on into the haunted house as he had anticipated: she had volunteered to go on the ride herself. Not realizing that he was fulfilling her desire to be alone with him, he had texted Karen, notifying her that he would be riding the haunted house with Clara and Clara alone.

Karen's immediate reaction was one of anger. Once she stopped and analyzed that emotion, she realized how unwarranted it was. After all, Benjamin had no interest in dating Clara. Karen accepted that it was possible, quite likely in fact, that he wanted to have sex with her. But what did that prove? Even married men had sexual fantasies about other women. It was harmless enough, or so Karen thought, as long as the men didn't act on it. Never did Karen believe Benjamin would act on it, what they shared was too special. It was true at times he was a real dick to her. Deep down, though, she believed he loved her and, for one reason or another, always convinced herself he did not mean the things he said or did when he was in a "dick mood".

Once in line at *Twisted Terrors,* Karen made up an excuse as to why she couldn't go on. "I don't feel like going on. I have this headache, and it's so loud in there. Going on might make it worse."

Benjamin's prediction that Clara would briefly insist Karen go on with them was accurate.

"The carts will easily fit three of us. Please, Karen! I don't think it's a long ride and –"

"No." Karen's stern tone assured Clara that her decision was final and she should not persist.

Benjamin was not the sort of guy who held hands with a girl, not even Karen. In the nearly two years he had dated Karen, he could count on one hand the number of times he had said, "I love you." He didn't assign much value to the profuse blathering that frequently accompanied teenage love. Benjamin reasoned it was far more meaningful to show one's love rather than express it verbally.

So, when Benjamin, midway through 'Twisted Terrors', covered Clara's hand with his own, he surprised even himself. It was so dark he couldn't make out her reaction. She didn't reject the gesture, didn't pull her hand away like he thought she might. Moments later, she responded by interlacing her fingers with his own.

The amorous gesture was not as spontaneously sweet as Clara felt it to be. Benjamin had been rather methodical, not with the sudden gesture itself, but with planning ways he might best go about earning Clara's trust. None of the possibilities included holding her hand. All of the ways were much more involved, complicated. While sitting so close to her, he had to resist the urge to simply slip his hand down her shorts. He concluded that would be much too aggressive, abrupt. To truly reach Clara, he knew he would have to be gentle, a mostly foreign concept to Benjamin.

Clara gripped his hand, and he had to admit he almost jumped. Not remembering the bright loud flashing light that signaled the ride was nearly finished. "Oh my gosh," Clara said, still holding his hand tightly, her other hand on her heart, which Benjamin imagined was beating very rapidly now. Clara did not have any romantic feelings for Benjamin - she would tell anyone that this was so. Later, she would try to convince herself of this. When she had held his hand, she had been caught up in the moment, nothing more. Just not thinking, and also a bit afraid, as she had never seen such terrors!

"You won't tell Karen, will you?" Clara had asked, letting go of his hand.

Benjamin had looked at her like he had no idea what she was talking about.

"You have the wrong idea," he said. "I have a girlfriend I love very much. I was only holding your hand to be a gentleman. I thought you were afraid -"

"Well, I -"

"I wanted to comfort you, that's all."

They couldn't continue their conversation, the ride had ended, and Karen greeted them with root beer and funnel cakes as they disembarked. Clara forced a smile, knowing that was the proper reaction. Benjamin himself had no reaction, averting his eyes and lighting a cigarette.

Clara was confused: yes, she knew he had a girlfriend, but still, she couldn't help feeling slightly rejected by him. Maybe he had only held her hand to be kind. Besides, what did it matter? It was silly, she thought, continuing something so distracting and fleeting as romantic feelings. After all, she was on a mission to deliver the good news of Jesus Christ. Throughout the evening, she had to repeatedly remind herself of why she had agreed to hang out with these two lost souls in the first place. Over and over she told herself that introducing them to her personal Lord and Savior was the focus here, salvation the obvious objective. How to bring it up again, though, without seeming too pushy? They were both already cognizant of her beliefs, and the interest in God they had shown during the Genesis meetings was gone. True, Benjamin had seemed receptive to the good news earlier in the day, until Karen had interrupted Clara, claiming the remote was missing.

Eventually, Clara thanked Karen for the funnel cake and soda and even went so far as asking if she wanted to be paid back.

"I don't have any money right now, but I -"

"Don't worry about it," Karen said, waving Clara's offer away.

As the trio stood in line to ride a rollercoaster (Clara had of course approved of "Drastic Dragon", noting afterward how there was nothing drastic or intimidating about this ride at all. There were no backwards loops, only a few sharp turns, and the drops on the ride were not very severe) Karen ventured to ask Clara if she wanted a cigarette.

"Oh, no," Clara said. "We're in public, and if someone saw -"

Karen laughed, not meaning to interrupt her honest explanation.

"What?" Clara asked. "Are you making fun of me, Karen?"

Karen didn't respond. She stopped laughing instead. Benjamin was sitting on the rail, seeming disengaged as they neared the front of the line.

Clara smiled the whole time. Sitting behind Benjamin and Karen, she screamed and giggled and threw her arms in the air. It was true Clara had been on a rollercoaster ride before, but never had she gone on one feeling so free and open to any and every possibility. On this ride with Benjamin and Karen, she forgot herself almost entirely, and all that remained for her to feel was the sheer exhilaration of being alive.

After the trio left the amusement park, an hour remained before Clara had to be home. Benjamin could think of several things he might do with Clara, but they all seemed premature, not quite right for tonight.

Clara was hoping they would ask her to hang out longer. Unsure what they might do, she only knew she wanted to spend more time with them. So, when Benjamin asked her for directions to her house, she felt a little disappointed. Why did he want to drop her off now, over an hour before 8:30? Hadn't they had a good time with her? Were they tired of her company? Possibly, Clara wondered, Karen had discovered they had held hands in the haunted house?

No matter, they presently pulled into her driveway. They were silent several seconds. Neither Benjamin or Karen were ones for pleasantries like *hi* or *goodbye* or *how are you*, and Clara seemed to be waiting for one. Quite clearly, she had no desire to return home.

"Do you think I smell like smoke?"

"Obviously, we can't tell since the entire car smells like smoke."

Karen had a valid point, but Clara didn't acknowledge it - in fact, she seemed not to hear her.

"If your grandmother asks, just tell her. Tell her your friends were smoking in the car and you were not."

Simple enough, Clara thought, however there was a slight problem. "But that'd be a lie. I did have a cigarette."

"Not really," Karen said. "You only took a drag or two."

Not altogether true: Clara had smoked over half of a cigarette. Nevertheless, Karen's point was taken well enough. Where was the harm in Clara smoking a cigarette?

"Well, I'll see you two tomorrow, OK?"

Clara opened the door, waiting for either Benjamin or Karen to respond. They said nothing. "I had a really good time tonight," Clara said as she stepped out onto the driveway. Still, they said nothing. As she began walking toward the house Benjamin beeped once and then peeled out of the driveway.

Chapter 11

Meem startled Clara. The second she walked in the front door, there she was, sitting in her rocker reading a magazine. Clara smiled. Meem stared at her. "Well, goodnight Meem." Clara forced another smile and then starting up the stairs.

"It's not even 8:00," Meem said sharply. "Surely, you're not going to bed already?"

"No, I -"

"Don't want to talk to me?" Meem asked, gazing back down at her magazine.

"I do!" Clara protested. "I have homework to do though! I also -"

"Oh, you're weak," Meem said nastily. "Offering an explanation like that. I might respect you if you were just honest and said how you really felt."

Clara looked at her with a blank expression, wanting to say something but thinking it probably wasn't a good idea.

"Say, 'Meem, I don't want to talk to you anymore or spend time with you because you're old. You're old, and I'll be leaving soon for college and want to get on with my life without you, want to be all -"

"No, Meem. That's not true, Meem!" Clara shook her head repeatedly. "You must know that's not true!"

Licking her index finger Meem started flipping pages in her magazine, aimlessly. She scowled at Clara and then continued flipping pages rapidly, hands shaking as she did so. "Just go up to your room. Don't sugarcoat what's inevitable, dear." Meem's voice flat and cold, all emotion drained.

Clara opened her mouth, wanting to protest further, to convince Meem everything she said was untrue. Instead, she decided to stay quiet. A decision based on past experience, for she knew the more she tried to make Meem feel better, the more belligerent she'd become, and things would only escalate from there. Continuing up the stairs -

"Aren't you going to tell me about these so-called *friends* of yours? What are their names again?"

"Benjamin and Karen." Clara thought she should provide the least amount of information as possible.

"Go on…"

"What do you want to know?"

"Are they Christians?"

"No," Clara said. "I already told you they weren't."

"I'm old, dear," Meem said loudly. "I FORGET things, you understand?" Beginning to feel uncomfortable again, Clara's efforts to not look at Meem failed, as Meem's wide eyes burned into her, demanding attention. Meem waited a few moments, believing such an intense pause might coerce Clara into offering more information. Clara was silent and then, finally, "I really do have a lot of homework. OK?"

Glancing at the muted television, Meem ignored her. "D-did you have a good night?" Clara asked. Meem turned up the volume on the television, and Clara didn't wait more than a few seconds before going up to her room.

In her diary that night she wrote:

> I come to You now Lord, please be with me Lord
> & comfort me. Jesus, I long for You. I am broken now,
> before you I fall. Lord, all I want is You in my life. I
> know that w/ You in my life I will always be happy
> & I can overcome anything. I just wanted to take this
> time to thank You Lord for hearing my prayers & for
> forgiving my sins. I feel your love all around me Lord.
> It is so amazing Lord how you gave up your life for all
> of mankind so that our sins may be forgiven & so we
> may live eternally. Lord, I love You so much! Please,
> Lord, lead me in the right direction. Please also guide
> Benjamin & Karen, Lord, & let them know that You
> love them. Lord, I pray that You help me to become one
> with You, so that I can serve You in all that I do. Lord,
> I give You my life & I want You to do whatever is in
> Your will w/ it. Take my life Lord & work through it

so that Your love & goodness may shine through me. Thank You so much for saving me Lord. Thank You for guiding me closer to You. Lord, help me to not rely on what I think is right, but instead to always remember You in all I do & turn to You for advice. Lord, I am so blessed to have You in my life. I long to become closer to You, Lord, & I pray that I would be able to reach Benjamin & Karen with the good news & salvation of Your Son Jesus Christ.

Love,
Clara

The next morning when she awoke she felt nervous, no sadness, simply a sense of anxiety, fear. Should she call Jeremy? She imagined the sound of his voice, how it would calm her down instantly. Clara knew the danger in relying on a single person to ease one's anxiety. Suppose that person left, went away somewhere? What if they suddenly didn't want to talk to you? She knew it was irrational, thinking he would abruptly leave without telling her or decide he didn't want to talk to her anymore. Of course, he would be going to college soon. Months ago he had made her aware so she might be somewhat prepared. His early notice was irrelevant, though – she still couldn't stomach the fact he would be going, couldn't stand the thought of him not being around much longer. From time to time she would still see him, she knew. Already he had invited her to visit sometime, also promising he'd be home an entire weekend this fall. They could communicate daily too, whether by phone or e-mail (Jeremy didn't have texting on his phone. In confidence, he had told Clara that Stephanie had been texting him up to 200 times a day. When Stephanie asked why he had ended his texting plan, Jeremy had been honest, which resulted in the silent treatment for three days. On the fourth day, when he had acted like he hadn't even noticed her not talking to him, she broke down, exasperated, saying could he please allow her to continue texting him? Promising she would text him moderately from now on, only when urgent and necessary. Still, he said no, refusing to reinstate his texting plan. She had been infuriated, and a second silent treatment had ensued, except this one only lasted a day.)

Clara did not call him. Yes, she knew he'd pick up, even if it was only 4:30 A.M., he never turned his phone off and likely wouldn't mind being awakened despite the hour.

For several minutes, the phone in her hand, she contemplated whether to call. Finally deciding not to, thinking she could anticipate the conversation: *what's up*, he might say after deciphering something was wrong, and clearly he would know something was given the hour, her tone of voice. Then, she would tell him everything, opening up to him completely, not holding anything back. After he listened to her for ten or fifteen minutes, she would feel better, relieved, even almost happy.

She didn't understand it - why did opening up to him make her feel better? During these rather one-sided conversations, he didn't even talk, or at least not much. He listened to her closely, that was true. Usually, he did not offer any advice unless he sensed she really did not know what to do and needed some guidance. Generally, though, she knew what to do and just needed someone to listen to her.

That day Clara rode the bus to school. Of course, Jeremy would've given her a ride, had she asked. She did not ask, though, why would she? He would not ever like her in the way she liked him, and those unrequited feelings made her feel slightly worthless. Even if he broke up with Stephanie, the chances of Jeremy going for a girl like Clara were slim to none, she knew.

Gazing out the bus window, seeing the trees and sky and houses blur by, Clara wondered why she had not asked Benjamin to pick her up. Certainly, she thought he would have. Did she still feel apprehensive, over the fact she might really be getting to know these two people who felt dangerous to her?

Dressed conservatively that day, she wore no makeup, nothing. Underneath her Capri pants a skirt that fell only a bit above the knee. Underneath her oversized red blouse she wore a low-cut sleeveless shirt.

Also, a push-up bra, which enhanced her breasts to a solid B-cup. She had thought herself rather daring when she bought the bra sophomore year, but she had never worked up the audacity to wear it, especially with a shirt like she had on today. She hadn't used the cache of makeup tucked away in her purse, not having the energy to sneak around that morning.

She wanted to ask Karen to give her a little lesson again. Maybe, she thought, she had applied too much eyeliner and mascara on the day Karen pulled her aside. Her complexion was similar to Karen's, only paler, so the contrast created with the eye makeup looked severe.

Approaching her locker that day, Clara heard the usual sporadic persistent sounds - laughter and shouts, lockers being slammed shut, the announcements stating that a particular student should report to the office. Too, she could see the extreme joy and excitement on most of the students' faces. Clara herself felt no real happiness or anticipation for the summer, partly because she had no plans and knew even if she got a job she'd be lonely, likely spending an inordinate amount of time with Meem.

Chapter 12

Jeremy had only the very best intentions. Truly, he did want to help Clara. She had to know, by now she stood no chance with him as a potential girlfriend. If he was honest he had no interest in her beyond friendship. She liked him so much, she had a hard time admitting how much, how attached she was to him. Certainly, he didn't mind such an attachment - on the contrary, he encouraged it. He believed Clara needed a strong male figure in her life, and he had been that for her, and would continue to be there for her, if only she would let him in a little bit more. She hadn't opened up to him in weeks. Their conversations, lately, had been superficial and their friendship was getting to that point as well. It was true Jeremy would be off to college in a month, hundreds of miles away, but that didn't change the fact that he could still be there for her always. Repeatedly, he had told her she could always call him, whenever she needed someone to talk with, but she didn't seem to ever fully accept that he genuinely cared for her and loved her as a friend.

Recently, realizing his departure was imminent, he had even told her they could Skype. She had stared at him, blankly, having absolutely no idea what he was referring to. (When he briefly explained to her what Skype was, she had giggled dismissively and said, 'Oh, yes, I knew what *that* was. I just didn't know the exact name for it.')

So, that morning, in homeroom, again Clara acted differently, not engaging him as she normally did, not even saying hi or acknowledging his presence. Jeremy understood it was very likely she was just upset with him for not spending time with her after school as he had originally said he would. Jeremy noted, however, that Clara had begun acting indifferent toward him for months now, the abundant warmth she had always shown when she was around him had slowly, steadily declined until now where she faced forward in her seat, listening closely to Mr. Pratt's announcements, acting like Jeremy was not even there.

Clara decided not to reveal her outfit that day. After homeroom, she did seriously consider ducking into the bathroom, but then she thought:

why the heck even bother? Who was she trying to impress? She believed she had only dressed so grown-up and worn makeup to experiment, to see how she might look. And then, there was the obvious fact that, having been denied this standard rite of passage, a natural curiosity arose, one that would've existed in the first place but was intensified as a result of being suppressed. Now that her experiment was complete, her curiosity sated, she wondered what she might want to try next. There were so many possibilities, all seemed very near her fingertips and yet, somehow, only marginally within reach.

When she was with Jeremy she felt anything might be possible. With Benjamin and Karen, she felt almost the same, not even knowing them very well, yet absolutely losing herself in their strong, consistent identities. And she liked to forget herself, if only for a short while.

In Trigonometry, Clara could not focus, too distracted by thoughts of her new "so-called" friends, as Meem had called them. Uncertain whether or not Benjamin and Karen had even come to school today, Clara wondered when she might see them again. Suppose they didn't come to school anymore, what then? Suppose they moved away and never let her know their new location?

Strange, Clara thought, completely absurd how she could be so attached to them, only having a handful of hours exclusively in their company. Nevertheless, Clara was worried and anxious about seeing them. Secretly, she was afraid they might not want to see her anymore.

What if they had, upon hanging out with her, determined she was a loser, unpopular and unworthy of their time. She wished she had their cell phone numbers, she wanted to call them, when she got home she wanted to call them right away. They knew where she lived, though, so surely if they wanted to see her they could easily do so. She didn't like the not-knowing part. Having no control over when they might decide to reappear in her life.

Clara could hear Mrs. Henderson's voice, she could also hear the marker *squeak-squeaking* across the dry-erase board. What Mrs. Henderson's words were, though, Clara could not say, for none of them seemed to register, none of them made any sense, and not only because she was teaching the last new lesson of the school year. All Clara could see was Mrs. Henderson's mouth moving and her motioning toward the board as she continued to talk, to explain, to elucidate. None of it mattered to Clara anymore. All that used to appear so important had value no longer: Genesis club, Jeremy, her relationship with God, her devotions, Meem, maintaining her perfect grades. What did matter then? Clara could not say, could not be sure, and did presently wonder what gave one's life meaning. God, of course, was the answer that came immediately to mind. God gave one purpose and joy and strength and peace. But what if there was no God? What if, after all, God did not exist? Never had Clara dared to question His existence, not even silently in her own mind. She had always accepted that He was there, somewhere, looking down on her and guiding and protecting her. Now, she began to wonder if what she had believed all along might not be true. Now, it was dubious as to whether or not God was really there, doubtful as to whether He really did listen to her prayers and love her like she loved Him.

"Clara."

Suddenly, she heard her name. Mrs. Henderson, calling on her to respond to a question she had not heard. "Yes?" Clara glanced up from her desk, not at all hesitantly.

"What was your answer for number 14?"

"What page?" Clara asked, seeing that her Trigonometry book in front of her was closed.

"Clara," Mrs. Henderson said, eyes widening, not at all unpleasantly. "We're on page 309."

Clara opened her book quickly, if a bit apprehensively, feeling other students' eyes on her as she leafed through the pages, turning page after page after page until - "That's the only equation I didn't solve." This was true too. Number 14 was the last equation assigned for homework, and Clara had not been able to solve it, even after spending an inordinate amount of time trying to do so.

"No?" Mrs. Henderson asked, glancing around the room. "Anybody else?"

Only one hand went up, and the student sounded hesitant. "I think I got it."

"Did you check your answer in the back of the book?"

"Yes," the student said. "I couldn't. Only the odd numbers have answers listed."

"Right," Mrs. Henderson said, signaling with her marker for the student to come up to the board. "You want to come up and show all the work you did to arrive at your answer?"

Clara wondered if Mrs. Henderson was disappointed in her. After class she thought about telling her that she had tried, really tried, to arrive at an answer. The answer to this problem, as with so many others she sought, had been elusive.

Chapter 13

The moment Mrs. Henderson got home she started correcting tests. She needed to stay busy. She needed to not think about Frank. She needed to not think about Clara. There were almost two full weeks before she had to turn in final grades. Frank was lounging in the study, ostensibly making business-related phone calls. In his hushed, insistent professional tone she could hear him talking. He would remain in that room all evening unless she went in to interrupt him, which she would not do. She didn't want to talk to hm. He would have to talk to her first. She had become so tired of initiating conversation, of trying to establish, or reestablish, a bond with him that had once been very strong. Clara had all of her contact information: phone number, e-mail address, and home address. If Clara wanted to talk to her, wanted some advice, she would get in touch. If Mrs. Henderson tried to pry into her personal life, which she had to resist the urge to do, she knew Clara would simply close up and then tell her even less. After all, she was 17 - shouldn't she be treated like the adult she was fast becoming?

Mrs. Henderson was midway through correcting tests when Frank, surprisingly, appeared at her side. She tried to ignore him, as he nudged her, slightly, setting his hand gently on her shoulder. It had been almost a full week, and she knew what he wanted. Oh, it was very much like clockwork. Her urges were more spontaneous, sporadic. Mrs. Henderson was not a creature of habit, not like Frank. It was rather early in the evening even for him. Typically, he initiated sex shortly before they went to bed, when she was about to take a shower, for instance, or he was finished shaving and making business calls. It was not even 9 P.M.

He said nothing. She said nothing. Whether or not he was smiling in that frank, forceful way she couldn't say. She herself was not smiling, was actually a bit uncomfortable. Glancing up at him for a moment was not the best idea. Their eyes locked, and she felt that old spark, that certain connection that she knew existed despite her wish to deny it

85

was there. His hand starting rubbing her shoulder, gently, moving onto her neck, firmly running his fingers through her hair, and she closed her eyes, tilted her head, slightly. Her ballpoint pen fell onto the stack of tests, and she could resist him no longer.

Afterward she thought of the same things that had been blotted out so urgently while making love. She dawdled over the tests, whether or not she should correct them. In the bathroom, on the toilet, she heard Frank resume his business calls, speaking so clearly and quietly. And then there was Clara, she focused on Clara, the daughter she still so desperately wanted but might not ever have.

Chapter 14

Clara did not go home immediately after school that day. She didn't want to go home, for she knew all that awaited her was Meem. For the first time she was willing to admit to herself that she was sick and tired of that woman. The only choice that remained, it seemed, was to block her out altogether. Listening to Meem, even if only for a little, inevitably resulted in her strident, contralto voice infiltrating Clara's mind.

After she was dropped off and the bus disappeared, Clara started down the road. She didn't know where she was going, had no destination in mind besides, possibly, the quaint cracked white bridge that ran across a muddy narrow creek. Although the water here was not at all pretty, everything else was serene and vivid: the trees with their thin bright branches swaying ever so slightly in the wind, the birds chirping quietly but distinctly since everything here was so quiet, and the thick high green grass that was surprisingly devoid of weeds, the grass that seemed to only be attended to once it was two or three feet high, the grass that presently caressed Clara's ankles. Behind it all was the subtly suffocating sound of water rushing slowly, steadily.

Clara sat down in the middle of the bridge, legs dangling off the edge as she gazed down into the water. No more than 15 feet below her, this water could be counted on, this water was consistent, this water would be far too chilly to venture out into, Clara knew, but she still might dip her toes into it. Even once it got to be summer, swimming in this creek would be impossible, as the water, even in the middle of the creek, was shallow and barely reached her knees. She had so much work to do once she got home. Once she got home, Meem would want to talk, would want to know where she had been. Also Meem would wonder about Jeremy, wonder why Clara didn't want to talk to him anymore, didn't want to call him or open up to him like she used to. Too, Clara would think about Benjamin and Karen, whether or not she could make a difference in their lives, how plausible it really was. Clara would not think about Mrs. Henderson or God or the Genesis Club and how she might best go about securing her place as vice president her senior year.

No longer would Clara think about how she might please Meem or please God or Jeremy, for truly she felt she was on her own now, felt she was doing God's will by reaching out to two unsaved individuals who no one else appeared to care for. The problem, Clara thought, with Genesis club, was that it had become very segregated, exclusive. The club did not reach out to others, for the most part, only associated with those who were already saved, already members. The club, Clara thought, was also judgmental, ignoring outsiders and not giving them a real solid shot to know Jesus Christ. It bothered Clara, irritated her deeply. There was nothing she could do though, was there? There were no meetings left in the school year and besides, when Clara tried to share a new idea she always felt it went overlooked. God knows she had tried, truly, to cast light on the issue of reaching nonbelievers - whenever she did, though, the president and vice president looked at her askance and then either cleared their throat dismissively or said, "We'll talk about that," indifferently and then inevitably the issue was never discussed. She didn't understand why the club should be so uninterested in developing an outreach program, and she had even mentioned it one time to Mrs. Henderson. Mrs. Henderson had said she didn't think they had the funds and she would look into it. A few weeks later, when Mrs. Henderson had not broached the issue with Clara, Clara had asked her about it. "Well, the whole problem is we don't have enough members who have the extra time for outreach. Besides, we do have an outreach - it's just not formally organized." Clara had pressed her, and she had said something about how the majority of students at Turner High School know about Genesis Club and know they are more than welcome to attend. "We cannot persuade a student to be born again if he has his heart hardened against God," Mrs. Henderson had said conclusively. Clara did agree with her, mostly. It was true, mostly, basic psychology: the more you try to convince someone else to do something they already don't want to do, the more likely they are to never do it.

Chapter 15

Benjamin and Karen were not thinking about Clara. She did not cross their minds once, and the only time they did think of her was when they were out on the front stoop smoking and Karen abruptly swung her head back, laughing and allowing smoke to seep out of her mouth.

"Well, what if someone saw me?" Karen asked, doing a spot-on imitation of Clara's soft, sweet voice. Benjamin watched indifferently as Karen continued mocking her.

"She never said that," Benjamin said.

"You know she asked someone somewhere a question along those lines." Karen threw her head back once more as her laughter dissolved and then ceased.

"I don't see why you ridicule her."

"You fuckin' make fun of her too."

Benjamin shrugged. "I did a few times. When I first met her. I didn't do it for the same reason you do it though."

Karen's puzzled look encouraged Benjamin to elaborate.

"You make fun of her to feel better about yourself. You feel like you are better than her because you want, you *need*, someone to feel better than. It's a way to boost your ego."

The puzzlement on Karen's face faded as Benjamin's assessment sunk in. She took one final drag off her cigarette and then tried to change the subject. "Are we going to school tomorrow?" she asked.

"You already know the answer."

Karen felt rebuked, a little, although Benjamin had no intention of making her feel this way. It had been a simple statement of fact. They would not be going to school tomorrow. Benjamin had plans to score some more methamphetamine. Karen was excited for tomorrow and not only because they would be getting high, although that certainly had a lot to do with it.

Her excitement arose out of the knowledge that she would be spending the entire day with Benjamin, and also knowing it would be the next to last day of school, which would enhance all of her joyful feelings. She did think that going to school high would be interesting, a good time for sure. Had no fear of getting into trouble, truly she did not care. Benjamin didn't care either, it's just that he didn't see the point in going to school and having to adhere to a schedule when they could simply stay home and do whatever they wanted. He had no specific plans regarding how they would spend their day. Usually when they skipped school and got high Benjamin at least had a tentative outline in his mind as to what they would do, and when, where. He felt less concerned now with creating a schedule, however tentative, he felt making one might be rather constrictive, restricting the amount of potential fun they could have.

"Do you think we should call her?" Karen asked.

"Why?"

"I don't know. We could ask her to hang out tomorrow."

Benjamin turned his head, lighting another cigarette. "That's a real genius idea, K."

Karen asked if he was being sarcastic, despite being relatively certain that he was. Benjamin explained: "You really think she's gonna want to get to know us, be our friend, if she knows we're using drugs?"

"She already knows we use drugs." It was a sharp counterpoint, one Benjamin didn't acknowledge, turning his head back toward Karen. "Yes, but using in her presence is different. Shows we don't care about her or her feelings. Shows we're not being sincere about wanting to change."

"Change what?"

"Our ways, everything. Shows we don't want to be saved."

"Do we?"

Benjamin chuckled. "No."

"Hell no."

"I do think Jesus existed."

"Do you?"

Benjamin nodded. "He had to have been an incredible man, little doubt in my mind. To have so many men and women follow Him and believe in Him, that he was God's son. But it was a fantasy, an illusion."

"Magic?"

"Kind of. Since it wasn't real."

"He tricked like masses of people then, he deceived them?"

"No," Benjamin said. "It wasn't like that. He wanted to help people that were hopeless - the destitute, lame, blind, hurting. He wanted to give them hope."

"Did He?"

"Well, yes. Those were people who had to believe in something, something to numb them from the reality that was their lives. They had to believe."

"Believe what?"

"Dammit, K. So many questions. They had to believe in an afterlife, had to believe in the resurrection, in heaven. Because their lives here on earth weren't enough, they were dealt a shitty fuckin' hand so the only way to go on, to have the strength and will to go on, was to believe in Him, to believe in heaven, a fantasy that was obviously pleasing and sustaining to them."

For a moment Karen closed her eyes, absorbing his words and opinionated logic.

"I don't blame them," Benjamin said. "I can understand it, I don't judge them. Which is so much more than I can say for them. Christians. Who are supposed to be the epitome of compassion and kindness and love and yet are often so judgmental it becomes a form of hate."

Karen didn't want to think about this anymore. She wanted to change the subject, but didn't know what she might say. Benjamin broke the silence: "I want to fuck." Karen averted her gaze immediately, not wanting her eyes to meet his own, as he could decipher the majority of her thoughts if he looked into them. She didn't know why she tried to hide her feelings so much - he so clearly knew her inside and out. Talking wasn't required for him to know what was on her mind. Right now, for instance, he knew she didn't want to have sex. And it wasn't because she wasn't attracted to him. Always she was attracted to him, physically and emotionally. It was the way he initiated sex lately - so forcefully. Bluntly, he said what he wanted.

Didn't he care what she wanted? Even if only occasionally, she thought it would be nice if he asked how she was feeling or, if that was asking too much, requested sex. True, sometimes when she was in the mood for sex she didn't want it to be gentle, didn't want to make love. True, sometimes she did want it rough, wanted to fuck. It was probably 50/50. The problem was Benjamin: when he wanted sex, he wanted to fuck 100% of the time. Never had he made love to her, well maybe three or four times, when they had first met. Then, slowly, so surely, the sex had become harder, rougher and less passionate. There was in fact no passion in the way Benjamin had sex with her, no love in the way he put himself inside of her. Consistently she felt like he was angry about something, angry and irritated.

"You coming," Benjamin said, didn't ask, as he opened the front door, holding it open for her which he did so rarely. Likely, he held it out of practicality, not any sort of courtesy - a couple drags remained on his cigarette and he wanted an extra few seconds before he extinguished it.

Karen thought she might protest, might voice her wishes, her concerns, or at least a few of them. Instead she said nothing, did nothing except walk inside the door that he was now impatiently holding ajar, his fingers tapping the glass on the door's rickety ripped screen window.

He blew the smoke above his head in two nearly perfect rings. His eyes were glued to her ass as she walked into the living room, which was really only a TV room but might have been also called a family room, a dining room, whatever. Benjamin's parents would not be home until very late, not that they cared if Karen was here or even if they were having sex in the trailer. He only became a bit alarmed over how loud Karen was when they had sex, so loud in fact that even playing metal music on the stereo didn't conceal her noises. The only thing that seemed to work was shoving a pillow over her face, or under her face, depending on the position. His parents, probably, wouldn't even care about that if it weren't for the fact that they were usually sleeping by the time Karen and Benjamin got around to having sex.

As soon as she was in his bedroom he slammed the door shut, and he didn't know why he had shut it so hard. Next time he thought he might close it gently, if only to confuse her, to make her think, *feel*, it would be gentle, gentle and loving. Several times when Karen had been anticipating sex, in the mood for sex, even on the verge of initiating sex, she had said softly, "You gonna give it to me babe?" and he had nodded and said, "Not in a good way." Another time when she had suggested they have sex, he had said, "You really want the wrath of God?"

Karen had become aroused over this rather rhetorical query, and she had been slightly apprehensive over how aroused she had in fact felt.

In his bedroom, on top of her now, Benjamin had no thoughts of Karen, his mind focused entirely on Clara. The blinds were closed and he had not turned any of the lights on. It was after 9 P.M., so he couldn't see Karen beneath him, not entirely, he could only make out parts and pieces of this body beneath him. This body beneath him was not Karen, this body beneath him became, for an instant, more than a body. This body beneath him belonged to Clara, and he imagined several of her features and how they differed from Karen: Clara was thinner, weighed at least 30 pounds less than Karen, though she was four or five inches shorter. Also Clara's hair was blonde whereas Karen had black hair (her natural color was brown but she dyed it.) He also could see Clara's face, her rather thin pouty lips, her small nose, wide eyes.

As he continued fucking Karen he saw Clara's reaction and how it would differ from Karen's. Being a virgin, he was sure she would contort and tighten her face, tighten her expression and then try to relax her expression. Too, she would close her eyes in agonized pleasure, close her eyes and open her eyes, close them, open them, trying to feel the pleasure more than the pain, gazing up into the ceiling and trying to detach herself from this feeling, this feeling, this feeling that Benjamin wanted to give to her, to confuse her, startle her, absolutely delight her. Since he would not attempt to muzzle her noises, it was likely she would try to suppress them, a bemusing mix of pleasure and pain that produced little loud moans and cries and *"Benjamin, Benjamin, Benjamin..."* Clara would scratch his back, for sure, resulting in an erratic long mess of marks that she would no doubt apologize for.

He wouldn't be a gentleman, which would entail telling her that she needn't apologize, it was her first time and she couldn't help scratching him. Instead, Benjamin would nod, allowing her apology to linger in the air, resulting in silence, absolute silence that only he would feel comfortable with. Clara, on the other hand, would wonder what she might say next, apologize again? Ask if he was mad, irritated? And if there was anything she could do to make him feel better? She would feel guilty, he was sure, not thinking at all about how he had hurt her, how he should be the one asking if she was OK, it being her first time, and was there anything he could do.

"Benjamin!" Karen cried, and still Benjamin imagined Clara beneath him, gripping his shoulders, legs wrapped around him completely, letting his body cover hers and feeling safe and protected.

"Benjamin!" Karen cried again, her head tilted back as she lifted her legs up further, her legs pushed far back beyond her head. "Benjamin…" And he covered her mouth, her nostrils too, for a moment. Her eyes widened because she could not breathe. She closed her eyes, she opened her eyes. She shook her head, scratched his back and slapped him. And he pushed himself further inside her, slowing down, slowing down, slow, slower, and then rapidly shifting speed, pounding away at her. At least 30 seconds passed before he decided to let her breathe again, this decision triggered by the fact that he had come.

"You bastard!" she yelled, shoving him off her.

He grinned.

"Dammit!" She was angry now as she climbed off the bed and began gathering her clothes off the floor.

Still grinning, Benjamin lit a cigarette, stood up, and walked out of the room.

Chapter 16

Meem said nothing to Clara, surprisingly, nothing at all. The moment Clara walked in the door, she could smell supper. Normally she didn't help Meem prepare supper, unless of course she asked, which she didn't, very rarely, as she couldn't stand another body in the kitchen with her, it was too small. Feeling very anxious, not knowing whether she should join Meem in the kitchen and talk to her and wait for the food to be finished, or whether she should attempt to go up to her bedroom and wait until Meem called her. Going up to her bedroom might be a bit suspicious. Clearly, Meem knew she had gone somewhere since she had not returned immediately after school. Meem likely wouldn't care, since she had only been gone about an hour, and what difference did it make? Meem's only objection would be that Clara had not informed her where she was going.

When Clara appeared in the kitchen, standing still by the half-wall assessing Meem's mood, Meem did not acknowledge her. At first, Clara thought Meem had not heard her, knowing she was hard of hearing. Clara decided to join her in the kitchen. When she sat down at the kitchen table, rather discreetly pulling a chair out and not speaking, she thought Meem would at least acknowledge her. Meem, however, did not even turn to see her, acted as if she wasn't there.

Showering something on the stove with pepper, Meem's expression was firm and fixed and void of all emotion. Picking her bifocals up off the table, Meem licked her index finger and turned a page in a cookbook. The quiet intense tune Meem began to hum made Clara nervous, a little. Should she say hello or ask her how her day was? Should she set the table? Each potential action she could take she analyzed thoroughly, trying to predict what response such an action would elicit from Meem. Minutes passed as Meem drained water from a colander, peeled big long fat carrots, diced onions, and dumped marinara sauce into a stainless steel bowl.

"Your mother called," Meem said.

Clara waited for her to continue, provide more information about the call, at least a few details, but she said nothing more. "Should I call her back?" Clara asked.

"That's up to you, Clara, but I'm sure if you don't she will call you back. Jesus knows how much that woman wants to rekindle a relationship with you."

Clara felt happy hearing this, though she tried to suppress how happy this news did indeed make her feel. It was never made so clear to her that her mother did want to establish a relationship with her. Usually Clara had felt the opposite was true. They used to talk at least once every week, Clara calling her one week and then her mother calling her the next.

Gradually, then, the calls became less and less frequent. Gradually, then, the calls became entirely one-sided, so it was Clara who was the one always calling her mother, and it was Clara who was always asking questions about her mother, asking what was going on in her life, how she was doing. Clara got tired of this, over time. A couple years passed before she decided it was in her best interest to not talk to her mother anymore. Whenever she became attached to her, she sensed her mother erecting an emotional barrier, her mother becoming distant and disaffected.

Sometimes still, she did wonder about her father, thinking about what he might look like today. Though she had seen several photos of him when he was in his mid to late twenties, she imagined how different he might look today, or might he look the same? People age very differently, she knew. In her mind she saw his closely cropped golden blonde hair, his hazel eyes which were rather piercing and mesmerizing, his dimples (they were very subtle), and the small scar on his cheek (he had been attacked by a pit bull in his youth). She used to daydream about him, especially at night, wondering what his voice might sound like, would it have a lot of inflection, monotone, or somewhere in the middle? Would it be deep and smooth or slightly nasal? She liked to think it would be the former. She liked to think it would be a calm voice, a calm and soothing voice that could lull her to sleep. A photo of him in a business suit (which she didn't understand since he worked in a factory) used to sit by her bedside until one day out of the blue it seemed she decided it was too much, decided she had been investing far too many of her emotions into this man she didn't know, this man who was a dead stranger. Where was that photo now? Still in the frame, she had placed it in the bottom drawer of her bureau, underneath a couple pair of Capri pants. On a semi-regular basis, she opened this drawer to steal a glance at it, to see his face again, his frame, his smile, and also to make sure it was still there, as it was the only photo she had. Last year, while conducting one of her standard checks, she saw it was gone. Her intuition advised her that Meem, for one reason or another, had taken it, though she had never asked her, knowing Meem would likely not fess up, even if confronted. Clara imagined Meem had been jealous, not wanting this essentially imaginary man to receive any of Clara's love and devotion, wanting all of it for herself.

"I think I will call," Clara said finally.

"She has a new number." Meem pointed to a scrap of paper sitting on the counter beside her cookbook. "That might be the only reason she called. Just so you can reach her."

Clara was disappointed, realizing the real reason her mother had likely called: not to talk, to see how Clara was doing, no, she called for a specific reason, would likely be very curt on the phone, saying what she had to say and then hanging up. Staring at the paper, Clara thought very seriously about ripping it to shreds. Over a year had passed since she had last spoken to her mother. Even then the conversation had lasted no more than ten minutes, and only that long because Clara had tried so hard to sustain the conversation, asking personal questions, hoping her mom might show interest in return, might want to know what was going on in her life. Instead, she had very succinctly answered each question, following each answer a stiff silence that enveloped Clara so much she felt forced to ask another question. During the course of this conversation, she had discovered several things about her mother. Her mother had moved to a different state, had a new "significant other", new hair color, and had finally informed Clara that "middle-age is a very open time" and that her significant other was a woman.

That night, Clara knew she should call Jeremy. He was on her mind, not all the time, as he had been in the past. Still, though, she was thinking about him, had things on her mind she wanted, *needed,* to discuss, things that were weighing on her, dragging her down. Meem was asleep. During dinner, she had avoided her as much as you can avoid someone who is sitting directly across from you at a dinner table. She had kept her eyes down on her dinner—the pasta, the vegetables, the tall glass of milk - she had kept her eyes closely on all of these things.

Very slowly, she had eaten her food, despite the fact that she wanted to be done as soon as possible so she could go up to her room and be alone. Now, away from Meem, her mind raced with thoughts that were obsessive and somewhat irrational.

Would she ever get married? No, her mind told her, absolutely not, though she had nothing to support this negative belief. Did Jeremy care for her? God knows how much she cared for him, how much she wanted to be with him, spiritually, emotionally, and in any other way that a woman can be with a man, forever. Forever. Always, she thought about him, often attempting to block him out. She had become concerned and a little worried about how much she thought about him, how much he occupied her thoughts, how much she wanted to be with him, spend time with him, how attached she had become.

Since she had met him, she went through intermittent desperate phases of trying to suppress her feelings for him, trying to push him out of her mind. Even when he was single, the sinking feeling she had proved accurate: he was only interested in being her friend, nothing more, nothing less.

Truly, she did appreciate his kindness, his caring considerate nature. It's just that she felt somehow like she wasn't worth it, didn't deserve him or his love. She loved him. Never would she deny this, not even now, in this moment, as she tried so hard to expel him from her thoughts. Did Jeremy ever think about her? Very rarely, possibly, when she was in one of her more upbeat moods, she believed he did think about her, not at all romantically. Pleasantly, possibly, she crossed his mind and she told herself then that he did care about her, as a friend, and loved her too.

Presently, she felt nothing, felt she was nowhere, at least not in her room, felt like she was no one, felt alone, isolated, disconnected from everyone and so very far away from Jeremy.

Slicing into the shaky silence she experienced suddenly she heard Meem's judgmental harsh voice. How could this woman possess such power, such authority? At least in Clara's mind, all the time, she heard Meem telling her she should do this or do that, and how she should do it, when, why. Constantly, she tried to silence Meem, terminate the grip she had upon her.

Jeremy, even now, was the only one who could come so very close to deleting Meem from her mind. Why did he have the power to do this? Clara supposed the why was irrelevant. The fact was he made her feel such a sense of calm, peace, like everything would work out in the end. And he was there, Jeremy, truly he was here with her now, inside of her, she could feel him and it erased everything, all of her thoughts, she went wholly blank. Clearly, he did not know he had such a brilliant hold on her, did not know that she often carried him with her wherever she went, not wondering anything about him really just knowing he was there, here, with her completely.

Now, she did want to call him, to talk to him, if only for a short while, wanted to hear his voice, wanted that voice to be with her, penetrate her entire being. She didn't want him to give her advice, necessarily, though she would gladly take any guidance he had to offer. He had the power to control her life, possessed a power to caress her wounds, to heal her, make her scars disappear. And she could trust him, genuinely, she felt like she could. For perhaps the first time in Clara's life, she felt she could trust a man entirely, tell him everything and not be at all afraid of being looked down upon or judged. She loved him so much, she loved him, loved him far more than she had ever loved anyone. Very close he came to making her love herself. With him, she liked herself, and that was certainly a good start.

So, why didn't she call him? The cordless phone awaited her, on the bureau, stared at her, or she stared at it, wanting to pick it up, wanting to give it attention, give Jeremy attention, listen to him and allow him to enter her heart and mind and soul. To pick up the phone would not be a hard task, not at all. To pick up the phone would be so simple and she would feel joy, talking to Jeremy, she would feel serene and loved and cared for.

After talking to him, regardless of what he said or what she said, she would sleep with this terrific white blankness, a blankness that was serene, a blankness that was heaven. Full of joy, this blankness would surround her, envelope her, and it would sink into her, or she would sink into it, fully, experience it, forever. And truly it would be happiness. Protected by this blankness, she would know love. Consumed by this blankness, she would know Jeremy, would be with him forever.

Her eyes were getting droopy. As she slipped under the clean white cotton sheets, she felt comfortable and relaxed without him. *But I am not without him,* she thought, *genuinely I am not.* Yes, Jeremy was still there, she saw him because he was here with her now, his face very bright and clear in her mind, as she fell so slowly asleep.

Chapter 17

Jeremy had nothing on his mind, no one person occupied his thoughts, he did not even think about Stephanie. He was searching for the results of last night's Yankees game. The results displeased him so he minimized the screen, leaning back in the swivel chair and gazing up at the ceiling, arms clasped behind his head in a lazy smartass assurance.

He tried not to think about Clara. This morning an acquaintance of his and an on-the-surface friend of Clara's had informed him that she had been with Benjamin and Karen, seen leaving after school with them. When he had first heard this, he was concerned but realized with how things had been going lately, there was very little he could do. So, he thought about sports, not only baseball, basketball too, and mixed martial arts, which he used to participate in and had in fact won several trophies, a multitude of trophies were scattered throughout his bookshelf that contained no books, at least not many of them. The bookshelf was an eclectic mix of DVDs and hooded sweatshirts and sneakers. These trophies he used to cherish had dust on them now, evidence that he very rarely thought about them anymore. Too, there were medals and plaques earned from playing various sports from the time he was in elementary school, and numerous varsity letters framed above his television, filling up a wide long space on the wall.

He did think of these letters, at times, felt a fading satisfaction over these achievements. It flowed through him, though, this satisfaction passed by and he no longer felt much pride over the fact that he was such a good athlete. He did feel a vague contentment but that too evaporated if he focused on it for any solid amount of time. The phone presently vibrated, and he saw it was Stephanie, not remembering putting the phone on vibrate. Even after school at baseball practice when he put his phone in his gym bag, he had not switched it to vibrate, or at least did not recall doing so.

"Hello?" Always, he answered the phone with this same seemingly distant greeting, as though unfamiliar with who was calling.

"I don't know what the fuck is going on with my cat. I swear, I think he ate a fat diseased rat. I found the carcass on the back porch, and it wasn't even a fuckin' carcass, Jeremy. There were guts left, that's all. Now Phoebe is vomiting all over the place. Twice inside so I put her out on the porch, and then she threw up two more times there. What am I supposed to do? I can't take her to the vet, well I could but that would cost like at least $1,000, right? So I -"

"Relax," Jeremy said. "It's gonna pass. Even if the rat did have a disease, she will probably be fine."

"You think so?"

"Yeah," Jeremy said. "Wait until tomorrow and see how she is."

"Will you come over?"

"Now? It's almost 11."

"My parents are asleep. I feel so alone, and Phoebe's not much company right now."

Jeremy sighed. "You come over here if you want."

Stephanie sighed, very loudly, very irritated. "I don't want to drive that far. It's dark—"

"No shit, Steph."

"– don't have any clothes on."

"Nothing?"

"I'm naked."

"What's your location?"

"The kitchen. I'm eating a banana with Nutella."

Jeremy felt himself getting hard at the thought of Stephanie eating a banana naked. He grinned but still felt a little annoyed with her. "Come over."

"Yeah?"

"Put on that long white coat you have and come in the back door. I'll leave it unlocked."

Stephanie sighed. "*Fiine.*"

She hung up, just like that. It irritated Jeremy how she did this. Never did she say 'goodbye' or 'see you later' or even just 'later', no, she always hung up. Not that Jeremy was one for pleasantries. He didn't appreciate small talk and did his best to avoid ever engaging in it, but it felt like Stephanie did everything she wanted to do on her own terms without ever even coming close to soliciting Jeremy's advice or guidance or direction. Not that Jeremy liked a girl who was clingy or needy, though those weren't traits he necessarily minded. Stephanie was too independent, he felt he wanted a girlfriend who was somewhere in the middle, one who absolutely needed him in her life, was fine with being alone yet at the same time needed him at the end of the day to feel secure and whole. Also, Stephanie was so self-centered! Never did she ask how his day was going, or had been. Never did she ask what he was up to, or what he was doing. No, it was all about her all the time. He felt suddenly a bit anxious for her to come over. He had plans to have rough sex, burying her head in a pillow as he had his way with her.

By the time Stephanie arrived it was almost midnight, and Jeremy had almost fallen asleep. He didn't hear her until she was on the bed beside him, licking his neck, giggling softly, grabbing his baseball cap from his head and putting it on her own. Jeremy chuckled, staring at Stephanie's long legs. Her coat was already on the floor, and she found it so cute and a little idiosyncratic how he had gone to bed wearing his hat.

The television played in the background. It was muted. Stephanie reached for the remote and turned it off. She wanted to hear soft, romantic music. Jeremy did not own any CDs that fit this description, but Stephanie, over the course of their relationship, had brought over CD after CD until now, in a shoebox under his bed, were at least two dozen CDs that they had listened to while making love. It didn't matter how Jeremy had sex with her, or in what position, as long as she was listening to music she felt like it was completely sweet and gentle.

Lowering herself, kissing Jeremy inch by inch, on his neck, chest, stomach (he did not have a six pack but his abs were very toned and developed), and then skipping several inches and resting her head between his legs, for a split second, his penis stiff and sticking up through the hole in his boxers. Lifting himself off the bed, Jeremy watched as she peeled off his boxers and threw them on the floor. In a purposefully languid teasing movement, she lowered herself and put him inside of her mouth. Jeremy too closed his eyes, expelling short rapid breaths of air, covering his face with his hands, partially, something he did when he was on the verge of climax.

As he sat up, Stephanie glanced up at him, her eyes meeting his as she lifted herself off him. She climbed on top of him and he pulled her hair gently, putting his tongue in her mouth and then taking his tongue out of her mouth, in, out, in, out, until he stopped and grabbed her, turning her around and driving himself into her, not even bothering with a condom for she was on birth control. She moaned, and he was very rough with her, not being at all gentle, which was how he usually started.

Jeremy reached his hand around and covered her mouth. "Shh," he said, still covering her mouth. She licked his hand, and he moved his hand away, rubbing his hand on her lips and then putting one of his fingers in her mouth, then two, and four. Sucking on his fingers, licking and kissing his fingers, Stephanie moaned softly, muzzling her moans as she said, "*Jerahh…*" gasping then, a sound that meant she was hurt. This went away quickly, and then she just moaned, a low steady hum of sorts that lasted about ten seconds and then stopped, for a couple seconds, and continued for another ten. Much more forceful now, he pulled on her hips as he entered her again, pulling her body all the way back onto him.

Chapter 18

The next morning when Clara awoke she felt a pervading deep sense of dread. She did not want to face the day, did not want to face anyone. Of course, this dread made it very hard for her to get out of bed. Gazing up at the ceiling, the only motivation she could muster to attend school that day was the fact that it was Wednesday, the next to last day of the year. All of her homework was complete, that wasn't the problem. She had also studied adequately for her finals. The problem was that she didn't want to face herself, didn't want to even look in the mirror, or have others see her. The anxiety she experienced, she supposed, arose from this feeling that she didn't know who she was, had no firm fixed sense of her own identity. It was a scary feeling, created a sharp sense of fear in her, her stomach, chest, made her heart beat a little faster, even making her palms sweaty at times. God knows when she was talking to Him she felt like she knew who she was, almost exactly. Fully, while doing her devotions or praying an impromptu prayer, she felt like she was someone, felt like she knew herself because God knew her. Didn't God know her? Surely, she told herself, He did, since she knew Him.

The covers she pulled further up her body, so they almost reached her chin. Her eyes were wide, staring at the ceiling, the rather subdued plain pink paint. She loved this color. It was relaxing and tranquil, at least this particular shade was. Other shades of pink were too bright, too flashy for her taste. Not that she had even chosen the paint used on the ceiling, she hadn't, Meem had decided. Clara had no input whatsoever in the color, or even how she arranged the room. Sternly, Meem had instructed her that the dresser must stay here, that the bed must stay there, and so on. At the time, being only a small child, Clara didn't care much, didn't have any thoughts on the locations of the furniture. Thinking about it now, she could see how her room might look if her bed had been set on the other side of the room where the dresser had been placed. She saw her bed somewhere else too: pushed against a side wall, immediately adjacent to a huge window that afforded quite a view of several large red maple trees. From where she was now, she could barely see out this window, the view obstructed almost entirely by the bedposts, so if she wanted to see the trees she would have to crane her neck and also lift her body up a little.

Her alarm clock had not gone off. She noted the time indifferently, seeing that there were a few minutes remaining before the loud jolting sound. Normally, and this morning was no exception, she set the alarm about twenty minutes before it was really necessary for her to wake up. Doing this gave her the opportunity to hit the snooze button a few times, a button she was fond of, a button she used regularly. Truly, though, she was not tired, had no desire to sleep, had in fact gone to sleep almost an hour before her usual time. Also, last evening, she had taken a nap after dinner. She did have a bottle of melatonin, a supplement she had been taking off and on for several years now. After struggling with insomnia for months, she had gone to the doctor and he had recommended the melatonin. She only took it as needed, after receiving poor results from taking it every night. It had been about two weeks since she had last taken any. Right now she very much wanted to take some - the only thing preventing her from doing so was school. Attending today was essential, there was no other option. She had two finals which she felt fairly confident about taking. Inexplicably, she had not had to study very much for the finals. The material she had absorbed very well in class, and outside of class while completing her homework. The anxiety she felt had nothing to do with the finals, or with the fact that the end of the school year was so imminent. Where did this anxiety come from then?

During her freshmen year, after telling Meem she felt so nervous a lot of the time she had trouble functioning, Meem had ignored her, telling her the anxiety she felt resulted from her inability to trust God. Clara of course responded by saying that she did trust God, trusted Him fully, prayed to Him daily and had obviously already accepted Him into her heart as her personal Lord and Savior. "You're not trusting Him enough, Clara," Meem had said again, and a third time. Eventually, after having to go down to the nurse during her 9th grade biology class when she felt she was having a heart attack, which turned out to be an anxiety attack, Meem had acquiesced. Very begrudgingly, she had scheduled an appointment for Clara to see a doctor, not a psychiatrist, for her insurance did not cover mental health issues. The doctor had prescribed Valium, which worked wonders for Clara. Under the influence of this soothing pill, which she still had no idea was a narcotic, a substance that was potentially addictive, she felt utterly at ease. Only as needed did she take it. All of her feelings of insecurity, then, her strong sense of unworthiness, this certain impalpable fear, vanished after taking the Valium. Never did she bask in the subtle euphoria of this pill, even when the doctor increased the dosage. All she knew for sure was that it made her feel better, and that was enough.

Ultimately, that morning, the Valium is what helped her out of bed. It had been a few days since she had taken any. Hobbling over to her dresser, as though she had some mysterious injury, she opened the top drawer and grabbed the bottle of pills. There were very few left.

Soon, she knew she would have to go to the pharmacy to get a refill. There were two refills remaining. She shook the bottle and the pills shifted as she began counting them. Nine.

She poured six out into her hand. Very infrequently, she did take a double dose, when the anxiety was especially debilitating, and the doctor had given her permission to do this. Feeling slightly guilty, she kept four and dropped the other two into the bottle. Rushing, for no apparent reason, as she had more time than usual to prepare for the school day, she went into the bathroom, filled a tiny plastic cup with water, and swallowed four Valiums.

If she would've known what being high felt like, she would've been high that morning, riding the bus to school and daydreaming during most of the ride, arriving at school ten minutes before the bell rang. She felt a bit unsteady, disoriented, as she walked to her locker, keeping her head down. Everything had slowed down, still was in fact slowing down, incredibly, as she reached her locker and felt like she was blissfully alone, separated from everybody and everything. Alone, she was alone here, even surrounded by people, and felt perfectly fine with that, content and calm and even almost happy.

Reaching into her locker, Clara grabbed a couple books. Reluctantly, then, she turned to see Mrs. Henderson descending a short flight of stairs before moving into the locker room. Clara turned her head fast, facing her locker, pulling the locker door open all the way to conceal her face.

There was no way she wanted Mrs. Henderson to approach her, not that she would, not likely. Typically, Mrs. Henderson waited for Clara to approach her. If she wanted to talk, in the past, she wasn't hesitant to pull Mrs. Henderson aside and start talking to her. Now, things were different. Now, although she felt like she had a lot to talk about, she didn't want to talk to Mrs. Henderson about it. She didn't know if she wanted to talk to anyone about it, if only out of fear she would surely slur her words.

Clara heard Mrs. Henderson's heels click-clacking down the hallway, and she breathed a sigh of relief, thankful she had not seen her, or if she had, had decided to ignore her. The fact was Mrs. Henderson had seen Clara, hadn't been looking for her, as she was in a rush to get to the office, carrying a copious amount of tests to Xerox. Too, Clara felt relieved when Jeremy, Stephanie at his side, walked on by. He, however, had not seen Clara, had not been thinking about her, at the time, so naturally didn't look for her. If she wanted some space, that was fine. If she wanted some time to think, be on her own, that was fine. Jeremy didn't have the time for mind games, he played enough of them with Stephanie or, rather, she played enough of them with him.

Slightly sore from the night before, Stephanie walked very slowly. Wearing flip flops, a conservative halter top, and short white shorts, she never considered how looking stylish without appearing to want to look stylish was the key to her looking stylish. Clara saw the familiar couple from behind after they were almost out of her sight. Clara had tried, in the past, very hard to emulate Stephanie's simple sophisticated style. Without much success she had tried to find reasonable buys at the mall and then at the outlets. The clothes were far too expensive, it seemed all the clothes Stephanie wore were designer, although their designer status was not evident. Never did she wear any clothes advertising the brand she was wearing, that would be tacky, better to keep them guessing, Stephanie thought, often wondering if she would win the yearbook superlative for 'best dressed' her senior year. Winning that award had already solidified its importance in her mind. There were many other superlatives, like 'most likely to succeed', 'best body', and 'best personality'. But who the fuck cares about someone's personality if she's smoking hot? Stephanie asked herself this numerous times. She herself had a sweet personality, on occasion, when she felt like it. Otherwise she could be a blatant unapologetic bitch. 'Biggest bitch', if that superlative existed, Stephanie knew she wouldn't be the one, God knew there were bigger bitches than she. Surely, at times, she debated in her mind, only very briefly, whether she wanted to be voted 'best body'. The obvious fact surfaced then that someone who feels they have to have a perfect body must be lacking in some other obvious very important area, like their face or intelligence. A 'Monet' is what these girls, or guys, though far less often, were referred to as, since from far away, based strictly on their bodies, they looked attractive but once you got up close they were a big old mess. The more colloquial pedestrian term, 'butter face', Stephanie never used.

About to close her locker, Clara remembered a manila folder she needed for second period. After she pulled that out, she spotted a piece of paper. It was folded once with her name written on it in magic marker. Small black cursive letters. Feeling her heart race, as much as it could race while being under the influence of the Valium, she pulled the note from the top storage compartment in her locker and opened it.

In the same handwriting, Clara recognized it as Karen's right away, the note read:

Meet us in the parking lot right behind the buses as soon as the day ends.

Everything around her that had seemed to be so much in slow-motion resumed to a regular pace - Clara was elated. The soporific effect of the Valium was canceled out by the energy this note induced in her. They did want to see her again! They did have a good time hanging out with her after all! She felt a strange sudden energy, radiating throughout her entire body, and she didn't feel anxious or melancholy, not at all. In this moment, she felt like she could do anything, really, if only she put her mind to it. First things first, she thought: *I will ace both of my finals today.*

Chapter 19

Clara had not felt certain she had done well enough on either of her exams to earn A's, but she knew she would receive at least a B on both of them. Exchanging pleasantries with Jeremy in homeroom had been discomforting, to say the least, he had not inquired about the time he knew she had spent with Benjamin and Karen. Clara wasn't even aware he knew she had been with them. His only wish was that she would open up to him again, for her own sake, not his, as it was so evident what was happening with her, the turmoil that was gradually pervading her life. She had his phone number, his e-mail, everything. He noted she had returned to her basic rather plain demure self. Wearing her same old clothes and not wearing any makeup, she looked so absent and distant, not depressed, exactly, but completely void of any affect. She did not ask him what his plans were for the summer, despite wondering, nor did she ask him if he was excited for college, even if she knew the answer, it would've been an appropriately engaging question to ask. Would they see each other over the summer? Every summer, they got together at least three or four times, going out for lunch or taking a walk in the park, going to the movies. For some reason, Stephanie used to not care if he spent time with Clara alone, or if she did care not enough to stop them from being alone together. What accounted for the change? Jeremy was not sure, though he thought it might have had something to do with the fact that Clara was transforming her looks, even Stephanie noticed she was becoming prettier.

Even without makeup, even without wearing moderately fashionable new clothes, she was changing, filling out a bit, not stick thin and awkward like she used to be but rather curvy from the waist down, her hips and ass possessed personality now. Even with her small breasts, it was not inaccurate to assess Clara as having a nice body, certainly, Stephanie knew, Clara would not be voted 'best body', not a chance. If she had larger breasts, though, Stephanie believed she might be a viable candidate. Certainly, Stephanie's body was not much more desirable than Clara's. In fact, Stephanie considered their bodies very similar, likely even equal, if she was honest. Clara had a better ass and Stephanie had bigger breasts, so the two features canceled each other out.

Of course, Clara was unaware her body was so appealing, as all she seemed to be able to focus on, when she dared to stare at herself in the mirror, were her small breasts.

Clara passed Christina and Tammy, who were giggling quite loudly over something, in the hall on the way out the door. She had not bothered to even say hello, averting her eyes as she moved outside. They had both seen her, were possibly going to say hi, decided not to since she seemed to be in such a hurry. And really she was rushing, as though afraid Benjamin and Karen would not be there, or at least would not wait even a minute for her.

The black car sat idly behind the buses, though, right where Karen said they would be. A beep wasn't necessary, Clara saw them right away. Still moving quite quickly toward the Cobalt, she moved her hand anxiously through her hair, this was one habit of hers, in addition to cracking her knuckles, to suppress her anxiety, or at least distract herself from it. The Valium had worn off entirely by this point and, even though she didn't feel as nervous as she was this morning, she still felt a modest amount of anxiety, produced, probably, over the fact that she would again be spending time with Benjamin and Karen, virtual strangers who she hoped she could soon call her friends.

Leaning over in his seat, Benjamin opened the door for her, Clara smiling widely over this gesture. Also making her smile was Karen, who had been so kind to sit in the backseat, allowing Clara to take the passenger's side seat. They were about a mile down the road when Clara decided she couldn't stand the silence anymore, her mind reeling wondering what they would be doing. "Where are we going?" she asked.

Still grinning, Benjamin shook his head, his black stiff hair not moving a centimeter even with all the windows down.

"It's a surprise, sweetie," Karen said.

"Oh, I like surprises!"

"Do you?" Benjamin asked.

Clara nodded.

"What's your favorite surprise?" Benjamin asked.

"Um, well, nothing comes to mind, I mean not right now. I'll think of it though and when I do I'll tell you."

Karen laughed, gazing out the window as they passed house after house and then neighborhood after neighborhood.

'Ellie's Skating Rink' was the unadorned straightforward name of the skating rink where the trio ended up. Benjamin and Karen had decided on this destination earlier in the day, during lunch at Wendy's. They had also decided they would attend school on the last day, tomorrow, each having two finals. They were still a little high, and it was true Benjamin had missed one of his finals today, Karen two. There would be no making those exams up, they were both aware but didn't care much since they knew even with a zero on these exams, they would still pass each respective course with at least a C.

The skating rink was not crowded. Clara felt very anxious, as soon as they pulled into the parking lot, seeing where they were, as she had never skated before and had a lot of reservations about falling and making a fool out of herself. Then, she thought, Karen and Benjamin really won't want to see me anymore. Karen and Benjamin did not skate very often, when they were much younger they did like to rollerblade or, on occasion, skateboard at the small skate park in town. Every so often, when they were high and wanted to do something easy and carefree and fun, they came to Ellie's.

"What size shoe do you wear?" Karen asked as they approached the counter.

Clara looked down at her sandals. "Seven."

After they had all gotten their skates, Clara looked like she had a whole lot to say except Benjamin wouldn't allow her to say anything. He took her hand suddenly, keeping her steady on her feet, for the most part. She stumbled very slightly, as he led her out onto the rink, and he held onto her tighter. Then she smiled so widely she couldn't help herself: with her hand in his she felt so safe, all her anxiety gone. Hearing the music, pulsating techno so she could barely hear a thing, she looked up at Benjamin and he grinned down at her, his eyes, defined by his customary austere eyeliner, smiling also. It was true she had numerous questions to ask, still looking at Benjamin for any instruction he might provide. He said nothing, and her hand tightened inside of his, her other hand gripping his forearm. He was so tall her head barely reached his shoulders. And then she felt quite confident, as she moved her feet forward in a pace that was moderate and fluid, she almost believed she could do this on her own. Though she didn't dare let go of his hand, not yet. She loosened her grip a great deal, after going around the rink twice, then let go of his forearm, feeling the music, wanting to dance, feeling her feet and legs become more relaxed.

This was not Benjamin's type of music, far from it. The music they played was mostly techno, pop, and mild hip hop. Out of these three genres, Benjamin liked the techno best. He appreciated the aggressive pounding beats that were somehow tranquil and warm. Clara had never heard techno before, as the only time she ever listened to music was in the car, sometimes, on the way to school, and also, much less often, at home on the radio. The radio was not fond of techno, apparently, for she never heard them play it. She didn't own many CDs, Meem forbade it, unless it was Christian music. One of her guilty secrets was she had collected a cache of CDs which she kept wrapped in an old wool sweater and hidden in a shoebox under her bed. There was Adele, Nicki Minaj (she was shocked to hear some of the lyrics on that one! Shocked and delighted!), Coldplay, Lady Gaga, and Fiona Apple. In secret, after Meem went to bed, she listened to these CDs alone in her room with headphones, appreciating these artists for the lyrics, mostly, and for making her realize that other people, even very famous rich people, experience pain and misery in their lives.

Benjamin pulled at her hand, which was only very loosely in his own. It was a silent instruction for her to keep up with him, as she was lagging behind, a little, was she tired? "Are you OK?" he asked.

"Why," Clara said, "Yes, I am. I'm just taking it all in. I've never been skating before!"

"You mentioned."

"Oh, that's right, I'm sorry."

"Don't be sorry."

And she was right at his side, her body touching his body, bumping against it, momentarily, accidentally, rubbing herself on him. Karen watched it all from a bench by the concession stand.

She wasn't at all upset, as Benjamin assured her after she couldn't fully assure herself, that Clara was so much less than her, in almost every aspect. Karen would be given a chance to skate with Benjamin, she was sure it was only a matter of time. Besides, it wasn't important, even if Benjamin decided he didn't want to skate with her, she would be the one going home with him tonight, not Clara, that pathetic little bible thumper. Karen did not feel sorry for her, not one bit. Karen thought it was possible she would like Clara, enjoy her company more, if only she would develop a backbone. Didn't she know that a person has the right to stand up for themselves?

Karen felt an innate burning desire to rough Clara up a bit. Wanting to push her, catch her off-guard, have her fall down, or slap her face once, maybe twice, just to push her to the point where she snaps, reacting in anger, an anger that Karen imagined had to exist somewhere within her, certainly she had various and sundry reasons to be angry, with all that she had been through in her life. Yet the only emotion Karen could identify absolutely and without question was sadness, a sadness that seemed to have dissipated the moment she got in the car with Benjamin. Karen wondered if her mood would have changed so suddenly had she been the only one picking her up. If Benjamin wasn't there, would Clara's mood have lifted? Karen didn't think so but she still pondered the matter in her mind. Deciding, finally, she had been thinking about this for long enough, she stood up from the bench. Patiently she waited until Benjamin and Clara were near her, and then joined them out on the rink.

Benjamin didn't acknowledge Karen at all. He kept his focus on Clara, looking down at her to make sure she was OK and not about to fall, which he still sensed, during certain moments, she was.

The smile on Clara's face appeared to be pasted there, permanent, so big it could not be real, except it was real, very real and genuine and contagious. Benjamin was smiling too. Karen noted this as she tried

at a pace that was not fast nor slow, moving rhythmically to the forceful surrounding sound of the bass, the treble, both of which rapidly shifted as they continued to skate. Benjamin felt such hate for Karen in this moment, such resentment. Clara was his, he had discovered her, she was his idea, and now Karen acted as if he didn't exist, did not matter. She would hear about it later. He would want her later. His face was blank, all emotion drained from him. He couldn't deny the joy he felt while skating with Clara, the uncontrollable lust, the grin that surfaced on his face when he had been with her. He wanted to have her, tonight too, except he knew that would not happen. It was far too soon. No matter how submissive she was, she would never acquiesce to any substantial sexual advance, at least not yet.

Soon he would make his move. Soon, he believed she would want him to make his move, and another one, again, harder. The grin on his face now was a sly one, calculating, not altogether real, and then gone.

That evening Clara went home with Benjamin and Karen. Relegated to the backseat (Karen happened to reach the car first and made it quite clear that the passengers' side seat was hers), Clara did nothing except stare out the window the entire ride home. The anxiety she felt this morning had returned, rising deep inside of her stomach, created as a result of realizing that she had not called Meem to inform her of her whereabouts. Meem would be waiting, it was probable she would be angry, sitting in the same rather tattered recliner, watching Wheel of Fortune and crocheting or knitting, her glasses lowered very far down on her nose, as usual.

She might not question Clara, at first, might not even acknowledge her, giving her the silent treatment as she sometimes did when she became irritated with her. In the past, this method had been effective in getting Clara to open up, to tell her things, to tell her everything, to not censor anything as she would if she thought they were on perfectly good terms. In the past Clara had always wanted Meem's approval, had always sought it out desperately. Now, Meem wasn't so sure. Now, Meem knitted furiously, her fingers gripping the needle, holding onto it as if it was her lifeline, her only grasp on sanity.

When the trio had neared Clara's house, no one said a word, not even Clara, though she thought about a few questions she wanted to ask, lots of things she wanted to say. No single thing seemed too important, so she decided to stay silent. Still, what she wanted to ask, to say, was heavy on her mind. It was beginning to weigh her down, driving her to want to confess something, anything. She asked not a question, though, said not a word, still gazing out the window. Was it that she didn't trust Benjamin or Karen with her most genuine abysmal thoughts? Was she afraid of their judgment, authority? They had no authority over her, so why did she think so? All she knew is that she felt it, the complete power they held over her, feeling them take control over her life, from the first time they had spent time together, at the amusement park. Even now, with them staying so quiet, she could feel their superiority, their power. What power? They said nothing the entire ride home. Pulling up into the driveway now, so many things ran through Clara's mind, but she still decided to remain silent.

Surprisingly, she had not thought about the whole intimate exchange with Karen. Once, when a few thoughts on the subject did come to her, she blocked it out of her mind, not wanting to admit how much she had loved every second of the encounter. Kissing Karen had been bliss, if she was honest: truly she had been in heaven, if only for a couple minutes.

Pulling into the driveway, Clara could feel her heart beat faster, already imagining Meem sitting almost horizontally in her recliner, (which was really a rocker, though Clara supposed Meem called it a recliner because, "Only geezers use rockers. *This* is a recliner, my dear, because I am *not* old! I am not one of *them!*") waiting for her, rocking and her *huh-huh-huh* heavy breathing as she did so. Trying to appear nonplussed over Clara's arriving home so late, Clara thought, at least initially, she would be silent, refusing to see her as she walked in the front door, moving, most likely, to the kitchen to heat up some leftovers. Later, Clara thought, as the pattern had been established and was quite consistent, Meem would shout several questions at her in rapid succession. Clara would not answer, not at first, having reached the point in her life where she felt comfortable enough to be alone, to simply ignore Meem and move right on past her. What would the old woman do? Smack her? No, never had she done that, and never would she dare. Her words, her disapproving looks, her silence was far more potent.

"Are you getting out?" Benjamin asked, not bothering to even turn around in his seat to see her.

"I – " Clara said, feeling nothing except her own heart and the tension that emanated from it.

"What the hell is wrong?" Karen asked. "Your eyes! They're so wide."

"Nothing." Clara reached for the door handle, fingers wrapping around it loosely, at first, and then squeezing, holding it as she had held Benjamin's hand, and Karen's, so firmly. "I have to go."

"That's obvious, sweetie," Karen said, not unkindly, leaning back in her seat and kissing Clara on the cheek.

"When will I see you?" Clara asked.

"Never," Benjamin said.

"Well, what do you mean?" Clara stared at Benjamin, then Karen, and Benjamin again.

"When we decide we want to see you," Karen said, turning away from Clara. Instead of saying 'bye' or 'see you later' or even just 'later', Karen took Benjamin's lead and stared stoically out the front window.

"Well…" Clara twisted her hands together as though inside of them there was clay and she had something real important to say. "I – I guess I'll talk to you soon then." Benjamin did not respond, Karen did not respond – they did not even look at her, they had already dismissed her.

Chapter 20

Clara's prediction of how Meem would react couldn't have been further from reality. Although based on the way she had in fact reacted in the past, Meem was not sitting in the 'family room' (as Meem called it, though since there was no family, Clara referred to it as the living room).

"Meem!" Clara shouted the moment she got in the door. "Meem!" She felt alarmed that Meem wasn't around, not in the kitchen or the small side room that Meem called the 'study' (which was really just an extra small room with a tiny old off-white couch where Meem read novels and knitted.) Nor was she in the laundry room. It wasn't even 8 P.M. Meem never went upstairs to her room before 9 P.M, not ever, unless she was sick. Could she be sick? Could she have just been unusually tired this evening? Might she have gone out somewhere? These questions Clara attempted to sort through, to no avail, as the anxiety she experienced was so pervasive she could not think straight.

"Meem!" she shouted once more, this time with the full intention of doing so. Glancing up the stairway, at the walls, briefly, the framed photos that contained mostly Meem and Clara, together and apart, a couple photos with Meem and her husband, who had died before Clara was born, and then there was a single photo of Meem, Clara, and Clara's mother. Her hand moved across the wall, touching one of the photos, two, three photos, the frames, as she ascended the stairs.

What if something bad had happened to her? Like a heart attack or a stroke, Meem rushed in an ambulance to the local hospital emergency room. More questions to process, more possibilities. At the top of the stairs, she saw Meem's bedroom door was shut, and it was only ever shut when she was in there. She knocked once, twice, a fourth time, louder and longer with each knock. She twisted the knob: locked.

"What do *you* want!" Meem cried, finally responding with choked sobs, controlled and quite soft, at first, and then unrestrained, loud.

The way she had said 'you' was very condemning and cacophonous, as though Clara was an intruder.

"Meem, I..." Clara fell very silent then, wiggling the knob again and knocking again, almost in a panic, wiggling, knocking, wiggling until –

"*You* little brat!" Meem sobbed bitterly. "I'm going to sleep! So, why don't *you* leave! Leave and don't come back!"

Clara sunk to her knees, beginning to cry herself, trying her best to suppress her sobs, control them a little. The attempt to disguise her upset feeling was unsuccessful. All at once, then, Clara felt so very confused and hurt, over her entire life, over Meem, Jeremy, Benjamin and Karen and their unsaved souls, how she didn't feel God was in her life, not anymore. Despite her best efforts to connect with Him, invite Him into her life daily, she just didn't feel Him anymore, He had vanished, abandoned her. Why? What had she done wrong? Apparently, she must have done something bad, except nothing in particular came to mind. She had been very good and kind and obedient her whole life and yet God was nowhere, at least nowhere near, no place where she could reach Him. Did she not deserve His love? Was she undeserving of His compassion?

She forced herself to stop sobbing then, on her knees, her head almost touching the door. Suddenly, she heard Meem's heavy feet hit the floor, stomping over to the door and unlocking it for her. Only partially did she open it, seeing Meem sitting on the bed with her legs queerly crossed, smoking a cigarette as she sometimes did, particularly at night.

"What do you want?" Meem's voice was very calm and even now, the tears cleared from her eyes, her cheeks still wet. Small steady puffs of smoke flowed out of her nostrils, her mouth mostly closed as she continued to smoke, taking three very rapid puffs. About a quarter of the cigarette remained. "I said..." Meem's loud voice trailed off, and she lowered her voice as she finished her thought quite quietly: "What do you want?"

Clara took several apprehensive steps further into the room, standing at Meem's side, right by the bed. Meem turned her head defiantly, staring out the window now, purposefully looking away from Clara, not wanting to see her immature filthy face. Cocking her head, Clara could see on Meem's chin tiny white hairs, barely visible, these hairs vaguely illuminated by the setting sun that cast farewell rays through the window. Even with the flimsy white curtain closed, the final light of the day shone inside the room. Clara moved closer to Meem, wanting to sit down beside her, ask her why she had been crying, if there was anything she could do.

Spinning around to face Clara, Meem's eyes were wide and wild with a certain abstract self-possessed energy. Rage radiated throughout Meem's body, and she could feel it rising inside of her: there seemed to be no reason for it, this anger, nothing tangible, she could not explain it.

Meem said nothing. Clara said nothing. They stared at each other for a good long while until Meem appeared tired, extinguishing the cigarette which had been smoked all the way down to the filter. Clara wondered if Meem would light another one, in the past, usually, on the occasions when she smoked, she smoked one right after another, seemingly unable to stop. Meem put a hand on her forehead, looking very exhausted and beat, out of it.

Falling back onto the bed, Meem rested her head on two pillows.

"Do you want a glass of water?"

"Get me another pillow, dear," Meem then said she needed to prop her head up. Clara did as instructed, grabbing a third pillow and placing it underneath the two Meem presently rested on.

"'Night, Meem."

Meem said nothing as she closed her eyes and turned over on her side. She was sleeping soundly within minutes, even snoring slightly.

Clara could not rest that night. For five distant dazed minutes, she stared at her diary, the two blank violet pages beckoning her to start writing on them. Her face was blank as she looked down at the cream carpet, it was so soft. Allowing her hand to sink into the fabric, she glanced beside her at her bed. There was no way she would be able to sleep. The Valium, in her bottom drawer, awaited her. Surely she could take those, an easy solution to this rather persistent problem, this insomnia that had ebbed and rapidly returned throughout most of her life. She did not want to go to sleep, though, not now. Jeremy crossed her mind, and she tried to disengage from him, to distance herself. But this boy would not go away, and the problem (or maybe it wasn't a problem, per se) was that he remained there in her head, in her heart, at least in this moment, her entire soul and body filled with the memory of him. She could recall most everything about him: his face, voice, what he said, what he didn't say, his smile, his big bright smile that could still, in this moment, make everything OK. Thinking of Jeremy, the anxiety she had been experiencing this evening became a lot more tolerable. Also the assaulting sense of sadness, it nearly vanished, in this moment. Most of her self-doubt dissipated too. Truly, though, the more she knew him, or felt she knew him, the less she knew herself. Knowing him increased her increasing knowledge that she had no identity, did not exist, not really. So she tried her best to push him out of her mind, tried not to think of him that night. Slipping under the covers, Clara didn't bother to write in her diary, didn't attempt to call Jeremy either. Still, as she drifted off to sleep, it was his face she saw, his voice she remembered.

The next morning Clara awoke before the alarm went off, again. It was the last day of school so possibly she was excited, certainly she was anxious, not as bad as yesterday though the anxiety still throbbed within her. Moments after getting out of bed, she thought of Jeremy, wondering why she had not called him, had in fact been ignoring him lately. But he was still there, inside of her, she felt him, who he was, what he would say or do in a particular situation, even as her mind zeroed in on the Valium that remained in the bottom drawer. Her mind obsessed over the Valium, it was a prescription so why did she feel it was a problem if she took one? Yesterday she had taken a quadruple dose. Taking such a high dose concerned her because she knew how good it made her feel, how relaxed, perfect. It was artificial, she knew: the feelings of confidence the Valium created in her, these fake feelings were not to be trusted, no matter if the pills were a prescription. So, she thought of Jeremy, again, stared at the phone, knowing it was not too early to call him. In her underwear she had gone to bed, unable to muster the energy to put on her pajamas or even her sweatpants. Thinking of him, last night, she had fallen into a slumber that was deep and uninterrupted.

For a minute or two she debated what she would wear that day. After all, it was the last day of the school year, she wanted, *needed*, to look good. Anybody's good guess was who she wanted to look good for. There was no one in particular, not Jeremy, not even Benjamin or Karen, no one.

Today, Clara would look good for herself, with a halter top, skirt, high heels, a sexy choker necklace, dangling earrings, everything. That morning she would not wear any makeup, having determined she did not like the stuff, not much anyway since, like the Valium, it was artificial, not to be trusted. Staring at her small backpack, filled with books, she debated whether all the essentials to her final new look would fit. Surely, they would, if not she could shove what remained in her purse. Yes, today Clara would look good for herself, and she didn't care who noticed her or didn't notice her. That morning, before she sneaked out the front door without speaking to Meem, she stared into the mirror and told herself she was good, entirely good, not only on the inside, this time it would be on the outside as well.

Chapter 21

When Clara arrived at school that morning, she felt herself slowly sink into the soothingly subdued feeling the Valium produced inside of her. Meem had not been awake when she had left, so sneaking out was unnecessary. The Valium she had decided to take at the very last second, standing at the front door, opening the front door, about to leave when something had stopped her. The anxiety had subsided by the time she had taken a shower and shaved her legs and brushed her teeth. Thinking of Jeremy had been unavoidable, really, and it was as though the greater her effort to push him out of her mind, the more she focused on him. A focus on Jeremy always lessened the anxiety, made it vanish, almost. So she didn't know why she had taken the Valium that morning. Most likely, she had taken it because she remembered the feeling, the soft euphoric rush, very vividly.

Feeling the Valium kicking in fully now, she imagined it would peak by the time she got to first period. Even after she had changed into her sexy chic outfit, she did not experience any of the confidence she had anticipated. In fact, she felt less confident now, knowing full well there were guys' eyes moving over her body, inspecting her, not seeing her entirely though since they chose to ignore her rather plain gaunt face. Clara knew she looked pretty good, at least from the neck down, not thinking about her nondescript face or her hair that was rather dry and damaged. The color of her hair was very real, natural. Normally, she didn't use any hairspray or gel and today was no exception. It's not that she felt self-conscious, she didn't really, not now since she presently could not feel, not with the Valium coursing through her veins like soporific liquid flame. Glancing up erratically as she moved toward her locker, she noted that guys were looking at her, seeing her, some even staring at her smooth silky legs she had slathered with coconut butter and self-tanner. She felt so exposed and free, the skirt she wore three or four inches above the knee. Too, she felt wholly honest, very open to what might happen on this final day of school, a day that was unoriginal, the same as every other day, if not for the fact that it would conclude the figurative final chapter in her life as a junior in high school. Despite feeling attractive and confident, she lowered her head, as she approached her locker, not wanting to see all the people. She put the combination in her locker then, feeling quite distant as she reached for two folders and two books. She observed the guys still looking at her, some even staring. A few girls walking by also inspected Clara, likely wondering just what the hell she was pulling, who the fuck she thought she was? Even Christina and Tammy, those pseudo-friends of hers, surveyed her appearance, for a couple moments only, and from a distance, not wanting her to know they were there, not wanting to have to stop and talk to her. Clara herself did not see these girls, not with the Valium inside her, not with being immersed in the fleeting joy she experienced as a result of being seen, noticed, even, dare she think, 'checked out'. She couldn't be certain anyone was really checking her out though. These bystanders could simply be looking at her out of surprise, or unfamiliarity, possibly not even knowing who she was, as Turner High School had a high student population.

By the time Clara had reached homeroom, she had forgotten herself altogether: she saw Jeremy. He looked very relaxed, sitting quietly with his legs spread laxly, hands resting on his desk. He tapped his emerald green senior class ring against the desk and then faced forward, the period was about to begin. He slid his hands under the desk and pulled his cell phone surreptitiously from his pocket, seeing he had received seven text messages from Stephanie since he had arrived at school that morning. He didn't bother reading them. Clearly nothing she said was urgent otherwise she would have called. Stephanie's habit was to feign a certain borderline self-righteous feminine strength, hiding many of her true feelings until they built up so heavily within her she had to call Jeremy and then see Jeremy, talk to him, for a good long while, telling him everything she had been keeping inside. After he listened to her for a substantial amount of time, inevitably she would want a hug, more likely a kiss, to have him hold her in his arms. She might rest her head on his stomach, gazing up into his eyes and waiting for him to initiate sex. About half of the time, following one of these confessional sessions, he did suggest sex, with body language and very close direct eye contact. When he did not bring up sex, it was generally not for any lack of desire. Generally, after listening to Stephanie closely for a long time, he would feel so tired he would go to sleep, with Stephanie in his arms often still talking.

He said nothing to Clara when she sat down in front of him, nonchalantly noting her new fashionable clothing, her hair that was pulled back in a high severe ponytail. Clara could barely contain her desire to talk to him. It was irrelevant what she might say, as later she would forget her words, for the most part, and remember his, likely the majority of them.

Minutes later, as Mr. Pratt rambled on, she could dismiss his presence no longer. She turned around slowly in her desk, afraid at first to see his face, his eyes, she tried to appear very confident, to hold her head high. Sitting as erect as possible, she reasoned a proper posture projected confidence. Then she slouched, a natural sitting posture for Clara. The fake perfect posture seemed too forced, manufactured. She also tried to lower her voice to a quiet consistent tone, for some reason associating a high voice volume with deficient self-assuredness, possibly only because her own voice was loud, usually, naturally uneven and shaky at times. Since childhood, she knew she stuttered too, having no idea why, ultimately concluding that the why question was inconsequential, since even if she knew the reason, nothing would change, the stutter would still be present. There was no cure for it. Over the years, it had gotten a great deal better but never went away completely. It was true she could improve her stutter, modify the way she ejected her words, possibly very quickly scan the words that she wanted to say before she spoke them so she could edit them, process them, and slow them down in her mind. The stutter would most likely never go away entirely, though. In all likelihood, the stutter would always be present.

Jeremy did not hear her words, not at first, he only saw her, her facial expression, that he imagined didn't match what was really going on with her. Too, he sensed the tension in her body. Even with the Valium that presently peaked she didn't feel relieved talking to him as she normally did. She was censoring what she was saying, wanting to project a certain cool confidence that she believed she should possess as a result of her new look and the clothes she wore. Jeremy could not be fooled, though, not for a second. He grinned at her as she continued talking, wanting him to see and believe her confidence. After she finished talking, Jeremy considered her words, how he didn't believe the majority of them. While talking to him she had focused her gaze on his chin, his lips, cheeks, focusing on anything so long as her eyes did not meet his, then it would be over, she knew, he would sense something not quite right. Why did she care if he knew things were not going smoothly in her life? Didn't she want to be helped? Want to feel better?

So he said nothing, not asking a single question. If she didn't trust him after knowing him all these years, then she would never trust him. After Clara turned around in her seat, Mr. Pratt still prattling on, Jeremy noted her hands. He was aware of how she singed them during especially rough times in her life, not usually using the sink at home, as that water couldn't be made quite hot enough to break skin. Most times, she used the stove, filling a pan with boiling hot water, after Meem was asleep, and then immersing her hands in it. One time, during her freshman year, around the time she first start performing acts of self-flagellation, she soaked her hands in that pan for 62 seconds. Hurting, naturally, at first, eventually she had just become numb. After 50 seconds had elapsed, the pain had returned, much sharper than before, as much of her skin had been broken and mutilated. She then had forced herself to endure another 12 seconds before finally removing her hands from the pan, sinking to her knees and sobbing, not having cried at all during the actual burning.

The next morning, when Meem had noticed the burns during breakfast, she had been alarmed but not quite worried, as clearly she thought the burns on Clara's hands were not bad enough to require medical attention. Not taking her to the emergency room, instead she had scolded her, not empathized with her at all, not inquired as to why she had done it, and Clara had offered no explanation, simply looking at her vacantly, not even feeling the pain in her hands, not much anyway, not yet. The following day the pain became unbearable, to the point she had asked to go see the nurse during second period. The gloves she wore on her hands concealed the burns. The nurse had been truly shocked, seeing Clara's hands and calling Meem, who acted defiant and dismissive on the phone. Mandatory counseling sessions had been arranged for later, and Clara was set up with a doctor who specialized in skin graphs. The doctor had claimed Clara had been lucky, considering how long she had kept her hands in the water. Easily, the doctor said, the burns could've been third degree. Her saving grace, apparently, had been the fact that she had put her hands in the pan while the water was still heating up, far from boiling point. The doctor admitted her to the hospital, the psychiatric ward, until the surgery had been scheduled.

Presently, anyone who saw Clara's hands could see substantial scarring, though the scars had faded over the years. Never had Clara burned herself severely, after that incident, all the times had been a lot less severe. She would keep her hands under the water (if she used the sink) or in the water (if the stove) until it hurt, hurt very badly, then, right before she broke skin, she would shut the water off or remove her hands. Of course when using the sink a much longer amount of time would be required for her to feel pain. When using the stove, not wanting to have surgery again, not wanting to hassle Meem, to worry her, or anyone else, she would only soak her hands in the water for five seconds, or seven, eight at the most.

Mr. Pratt finished the announcements, finally. Clara too had finished talking to Jeremy, who responded, or did not respond, with a slow sure nod of his head. Surely, he would see her this summer, more than happy to spend time with her, if only she would ask. Even willing to see her behind Stephanie's back, since Stephanie no longer approved of his being alone with Clara, only approved if she was present. Clara did not ask. For a moment he wondered if he would hear from her this summer. Based on the way she had been communicating with him lately, he imagined he would not. In the past, every summer they got together to go out for lunch or dinner or the movies. Jeremy had not heard about her recent trip to the skating rink with Benjamin and Karen. Possibly, if he had been aware of the increasing amount of time Clara was spending with those freaks, he would have likely at least inquired about it. Before Clara left homeroom for first period, she noted Jeremy's muscles, how they bulged, looked bigger than usual, as if he had just lifted weights before coming to school.

It was true Clara wondered when she would see Benjamin and Karen again. During the school day, she wouldn't encounter them, not in the halls, not during lunch, not having any mutual classes. Walking to first period, she slouched without meaning to, did not walk upright as she intended to, had trouble adjusting to her new height of, approximately, 5'5 ½' (her heels 3 ½"). Feeling fully prepared for the Physics final, having spent at least a dozen hours studying over the course of a week, still she questioned herself. Would she earn the A she desired? Math she preferred to science, having more a natural ability for it, though she excelled at both.

As she approached the classroom she still felt high, two books held at her side, as though she was a guy, not holding these items at her chest, as most girls did. The Valium continued to affect her deeply, the high still absorbing her. But she did not feel disoriented at all. She felt very smooth, and calm, thinking about her new confidence until she reached the first period classroom. Here, the door was halfway open, a student standing there not bothering to give it a courtesy push, as the door nearly shut on Clara's face. Quickly she stuck a hand out, pushing the door open for herself. As she entered the classroom, she saw the teacher already in the process of distributing the tests, handing one to the front desk of each row, allowing the first student in each row to pass the tests behind them.

Not normally a fast test taker, Clara surprised herself today, having had completed the test 15 minutes before the allocated time passed. Too, the second final exam of that day she had completed well before the class period ended. Students at Turner High School had been dismissed shortly before lunch would have started on a regular day. Clara had no plans as to how she would get home. Not wanting to ride the bus, though that seemed the only option right now. Unaware of Benjamin and Karen's whereabouts, she wondered if they had even attended school today. There was no way she could know since she had no idea where their lockers were, even with them knowing the location of hers. The thought of returning home to Meem she dreaded, that small old yellow house that stifled her. Where were they? Benjamin, Karen. When would she see them again? What would they do when she did see them? Climbing the stairs, moving onto the bus, she couldn't help thinking about the possible answers to these questions.

Chapter 22

Benjamin and Karen had in fact gone to school that day. The entire time they were high, having taken methamphetamine to school, blowing some in the bathroom in between periods, even daring to take bumps of it during class under their desks on one of their textbooks. They were still quite high as they arrived back at Benjamin's trailer immediately after the school day had ended. For a moment they thought of Clara, imagining she was thinking of them also, knowing she had had an absolutely divine time, trying to hide how happy she felt. Not even bringing up the subject of God or salvation once (surely later she felt guilty over how her real purpose in befriending them had been neglected) Clara had enjoyed herself so much she would tell anyone she simply forgot about religion and God altogether.

The black cats meandering alongside the dusty unpaved road in front of Benjamin's trailer appeared hungry and lonely. Even though there were three of them, they looked lost. These cats were dirty, too, unclean at the very least, and probably vermin infested. Benjamin wondered where they had come from. Out of nowhere, going nowhere, it seemed. As he took a step closer to them, he confirmed they were strays, as they had no tags, no collar and were bone thin. Karen asked if Benjamin had any tuna or milk.

Benjamin shook his head as he approached the cats, one of which had already darted off, another on the verge of doing so, while the third sat still in what could have been terror, or confusion. Karen's hands worried the front stoop's cracked and chipping wooden railing, white flakes floating like confetti to the ground unnoticed as she watched Benjamin, having no clue what he might do. She'd of course heard the story of how he had slaughtered a kitten and kept the bones for a necklace, believing *that* was a rumor, believing *that* never happened. She leaned over the railing, slightly, slumping her shoulders in anticipation. Honestly, she thought he was going to bend down to pet the cat or, very possibly, keep her a few days and maybe nurse her back to health before dropping her off at an animal shelter. This vague hope in Karen made her badly want to believe he was a good person, that he had the ability to be a good person.

Benjamin bent down and grabbed the cat by its neck, squeezing the excessive amount of flabby dirt-flecked fur, pulling the cat into the air as the cat meowed, the fur standing up on its back and tail. The cat hissed, cried, helpless to do anything as Benjamin proceeded to lower it onto the ground. He was very gentle, then, as he softly set the cat down onto the grass. "Good kitty kitty," he said, suddenly tightening his hands around the cat's throat as he started to strangle it. "Ben*jamin*!" Karen yelled, still standing on the front stoop, watching as he stared into the cat's wide blank eyes, searching senselessly for some sign of fear and seeing none. The cat only hissed and meowed, hissed, meowed - meowing until the hissing ceased and the meow was truly abysmal – continuing until it turned into a repellent persistent growl. "What the fuck are you doing?" she shouted, racing off the stoop and running to his side. Benjamin tightened his grip around the cat's throat, and the cat went limp, silent. Benjamin, too, was silent, as Karen continued screaming at him, pushing him, trying to tackle him, make him stop. Her efforts were of no consequence, as the cat was already dead.

Walking toward the front stoop there was no real reaction on Benjamin's face, even as her anger washed over him. Fists clenched, teeth gritted, she followed him inside, words finally rising in her throat. "Do you think you –"

"I *don't* want to hear it, K. Just shut up, okay? Shut the *fuck* up!" Anger radiated from him, not only contained in his words, no, she could detect it in his entire body: the tension, fury. He started back toward his bedroom, and she sat down on the couch, allowing her head to sink into her hands as the tears unfocused her eyes. He slammed the door, and she inexplicably wanted to ask him what was wrong, was there something she had done? How might she make him feel better? Could she offer herself up to him? Surely, she might do something to make him feel better.

The music started playing, loud heavy metal music that silenced all of these questions in Karen's mind, at least for the time being.

In that moment of clarity, she took in her surroundings, staring at the television remote, the fishless waterless fish tank that was flecked with maroon paint, the empty two liter bottle of Mountain Dew that Benjamin's mother had turned into a piggy bank, half-full of coins and decorated with streaks of gold and silver and faux feathers and beads. Too, she noted the old beige carpet that needed vacuumed badly, needed shampooed too, the beige color that had faded to a murky brown. It must have been months since it had last been vacuumed, or even over a year. She could see herself in the television's screen, a big black screen that seemed like a mirror – she frowned at her reflection, there was no hope in it, nothing that even came close to joy, and it bothered her to know her emotions were controlled by Benjamin, by what he said to her, or didn't say to her, how he made love to her, or didn't make love to her, his facial reactions, or lack thereof. He did not love her, she felt she knew that now. She believed he had loved her at one time, around when they had first met, as they were getting to know each other, when he was still pursuing her, not that he needed to chase her, not at all. The time it took for her to give herself to him entirely was very short in duration. Now, he knew he had her. Now, there was no getting away.

If she wanted to leave, it would be a very difficult task, as Benjamin had hold of her now, body and soul. Whatever 'soul' meant, Karen didn't know, figured it was probably only an idea, the soul of anyone being so elusive and mutable. Though Benjamin's soul was very reliable and singular. Benjamin was constant, never did she sense he changed, no matter the various shades of eyeliner he wore, the lipstick or his mercurial taste in clothing.

Karen thought it would be impossible to leave him, as her entire being was so tied up in his. Too, half of her belongings were in his room, not that she was a materialistic person, she wasn't, she didn't really care whether he kept her clothes and CDs and books. What she cared about was that by leaving these things with him, she would be leaving a piece of herself with him, though that was unavoidable at this point, she knew. Even if she retrieved every last thing she had brought to his trailer over the years, he would still be with her, who he was and how it cancelled out who she thought she was, or wasn't. Also there were his belongings in her bedroom, though far less in quantity, he had, on occasion, brought various and sundry possessions over to her house since they had first began dating.

When she first met him, near the end of ninth grade, she had not known herself, not very well so. She had been experimenting, trying to find out who she was, where she fit in. Believe it or not, for a couple months, she attempted to fit in with the preps, buying clothes at American Eagle and Hollister and Gap. There was also a point in time when she thought she would be one of the stoners, those disaffected kids who looked so blasé all the time, wearing hemp bracelets and Bob Marley tee-shirts and having eyes that were constantly bloodshot. Now she considered herself pseudo-goth, because sometimes she still liked to dress pretty, even at school, sometimes liked to wear clothes that were feminine and bold. It was true that the majority of people who had any knowledge of gothic subculture thumbed their noses at pseudo-goth, assessing those who fell into this particular category as being superficial posers. Karen herself was not superficial, if she was honest she thought she might have been a poser, at least in the beginning, though she liked to think she wasn't anymore, liked to believe that now her transformation was complete and genuine.

The music stopped, suddenly. A severe tension radiated throughout Karen's entire body which she could not control. The more she attempted to loosen its grip, the more it invaded her. The tension was not anxiety, exactly. It was more of a fear, and the source was unclear. Badly, she wanted to know what Benjamin would do next, what was on his mind.

Already she had forgotten about the cat, or at least no longer concerned herself with why he'd done it, thinking the reason irrelevant. Clearly, he was disturbed, angry, had to take it out on something. He could have chosen to take those feelings out on her, Karen knew. She thought she should probably be thankful for the scapegoat that had been the cat. She could find no gratitude, though: she felt awful that an innocent helpless animal had been killed for the sake of improving Benjamin's mood, which hadn't much improved since the vicious attack. He still appeared very dour and distant.

Karen got off the couch, feeling rather daring as she snuck a glance inside Benjamin's bedroom, seeing him even as he could not see her. Her hands were pressed against the doorframe, the television and television stand partially concealing her as she watched Benjamin, sitting on the edge of his bed with his head buried inside his hands. She could not see his facial expression, though the posture itself suggested he was feeling quite grim. She wanted to make him feel better. What could she do or say? She understood how co-dependent that was, feeling responsible for his bad mood.

She moved hesitantly into the bedroom, not knowing what to do, or say. So, she did nothing, said nothing. She simply stood there looking at him. Very apprehensive and uptight as she lowered her eyes, finding herself unable or unwilling to meet his hard gaze with her own rather tentative one. Even with his eyes still on her, she stared down at the floor.

"K." Benjamin's tone was very soft and firm.

She looked up at him, slowly.

"I want to make love to you, k?"

A smile on Karen's face then, one so big and wide and then all her tension was gone. She could feel his love so fully now, forgetting all the cruel hateful things he had said and done to her over the years, forgetting his hate entirely. Still sitting near the edge of the bed, he put his hand out, and Karen took it, sitting down beside him and then on his lap. He wrapped his arms around her, holding her tightly, cradling her in his arms that were so strong and lean. Then he was kissing her, on the neck, biting her so briefly, gently, and then kissing her lips, slipping his tongue inside of her mouth. Karen remained passive, allowing his tongue to enter her, probe her, move around inside of her, not responding, simply allowing him to have his way with her, direct and guide her.

As he dropped back onto the bed, he removed his tongue from her and pulled her back with him. Lifting up her shirt, then, he made a sudden gesture for her to take it off all the way. She complied with his silent suggestion, and he unbuttoned her jeans, sliding down in between her legs, lowering himself as he took off her jeans and removed her underwear. Entirely naked now, she put her arm on Benjamin's leg, massaged his thigh, for a moment, as he kissed and rubbed her breasts, licking them all over. Her nipples were very erect. Benjamin pulled his jeans down halfway before kicking them off onto the floor. Sliding out of his shirt, he pushed Karen gently down onto the bed, breathing on her heavily and kissing her. He didn't bother with a condom as he entered her. Kissing his mouth, she put her tongue inside him, meeting his tongue with her own as he made love to her. His thrusts were so gentle and she felt now that he did care for her, that he loved her and always had loved her.

Chapter 23

Immediately after the bus dropped her off, Clara went home. Meem did not greet her. Sitting in her usual easy chair, watching television, knitting, Meem ignored her. Clara tried to tell herself she didn't care, that Meem didn't matter, Meem's love was not essential in her life, just as Jeremy's love was insignificant, Benjamin and Karen's too. Truly, though, she did not feel this way. She did want their love, all of their love, wanted her mother's love too, her mother she presently glanced up at. Her mother, hanging on the wall, did not smile in the photo. The expression that emanated from her mother's face did not suggest sadness nor did it contain any hints of happiness. The expression evoked a poker face, rather disaffected. As her mother looked down at her, Clara could feel her unfair disapproval, as she could feel Meem's disapproval, burning into her, even as Meem glanced downward, continuing to knit as she moved the needle unsteadily, her hand slightly shaking. Did Meem actually disapprove of Clara? What would the reason for that be? Or was this simply Clara's own impression, her projection? Since she often did not accept herself, did not like herself, she thought others in her life who were important to her would not accept her, would not like her. She wanted to conquer this, feeling the need to be accepted by others, liked by others. It was true she did want to be accepted, obviously still wanted to be liked, but she did not want her self-worth to be determined by the acceptance or love of others. How to modify this intrinsic part of herself? How to alter this throbbing desire for love that she had felt so deeply from the time she first moved in with Meem?

First things first: ascending the stairs, she did not engage Meem. Contrary to her innate desire to want to do so, she did not talk to her. As she moved into her bedroom, she tried her best to dismiss the fact that Meem had ignored her entirely, told herself she did not care, that Meem's opinion of her was insignificant. Falling back onto her bed, she gazed up at the ceiling, focusing on the dozens and dozens of tiny and medium-sized plastic glow-in-the-dark stars that she had covered her ceiling with when she was a child. Without Meem's permission, she had purchased the stars and distributed them. Later, when Meem had discovered the stars, she had yelled, thrown a fit, for a good long while. Passively Clara had listened, at the time, too excited over the stars to care that Meem had lost her temper. Meem would be losing her temper again soon, she knew, the pattern had been established: Meem gave her the silent treatment over a very variable length of time that was of course at her discretion and then, the resentment built inside of her until it had become unbearable and she inevitably exploded, shouting questions and comments at Clara until Clara would break down and reveal everything she had been holding inside. Now, at least the last few weeks, Clara had erected an imaginary wall between her and Meem, not opening up to her at all, not telling her how she was feeling, or why, not asking her questions and in fact only speaking when she was spoken to and only offering answers that were succinct.

Jeremy, for some abstruse reason Clara decided not to analyze, did not occupy her mind at all, did not even cross her thoughts. Sure, she thought about him once or twice as she sat on her bed, sitting with her legs crisscrossed and her hands on her face. Jeremy did not linger, though, not as he normally did. She simply wondered, for a moment, what he might be up to right now and if she was ever going to call him, as she knew he would be leaving for college soon. Already he had informed her that he was taking summer courses, so in less than a month he would be gone. Then, Benjamin and Karen surfaced in her mind. Although she did think of them much longer than Jeremy, she was able to gloss over them too, like they were clouds that were distant. Attractive, clouds she could momentarily appreciate and then allow to float by. She was surprised Meem had not mentioned anything about her looking for a job, not in over a week. Clara did not care, since she was motivated to get a job herself, if only because she didn't want to be stuck around the house so much with Meem. A little extra money would be nice too.

What sort of job did she want? What jobs were available to someone still in high school? She decided to go downstairs and browse through the classifieds in the newspaper. On her way down the stairs, she decided instead to walk right out the front door. Her house was not too far from downtown, the business section less than two miles away.

As she started walking down the desolate road, Clara wondered why she hadn't simply just asked her grandmother to borrow the car. For sure, Meem would have said yes, after all it had been her idea that Clara should get a job to begin with. *Ask and ye shall receive*: this rather succinct verse from the book of Matthew surfaced suddenly in her mind. She often had no control over it, how the bible invaded her mind, her heart. She dismissed the bible verse. Her not asking likely had nothing to do with her pride, for God knew she had almost none, besides that which her sincere sometimes aimless and sometimes focused devotions provided her. No, she had not asked simply because she thought Meem did not love her, had in fact likely never loved her, had only wanted to raise her up because she herself possessed an emotional void she wanted to fill. Was this true? Or only Clara's perspective? Ultimately, Clara had come to believe that Meem taking care of her was selfish and self-centered, believing Meem only thought about what was in it for her, considering what kind of indelible impression she could make on Clara, how she might make one that would stick forever, and how after she went to be with the Lord, her memory would live with Clara forever. *But I will not remember that bitch, at least not very well,* Clara presently thought, not after Meem had been so harsh and judgmental and manipulative.

Stopping inanely at a stop sign, as though she was a car, too distracted with her own thoughts, Clara could not help but wonder how her life would play out - would she ever find the man of her dreams? Would she get married and have children? Would her husband be there for her, always, would he cherish and love her and be faithful? How would she go on without Jeremy? Would they keep in contact? Who would she be buried with, if she was, for whatever reason, unable to marry?

Finally Clara continued down the road, moving forward after standing at the stop sign for at least half a minute while processing her thoughts. For a second, Clara thought she would hear Meem shouting after her, calling for her to come back, and Clara, if this happened, would not look back, even if Meem decided to poke her head out the front door. Standing on the stoop and whistling for Clara as though she were some sort of stray dog, like she used to do when Clara was a child, on the swing set, or in the sandbox, generally interrupting her just as she was starting to have fun. If Meem did call out after her, Clara would ignore her. Of course, she might very well acknowledge to herself what Meem said, as that would be unavoidable, as Meem's loud voice volume made it impossible not to hear her, but she would quickly dismiss it.

Meem did not appear outside of the house, though. Clara quickened her pace, very nearly jogging now. A silver long boxy car that looked like a hearse passed her by, the driver wearing glasses and looking very staid and stern. Another car, nearly identical to the first, crawled past her, and now she felt like she was witnessing a funeral procession, except there was not a third car and they were not hearses, they were only sedans, the first one a Taurus and the second a Buick. It made Clara almost smile, to know now that even if Meem came out after her, she would be completely out of her sight. The houses that were a mixture of plain rather small bi-levels and ordinary two-stories she passed with increasing speed until she was running, panting, practically gasping for breath, holding her chest as she pushed herself faster, harder. Faster, she ran so much faster then, sprinting down the road, her fists clenched at her side as she tried to breathe more evenly. Soon, she stopped, slowly lowering her head with her heart, resting her hands on her knees. She wheezed briefly, feeling like she could not breathe, feeling herself on the verge of collapse. It had been a long time since Clara had formally exercised.

Not allowing herself to rest for long, she walked past a final row of houses, a new neighborhood that was rather separate from hers though still somewhat connected, if only because the yards ran together and there were no fences or posts serving as barriers. Clara gazed ahead, moving at a pace that was very moderate. Soon, this neighborhood would fade, the homes would be behind her and Clara in town.

Downtown, the traffic light was green, but as she approached it the light turned yellow and then red. Clara did not stop, not like she had done at the stop sign, no, she kept moving. Her mind was suddenly very clear, and she did not think about anything, her obsessions were gone. It might have been the sun, beating brightly down upon her face, or the fact that she had just ran, resulting in a release of chemicals in her brain that made her feel good, temporarily, and very calm.

Seeing a number of different large colorful signs now, seeing so many cars driving by her at a pace that seemed to match her own, not fast though by no means slow, the anxiety in her chest rose up from her stomach and spread throughout her entire body, increasing as she saw so many people, all different kinds of people, not crowding the sidewalks at all, the people were dispersed conservatively throughout the town, peering into the windows of stores, walking into stores, walking out of stores, smoking cigarettes, eating hoagies, smiling, frowning, looking like they cared, looking like they did not care, pressing a faded metallic button so they could cross the street, some crossing the street without the button, joyfully jaywalking. Children holding the hands of their mothers, their mothers who wore large sunhats and sunglasses, their tall mothers, their petite mothers, their mothers who stood at a normal height, their mothers who were plump, thin and average. Too, there were fathers around, walking with their children, their teenagers too, some teenagers loitering outside of a market, marking this corner as their own by defiantly standing there. A few of the young people Clara noted. Three good-looking boys clutched skateboards like schoolbooks, holding them very near the side of their stomach, pressed against their armpits. They were probably a couple years younger than Clara herself.

Clara was jaywalking now, not seeing any store that suited her, no business that appealed to her. Clouds appeared in the sky, almost out of nowhere, these clouds gathered density and thickness, turning the clear blue sky gray. Clara thought the shift must have been more gradual, more deliberate, reasoning she must have missed it, too inundated with all the people, not that the streets were crowded, or the sidewalks. Some stores were closing, she observed, it was well past five P.M., the business day was officially over. She watched numerous employees exiting the stores, seeming to hold their heads held a little higher, knowing it was

Friday and they would be returning home to their wives, husbands, children, lovers, friends, or parents. Clara would be returning home to Meem, that much she knew. Planning to fill out several job applications, presently she was unaware of where she would apply, not knowing specifically what businesses were hiring. Would she tell Meem anything about her day? No, she decided, not even if she asks. Upon her return, Clara could anticipate Meem's reaction: shouting questions at her, demanding to know where she had gone, what she had done, and why she had not informed her. Now, the only thing Clara wanted to do is look for interesting stores where she might want to work.

The triangular maroon sign Clara saw cattycorner from the post office, an organization she gave no consideration to working at. She felt it was too official, too serious, stamping stickers on boxes all day and punching numbers on a register and writing abbreviated addresses on little slips of paper that were delivery confirmations or insurance receipts. No, she could not see herself doing that, not while having to maintain a superficial smile, though the post office workers she could recall did not seem at all fake - no, she sensed when they were having a bad day, never did they try to conceal it, typically they allowed their mood to show. So long as they were not rude to customers, Clara thought it was fine for an employee to appear melancholy if that's how they were feeling. There were some employees at certain businesses, especially those telemarketers or the customer service representatives at credit card companies, that did seem to manufacture consistent courtesy, concealing their mood entirely, only permitting the tone of their voice to contain a light pleasant cheeriness. Clara couldn't comprehend such a position, unable to imagine how they could fake so much day in and day out, so mechanical in their daily duties. What the heck kept them going? The paycheck, ostensibly, though Clara had no idea how much they were paid. Some telemarketers were very friendly and some were quite detached and even somewhat cold. What accounted for this discrepancy? Clara wondered, for a moment. No answer came immediately to mind and for the sake of moving onto a new subject, she figured the cheery upbeat ones earned more money.

Clara presently stood directly below the maroon sign that read *Christy's Cakes,* but did not dare enter, not yet. There were circles of sweat under her armpits, circles that were very big and obvious with her short-sleeved shirt white. Well, there was nothing she could do about those! She could do something about her sunburned lips. Slipping lip gloss out of her pocket, she slathered her lips with it. Her hand deliberated on the doorknob, and she hesitated when she saw her reflection in the full-length glass door. "Move it," a boy beside her said as Clara simply stood there unaware she was blocking the entrance of the bakery. Taking several short rapid steps backward, Clara moved onto the edge of the sidewalk, gazing out at a long line of cars waiting at a red light. When it turned green, the cars did not move. Horns blared behind a white convertible that Clara saw was responsible for the hold-up: a young man around her age leaned over in his seat, kissing a young woman, his only passenger. The young man pulled his mouth away from hers, glancing in his rearview, adjusting the mirror to afford him a better view as he slammed on the accelerator. Clara couldn't take her eyes off the woman's long black hair, billowing out the window like smoke – her hair very smooth, shiny. As the white car vanished down the road, Clara decided that now would be the appropriate time to enter the bakery, if not now she might never summon the nerve that would allow her to enter an unfamiliar business and request an application. She felt eyes on her already, the patrons and staff, assessing her as she moved further into the store. She hoped the application would be brief, only one or two pages, though she supposed it might be three or even four pages. Never had she wholeheartedly applied for a job, only one time a few weeks after she had turned sixteen. She had started one and never finished, leaving the application on the customer service counter, partly completed. Later, she tried to analyze why she didn't turn it in, but the reason eluded her. Days later she would wonder again, wanting to know why she had ultimately decided not to finish.

At the time, she didn't need a job, Meem not saying a word about her getting one. But Clara wanted to work, if only because she wanted to make a couple good close friends. Realizing she had none, at the time, she had viewed work as a social opportunity, not caring too much about the money, since Meem paid for her car insurance and everyday living expenses, even providing a weekly allowance that was consistent despite being quite small.

As Clara approached the counter, seeing the cashier bent over resting on her elbows reading a newspaper, she felt now like looking for a job had been her idea all along, like it wasn't Meem who had initially suggested she get one. After Clara requested one, the cashier slid an application across the counter, setting a clicky pen beside it and by the time she said a few words Clara did not to catch, the push-button was pressed. Gazing at the cashier's nose as she accepted the application, Clara asked if she could fill it out here. The cashier flashed a smile and nodded, motioning for Clara to move to the side of the counter, there were a couple customers waiting behind her.

There were three pages in the application. As Clara flipped through it, she noted the numerous empty slots that required her personal information: address, phone number, job history, references, education, and so on. She continued to browse through the application, glossing over the pages, not quite ready to start recording her information, not quite prepared to submit herself to the austerity of the whole thing. Even though the application required nothing intimately personal, Clara felt very apprehensive about filling it out.

Rapidly, the cashier pressed buttons on the cash register and a receipt surfaced, the customer taking the initiative to rip the receipt from the box it had ascended from. "Thank you," the customer said after the cashier herself had said the same pleasantry, flashing a smile to dismiss her and then nodding politely, hearing the monotonous mechanical low *beep-beep-beep* as she scanned the customer's boxed premade cakes as if they were groceries (too, *Christy's Cakes* designed unique original cakes, designed to meet a particular customer's specifications, in fact sold more of those than the premade ones, which were mass produced in the relatively small family-owned store).

Summoning a certain uneven motivation from deep within her, Clara finally put pen to paper, writing rapidly as she began filling out the application. She did not think about her name or address, phone number, or even her job history, which was understandable, since she had none. Filling out the application, she released the information through her pen without thinking much at all, rather detached as she continued recording her information. When she reached the reference section, she stopped for a moment, not certain what she might write, for the section did not specify whether they wanted a professional or personal reference, or both. Such specification was irrelevant, though, since Clara herself had no professional references. There was space to list three references. Immediately, Mrs. Henderson came to mind. Listing her would be no problem. Calling her to ask permission would be unnecessary, for Clara knew it would be fine by her. The second reference eluded her, at least for the time being, as she stared at the white blankness of the application, tapping her pen against the paper and then thinking about Jeremy, wondering if she could use him as a reference. He was in no positon of authority though, unlike Mrs. Henderson, and he was only a friend. What about her therapist? Clara no longer saw a therapist, since Meem's health insurance had changed. Her therapist would not mind being listed as a reference, Clara thought, however would that be right? Shouldn't the fact that a person sees a therapist be kept private, confidential?

After writing Mrs. Henderson's phone number down, describing the nature of their relationship, and how long they had been acquainted, Clara continued on to the next section, which she completed very quickly.

It only asked her what position she was interested in (there were only two different positions to choose from) and when she was available to start. Respectively, she circled both positions, as she had no preference, she would work behind the scenes, she would do the hardest most anonymous work, which was conducted in the large sterile kitchen, if it meant she could have a job. If she had to choose, she would prefer being a cashier, as she felt being in the public eye would be important for her personal growth and development. If she wanted to overcome this social anxiety, she knew she would have to work at the counter, greeting customers and making small talk, perhaps even asking a simple personal question such as '*how is your day going?*'

When she handed the completed application to the cashier, who was not waiting on anyone, she noticed the bakery had cleared out. Only two customers remained, admiring the fancy cakes revolving around inside the tall glass display cases. She briefly considered the money she would earn if she was hired. Sometime in the future she wanted to earn a college degree, but as she watched the lushly florid cakes spin in their case, all she could think about was getting married. She didn't know where this strong desire had come from. Another full year of high school remained, and so far Clara had never gone out on an official date. She wasn't familiar with the whole game of flirting either. All she knew is that for the rest of her life she wanted to be with one man, loyal and devoted to him, completely monogamous. She would take her wedding vows very seriously, of course. Clara wanted to ask the cashier when she might hear something about the job, when she might know when her interview was, if they did in fact select her as a potential candidate for a position. The cashier nodded her head to acknowledge the application, and then simply looked very closely at Clara, inspecting her, for a moment. Clara thought she should smile, or at least say something to the cashier, anything, if only to appear personable. Clara chose to say nothing, though, as she watched the cashier disappear into the back room, the application still sitting on the counter.

As Clara exited *Christy's Cakes*, she did not consider the job she had just applied for but, rather, the man she would someday marry – who would he be? She imagined what his personality would be like, and his appearance. Would he consistently treat her well? And would they always be together, forever?

Chapter 24

Meem said nothing to her. All the lights in the house were off by the time Clara returned home, and she did not call out for Meem, did not even search around the house. It was true Clara wondered where her grandmother might be. She could picture Meem in her bedroom, possibly smoking a cigarette with her legs crossed, gazing intently into the maroon walls. The image of Meem in her mind passed quickly, and Clara knew then that she did not matter to her as much as she used to. For perhaps the first time in her life, she had begun to feel free of Meem for good.

"CLARA!" Meem shouted from upstairs.

Clara could not help thinking that Meem would want to scold her severely, asking where she had been, what she had been doing, why she hadn't informed her first. Not responding, for a short while, simply standing still in the living room feeling the silence, the judgment, throughout the entire house. She felt like she could not move.

"CLARA!"

Wanting to run out of the house, thinking she might hitch a ride with someone and let them take her far away - somewhere, anywhere, even out of the state. Step by step, then, very slowly, Clara ascended the stairs, her hand moving over the railing, brushing the shiny, timeworn wood, eyes wide as she continued climbing.

Meem did not call for her again, even when Clara had reached her bedroom. Seeing Meem sitting on the edge of the bed with her jaw hanging wide open. She looked very tired, and yet, at the same time, strangely alert.

"Get me my pills."

Clara didn't know which ones, there were so many scattered across Meem's bureau. Large bottles, small bottles, medium-sized bottles, some of them knocked on their side, and two bottles sitting rather oddly upside down on their caps. Clara imagined Meem with her glasses off in the dark, not realizing she'd made such a mess of her meds. "Which pills?"

"The Klonopin."

"How many?"

"Two."

Clara did as she was instructed, pulling two pills from the bottle and then placing them into Meem's extended wizened hand. Rather intensely, angrily almost, Meem stared at her. "Well, where's my glass of water?"

As Clara stumbled out of the bedroom, her hands slightly shook. Moving into the bathroom she proceeded to fill a small plastic cup with water. The anxiety that had been mostly absent until now returned, and she thought about the near-empty bottle of Valium in her bedroom. She considered the Klonopin too, knowing Meem would not notice if she took three or four of them out of the recently filled prescription.

Clara rushed to her grandmother's bedside - "Here you go, Meem." She handed her the cup, watching Meem pop the pills in her mouth and chase them down with water. Meem extended her hand, shaking slightly with the palsy of age, and then gave the cup to Clara. Very quickly, then, she dismissed Clara by pointing toward the door. Clara hesitated, for a moment, wondering why Meem had not asked her anything. Had she stopped caring about Clara? Clara lingered in the doorway, thinking of something she might say to Meem, she could ask a question, maybe, but nothing came to mind. Stepping out into the hallway, she decided not to take any of the Klonopin - although now she wished she had. The anxiety throbbed within her, overwhelming her now as she thought about Meem and how she was going to bed, imagining her empty bedroom and how it was getting dark now. Clara had no plans, she had nobody to see right now, nowhere to go. She thought about how the school year was over now, how she wouldn't be seeing Mrs. Henderson anymore, unless she called her, or e-mailed her, and that seemed unlikely at this point. The moment Benjamin and Karen crossed Clara's mind they disappeared from it, for Clara knew she had no control over when she would be seeing them next. They had not given her their phone number, and surely if they wanted to see her again they would contact her. Even if they didn't have her phone number they knew where she lived. They could drop by anytime, and Clara did feel a little concerned about what would happen if they did so. Meem would throw a fit, would be absolutely appalled, outraged, maybe yell at them, or call the police, not the least bit afraid of them as Clara was. Knowing them just a little, Clara was at times preoccupied with what they thought of her and how they might treat her in the future, how long they would be in her life. Clara believed very strongly that God puts people in our lives, but she also thought that sometimes He removes them as well.

Then she thought of him. Jeremy. Moving into her bedroom and sitting down on a basic wooden chair in front of her bureau, Clara didn't look into the plain long large mirror, uninterested in her own reflection. Sighing deeply, Clara tried to breathe steadily and evenly as she stared down at the unclean carpet. There were several dark spots and Clara did not know where they had come from, did not remember spilling anything in particular. Still, Clara could see Jeremy in her mind, his face appearing very vividly to her and then quickly fading away, like a cloud. She would not allow herself to think of him anymore. Her head still hung down on her hands, lowered a bit between her legs, and she could not cry anymore. There were no tears left within her. So what should she do now? She felt like she needed someone to guide and protect her. Was this a reflection of her own insecurity? What was she afraid of anyway? Life was a mystery, she believed, and God did not know everything. Lowering herself back onto the bed, she rested her head on a pillow and stared into the blazing ceiling light. For the first time, since she had accepted Christ into her life and been saved as a young girl, Clara was beginning to start to think and feel that God might not be there, after all. Maybe God was only a function of mankind's fanciful thinking. Clara knew she had a strong desire to believe in *something,* anything, so long as it was a power greater than herself. She also knew how badly she needed God's love. Clara suddenly felt unsafe, like she was in danger. Jeremy? Yes, she thought about Jeremy. It was true she did miss him already, although that didn't change the fact she didn't want to talk him, didn't want to see him, maybe not ever again. She wanted to sleep now, but she wasn't tired. If she shut her eyes she thought she would simply lay there, staring at the red-veined insides of her eyelids and scratching her legs that seemed to itch constantly. She reached out and turned off the light.

The stars were glowing, the ones on her ceiling, so many of them, scattered rather aimlessly in no particular pattern. She could see the stars outside, too, shining so very faintly through her windows. She did not shut her eyes, instead she turned on her side, feeling like she was going to cry. The tears did not come though, maybe there were no tears left. She allowed herself to think of Jeremy then, and as she did, she felt a sense of calm, peace, and the anxiety faded. She felt Jeremy did love her, in this moment, she truly believed that. He loved her as a friend, she was sure, but she also accepted that they were not meant to be together. A sudden calm rose through Clara now, and she decided she was going to do her best to let go of all her sadness. In a way, she was starting her life anew. Benjamin and Karen suddenly sprang to her mind unbidden. She wondered what they were doing. Where were they? When would she see them again? Would they simply drop by one day without her knowing?

Chapter 25

Benjamin and Karen did not experience even a small amount of nostalgia, now that the school year was over, nor did they think much at all about how summer break would now officially begin. They were both high. Benjamin dabbed at his eyes as pockets of tears filled them, tiny drops of wetness flowing down his face.

Karen was not as high as Benjamin nor did she pretend to have gotten much out of the crack they had smoked. Karen had never smoked crack before, but knew it was essentially speed that would create a definite euphoria within her, making her laugh and smile and talk a lot. She had become quite familiar with the high crack delivered – it was quite intense, though very short-lived. Methamphetamine was a much better drug, in her opinion, since the high, though not as strong, lasted for a far longer time. She grabbed Benjamin's hand, gripping it as she gazed up into his eyes, surprised at how calm she felt. She did not feel at all on edge or anxious, even as her heart pounded much faster than usual, the small slightly ripped black breast pocket on her tight tattered tee-shirt moving slightly away from her body with each steady, predictable beat.

Taking a deep breath, several long heavy inhales and exhales, Karen watched Benjamin as he took another hit. She was not interested in smoking anymore, since she had taken a big hit the first time and didn't want to get high again - she planned to drive home shortly. A few minutes later she felt Benjamin's hands on her, moving slowly over her body. Karen wondered if he wanted to have sex with her now. She was definitely not in the mood for sex. By the time she heard Benjamin's parents going to bed in the room beside them, her high had evaporated. Even after she took her clothes off and sat next to Benjamin with her legs crossed wearing only black underwear, sex was not on the agenda. Nothing was on the agenda. It was nearly midnight and they were both still coming down. Very little crack remained in the little baggie on the table in front of them. Only enough, perhaps, for two more hits, one for each, that was all.

The rain outside came down harder now, pitter-pattering off the rustic rusted roof. Karen heard it very clearly, had heard it even when it had only been a drizzle. Benjamin seemed not to hear it, seemed to be disengaged from his surroundings staring at the plain beige wall, not turning the channel despite the remote being right next to him. Despite MTV being on. Benjamin detested MTV. The top ten were playing, a show that featured the ten most popular pop songs in America currently. Benjamin lit a cigarette and finally grabbed the remote. He began flipping the channels incessantly until Karen wanted to grab it from him. Channel after channel he flipped through, not allowing the new channel to be established before he turned to a different one. How were they going to spend their summer? They had nothing much planned, not even a short vacation, and their parents didn't care whether they got a job or not so long as they didn't come asking for money, which they very seldom did. Benjamin sometimes sold drugs on the side when he wanted to add to his eclectic wardrobe or get a new tattoo or piercing. Karen had money most of the time too, but Benjamin imagined she obtained the majority of it from her parents.

The moment he extinguished his cigarette, he lit another and watched Karen as she moved outside onto the front stoop. It was still pouring and Karen, wearing only her underwear, began a rain dance, closing her eyes and gazing up into the sky as she shook her body slightly, swaying from side to side and feeling the rain as it poured all over her, soaking her underwear, her stomach, breasts, neck, face. Benjamin had to admit he could not take his eyes off her. She appeared utterly possessed, enraptured in the darkness and the rain that cascaded down her body.

The last thing Benjamin ever imagined he would do is join her. Peeling off his ripped jeans and tee-shirt, he noted he had an erection. He moved off the couch and out onto the front stoop, watching Karen as she continued to rock her body side to side, swaying back and forth, so immersed in the rain she didn't even hear or notice him. As he stood a few feet behind her smoking a cigarette and observing her impromptu dance, thunder and lightning started very suddenly. Karen stopped her dance for a moment, gazing up at the sky in a subdued delight and wonder. She had no desire to kiss Benjamin, didn't want him to hold her, and didn't want to touch him either.

The slight depression she normally experienced after coming down off any stimulant, however gentle, did not surface. Not feeling happy either, she felt calm and content, knowing the school year was over, knowing it was summer, thinking how she had no plans, what might she do with all her free time? The library wasn't far and since she didn't own a car, walking there would be no problem. Also, the mall was less than two miles away. Although she had very little money and didn't like to shop much to begin with, she could always go there to hang out and people-watch, as she used to do so often with Benjamin.

Stepping off the stoop, Karen moved out onto the front lawn which was very small and covered in more dirt than grass. She was barefoot. Benjamin joined her there wearing sandals.

Kicking his sandals off, he felt the rain pour all over his body, his wet lean muscular body, touching Karen's body, fingering her ribcage, breathing on her neck, his dick poking into her lower back as he stood behind her. He thought he might fuck her right here in the grass. Just slide down on top of her, spread her legs up in the air and then very carefully fuck her, with a certain precision that was unusual for him, giving it to her just how she wanted it for once. If she wanted slow and gentle and deliberate, he would do that for her. If she wanted fast and hard and sloppy, he would do that for her too. For once, although he would still be in control, he would allow her to direct the sex.

How would she want it? Would she react positively to his initiating the sex, as she still seemed absorbed by the rain, the sky, the pleasantly adulterated semi-silence.

Karen could feel him behind her, still approaching her gently and steadily. He kissed her neck and then pulled away. She had stopped moving. Her eyes were closed and she had her head tilted backward. The soft bright light that emanated from the black sky she could feel inside her, so deep within her it distracted her from Benjamin, his entire presence forgotten.

The rain had eased somewhat - though it was still pouring down upon her. Karen could feel the rain drenching her, soaking her black bra and tee-shirt and underwear. Despite it being so dark, Benjamin could nearly see through them, observing the distinct outline of her vagina, her engorged clit. She had become aroused with little stimulation. Benjamin hadn't been required - his hands, his voice, fingers, dick, nothing. Was it the rain? That might have been responsible, partially. It could have also been the night, the fact that it was very dark outside. Benjamin wondered if Karen had been thinking at all about him, when she had become aroused.

The rain came down faster now. So severe it felt like hail and not rain, and Karen's skin hurt from it, felt stung, pelted. Still, she danced, moving her arms out on both sides of her and spinning around until Benjamin grabbed her arms to stop her. "You'll get dizzy," he said, moving close to her, thinking he might kiss her. She laughed.

Chapter 26

Mrs. Henderson was relieved, feeling as if a certain overwhelming burden had been lifted from her. All summer she would have to do whatever she pleased, all summer to spend time with Frank, even if she didn't want to spend much time with him she knew he would be there, that he would make time for her, despite his consistently hectic professional life. If she needed him badly enough he would be there for her, but did she really need him? Not really.

What did she want? To be alone, maybe, to collect her thoughts, allow the realization to sink in that the school year was over and she would have lots of free time on her hands. She didn't have many hobbies. On occasion, she liked to read, romance novels mainly. They were an escape from her own life, distracting her from the fact that the passion in her married life with Frank had dissipated. Perhaps, Frank's emotional absence was a factor in their marriage that she had somehow unconsciously created. Did she want a divorce, to have more independence in her life and maybe even be free from him? She wasn't sure, but the distance between them made her feel so empty.

Where was Frank this evening? Mrs. Henderson presently wondered. Inevitably, he was on his phone, likely talking to a client. Possibly at the local Starbucks, where he spent time on occasion, working most times, never idly drinking coffee or sipping espresso, no. Frank was almost always conducting business, sometimes even venturing to the local bar, downing martini after martini, never becoming intoxicated but always working to make the deal, always sure he never appeared impaired. On some rare moments, typically when he was alone with Mrs. Henderson, he did admit to a plaguing discontent, a sense of dissatisfaction with his job and the way it had taken over his life lately. His job did not give him the same sense of fulfillment that it used to. At the end of the day, did all the money he earned, the millions of dollars he had in the bank that would never be drawn upon, mean anything? If all this money did mean something, what did it mean? All this money, so much in their joint savings and checking accounts, so much invested in the stock market, what did all of it amount to, really? Mr. Henderson could not answer this question nor could he say why his wife worked, it must have fulfilled some purpose within her, must have given her some sense of purpose, for obviously she knew her working was unnecessary to sustain them.

When she thought about having the entire summer off Mrs. Henderson felt restless and uncertain. She had very few friends. She did have several women she saw on a semi-regular basis, sometimes talking on the phone, but typically never about anything substantive. Nothing about their conversations was very real to her. She didn't feel these women really knew her. Mostly, it seemed they got together to complain about their husbands, not to discuss ideas, solve problems or discuss their faith. In private, Mrs. Henderson often questioned her own religious beliefs, reflecting on how she had lost her connection with God over the years. Very infrequently, she still attended church, alone, usually, sometimes with one of her friends, their husbands never bothering to join them. Frank used to attend church with her, years ago. Now those days were long gone, and a part of her missed them, and him, the close connection they shared. It was true there were no problems in their marriage to speak of, they were both faithful to each other, loved each other, didn't they still love each other?

Sometimes, she questioned that love. Usually this happened when her love for him was very strong, when she put her entire heart and soul into loving him and then felt the futility in doing so, wondering what loving him so much really accomplished, what purpose it served within her. She supposed it did fulfill a purpose, to a degree, making her feel her life had more of a meaning, also making her happier and more vibrant and alive. After a certain amount of time had passed, she would inevitably sense him pull away, he would become emotionally distant. During these times she felt somewhat hurt and abandoned, fearing he would leave and sensing he might have another woman in his life. This was a sign of her own lack of trust, she knew, a result of losing her father to Lou Gehrig's disease at a very young age. When she was old enough to think about God and question the Presbyterian Church she had been raised in she really began questioning whether God existed, why God would be so cruel as to take her father away. Maturity helped her to understand God was not responsible for her father's death, no one was responsible. As much as she wanted to blame someone, she realized that terrible things do happen in the world and those things have nothing to do with God. Nearly a year after her divorce from her first husband, when she was 30, she met Frank through a mutual friend. They had only dated six months before he proposed. Maybe it was the fear of carrying her father's disease in her blood and potentially passing it to their children, maybe it was the fact her first marriage had failed, but shortly after getting married for the second time, she had begun thinking a lot about the existence of God. She knew it was not fully rational to continue obsessing over her religious and spiritual beliefs. It was not as if there were some neat conclusion she would ever reach, or any definitive answers she would receive. For a long time, she didn't share any of these thoughts with Frank. She knew her own emotional issues were not his burden to carry. Eventually, though, she broke down and told him everything about how she had been raised, about all her fears, about her wanting to believe in something greater than herself. Frank had not responded to her opening up to him. He had simply listened intently, and then his cellphone began ringing and he walked out of the room.

Chapter 27

Benjamin and Karen had nothing to do besides get high, and that was all very well and fine with them. Their drug of choice for the evening was not methamphetamine. Benjamin had decided he had experienced quite enough of staying up all day and all night for nearly a week straight. Badly he wanted to sleep. The Xanax he had procured from a middle-aged man, a virtual invalid, who held a valid prescription for the benzodiazepine, presenting a legitimate need for the stuff since he suffered daily from severe anxiety. Benjamin had shared enough substantially terse conversations with him to know his anxiety was real, not at all imaginary, or psychosomatic. The man's psychiatrist considered it profound enough to have doubled his dose. Sneakily, the man also saw another physician, this one not a psychiatrist but a regular medical doctor who prescribed Klonopin in similarly high amounts as the psychiatrist prescribed the Xanax.

Karen watched Benjamin lay down on the sofa, reaching into his pants pocket and revealing a small plastic baggie filled with pills.

"Is that Valium?" Karen asked.

"No," Benjamin said. "Xanax."

She quickly sat down next to him. Immediately after snorting three super slim long lines each, both Benjamin and Karen were ready to sleep.

When Karen woke up it was still night, blackness enveloping the room. She concluded there were no stars out, no moon either, as even with the blinds shut, if stars were out, if any amount of moon loomed above, the room would be at least partially lit. And she would be able to decipher the outlines of things such as Benjamin's dresser, the music posters on his walls, the bed frame, bed sheets, et cetera.

She could see nothing. She debated whether to turn on a lamp, perhaps the lamp on the end table? Not wanting to risk waking Benjamin, fully cognizant of his being a very light sleeper, she stepped slowly out of bed, realizing now how she was naked. She had no memory of taking off her clothes, or anything else from the night before, no recollection beyond arriving at his trailer and talking very briefly (about what, she could not say) and then nothing, blankness.

Chapter 28

The graduation ceremony would begin in an hour. Clara would not be going with Meem. She thought she should tell her where she was going, not out of any courtesy or desire to regain her approval, but because she thought there was a chance Meem could have a serious breakdown if she discovered Clara was gone the whole night and didn't know her whereabouts. It was true Clara had gone out many times without telling Meem - these times, however, had only been for a few hours, never had she been gone for an entire night. A few days ago, Jeremy had invited her to attend a graduation party. All the popular kids at school would be going, and Clara had been so ecstatic when Jeremy had asked her that she feigned nonchalance: a sure sign of her extreme excitement.

That evening, Clara had spent very little time planning her appearance. Briefly brushing her hair, Clara gazed into the mirror. She applied some foundation and a touch of eyeliner. A brief smile surfaced on her face, and she had no control over her sudden unexplained happiness. At last, she felt she had a certain measure of control over her life, that she was living her life the way she wanted to. The part of her that felt daring and free, the side of her that did not analyze what was right or wrong in the eyes of the Lord, the part of her that was rapidly growing and gaining power, persuaded her to not tell Meem where she was going, or even that she was going out at all.

Clara presently slipped out the front door. Meem was in the kitchen eating dinner, apparently still upset with Clara as she had not even called for her to come down from her bedroom to join her. Clara was aware of Meem's hiding spot for the car keys. She had known ever since Meem had decided she couldn't go anywhere without her knowledge. The only reason she had never taken the keys before centered on her belief that it would be wrong in the eyes of the Lord. Now, looking down at her outfit, feeling rather detached from her physical appearance although nonetheless noting that she wore an oversized tank top and jean shorts that were on the tight side, she reached inside the tissue box on the end table right beside Meem's rocker where she knitted and crocheted. Reaching all the way to the bottom, she felt the keys and pulled them up into her hand.

"Clara?" Meem called for her from the kitchen.

Clara hurried toward the front door. Seeing the car had been parked in the driveway and not in the garage, Clara smiled very widely, thinking that this was just her lucky day, as Meem would surely hear her and come out after her if the car was in the garage, since that would require Clara opening the garage door, which would create a certain amount of loud annoying noise.

She opened the car door quickly, knowing she had to get out of here fast. Glancing back at the front door, she smiled, seeing that Meem was not there. The moment the keys were inside the ignition, the moment Clara started the engine, the smile on her face grew.

Chapter 29

At the graduation ceremony Clara decided against sitting in the bleachers. Moving across the cinder track, Clara stepped up against the railing that reached her waist and had paint chipping off it. She looked out onto the football field, feeling so excited to see Jeremy and no one else. In this moment, she did not want to see Karen or Benjamin, did not care if she ever saw them again. In this moment, there was only Jeremy.

Clara couldn't wait for the ceremony to begin, eager to talk to Jeremy afterward, possibly even spend time with him at the party he had invited her to, if there weren't too many people demanding his attention. Clara felt lucky that she had been invited, very grateful. Despite not being close to him lately, Clara still adored him, admired him, wanting to be with him always. She dreaded the thought of him leaving for college. Very badly, she wanted to restore their relationship. They used to be best friends.

The stadium, quite crowded already, would be packed full by the time the students began promenading onto the field. She was not looking forward to the procession, knowing very well how long it would last, with a class of over 700, and Jeremy having a last name that fell near the end of the alphabet. For a moment she wondered about Christina and Tammy, those so-called friends of hers. Where were they? Was she going to see them at all this summer? What about Mrs. Henderson? She wanted to see her, not necessarily right now, although sometime soon she wanted to spend time with her.

Surely, Mrs. Henderson was at the ceremony tonight, possibly had not arrived yet. Likely, she would not see Clara in the crowd, they had made no plans to see each, either tonight or over the summer. Both shared the implicit knowledge that the other would be there, but they had not discussed it, or designated a spot for them to meet. Formal instrumental music started to play suddenly, signaling that the commencement was about to begin. The music increased in volume, and then the students appeared, moving across the field, some smiling, others more serious, gazing out onto the track at all the people in the bleachers.

Clara absently tapped the track with her foot, the grass too, standing near the edge of the field and doing her best to remain patient as she awaited Jeremy.

She felt so excited! As she continued to wait for him, knowing that at least half of the class had exited the building, knowing that at least half of the class had already ascended onto the high-risers, knowing that soon she would see his face, his smile, inevitably she thought he would be smiling. Not that he was a person who smiled a lot: given the occasion, though, given the fact this was a celebration – a very formal rather solemn celebration, yes, but a celebration nonetheless - he would be smiling, grinning actually, a better way to describe the appearance of his face when joy, even contentment, consumed it.

Tears welled in Clara's eyes, which she tried to suppress. How sad she felt! Mostly, over the fact he would be leaving in two short weeks. That reality was just registering now. Not wanting to acknowledge how much she would miss him. Oh, how she loved him! Wanted to be with him! Spend time with him, kiss him, hug him, hold hands with him, go to an amusement park with him, ride all the big scary rides with him, the ones she was too afraid to ride on by herself, thinking of all she wanted to do with him, all she wanted to say to him. Yet, when the time came she felt the words would evade her. When the time came, she thought her reticence would keep her quiet, prevent her from expressing her true feelings for him.

Still, a part of her wanted desperately to tell him, dared her to tell him, asked why shouldn't she tell him? What did she stand to lose? Nothing, she concluded. Nothing at all.

Chapter 30

Benjamin and Karen had not attended graduation. In fact, they had no knowledge the ceremony had been held this evening. Even if they were aware of the date and time, they would have no desire to attend – the ceremony didn't involve them, so why should they?

The Xanax was all gone and the man who sometimes sold Benjamin Valium, among other things, claimed he had a short supply remaining. No reason given, and Benjamin hadn't asked, all the man offered was he wanted to keep the remaining pills for himself, for his own use. It was true Benjamin had other sources to buy drugs from and also, since he used to occasionally deal drugs in rather small amounts, mostly for the thrill, the adrenaline rush, but also, for the fast money selling drugs produced, he, like the drug dealer he had called only an hour or so ago, had a small cache of drugs hidden in his bedroom, set aside for a special time, a desperate time, when he could not afford drugs, find them, or both, although the former likely more accurate, since he had several numbers in his phone, names of people he knew would be holding. Fairly certain all he had left was a miniscule amount of cocaine and a fair amount of pot. The only reason he didn't get some drugs out now was Karen. For starters, he was short on cash, so could not easily afford to buy more. Also what drugs he did have he wanted for himself, did not want to share with Karen – Karen, who was a fool when she was high. Karen, who strangely lost her libido, when under the influence of any narcotic, only wanting to cuddle, having to be coerced into sex. Karen who, when under the influence, laughed constantly, completely giddy for no good reason. Under the influence, she got on his goddamn nerves, plain and simple. He wanted to get rid of her. A part of him wanted to be free of her forever. At the same time he wanted to keep her around for sex. The more he considered this, the more he wondered why he felt this way: easily, he could find someone else to fuck.

Why not simply break up with Karen? Tell her he didn't want to be with her anymore? Tell her in no subtle way that things were over

166

between them? He could not say for sure, why he could not just come right out and tell her, although he supposed the reason had to do with the fact that he liked her a lot, regardless of how much he wanted to deny his feelings for her, he knew, at the end of the day, he did love her, he loved her a great deal.

Benjamin did think of Clara, a little, unable to deny he was curious what she was up to, with who? Probably no one, he thought, probably alone reading the bible down on her knees praying her fifty 'Hail Mary's'. Benjamin had to chuckle at that, how utterly pathetic of her, to have such a sincere belief in God, how inane! Did she honestly believe all that shit, in the depths of her being, did she believe she might save their souls from eternal damnation, from the fiery pits of hell? Did she truly believe in hell? Still chuckling silently thinking about the uneasy look that constantly consumed Clara's face, Benjamin imagined what it would be like to put his dick inside of her, how good it would feel to tear her apart, rip her open. Would she cry? She would yell and moan, definitely, perhaps even scratch his back, chest or arms, maybe break some skin, make him bleed. The pain these scratches created would not bother him much, for the pain he would inflict upon her would be far greater.

Karen slept on the couch. He hated watching her sleep: she looked too serene, content. Why should that bother him? Make him feel an innate burning need to disrupt her slumber? His sadistic streak, of course – running on rather endlessly, he supposed it was intrinsic. Not feeling aroused, as he watched her sleep, he felt no sexual excitement at all. The disgust and fury he felt had been growing slowly over their entire junior year: he hated her identity, or extreme lack thereof, hated how she clung to his identity, looked to him for security, affirmation, looked to him to see who she was, or wasn't. Much more than any of this he hated how, despite her strong independent show, she was, in reality, quite emotionally weak, extremely needy of him. He might respect her, or at least come close to doing so, if she simply stopped pretending, if for once she was real, for once she just acted like whoever she felt she was at any given moment, not censoring what she thought or how she felt, not changing herself to suit his needs, not modifying and adjusting herself to become who she thought he wanted her to be.

But no - Karen being Karen seemed an impossible feat she could never come close to achieving. The irony he had slowly recognized. Despite Karen's appearance, inside she wasn't too different from Clara herself. Like Clara, she was malleable, quite vulnerable, sensitive, reluctant about her own identity. Like Clara, she was laughable, not someone to be taken seriously. Like Clara, she looked to Benjamin to validate her: perhaps this was her most pitiful attribute, certainly it made her foolish in his eyes.

Looking at her now he realized he didn't even have the desire to have sex with her. The thought of her naked rather disgusted him. He had had her hundreds (thousands?) of times, and now he wanted something, *someone,* new, a challenge, preferably. Was it the matronly way she dressed?

Recently, she'd bought some new clothes and had been wearing clothes she already owned that were about two sizes too big, all in an obvious effort to hide her ever-expanding figure. Over the last school year she'd gained approximately 40 pounds, and ten of those over the past month or so. It was true that, before Karen's allegedly unintentional weight loss, she was a thin girl, too thin, perhaps. Benjamin felt disgusted with her, unable to fathom how he had dated her this long, committed in theory for almost two years. He would have to hurt her, that's the one thing he understood. She was repugnant to him - as she lay down spread out on the couch, looking serene, even almost happy, to the extent one can appear happy while sleeping. Her head was propped up on a pillow and her right foot dangled off the edge of the couch - repellent and ugly to him. How he loathed her! Loathed how she had recently begun calling him 'babe'. How she made herself at home at his trailer, helping herself to anything in the cupboards, anything in the refrigerator, the pantry, without his permission. Loathed how when she woke up, nine times out of ten, she'd gaze over at him smiling and then ask for the time. Truly unbearable it seemed to him - the entire summer stretching out before them, seeming infinite and empty with nothing at all planned. Karen would want to spend every waking moment with him, he knew. Well, that wasn't going to happen, he would just have to let her know, too.

Clara surfaced in his mind – would he see her again soon? It was true he knew where she lived. He felt no reluctance about simply stopping by one day unannounced. Sure, she would be startled, shocked even. Maybe he'd call first. Already he had her phone number memorized, the number a very easy one with three of the same numbers in the last four. He saw Clara naked then, suddenly, completely naked. His dick was hard.

He immediately sneaked off to the bathroom, unzipping his pants and rubbing himself through his underwear. After the door was shut he wondered why he didn't just stay where he was? Right by Karen, jerking off at her side, watching her sleep then coming on her face? He grinned to think how that would wake her up. After all, his mother was at work, not off until midnight. On the verge of climax, he moved out of the bathroom and approached Karen who was still sleeping.

Chapter 31

Mrs. Henderson did not see Clara. The ceremony had commenced and for a moment she wondered if she might have the chance to talk to her afterward, figuring that was improbable since Clara's habit was to sneak off after a big event, her head likely lowered, staring at the ground as she made a beeline for the exit, wanting to get away unnoticed. She had to admit she had become exhausted trying to repair that girl's self-esteem, trying to persuade Clara she was worthy of a good and happy life. There was nothing more to say, nothing more to do, and Mrs. Henderson understood fully, perhaps for the first time, that she could not save Clara. Save her from what? Well, she had heard from several sources that Clara had befriended Benjamin and Karen and had even spent time with them outside of school on three different occasions. Initially, Mrs. Henderson believed Clara had no ulterior motive in wanting to get to know Benjamin and Karen - that is, she didn't want to get to know them because she was lonely and insecure and needed a friend, or friends. At first, Mrs. Henderson thought Clara genuinely did want to introduce them to Christianity, genuinely did want to witness to them and save their souls so they could go to heaven. Now, Mrs. Henderson wondered why it was necessary for Clara to spend time with them privately outside of school. Witnessing to them could've easily been accomplished on a single occasion on school premises, even before or after a Genesis club meeting, if that happened to be the most convenient time. It was true Mrs. Henderson still wanted to help Clara. She had no idea what that help looked like, but she knew the girl needed help. *Everyone* needed *some* help, God knew that.

No plans had been made for her to see Clara over the summer. Last summer, they had met twice for lunch and then again for dinner. The first time had been arranged before the school year had ended. Mrs. Henderson had hinted at the idea, had almost suggested they get together, not wanting to come right out and say so, wanting to be subtle, not wanting to scare Clara off, for Mrs. Henderson was a teacher and Clara a student, Clara being self-conscious, Clara caring a great deal about how her classmates perceived her, caring so much that she would forfeit an opportunity to spend time with her favorite teacher just so others wouldn't think poorly of her. So, days before the final day of last school year, Clara, apparently deciding finally not to care what anyone thought or, probably much more accurately, determining that most students would never find out, had approached Mrs. Henderson after class and whispered that yes, she did want to meet for lunch sometime, when would she be free? Then, last summer, after they had had lunch that first time, before they parted, Mrs. Henderson had said they should "do this again" and Clara had eagerly agreed, nodding her head repeatedly, eyes widening in anticipation. A date had been set and, following lunch on that second occasion, since no subsequent meeting had been set, Mrs. Henderson had waited, curious to see if Clara would be proactive in asking her to meet again (and Mrs. Henderson was sure she did want to meet again, if only for the fact that a huge smile had consumed Clara's face almost the entire time while they were having lunch, Clara had said she would call her seconds before they parted, asking if that would be all right, knowing very well that would be fine but asking nonetheless. Asking too whether they might have dinner this time, if only for a diversion, and then Clara even going so far, with their backs both turned to each other as they walked in different directions in the parking lot, as to ask: "Could you bring your husband along?" Mrs. Henderson stopped, her hand fishing her keys out of her purse, and looked up, turning around to face Clara, quite confused by the request. "Frank," Clara said, as though Mrs. Henderson didn't know her own husband's name, "Could you bring Frank along, too? For something different, you know." Mrs. Henderson had simply nodded, at the time, feeling very tired and offering no real response other than a slight smile as her hand returned to her purse digging around for a moment before finally grabbing her keys. "OK," Mrs. Henderson had said. "OK." Frank had said no, he just didn't have the free time, to which Mrs. Henderson informed him that Clara's schedule, as well as her own, was very open, very flexible. "You can find the time," Mrs. Henderson had sad.

Frank was firm when he said no, and then added: "I don't even know this girl. Why would I want to meet one of your students?" Mrs. Henderson had not given Frank the back story on Clara, since they rarely talked anymore, this enduring silence between them having started the fall before last summer, triggered by Mrs. Henderson's belief that, over the years, ever since his career took off, he had become selfish and cold and uncaring. Rather than tell Frank why he should join them, she had allowed his rhetorical question to slide. At the time, he had added, rather sweetly, sweet as he seldom seemed, "Besides, I'd rather just be with you. Dinner out somewhere with you. Or dinner here with you. Alone. Us. *Alone*." And he had kissed her on the lips, slipping his tongue in her mouth as though that would settle things, which it did, for a time.

So, she did want to see Clara, wanted to spend time with her, to help her, but how to initiate such an interaction? How to extend help to someone reluctant to accept it? Since Clara had erected a wall, she no longer opened up to Mrs. Henderson, was no longer even open to opening up. In short, the Clara Mrs. Henderson knew existed no longer. Much more than the obvious physical transformation, which was easy to overlook and see through, Clara had changed herself emotionally, it seemed, her personality gone. The void within her was apparent. There was no discernible expression on her face. Mrs. Henderson could not read her as usual. Clara didn't look sad, necessarily, or happy, serene or discontent. She didn't look any particular way. Mrs. Henderson had noticed in class and during the last two Genesis club meetings, Clara had looked absolutely blank, empty, dead.

Mrs. Henderson had considered asking her what was wrong, but they had been through that already. Such a question was trite and juvenile, Mrs. Henderson knew, no way would it succeed in getting Clara to divulge her feelings. She considered calling Dorothy. Over the years she had only ever shared a few substantial conversations with her, and they had amounted to little, as Meem seemed disengaged the whole time, disinterested in what Mrs. Henderson was saying, giving one or two word answers to all of her questions. Why didn't she call Dorothy? She thought that if she called and Clara found out, Clara would be very upset, feeling that her trust had been violated, which would result in her confiding in Mrs. Henderson even less once the new school year began. So, she didn't call.

All of the students had exited the school now, and the risers were filled to capacity. As the last few students filed in front of the first row, Mrs. Henderson noted the music: abruptly the song rose in volume before ceasing completely. Had this been a mistake?

Clara did not see her, even though Mrs. Henderson walked right past her, having arrived late to the ceremony, near the middle of the procession. Clara had been standing at the railing, her back turned toward her.

When Jeremy appeared she felt herself go weak in the knees. Her anticipation had been immense, her heart beating very fast, feeling suddenly very anxious as she thought about how he would be gone soon. Considering the knowledge of his imminent departure, the empty feeling within her returned. She felt quite ill for a moment, like she might faint, and that's when she forced herself to focus on Jeremy. Jeremy and only Jeremy: his face, his eyes, body, wavy light hair, his voice, everything. In this moment, as she forced herself to clear her mind and think of only him, she felt none of the anxiety she felt when she imagined herself apart from him, or when she attempted to be strong and do things on her own. Yes, she accepted that soon he would be leaving: possibly she thought she should at least acknowledge that reality. The announcer began speaking, and Clara knew she shouldn't think of him anymore. She shouldn't think of being married to him anymore, she shouldn't think about having his children anymore, waking up in the morning by his side and then seeing his face right next to her before she went to bed each night. That would never be realty. Immediately feeling sad, Clara began to think of Benjamin and Karen, for she knew, or at least thought it very possible, they would be there for her over the summer, wanting to spend time with her and help her forget that Jeremy had left.

Jeremy had little on his mind. He was blank, which is to say he felt nothing, really. This day he had anticipated for so long now felt anti-climatic. All the excitement and joy he had been feeling today and all week seemed now somehow out of reach, distant. Jeremy was already thinking of the next step, only for a few dreamy, distracted seconds, though, as he wasn't one to think too much of the past or future. Jeremy stayed in the present, mostly, and with little effort. He did like to plan, though, thinking it wise, a grown-up concern. The next step: college, and not much time until he would be leaving. This would be the most difficult step, like going to work, most of the battle existed in simply leaving the house and driving to the work site. Once in his car, driving a bit over the speed limit on the highway, he imagined it wouldn't be too hard saying goodbye to Turner High School, as well as his parents, friends. He had to concede he was a little anxious about leaving, feeling even more apprehensive than he had felt on the night of the state final football game. He was sure everything would be fine, it was just that college held such an element of anonymity: once he got there no one would even know who he was. It would be like he didn't exist, essentially.

Wouldn't he relish this independence and freedom? Some of him would, the rest of him might miss everyone knowing him, everyone knowing he was a star athlete and all-around excellent guy. Sure, college offered him the opportunity to establish a new name for himself, but even if he was successful in doing so, it wouldn't matter much because it wouldn't be the same: the university was large and yet, compared to other schools like Penn State or even Purdue, quite small. Even if he became the team's star quarterback, the majority of students on campus would not know him, he would still remain rather anonymous. Jeremy understood in college no one cared what you did, not really. For instance, if he decided one day to not attend class, the professor would not care, would not say a word, likely, because his absence would not be noticed. Not that his aim was to be noticed, necessarily, he simply wanted to feel some connection to others. Being a very social person, he sometimes liked feeling a sense of oneness, solidarity. If he was honest with himself, that's the only reason he still attended church: he appreciated the established sense of connection, seeing all the familiar faces. In two short weeks, most of those people would be in the past, abruptly absent from his life since he would no longer see the vast majority of them. And slowly, then, as time passed, they would fade into memories.

Chapter 32

A fair amount of time passed before Meem realized Clara was not home. Blissfully unaware of her surroundings, she shoveled food into her mouth, returning to the counter for seconds and even thirds as she watched the local news. She listened intently at first, then let her thoughts drift onto other things - when the repairman was going to come to fix the upstairs bathroom's leaky faucet, whether she might start attending church again, whether she had another pack of cigarettes in her dresser upstairs or would she have to go to the market, where she might donate the quilts and afghans she had made or should she sell them somewhere? Perhaps donate half and sell half, as God knew she needed the money. Finally the pressing question of how she would spend her last years once Clara was gone?

As much as she didn't like to admit it, she did rely on Clara for a great many things such as taking her to appointments, picking up her prescriptions, making trips to the post office, cutting the lawn, shoveling snow, and so on. More than all of these things, though, she relied on Clara for emotional support, whether Clara realized it or not, Meem needed her company, companionship.

What would happen when Clara graduated from high school? Marriage was on her mind, that much Meem knew, thinking her an absolute fool to believe marriage would solve her problems. The truth is it would likely only add to them, that naïve fool thinking some man - no matter how perfect she *felt* he was, no matter how high the pedestal was she placed him upon - would complete her and consequently make her happy and fulfilled forever was rubbish. Such nonsense needed to be struck out of her head, and more importantly, out of her heart. Clara genuinely believed finding the right man was the key to a prosperous, joyful future. Was there something Meem might do to change her mind? To make her believe she could never get the kind of commitment she desired, to make her believe no man would ever want to spend his whole life with her. But Meem knew one type of man who could sweep in and carry Clara away. This particular man would find Clara extremely attractive, a knockout really, with her most appealing features being her desire to please, her utter selflessness, her submissiveness and lack of identity. The type of man she would end up with would see her as clay to be shaped in his hands, molded into what he wanted her to be. Then, after a time, he'd modify and adjust the Clara he had created, discarding what he didn't like only to add more of what he wanted.

"Filth," Meem said suddenly staring at the small television set, seeing the bottle-blonde big-breasted newscaster babbling, wide-eyed into the camera. "This whole world." Meem averted her gaze from the newscaster as she shoveled more food into her mouth. "Clara," she said quietly, to herself, rather absently, realizing she had been eating for well over an hour now and Clara had not joined her. It was true she had not called for Clara, not as she typically did.

"Clara!" She was yelling now, yelling abrasively. Clara's name was like a marble in her mouth, very garbled since her mouth was full of mashed potatoes and turkey and stuffing. "CLARA!" She chewed more rapidly now dropping her fork and standing, shutting the television off and staring at the clock. "CLARA?"

She moved into the empty living room looking into the gloom and feeling the silence. Moving toward the stairway, she rummaged the pocket of her tattered sweater-vest for a cigarette, feeling into the recesses of the baggy wool pocket and finding nothing but lint. Furious now, she gazed up the stairway and shouted, "CLARA?"

Silence.

"CLARA! Goddammit…CLARA!"

Chapter 33

When Karen awoke it was late and Benjamin had long since turned his attention elsewhere: a show called "1,000 Ways to Die" played on Spike TV and Benjamin was fascinated with the various and sundry ways people died - truly, he wondered if some of this had not been invented, not quite able to accept all of this at face value, thinking, at the very least, some of these deaths had been severely embellished. Many of these deaths Benjamin laughed at, very hard and for a long time, what shit-for-brains some of these people were, what imbeciles! Most deserved to die for their stupidity. There were a handful he thought should be selected to receive a Darwin Award. Some of these had to be fiction, or they would've been chosen for the dubious honor, although he was fairly certain a good deal of the Darwin recipients were fabrications – a marketing ploy to sell books and videos.

Karen glanced at him and then looked away quickly, as though she didn't want him to see her, wanted to hide her face from him, from his judgment, his authority. Over an hour ago Benjamin's mother had come home. As usual she had not said a word to him. She had noted his presence and dismissed him, moving into the kitchen to grab a half-eaten Snickers bar from the refrigerator. She ate that in two hurried bites and then washed it down with a glassful of milk. The entire trailer was dark, although moonlight trickling through the window and the small television set provided the meager illumination Benjamin's mother needed as she scratched off three, apparently losing, lottery tickets. Each loss was punctuated with an expletive muttered under her breath.

After two more lottery tickets were fished out of her purse, scratched and trashed, she moved past Benjamin, purposely ignoring him to walk down the tiny hallway, opening her door and shutting it gently. A cold-hearted bitch, Benjamin thought, a malevolent manipulative irrational bitch who drove my dad away. His dad who he had never met, his dad who very easily could be dead now for all Benjamin knew. He had been dead for years, Benjamin felt, his father had never truly lived, had been dead from day one, dead from the word *go*.

Chapter 34

After the ceremony Clara had her chance to congratulate Jeremy. Still standing on the football field, mom on one side, dad standing further from him on the other, a myriad of friends surrounding him, Jeremy grinned and listened to their words patiently, graciously. Clara did not mind how invisible she felt, did not particularly mind how no one standing near Jeremy saw or even acknowledged her. She hadn't transformed her appearance, as she had been doing lately. She wore no makeup, and her hair was not styled or sprayed or smoothed with argan oil, and her outfit was very conservative. She simply hadn't the time since she had remembered the ceremony at the last minute.

Wait for him, yes, that's what she would do now. Since others had approached him first, many of them reaching him just a little before her. She would wait until it was her turn to talk to him, to be near him, to hug him, if Stephanie was not close. Not just hug him either, this time when she put her arms around him she wouldn't let go, knowing this action would convey how much she loved and needed him.

Where was Stephanie anyway? For a second, noting Stephanie's absence, Clara thought she might be bold enough, might just have the audacity to carry out her plan, to tell Jeremy how she truly felt for him, to begin making out with him too. Her plan seemed extreme in this public arena. She acknowledged it was only a fantasy, one she could never bring to life. Clara's thoughts stopped suddenly. She had finally reached him. Jeremy looked at her warmly, nodding hello and quietly smiling. "Hey," he said. Clara stood before him now, reticent and completely silent. She felt like she had lots and lots to say, yet in this moment she was unable to find the words.

Chapter 35

The large dilapidated grandfather clock in the living room chimed off-key into the darkness. It was 10:15 and Meem could feel her rage coursing through her veins. She did not consider that Clara was nearly of legal age and consequently entitled to exercise a degree of freedom, deserved to make at least a few of her own decisions, deserved to have a life apart from Meem, despite living under her roof. Goddammit, though, that little brat! Her sheer nerve! *Going out God knows where and not letting me know!*

Meem had a cigarette in her mouth and was smoking furiously, inhaling absently, exhaling aggressively although allowing an inordinate amount of time to pass before each exhale, holding the smoke in and letting it escape through her nostrils. She knitted in similar fashion, with extraordinary anger and determination, another quilt nearly finished. How could she best get the message across to Clara that *she* was in charge, *she* was the boss, and Clara merely a subordinate? How to put the fear of God inside her again? Various ways surfaced immediately, each one she gave careful quick consideration. A few were too easy, juvenile actually, and consequently Meem thought Clara would have little difficulty ignoring. After almost fifteen minutes passed, an idea finally came to her that she thought would work.

Even as she smiled, her fingers worked angrily, knitting as though her life depended upon the completion of this quilt. In her spastic fury, her glasses slid further down her nose, barely staying on her face, "Bitch," she said, thinking she might buy one of those cheap straps to hook around her neck, at Walgreens, she recalled she had seen a whole rack of them. "Little bitch." Still, she did not adjust her glasses, forgot her glasses quickly, rocking in her rocker, detached from the quilt even as she worked on it passionately, only peripherally engaged with the design, the pattern, as she thought of Clara now, only Clara. That dummy would pay, by God would she pay! Meem was sure of that!

Chapter 36

The party had started without Clara, which was fine, since she wanted to arrive unnoticed. Many of the popular kids would be here, she knew, and she always felt uncomfortable among them. Where was Jeremy? Immediately after she ceased thinking about him she saw Stephanie. It was impossible to ignore her so she simply tried to push her out of her mind. Strangely, Clara couldn't deny, even with feeling bitterness bordering on revulsion toward Stephanie, she was drawn to her, her effortless beauty, her easy *as-if* confidence. Did Clara want what she had? To a degree, certainly, yes, how could she claim otherwise? If there was no point in lying to others, what the heck was the point in lying to oneself? Of course she wanted what Stephanie had, her boyfriend and her looks, although her boyfriend far more than her looks.

Still not seeing Jeremy, Clara thought of that boy who had brought her to the party. Already he had disappeared. Not knowing him, really, only vaguely aware of seeing him at school in the hallway in between periods. Boldly after the graduation ceremony she had come right out and asked, knowing he was a junior, a rather popular one she assessed him, more importantly knowing he was a good athlete, lacrosse, she knew, baseball, maybe, was he going to the party, yes the one in the woods? He was, oh, well, she had been invited too! If it wasn't too much trouble could she get a ride?

The ride to the party was silent and serene. Feeling like making conversation, Clara thought there were questions she might ask, several things she might say, none of which seemed important in this moment, though. The conversation she was about to start had no purpose, she realized, other than filling the silence.

The ride, no more than five miles, was not serene at first. Two minutes had passed before she felt all right with the silence. She knew this because she had glanced at the clock when she had climbed into the driver's side seat, which is to say as soon as she started feeling uncomfortable. The boy hadn't been driving particularly well, though she hadn't noticed until after she started feeling pretty much at ease. Possibly, he was a good driver, Clara couldn't tell because he was distracted with his cell phone, at first texting and then talking to some girl (she could tell the person on the other end was a girl from how he ended the call with the word 'babe'). He had veered slightly off the road, tires moving over the yellow lines, when she thought of Jeremy, her eyes widening, wanting to say something, wanting to yell at him to pay attention when she thought of Jeremy. Thinking about Jeremy almost until they had gotten to the party. Now where was he?

Jeremy...? Nowhere.

Stephanie, everywhere it seemed, attracting the attention of everyone who mattered, which at this party, based on high school standards of popularity, was the majority of the crowd. The partygoers, well over a hundred of them, did not fill the endless dark in the middle of the woods. Most stood around in small circles or, in the case of the jocks, what appeared to be huddles.

Despite feeling nervous, mostly because there were an awful lot of people here, but also not knowing how she might get home, Clara considered herself lucky to be among these students here, so lucky to have been invited! Now if only she could find him.

Looking down at the ground, at first fearful to look around, she finally forced herself to see the trees that surrounded her. And then the students, too: moving past a group of smokers, she heard them chatting and chuckling/giggling (depending upon whether a boy or girl), most of them standing around, some of them sitting, all of them drinking, every student Clara saw with a plastic cup in hand. There were numerous beach chairs, most occupied, and a large tattered gray sofa Clara imagined one of those strong young jocks had hauled out here, also occupied by five students although room remained for at least one more. Then she spotted the kegs, an old wooden table lined with liquor bottles, as she began walking faster, still looking ahead, seeing everyone though no one in particular. She stepped over a pile of crushed beer cans, briefly wondering where they were from, since there were only kegs here, at least so far as she could see.

The ground, wet from the night before, absorbed her white sandals, and she sunk slightly, regretting not only the type of footwear she had chosen but also the color of the footwear she had chosen. A slight sense of panic rose high inside of her. She wondered what she would do if she couldn't find Jeremy? Quite sure she could find someone else to take her home, the issue was she did not want to go home, not to her home, she wanted to go to someone else's home, if only because she knew Meem would be waiting up for her, even if she didn't get in until one or two A.M. Walking past three smallish groups of people, Clara suddenly reached onto the table beside her where the kegs were, grabbing a plastic cup off one of the many unevenly high stacks that someone had haphazardly distributed, a few of them so high they appeared like they would soon topple.

A young man Clara did not recognize manned the keg table, simply standing there observing each student as they filled their cups with beer. As she filled hers she looked at him for a moment, noting a small shiny cross dangling at his throat. With his arms folded over his robust chest, he looked straight ahead nodding as Clara smiled.

After the second small sip, Clara felt she might throw up, not knowing what type of beer it was and of course never having tasted beer. Now taking another sip, a bigger one this time, which made no sense, since the taste obviously upset her, gulping the rest of the beer, draining the cup feeling her gag reflex, again, feeling like she might throw up. She closed her eyes, allowing a small amount of time to pass before opening them again. She focused on breathing in, out, paying complete attention to her breaths as she took them, making the breaths methodical and measured. This process relaxed her, calming her until the urge to vomit passed.

Not seeing anyone she wanted to talk to or, perhaps more accurately, not seeing anyone who wanted to talk to her, she got another cup of beer, this time thinking about what she was doing, recognizing the way the first cup had made her feel already. A certain warmth radiated throughout her body, feeling very much like she had taken a Valium, making her feel more confident, calm.

Fully aware that she wouldn't appreciate the taste, she chugged this second cup. Two guys watched her, several more looking at her as she did this. Clara then grabbed a third cup and did the exact same thing.

"Clara."

It was Jeremy – immediately she knew, turning around seeing him standing there looking at her and smiling. He stepped closer to Clara, putting his hand on her shoulder for a moment, steadying himself, she thought, although when he spoke his words were not slurred at all, his thoughts were not disoriented, his thoughts were very logical, in order. In this moment, she could not hear what he was saying, mostly because of the three cups of beer coursing through her veins. She wanted to grab another cup. Jeremy wasn't saying a word over the fact she was drinking. Never had he seen her drink before, and he didn't seem to be surprised.

"Yes," she said, looking into his eyes, then looking at his arms, his muscles, chest, feeling herself slip away, her thoughts gone, her identity fading, thinking only of him, feeling so connected to him, hearing his voice as he spoke even though she did not hear his words. Hearing his voice, feeling him as he stood in front of her even as her hands were at her sides, feeling him inside of her.

Clara tried to listen closer now, and managed to hear him say several things: how he had decided to go to college almost a week before the time he had originally told her, how he had been fighting with Stephanie lately, how he didn't know if he wanted to remain with Stephanie since they would be hundreds of miles apart (and, no, he said, his uncertainty, at least most of it, did not revolve around the fact that they had been fighting) and, finally, how he was very close to being drunk. These things he told her, Clara imagined, he would have said even if he was not nearly intoxicated. She had been around him before when he had been intoxicated, or very nearly so, and he was not the kind of person who disclosed anything that he would regret, or even question, when he was sober.

She looked at him. She stood there and looked at him. The cup of beer in his hand he had nearly drained, she wondered how many cups he had consumed and considered asking then realized what did it matter? She was not his mother. Besides, when he went to college he would be drinking a lot more. Still, did he have a designated driver? He should not drive himself. In the extremely buzzed state he was in, driving home would not be safe.

"Want some more?" he asked, seeing Clara's cup was empty. Clara had not realized she had slowly emptied the contents of the cup while he had been giving her the bullet points of his life. Nodding, not perhaps completely consenting to nodding, she walked with him over to the keg table. Very enthusiastically, he pointed to the many rows of cups, then to the kegs, as though Clara could not decipher their location on her own, as though she had not already gotten beer on her own.

For more than a moment Clara questioned whether or not she should have more beer. Jeremy answered her question by reaching for a cup, quickly filling and handing it to her. Clara nodded her thanks, holding it with both hands, and then looking up at him to try and see what she should do next. No direction was offered, not even a subtle one. Wanting to kiss him badly, she turned around instead, seeing Stephanie perched on a beach chair, legs crossed with her hands clasped resting strategically on her knee, sitting underneath an umbrella that served no purpose other than to make her look hip (unfortunately, Clara had to admit, the umbrella accomplished its purpose).

Gazing out at the party crowd, Stephanie chewed bubblegum and drank some beverage, presumably an alcoholic one, from a skinny pink thermos.

Clara was tipsy, wanting to go home and have a serene dreamless sleep. Instead, emboldened by the alcohol, she moved closer to Jeremy. "Want to come over to my house tonight?" she asked suddenly. "After the party I mean." It was too late, she understood that, having no idea what her intention was, only knowing she wanted to be close to him.

"I can't," Jeremy said. "Stephanie's staying over."

Then Clara's mouth was on his, and she was kissing him hard on the lips, about to slip her tongue inside his mouth when he pulled away. "*Clara!*" Not looking mad or sounding upset, she thought him simply surprised, too baffled to react beyond exclaiming her name. Walking away from him, she said nothing, understanding now: he did not want her, not like she wanted him. He would never want her, not like she wanted him. He had a girlfriend *who is much prettier and more popular than I'll ever be.*

Her back was turned on him as she moved toward the keg table thinking she might ask for another cup of beer. No, she said to herself, I don't need to *ask* anyone for a glass, I don't need permission to drink more, I can get more if I want to, if I want to I can have a fifth glass!

She passed on this impulse, wanting badly to go home so she could climb into her bed and be away from all these people.

In front of her now she saw Stephanie. How had she missed the kiss? For an instant Stephanie saw her, then looked away quickly, not acknowledging her. "Hi Stephanie," Clara said as she moved past her, not expecting a response, her expectation proving accurate. Stephanie said nothing or, if she had said something, Clara could not hear her, as she picked up her pace, weaving in and out of small groups of people, medium-sized groups of people, large groups of people, feeling a little unsteady on her feet. She reached out for the young man who stood closest to her, putting her hand on his wrist. He pulled his arm away, not unkindly as she persisted, her hand on his arm, this time he stared at her, rather blankly, staring at her. She didn't know him, obviously, he didn't know her. She wondered if he had whether or not it would've made a difference in his reaction. She watched the cup of beer he carried, focusing her gaze on that, thinking if she did this she would not fall, would not lose her balance, she would stay on her feet. Still holding onto him, she tightened her grasp around his arm, perhaps too tightly, and apparently that was enough. He yanked his arm away. Glancing at the two guys at his side and the two girls across from him, assessing their reaction and, seeing none, he relaxed.

Jeremy did not follow her. Holding onto his cup with one hand, lighting a cigarette with the other, he thought, for a moment, about following her when one of his teammates from baseball approached him, peppering him with questions, lots of questions. He watched her as she moved further and further away from him, Jeremy fully aware that questions were being asked, hearing the first two or three very clearly, answering them tersely. The effects of the five beers he had consumed over the last half hour were just now registering, and he felt slightly light-headed, dizzy, hearing more questions, all of them very simple, only requiring him to shake his head 'yes' or 'no'. And Clara was gone, out of Jeremy's sight.

Chapter 37

Meem heard her before she even walked in the front door. Smoking in her rocker, very nearly asleep with the lights off, Meem woke up feeling startled and very alert, holding her chest, her heart pounding. "Bitch! Stupid, stupid bitch."

The young man, another classmate of Clara's she did not know, pulled into the driveway rather rapidly, almost driving past it when Clara exclaimed, "Stop! Right here!" Slamming on his brakes, he yanked the wheel hard and far to the right. Clara had been worried about Meem and how she might react, how she might reprimand her for not only going out without permission but also for coming home late under the influence of alcohol. And it would be clear she was under the influence. Meem would chastise her, for sure; punish her, definitely, Clara wondered about this - what might the punishment be, enforced how? How could she possibly dodge the consequences of her behavior?

Shutting the door gently, Clara waved her thanks and said, "I'll see you," so softly she was sure the young man didn't hear her. She didn't wait for his reaction, only caught a glimpse of him as he grabbed onto the passenger's side seat head cushion, spinning around in his seat as he backed down the driveway. For a moment, she thought about this young man, wanted to know his name, his phone number, realizing she wouldn't ever see him again and feeling sad, extremely sad, recalling a certain strong sense of connection that had been established during the ride home that had lasted about 15 minutes. Very few words had been exchanged, fewer than with the first boy she rode with to the party, but the connection with him had been stronger than the first one. She could not explain that chemistry, how it had been established, how potent it was, how strongly she felt a connection to him.

The back door! Yes, the key Meem kept under the doormat, Clara thought she could simply sneak in the back door, as quietly as possible, then creep upstairs to her bedroom. Dealing with Meem in the morning was unavoidable, though at least by then she would avoid the punishment for drinking. Grabbing the key from under the mat, she seriously doubted her plan's success, if only because she was sure Meem would not be asleep. Meem always waited up for her, the only difference now was that Clara had never been out this late.

She shut the back door soundlessly, tip-toeing into the kitchen, feeling anxious, if only because of the severity of the silence, the darkness. Then - *click!* The living room light, dim as it was, seemed a searchlight to her as it turned on. Clara stood absolutely still in the kitchen, knowing she'd been caught.

"Come in here." Meem's voice was hoarse and deep, barely audible. Clara held onto the kitchen counter, not moving. A long moment passed, then *click!* - Meem had turned the lamp up to a greater brightness, "Come!" Realizing her only option was to do as Meem said, Clara moved into the living room. With that realization came clarity. She was ready to face Meem, ready to hear what she had to say, ready to dismiss her if she was too condescending and even, possibly, if she wasn't.

Click! This third click the final one, so bright now, Meem's bloated face haloed in light, looming out of the darkness. Clara took several steps toward her, still tip-toeing absentmindedly. Crushing her cigarette into a ceramic ashtray, Meem squinted, surveying Clara thoroughly, seeing her from head to toe, then lighting another cigarette as she leaned back and started to rock, slowly. Clara looked down at the dark carpet, a sleepy frown on her face, one that Meem could not see: Clara stood too far away. Meem raised a hand and moved her index finger, exaggerating the back-and-forth motion of her index finger, reeling Clara in toward her, for a long time, since Clara did not budge, simply stood there watching Meem as she continued signaling for her to move closer.

Finally, Clara did, only two small steps so Meem could see her more clearly. "What do you have to say for yourself?"

"I -"

"You?"

Clara didn't know what to say. Moreover, she knew she should not speak, fully aware she had been slurring her words when she had been talking to Jeremy. "I don't..." Silent then, she stared at Meem for a second, then looked away at the bookshelf beside the rocker, focusing on that, trying to read a few of the titles, if only to distract herself.

Meem could have skipped to the point. Instead - "You don't?" Playing with her now, finding it easy to be cruel to Clara, "Don't what?"

That was it. Fuck this, Clara thought, turning her back on Meem and moving toward the stairway, fuck her!

On the fourth step when Meem screamed after her - "Where the *hell* do *you* think you're going?! To HELL, that's where, straight to HELL!"

Standing very still now, Clara felt the tears well in her eyes, having no control over them, most of the time having little control over the sadness inside of her. When confronted so severely by Meem, though, the tears flowed, impossible to hold back. Clara rushed up the stairs, taking two steps at a time, anxious to get to her bedroom, lock the door, and hide underneath the covers with the lights off and stars shining.

Meem was right behind her now, somehow, reaching out just as Clara reached the top of the stairway. She grabbed Clara's hair, holding her ponytail tightly in her hand, yanking back on it as Clara fell in the hallway in front of her bedroom door, falling fast because she was drunk.

Sobbing now, releasing the tears inside of her she had held back for so long, trying to be strong, wanting to be strong, needing to be strong for a reason she could not identify.

As Meem stood over her, looking down at her, squinting at her, her glasses gone, possibly they had fallen off her face as she had pounded up the stairs, glaring at Clara now as Clara continued to sob, seeing double, for a moment, seeing Meem with two heads, Meem blurry, fuzzy, for a moment, then returning to normal.

"Don't *ever* do that again! Understand? *Stu*pid brat baby!"

All of Clara's tears had been released and now she wheezed briefly, gasping for breath.

"GET *UP!*" Meem reached down and swung her hand at Clara's face, seizing her hair in an attempt to raise Clara onto her feet. Clara suddenly reared back and slapped Meem's leg.

Clara crawled up onto her knees, Meem still gripping her ponytail, Clara hitting Meem on her upper thigh, then her hip as Meem took a step back, gritting her teeth, eyes widening in surprise at Clara's aggression. In a rage, she lunged after Clara, fists clenched and swinging.

Clara dodged her grandmother, on her feet now - "BITCH!" Clara screamed, "You miserable *old* BITCH!" Meem spit at Clara, aiming for her face, her aim failed, spittle dribbling down her chin onto her neck, a surprising lot of it too. Clara took a step toward Meem, face to face with her, and looked her right in the eyes, waiting for her to say something. "You'll turn out just like your come-dump mother," Meem said, her voice void of emotion, her face lacking any discernible expression. Clara swung at her suddenly, slapping her across the face, putting her hand over her mouth so shocked she had reacted this way, slapping her by reflex. Clara was unable to recall ever feeling anger, an emotion entirely new to her. Taking several steps backward, she tasted the satisfaction of her own rage fulfilled. That slap had crossed a line for both of them. As Clara moved toward her bedroom, she kept her eyes on Meem, watching her as she stumbled backward holding her chest pointing a finger at Clara, "*YOU...*"

Clara reached for the doorknob and discovered it was locked. Clara looked at Meem, unafraid, seeing the old woman stare back at her blankly. "Why the *fuck* is this locked?" Clara wiggled the knob again, pushing with all her strength trying to open the door. "OPEN this door *now!*" Tilting her head back, Meem started laughing. Clara moved past her down the hallway, and Meem followed her slowly. There were a cache of bobby pins in the bathroom, one of these would open the door, Clara knew. Knowing Meem had locked her door to aggravate her (she had done this several times before), Clara thought she would return the gesture the best way she knew how: overcoming the obstacle, and shoving the fact that she had done so right in Meem's face.

"What are *you* doing! Where *were* you! Who do *you* think you *are!*"

Clara brushed against Meem's body, Meem making no effort to block Clara's path, not that any such effort would have mattered. Clara was obviously stronger and more agile. Pushing a bobby pin into the keyhole, Clara smiled, knowing she had thwarted Meem's plan.

Meem stood there. For a moment, she thought she might retrieve a bobby pin herself to open the door which Clara had just shut and locked. Thought she might yell at Clara some more, let her really have it this time, break her down and destroy her spirit for good. Instead, she stood there staring at the white door, staring at the slit underneath the door where she occasionally slipped notes telling Clara to bring her breakfast in bed because she was not feeling well, telling Clara to wash the dishes when she awoke, to mow the grass, do the laundry, clean the bathrooms (*yes, dear, that includes scrubbing the toilet and the bathtub as well!*) Standing there furious now seeing the light under the door, wondering just what in the hell Clara had been up to, where she had been, why she had defied her one and only grandmother! Meem wanted to rip her hair out, that would teach her a lesson! Or better yet: sneak into her bedroom one night and shave her head. Clara's reaction! Meem could just see it, how horrified she would be, waking up in the morning and seeing herself in the mirror, very shocked although the blow would likely be lessened by the fact that the school year was over and Clara wouldn't have to face her peers.

The lights were extinguished. Meem heard a drawer being opened and shut, another drawer - opened, shut. She considered opening the door and going after Clara, chastising her until she broke down and became obedient and submissive once again. Well, she could tell her she was going to hell, a nasty manipulative prediction that had worked many times before, what else might she do? She had already taken away her car, thinking that would deprive her of this newfound freedom she was seeking for whatever reason. Taking her car wasn't working, not so much anyway. Seemed to be having the opposite effect, Meem noticed Clara had been more adventurous lately, going out without asking, responding to any restriction with rebellion. Meem could understand that. Meem had been the same way, how many years ago? Ages! What she couldn't understand is where Clara had worked up the nerve to be so defiant lately. Maybe those two new so-called friends of hers, Benjamin and what was that girl's name? Casey? Were they influencing her, were they responsible for her newfound confidence? Meem could not stand this, how self-assured she seemed! How she detested Clara! Everything about her really, at least now, now that she *acted* confident, *acted* like she didn't need or even want Meem's approval, Meem's guidance, direction. Whatever! Meem planned to let her have it one day, one day real soon she would make it abundantly clear who was in charge! Soon, she didn't know what she might do but, something! She would do *something*. Figure out some way to make Clara crumble.

Chapter 38

Clara could not sleep that night, which was no big surprise. Meem couldn't either - she sat in bed resting her back against three pillows that were propped up against the headboard. She glanced at a bible that sat on the bedside table. It was dusty. Rosary beads reflected in the mirror above the bureau. They were dusty. Stray bills were scattered across the bureau as if Meem had recently played a game of poker. Her organizing style was haphazard, rather hit or miss. One room organized one week, the same room a big mess the next. All of the rooms were never cleaned simultaneously, always at least two of the rooms throughout the house were a disaster.

Where were those pills when Clara needed them? No refills remained and of course she could not tell Meem, that would require her opening up to her and she would demand to know everything that had been going on in her private emotional life, including why the pills were gone so soon. It was true Meem's memory was fading but she always seemed to remember those things she could use to hurt Clara.

That morning, Clara considered her inevitable punishment and how she would face Meem now that her liquid daring had dissolved. Certainly, she would be punished, no doubt Meem had decided upon one already. (Truth: she was still deliberating an appropriate sentence). As Clara considered potential punishments, she realized there weren't many possibilities. What consequence could Meem create that she hadn't faced already? Nothing remained for Meem to take away from her. In a sudden burst of optimism Clara thought: *I have nothing to lose, really. What other direction's left for me to go but up?*

Chapter 39

Mrs. Henderson had not seen her reluctant protégé at the graduation, but when she awoke, Clara was the first person on her mind. Maybe she hadn't been on time for the ceremony, although Mrs. Henderson had not surveyed the crowd very thoroughly, nor stayed after the formalities. Now, waking up with her husband snoring at her side, she still found herself worrying about Clara. Perhaps she should check on her or something, if only because she was aware of Clara's recent interaction with those two hopeless ne'er-do-wells. Heaving a breath of resignation, Mrs. Henderson had to concede: *Clara is not my daughter. Although I very much want a daughter, or a son, I do not have either one, and likely never will.*

As she stood in front of the mirror that morning scrutinizing her face and neck (seeing very minor signs of fine lines and wrinkles, the only mistakes in her face, dismissing her extremely smooth complexion, her flawless skin tone) the thought of Clara would not leave her alone. Mrs. Henderson wanted to help her, wanted to demand that Clara allow her to help. How might she convince Clara to accept her more mature, experienced guidance?

Looking in the mirror, not focusing on her face as she stared blankly for long, silent minutes, she continued to turn the question over in her mind. Movement now, Frank, turning onto his side, the snoring ceased as Mrs. Henderson picked up a comb, started to brush her hair, for a moment wondering why? This morning she planned to wear makeup - just some foundation and a little eyeliner - although she had no idea why. She would be home alone all day after Frank left for work, and no one would see her save for a short trip to the grocery store. Just the same, she would wash her face in the shower with an expensive facial exfoliant and apply anti-wrinkle day cream and anti-wrinkle eye serum. Who did she want to look perfect for? Truly, Mrs. Henderson's aim was to look perfect, which she knew was impossible unless she had plastic surgery (she thought her nose was too big and already she had wrinkles on her face that she knew a facelift or Botox would correct).

Frank rolled over again, stomach pressing against the bed, apparently this position uncomfortable for he immediately turned on his other side, then, finally - "Hey you..."

Forcing a small smile, Mrs. Henderson saw him looking at her, looking at her reflection, looking at his own reflection, briefly. Mrs. Henderson turned around, took a step toward the bed.

Patting a spot beside him on the bed, Frank said, "Here, honey."

The very last thing she wanted to do was join Frank on the bed. She wasn't in the mood, hadn't been in several days, and she didn't attempt to analyze why. This was simply the way her libido worked. "I have to...run errands."

"After." Frank motioned toward the bed again, more forcefully this time, reaching a hand out toward his wife who had taken another reluctant step toward him, which she didn't understand. If anything, given her desire, or lack thereof, she should've taken a step backward. Suddenly, though, she felt aroused, standing there wearing only her panties, maybe it was Frank's smell, a smell that seemed strongest in the morning when he was slightly sweaty, his natural man-odor.

Going against her better judgment, knowing what she didn't want to do, she sat on Frank's lap, her back toward him as he held her, cupping her breasts, kissing her neck as she tilted her head back and stared at the ceiling. He tweaked her nipples, very softly at first, then much harder, firmer, pulling her closer toward him, pushing her up onto her feet and motioning toward her panties. Too impatient to wait for her to remove them, he pulled them to the floor. "What do you want to do to me?" she whispered, turning her head around just far enough so she could face him. His penis pressed against her ass, its heat throbbing onto her lower back in time with his quickening pulse. Did he want to have anal sex with her? Typically, only on special occasions did she allow him to enter her this way, the only exception being if she felt exceptionally horny, as she did now, not knowing exactly why. Of course, she didn't know for sure that's what he wanted, not until he whispered in her ear. Realizing she was right, she did not smile. Even feeling aroused, she did not smile. Closing her eyes she could only sigh, trying not to think of how much this would hurt. She pictured herself gripping the headboard, facing the headboard, passively noting its intricate design as Frank grabbed at her hips pulling her fiercely into him, slapping her ass as she moaned and cried out his name in both pleasure and pain.

Chapter 40

Stephanie had spent the night, claiming she was too tired to drive home after they had sex. They hadn't gotten home from the party until around 3:30, and Jeremy had been surprised how horny she'd been, climbing on top of him as soon as they arrived home. Not that Stephanie never made the first move, she did, just never when drunk, usually never when she was tired either. And when they had gotten home she had clearly been both, yawning and stretching her arms over her head before falling back onto the bed.

There was no hangover in the morning like he had anticipated. Hangovers for him were very hit or miss so he could seldom predict when he would experience one. Often it seemed they had little to do with how much alcohol he consumed: five or six beers could produce one, then other times after two six-packs he'd be fine. Last night he had observed Stephanie refill her thermos several times with beer so he thought it likely she had a hangover. Looking at her large breasts, he whispered in her ear. She appeared to move, for a moment, moaning, then opening her eyes.

"Hey babe."

Turning over on her side, she smiled at him, her eyes still filled with sleep. He moved on top of her, and she could feel that he was already hard, although she supposed he had possibly been so when he had awoken - 'morning wood' the guys called this dubious phenomenon, yes, she was aware.

"Not now," Stephanie said, her whole body stiff, like Jeremy, who pressed his own stiffness against her belly as he moved himself further on top of her, brushing a piece of hair out of her face. She placed a hand on his chest, a barrier he wondered why she felt the need to erect.

"What is it?" He kissed her breast, her other breast, her upper chest, her neck.

"Stop." Both hands up against his chest now, pushing him away with as much strength as she could muster being pinned against the bed.

Again, he asked what was wrong. Nothing, she wanted to say, nothing, however she knew that would be untrue. Everything, she felt, everything was wrong. She just couldn't put her finger on any one thing. But yes, she could: college. Very soon they would both be headed to college, in different states no less, hundreds of miles away from each other.

"Talk to me," he demanded, gently.

The last thing she wanted to do was open up to him. Doing so would only make her more hopelessly attached, and what would be the point in such an attachment? Over the last month or so, she had stopped divulging her feelings, her emotions, slowly detaching from him. Breaking up was inevitable, did he believe that too?

"I have to go," she said, having extricated herself from him, stepping out of bed and searching for her clothes. As much as he wanted to try and stop her, tell her to stay, continue asking what was wrong, he said nothing. Once she had changed she kissed him quickly - what seemed to Jeremy a perfunctory gesture, like shaking hands with a business partner - then walked out the door.

Chapter 91

Benjamin detested her, could not stand her! The little things, mostly, are what got to him, like the way she helped herself to the food inside his refrigerator, the way she always left the television on when she couldn't sleep and ended up on the couch in the living room claiming the white noise put her to sleep. The way she looked at him first thing in the morning, staring at him, touching him briefly kissing him on the lips when he barely had his eyes open. The way she left all her clothing and toiletries scattered around his bedroom and bathroom and sometimes even his living room, as though she had moved in. Also how she never put the fan on after she showered, leaving the floor slippery wet and the mirror above the sink steamed. There were other things that aggravated him too, but these were the ones that immediately came to mind.

Right now she was reading a book in his bedroom. On the couch he sat pensively moving a tiny baggie of methamphetamine around in his hand, imagining when he might get high, knowing he would get high today, although afraid to face facts: he was unemployed, had no money, virtually, the only way to earn money being to sell drugs. He had not sold drugs in over a month, having sold a high quantity to two slightly older men looking to become dealers, feeling very complacent after these two sales, his pockets fat with cash that had now disappeared. Was he afraid of getting caught? Never would he admit this to anyone - it was true, though, he was afraid of being arrested, well, not being arrested, it was jail he feared. His biological father was still in prison, or so his mother said! Who knows if this was true? Benjamin knew it was possible his father was dead and realized it was very possible his mother didn't know what had happened to him. After all, she admitted years had gone by since she had last spoken to him, which might also be untrue, although Benjamin didn't see why she would lie about that.

Not at all in the mood for sex, at least not with Karen, although he supposed he could simply picture Clara the whole time, he walked into his bedroom and said, "Your visit's over."

Glancing up from her book, Karen smiled, not even looking confused. Clearly, she thought, I misunderstood him. "Hey," softly she said.

"Did you hear me?"

"My visit's over," she said, still smiling. "What do you mean?"

"Exactly what I said."

"I—"

"I want you to leave."

"Benjamin," Karen said, her confident smile gone now, kneeling on the bed now leaning up toward him and arching her back slightly. "There's this new sci-fi movie playing at the -"

"Didn't you hear me?"

Karen looked at him, sadly. "What's the matter?" She manufactured a smile, thinking this might make him change his mind. "*Benny...*" she whispered his nickname that she seldom used, since he was mercurial regarding his thoughts on the attenuated version of his name, claiming he loved it one week and detested it the next.

"*Don't* call me that. *Don't* fuckin' call me that ever again, you understand?"

Karen said nothing, only looked at him, blankly. Looking away now, down at the floor, her clothes scattered about, her having stayed here for over a week now.

Knowing it was time for her to go, yet not knowing how to react, not exactly, not knowing what to say, if anything. Should she try to ask why, request a reason regarding his wanting her to go?

That might make it worse, she imagined he would get annoyed, as he typically did when she asked him any question he deemed superfluous. So, she would say nothing, absolutely nothing. She would go, she would gather her belongings, leaving the toiletries, at least some of them, being confident that their relationship wasn't over. Soon he would call her, ask to see her again, ask her to come over, tell her he wanted her again, wanted to hold her, love her, make love to her (yes, he would assure her he wanted to make love, not fuck, no, he would likely have to say he wanted to make love a third time).

She hadn't brought a bag along. Every day, she had taken an outfit out of the car, or two outfits, sometimes. Her hands were overflowing with clothes and Benjamin did not offer to help, walking out of his room and moving into the living room, the baggie of white powder still in his hand. Karen followed him, not daring to look at him, not wanting to see the hate in his eyes.

Two tee-shirts and one pair of jeans fell out of her hand and onto the floor. "Don't call me tonight either," Benjamin said.

"What?" she asked, even though she heard him. He knew her well enough to know her asking him to repeat himself was a reflex and not a real question.

"Also, don't leave me messages on Facebook. Don't like any of my statuses or comment on any of my statuses, if you do, I'll block you. You understand?"

Karen glanced down at the floor, seeing her two shirts, her jeans, not even thinking that she might pick them up, not even caring, or not realizing, perhaps, she had just purchased one of those shirts last week at Hot Topic, thinking too much of Benjamin and what was going on now. Why was this happening? What had she done wrong and how might she fix this? Would Benjamin want to see her again? Surely, he would want to see her again, but when? When would he call her since he said she shouldn't call him? Perhaps, she thought she should go ahead and call him anyway. She wondered how much time would go by until she talked to him again, saw him again.

Opening the door, Karen still thought she should say something, she didn't know what. As though unsure whether he had inflicted enough pain, Benjamin added: "Don't text me either, K. You do you'll see what happens."

The door slammed shut behind her, she had let go of it so suddenly, feeling a certain strong sense of fear, anxiety, feeling very suddenly like she had better hurry up and get out of here.

Quickening her pace, moving toward her car, she dropped another shirt, not bothering to pick this one up either.

Chapter 42

When Meem shouted, "PHONE!" up the stairs, Clara awoke immediately, very startled, having had an unpleasant dream she could not now recall. She was sweating, her tank top and shorts both very wet. The rising nauseating sense of dread she felt inside of her was no surprise. Of course she still felt very curious about what punishment she would receive, how might Meem enforce it? Clara was pretty sure Meem would never kick her out, not while she was still in high school, once she graduated though...?

"PHONE CLARA!"

Pushing the covers off her, Clara climbed out of bed and rushed toward the stairway where Meem stood, gripping the phone, her hand slightly shaking as she extended the phone further toward Clara.

"Who is it?"

"Who do you think? Just think about this, Clara. Who is the only person that ever calls you?"

Clara considered, well, that was true, she had to concede, her mother was the only person who ever really called, albeit on an inconsistent basis. Clara used to call her, until one day her mom informed her very matter-of-factly that she shouldn't call her anymore. *She* would call Clara when she wanted to talk, the phone calls must be on *her* terms, that much she made clear. "But I..."

Clara had started to argue when her mom quickly cut her off. "You heard me! Don't make me repeat myself because I'm not going to." Clara sighed wanting to cry, why didn't her own mother - a mother who is *supposed* to be caring and loving and compassionate - not want to talk to her? Clara didn't understand this, and knew better than to request a reason. "Well, may I e-mail you at least?" she had asked.

"I don't have an e-mail, Clara, you know that!" This was a lie. "If I had one I would've given it to you." Clara did not question this since she desperately wanted to believe her mother was good and kind and true.

When she accepted the phone from Meem Clara looked at the wall, purposefully ignoring her grandmother, thinking about what she might say to her mother. "Hello?" This was a good start, Clara thought, a very basic greeting, one that did not acknowledge she was familiar with the person on the other line, for a moment thinking of Jeremy, this being the way he always answered the phone.

"What are you doing?"

"I, I just got up, you woke me up."

"Oh, so it's my fault you don't sleep well, is that it? Always, Clara, you have to blame someone else, you're an adult now, legally almost an adult, so it's time you accept responsibility for yourself! Time you stop blaming others! Soon you'll have to -"

"*Mom -*"

"No, Clara, you need to listen. You've never listened to anyone your whole life, and that's part of your problem. She's been telling me you have been spending time outside of school with these two new people, what are their names? Well, she just tells me they are bad news, into drugs and stuff, you know Meem can't handle that, you get involved in that shit, you know what will happen, you know -"

"I know."

"So, she also told me you've been not listening lately - defiant, temperamental. Well, you always were that way, ever since you were born, that's why I couldn't handle you, you always had such a mind of your own, always wanted to do things *your* way, never listening to anyone else! You know if you would've been more obedient and respectful, I might not have given you up to that old woman, yes I know she's my mother, did you know she used to slap my face when I was little, Clara, did you know she -"

"Mom, stop. You gave me up because you had to. Children and Youth wouldn't allow you to keep me any longer, the environment wasn't suitable for -"

"I guess you know Meem suggested I call you?"

"No, I..." Although Clara had suspected, as Meem had directed her mother to call her many times before over the last decade or so just to set her straight, tell her to behave and listen to Meem.

"Listen darling…" she stopped, taking a long drag off her perpetual cigarette. Clara could hear her inhale and exhale and, as she did, thought how much she disliked being called 'darling'. This pet-name she considered a slight, a way for her mom to talk down to her, belittle her and make it easier to hang up.

"I really have to go now…"

"Where are you going?"

Pause.

"M-mom?"

Very stern: "That's none of your concern."

Click!

"Mom?" she asked, despite being positive the line was dead. This was far from the first time her mom had simply hung up on her. She clearly didn't care, Clara thought, else she wouldn't say she had to go. She would *want* to continue talking to me, else she would ask how I was feeling or if there was anything more I wanted to talk about? *If* she cared for me, *if* she loved me, she would ask me at least one or two personal questions when she called, she would want to talk more than two minutes and want to see me too! *If* she cared for me, *if* she loved me, she wouldn't have allowed me to be taken away in the first place!

Clara set the phone onto the railing. Then, thinking this wasn't a good place, afraid the phone might fall, she moved it toward Meem, whose hands were both closed, in no position to accept the phone, purposefully, Clara thought, seeing Meem close her hands even further now, her hands both almost fists now. Bending down, Clara set the phone onto the second step of the stairway. Looking at Meem was unnecessary, she could feel her eyes burning into her, could feel her glaring.

As Clara moved out into the kitchen - "Tell me what she said," Meem demanded. Possibly, if she would have asked, Clara might have offered an answer. Instead, she said nothing, opening the pantry and pulling out a box of Triscuits.

Meem's steps were heavy and hard against the hardwood floor, Clara heard her approaching, feeling fearful, somewhat, nothing like she would have felt months ago had she committed these same transgressions - going out without permission, attending what Meem called 'an alcohol party', staying out so late past her 10 P.M. curfew, drinking alcohol in excess, which was the worst offense for sure, at least in Meem's eyes. Meem's reaction was one more of fury than disappointment, since Clara knew Meem thought drinking alcohol in any amount, especially drinking while underage was a sin.

"Did you hear me?" Meem asked, a question this time somehow sounding more demanding than the demand.

Clara nonchalantly shook her head. It was the boldest thing she could do in the moment. Feeling Meem approach her from behind, she shook her head a second time, feeling a bit tense now she had to admit. There was no telling what the old woman would do, knowing full well what she was capable of - verbal abuse, physical abuse. Although last night was the first time she had slapped Clara in a good long while. She had done it a number of times before, and who knows how many times she did it when Clara was a child, times she couldn't now remember. She stood there, her back turned toward Meem, chewing on a Triscuit, then putting another one into her mouth, pretending she couldn't feel Meem's awful presence behind her. If any closer Clara imagined she would feel her breath on her neck. With a strength Clara didn't know she had inside her, she spun around, faced Meem, and looked her directly in the eye, "Didn't you see me shake my head?

That means no, all right, N-O!"

Meem's hand was already in the air, somehow, high above Clara's head, then coming down hard across Clara's face. There was no time, nor room to duck, but the blow drove the girl back hard against the countertop. She reflexively tried to move back but only forced the counter further into her back. Anxiety overwhelmed her as this irrational fear she had of Meem paralyzed her, not allowing her to realize how easily she could escape, not realizing how simple it would be to simply push the old woman out of the way or punch her in the gut. *No,* Clara thought, *no I would never do that, not ever, not to Meem!* But the thought continued to worm its way into her mind. Clara imagined Meem's reaction if she hit her, imagined watching Meem fall over from the force of the punch. *That* might kill the old bitch. Come to think of it, a severe slap might do the trick. Clara imagined seeing herself slapping Meem across the face, then Meem losing her balance and falling onto the linoleum floor, maybe smacking her head against the refrigerator or even the foot pedal on the steel garbage can. Meem would pass out. Maybe Meem would die right there on the floor as Clara looked on, wondering how she might explain this to the police. She imagined it would be an accident, so if that happened she could be honest, if that happened she could tell the police exactly what had transpired, there would be no reason to make up a story since - *Ohh!* she stopped thinking about *that*, didn't want to think about *that!* Why was she still thinking about this?

Meem stood still. Clara stood still. They faced each other, both looking very solemn as moments passed feeling like hours to Clara. "What are you gonna do," Clara heard herself ask very suddenly, "Huh? WHAT?!" She moved her body fiercely forward, challenging Meem. She moved her body rapidly to startle Meem and found this worked very well, as the old woman took two quick steps backward. Seeing the rage on Clara's face made her entire body tense.

For the first time in Clara's short life, Meem felt a fear she had never experienced toward the girl. She truly didn't know what to do, how to react to Clara standing up for herself. She found herself speechless, her mouth hanging open, unable to move. Clara finally stepped past Meem, who grabbed her arm, trembling to hold on to it, then raised her hand to strike again. "So! GO ahead! HIT ME!" Clara was stunned how furious she sounded, not realizing how much anger was inside of her waiting for a reason to be released. Meem let go of her, took a step back, her hand clutched to her chest, looking at Clara now as though she should take pity upon her. "Didn't think so!" Clara shouted right in her face, then stormed out of the kitchen, through the living room and out the front door having no idea where she was going. She had no clue what she was going to do. She only knew for sure she did not want to return here. Never did she want to come back to the hell that was her life living with Meem.

She stopped on the front stoop, gazing out onto the road to watch a car drive by so slowly she thought it might idle. The car kept going and the driver waved. Clara wondered if the driver knew her or was only extending the wave to be friendly. Clara did not expect Meem to come out after her, and as she started walking alongside the road, her expectation proved accurate. The front door did not even open. Did Meem care about her at all? Yes, Clara thought, but mostly because she wanted Clara to be available to serve her in her final years. Meem did not care about Clara's future, she cared only about her own future, cared how she might deceive Clara into giving up her dreams of marrying and having children, how she might convince her those dreams were foolish, utterly idiotic!

Clara did not look back, not even a glance over her shoulder. Too focused on the road ahead of her, she walked slightly to the right of the yellow line, trying to keep her feet moving as she felt a little nauseated from the anxiety the confrontation had produced within her. She had to figure out where she was going, how she would get there. Hitchhiking was always an option, although she imagined wherever she wanted to go wouldn't be too far away, the place she most wanted to go probably right here in this town, well, the person - that's when she thought of him. Benjamin.

Chapter 43

Since Karen had left, Benjamin had blown four long thin lines of methamphetamine. Glancing in the baggie he saw that three perhaps four lines remained. Soon, he would blow those. He felt very horny, immediately Clara surfaced in his mind, a part of him couldn't help wondering what she was up to, what she was wearing. He imagined the panties she wore were white, imagined she didn't own panties that were any color besides white. It was true he had noticed subtle changes in her appearance lately, wearing makeup and a sexy outfit one day, wearing no makeup and a plain simple outfit the next. How could one person possibly possess so much innocence? Could her innocence really be considered real, valid? More importantly, how might he penetrate this innocence? He found himself aroused, hardly thought about her and hard already, wanting to fuck her very badly. The lines he had just snorted added to his libido. Speed always made him horny, always made him feel like he could fuck like a champ for hours without needing so much as a glass of water. Now, he wished he had waited to tell Karen to leave, only wanting her here now so he could fuck her and pretend she was Clara, fucking her from behind having her sit on his lap her back toward him as he pounded away at her. How Clara would moan, how she would beg him to go easy on her, how she would enjoy him inside her despite feeling like she shouldn't. Benjamin imagined the religion that had been ingrained in Clara's brain would result in an inability to enjoy sex. Oh, how he would rip her apart, break her in, destroy all of her ideas about what sex should mean. Benjamin couldn't control himself any longer: he slipped off his pants and ripped off his underwear. He had only been jerking his cock two minutes before he came.

Chapter 44

Karen cried when she got home. The entire ride home she felt the tears building up inside her, but she told herself not to cry, to be strong. She would see Benjamin again. A decent amount of time would have to pass, she knew, as he had done this several times before, out of the blue just asked her to go, acting like he didn't want to see her again, like he didn't care for her, making her feel like he never had. She didn't like the heavy metal CD she blasted on the way home. While she did appreciate some metal, much of it bothered her, made her uncomfortable for a reason she couldn't identify. The constant screaming always sounded full of hate, the "death growls" (Benjamin had informed her of this proper name), the angry lyrics, the volatile tempo, aggressive instruments with the warped way the guitars were downtuned, the rapid rage-filled drumming all bothered her. She would never tell Benjamin though, for fear that he would think she was weak, or immature.

Hearing her mom call out from the kitchen, "honey, you're just in time, I made this pizza with the homemade crust and Aunt Margaret's here, she wanted to…" Her mom stopped when she heard Karen ascend the stairs. She walked to the bottom and called up after her, "Honey?" Karen slammed the door shut, not wanting to see her mom, not wanting to see anyone ever again. She wanted to be alone, wanted to sleep. She just didn't want to face this life of hers anymore, couldn't face her senior year of high school, couldn't face Benjamin, couldn't continue putting up with his games, couldn't - "Karen!" her father this time, standing near the bottom of the stairway, even with the bedroom door closed Karen could tell, "Karen!" his voice closer now, perhaps he had ascended a few stairs. She wanted to shout at him to leave her alone, not to bother her, to just let her be!

Anticipating he might come up to see what was wrong, Karen locked her door and then she was back in bed, pulling the covers up to her chin, listening to her iPod. Skrillex, a techno/dubstep group she first heard at a rave the summer before junior year, always relaxed her, the beat thrusting her into a new time and place, creating a different consciousness, giving her a sense of calm.

He did not come after her, nor did her mother. A little hungry, Karen considered going down to grab a few slices of pizza. But no. She didn't want to face Aunt Margaret. That chatterbox that would ask a half dozen personal questions at least, certainly asking questions that even Karen's own parents didn't dare ask. Her parents didn't know half of what Karen was up to. Her parents were very liberal. They'd met Benjamin a few times, seeing him in his full gothic garb, and only later asking Karen if he "went around in those clothes all the time" or "just sometimes?" Hearing Benjamin's history - his absent father, his crazy domineering mother - her mom commented to Karen's father, "you know that boy will grow out of it, this *phase*, he's just angry with his father, angry he was never around, angry so he wants to rebel, *is* rebelling," Karen's father just listening very quietly drinking a bottle of beer and nodding. Karen's mother continued not knowing Karen was standing at the top of the stairs listening, "I just hope he doesn't do drugs. You know a lot of those kids that are, well, 'gothic', do lots of drugs. I did ask her and she said he's not into drugs, he's a good student, but he just likes to dress differently. There's nothing wrong with that, so long as -"

Karen's father had interjected, finishing her sentence although changing her sentence so finishing it in a different way, "- as she doesn't end up with him." Karen's mother had objected, "He's very smart, you know that. She says he's college-bound, and with all the A's Karen says he earns -"

Karen heard her father sigh loudly, effectively interrupting her mother. Such sighs always denoted sharp disapproval or discontent. Her father deliberately paused knowing if he waited what he said would have more impact. Karen heard him set his bottle of beer down on the glass end table - "You really think you can listen to what she says? This kid could be flunking his subjects for all we know. We don't know anything. All we know is what she *tells* us. She could be smoking pot with this guy and -"

"I don't think so, Jeff, I really *don't think so*. We have to trust she'll make the right decisions, we have to...give her the necessary space and...freedom to make them. You try making arbitrary rules, you try being strict and you will alienate a strong-willed oppositional defiant girl like Karen. We just have to wait. Give her some time, Jeff. If this guy turns out to be a, a –"

"A shithead?"

"Thank you, yes - a shithead. I trust she'll stop seeing him then, you know, Jeff, I trust she will."

"What about the drugs?"

Mom sighed. "We've gone over this a hundred times - he doesn't do drugs! I asked her and I could tell she was being truthful when she said he had tried pot several times last school year but *only* to experiment, *only* to see what it was like, and what's wrong with that? God knows we've both tried -"

"We didn't dress like circus freaks. We didn't -"

"Jeff, it's a *phase*, it will pass...you think he'll dress like that when he goes to college?"

"How do I know?"

Karen's mom sighed impatiently. "I'm done with this discussion."

Soon Karen had gotten numerous tattoos. Her parents had been unsure where she had gotten them, thinking she must have illegally done so, since she was only 17. Seeing too she had purchased an entirely new wardrobe from Hot Topic, he had first wanted to ask where she had gotten the money. Then he remembered the Anderson's, a local family she babysat for. When she had come home one day with multiple piercings on her face, her father had been furious. That night when he told his wife Karen was clearly having trouble in her life, she had acted oblivious before dismissing this conclusion. "She's just going through a phase, Jeff, what do you expect? She's in high school. Aren't most students her age having trouble?" Her indifference over matters pertaining to Karen seemed to always come too easily. He had appeased himself, to a degree, with the certainty that they had been good parents. Any punishment would be unwarranted, he had decided eventually. Karen was a good daughter, usually, and not disrespectful.

Karen presently turned off her iPod, remembering a decoy bottle buried in her bureau. The bottle of Vitamin B12 contained none of the pills specified. Inside instead there were five prescription Dexedrine pills. Benjamin didn't know she had procured these about a month ago from a fellow in her study hall. On occasion, she did buy drugs behind his back, a fact she hid for fear he would be angry: he loathed when she did things on her own without his permission. In her study hall one day this person had approached her, obviously aware she took drugs for he wasted no time asking if she'd like to try some of these. Opening up a side pocket in his cargo khakis, Karen had peered inside to see two prescription bottles. Her eyes had lit up, very eager to know what he was holding. Since the study hall monitor was not too far away from their table, he had informed her in a whisper. Karen decided to buy the Dexedrine. She had heard of this drug once before when she had conducted a Google search on amphetamines. Dexedrine, she had learned, would produce a high similar to cocaine just not nearly as strong. At the time she had tried coke on five different occasions, not doing it more often simply because it was too expensive. "Are you sure?" the young man had asked, as if Karen wasn't capable of deciding which drug she wanted to try. "Why don't you buy some Vicodin?" he asked, "it's a painkiller that will make you feel like –" Interrupting his description of the drug, Karen had told him she had done Vicodin several times before, not thinking very highly of it, then asking him if he was aware the drug consisted mostly of over-the-counter pain reliever? "Fifteen dollars for five," he had said, effectively ending their conversation but not before he made her aware he was being quite generous in giving her five pills for that price.

Knowing that the Dexedrine would enhance her mood considerably and give her extra energy, she had saved the pills for a 'down day', one where she was feeling particularly sad and lifeless. Today was definitely one of those days.

She swallowed two, which she knew would produce an acceptable high, since she hadn't tried any stimulants in five months. Soon, too, her mood would be elevated, endless energy coursing through her veins as she considered running in the rain. Badly Karen wanted to lose the weight she had put on, the only problem being she loved food and loathed exercise. At least 20 minutes would pass before she'd feel any effects from the pills. The instantaneous rush is what she wanted. Off her dresser she grabbed a five dollar bill and rolled it. With her driver's license, she crushed a third pill, sorting it into two long thin lines and then quickly blowing it.

Karen did not go for a run. Even after the pills kicked in, she just didn't have the motivation to do so. Slipping on her headphones and cranking up the volume on her iPod, Karen experienced a sudden surge of energy, not knowing what she might want to do with it, not wanting to run or even go for a walk, both of which sounded quite boring to her. Although laying here for the remainder of the day also seemed monotonous. It was only a bit after 6:00. She had no plans, no job and no real hobbies, having become accustomed to participating in whatever activity Benjamin happened to like at any given time. At first, when she met him, it was rollerblading on strictly dangerous terrain (several times Karen had badly torn up her knees and elbows) and attending local shows by punk/ska groups. On occasion they still attended the punk shows, not ska though, as Benjamin had decided he detested that type of music. Then, after about a year, he started skateboarding so she started skateboarding. Never did they rollerblade again, dropping the hobby like a bad habit, claiming rollerblading was for "fuckin' losers", Karen immediately wondering how he could condemn something he had been so fond of only two days before. Around this time, Benjamin also began to paint, using watercolors and acrylic paint, mostly. So, Karen started drawing with him, telling him she found herself much more artistic than she ever imagined. When she asked him if he agreed with her he said no. Karen had then changed the subject, not wanting Benjamin's rebuff to hang around in the silence, telling him she found painting to be very therapeutic after a moment asking him if he felt it was also. He had said no and then told her not to talk anymore, as he wanted to concentrate on his painting. Karen had felt quite rebuffed, rather resigned to the realization that if she continued to talk he would keep criticizing her. Now, almost a year since he had immersed himself in painting and skateboarding, Benjamin still liked art, just not creating it himself. He took great pride in his own body becoming a work of art, being tattooed and pierced countless times. His goal he claimed was to have a quarter of his body pierced by the time he graduated high school. Karen wondered how he was able to get these tattoos since he was underage, but she never asked since he had already managed to get lots of tattoos already. Seldom did he ever paint or draw now and no longer did he skateboard. At the beginning of junior year he had purchased a used drum set at a novelty thrift store. Assaulting the drums with his sticks had become his new hobby, she noted soon after the purchase how obsessed he had become, unable to tell whether he was any good or not. Benjamin wasn't playing to try to be good, Karen believed, he was playing simply to release his aggression. Then suddenly one day near the end of February, Benjamin had gotten rid of the set. When she had asked why, he told her to mind her own business.

Naturally she thought he was angry and annoyed with her so she had not said anything further. He had grinned very widely then and said, "Jesus, K, I'm kidding." Karen had felt very relieved, not only because she knew he wasn't upset with her also because she understood she would no longer have to listen to his incessant hateful drum-playing. No longer would she have to put up with his frequent interruptions of her while she was in the midst of talking to him. And not just talking: typically when he interrupted her that purposefully he did so when she was opening up to him, explaining something about her feelings she thought rather important.

His only real hobbies soon became activities that couldn't even be classified as real hobbies. He enjoyed doing drugs, talking about doing drugs, and selling drugs. He had also developed a fondness of pornographic movies that featured particularly violent simulated rape scenes. Karen knew Benjamin looked at porn - she just wasn't aware of the frequency and content.

So, what would she do? In this moment realizing she had no one who she could call, no real friends to talk to, no one to hang out with. Of course she had the guy's number who had sold her the Dexedrine, but he was only an acquaintance. Her life with Benjamin had become restricted, to the extent she had pushed away the few friends she did have. Feeling thoroughly satisfied in Benjamin's company, she had not felt any real desire or need for friends. She regretted that decision now. Attached to him as if there was no one else, all her emotions and self-worth dependent on him, she now found it impossible to escape. Ending their relationship effectively erased her own identity. So, she wouldn't break up with him, she couldn't, not just yet. Did she have a goal of breaking up with him? She wasn't sure, could not decide, in time she believed the answer would come.

Chapter 45

Clara ended up at *Christy's Cakes*, wanting to check on the status of her application. The sign on the door almost caused her to walk away discouraged. Cupping her hands on the side of her face, gazing through the glass door into the store, she saw two middle-aged women talking behind the counter. She already felt down – after all, over a week had passed since she had handed in her application. Surely they would've called her by now if they were interested in hiring her. Feeling courageous, she knocked on the door, lightly, the *Closed* sign that hung from a thin piece of golden twine shaking slightly. One of the women looked up immediately, her eyes widening in surprise, or aggravation, this being the end of her shift. Clara imagined a small local store such as this closed on Sundays. She had decided to come here on an impulse, not having considered their hours would likely be different since it was the weekend.

The woman rushed to unlock the door, glancing over at a clock on the wall as she did so. Clara did not know what to say, how she might introduce herself. Seeing the woman check the time she began to worry about Meem, about the punishment she might receive. Clara felt herself freeze when the woman said, "Yes?" in a firm low tone.

"About a week ago . . ." Clara cleared her throat. "I handed in an application. Well, I - I thought maybe you would've called me by now to arrange an interview."

"You did, did you?" The woman manufactured a smile, not motioning for Clara to come any further into the store, staring at her more directly as though to establish her authority. Clara stared at her forehead to avoid eye contact. "What's your name, young lady?" The woman's playful tone made Clara uncomfortable. "Clara."

"Clara what?"

Clara opened her mouth when -

"Welliver!" The woman appeared excited over this retrieval, closing her eyes briefly as she summoned additional memories. "You have no

216

prior job experience, no references besides one of your schoolteachers and your grandmother who doesn't count since she's obviously a relative…"

"That's right."

"I wasn't finished." The woman had given every indication of being finished with what she had to say however, allowing her voice to trail off then staring at Clara, assessing her reaction, wanting to see if she would say something just to interrupt the silence. Clara said nothing. The woman said nothing for a good long while.

"I'm a real good worker," Clara said finally, not to break the silence since it had already lingered for so long as to negate its intended effect. No longer did Clara wonder what the woman would say next, or what she herself might say. Focusing only on the soft music in the background, the music contemporary and instrumental, made her feel almost entirely at ease. She decided to inform the woman of her good work ethic, which resulted in no response. Breathlessly: "I earn almost all A's in school, I help Meem, my grandmother I mean, around the house, all the time, too!" The woman said nothing. Clara continued enthusiastically: "I plan to go to college one day and I love animals! I think I might want to be a veterinarian. I'm pretty good at math, and I know the courses required to become a vet would require a lot of math and—"

"Clara . . ."

Clara smiled, thinking the woman might ask her to sit down for an unplanned interview.

"We're not hiring."

"You're not?" All hope and joy were drained from her face.

"We're not." The woman looked out the store's front windows, a subtle signal that Clara should go. Slowly, she moved out the front door. As she walked away from the store, she felt very anxious to return home, if only because she was eager to face Meem.

Clara would swear she had every intention to return home. In fact, she had nearly reached her driveway when she saw Karen parked right beside her mailbox. Never had she seen what kind of vehicle Karen drove. It was a white Jeep that looked brand new. Clara did not want to see her, too focused on Meem, also thinking about how she had just been denied a job.

"Clara, hey," Karen said.

"Um, hi."

"You're probably wondering why I'm here, huh?"

Clara nodded.

"I wanted to hang out." Karen smiled, too widely for Clara to take her seriously. Clara sensed she wanted something from her.

"Hang out?" Clara took a cautious step closer to the jeep's passenger side window that was rolled down halfway. Karen pulled up the lever on her seat so she was sitting upright and no longer reclining.

Karen nodded, assessing Clara's reaction. Clara continued to mask the joy she felt, though she was very happy Karen had dropped by to initiate time they might spend together. Not worth the effort, she finally decided, wondering why she disguised how much she wanted to hang out with Karen. Truly, she felt Karen liked her now. Lost in the electricity of the moment, she rather naively believed Karen wouldn't want to hang out with her otherwise. Certainly, she wouldn't drive all the way to her house and – wait, she suddenly panicked, wondering if Meem had seen Karen?

"Did you go to the front door?" Clara asked, suddenly noting Karen's apparel for the first time now, seeing she did not wear the usual heavy black eye makeup, nor did she wear what she called her 'whore-red' lipstick. Yes, several of her tattoos were exposed, but Meem, distracted in the moment by this young pale black-haired stranger, might not even notice how inked up she was, and even if she did, so what? What was the worst that could happen? To Clara, it seemed the worst had already happened: she had not only been in the most severe verbal confrontation she had ever been in with Meem, she had also been involved in her first ever physical altercation.

"Yeah," Karen then asked her why she wanted to know.

"No reason." Clara didn't want to tell her how Meem still held lots of authority over her, possessed so much control in her life that if she disapproved of Karen Clara might not be able to see her, especially now that school was out. Unable to resist: "Did you meet her?"

"Your grandmother?"

Clara nodded.

"Well, yes," Karen then said they had talked for a good long while.

"Really?" Clara did not ask, really her rhetorical question was a reflex. "How long did you talk?"

"A decent amount of time I said, I didn't put a timer on it."

Clara wanted to ask several more questions, to find out what they had talked about. Had Meem mentioned she was upset with Clara? Did Meem appear upset herself? What questions had Meem asked, if any? From past experience Clara knew she asked a great many questions to anyone she befriended, also practically interviewing that person's parents.

"What do you want to do?" Clara asked, surprised over how easily she had dismissed her questions. She had concluded they were rather unimportant, irrelevant to the moment, to the fun and good times that might be awaiting them this evening.

Benjamin was infuriated when Karen arrived at his place. Not only did she come without his permission, completely unannounced, after he had specifically told her he didn't want to see her for an indefinite period of time, she also walked right in the front door without knocking. Typically, she knocked three times in quick succession, that way he knew who was at the door (he had reluctantly admitted that ever since he had started dealing drugs sophomore year, sporadic as his efforts were, he had become a bit paranoid) also that way he didn't have to get up from wherever he was and stop doing whatever he was doing ("yes, I'm lazy sometimes, K, it's okay to be lazy…sometimes.")

Surveying her as she stood smiling at the doorway, he wanted to grab her and fuck the hell out of her. He could feel he was slightly stiff already. If he did pin her down on the couch and take her unaware of what was going on until he was inside her, he imagined she wouldn't even have the time to get wet. He said nothing as he took a step toward her. Looking at her very seriously, he still considered grabbing her and fucking her and then telling her to leave and never come back. That's when he saw her. Clara moving inside behind Karen, everything about her apprehensive - the way she had taken a long time to finally come inside, the expression on her face, the way she glanced every which way around the trailer, her eyes seeming to twitch nervously as she did so, avoiding eye contact with Benjamin and even Karen herself, staring down at the floor now looking around no longer.

"Clara," Benjamin said.

"Yes?" Clara glanced up at him.

"Long time no see."

"Yeah, I know!" Her tone had changed, also her facial expression, both quite hopeful now, enthusiastic, interpreting his comment as an indication he had missed her, since it hadn't been that long since she had last seen him. "I missed you!" She blurted this out, immediately thinking she shouldn't have said it, if only because Karen was standing right there and also she didn't want Benjamin to know how much she wanted him, how much she wanted him all to herself.

"Did you?" He stared at her quizzically, allowing the question to hang in the air as if it was a complicated one that would require a good deal of thought to answer.

"Let's do something fun!" Clara liked how she had taken control of the conversation by changing the subject, even if her redirection did not actually present a new topic, only offered a vague suggestion. Benjamin asked her what she wanted to do and she said, "Um…" Distracted now noticing Karen had disappeared, she asked, "Where'd she go?"

"Does it look like I care? Here, sit down…" Benjamin himself sat down on the couch then softly patted the cushion next to him. Clara obeyed, sitting beside him, wondering where Karen had gone.

It was a surprise to Clara herself she did not feel nervous. Maybe it was because Karen wasn't present, so she had no worries about being perceived as coming onto Benjamin, even as she made a concerted effort to suppress her urges to flirt with him. She thought about kissing him, his tongue inside her mouth. Then she imagined sitting on his lap, wrapping her arms around his neck as he held her, kissing her neck, kissing her mouth – *stop!* "Tell me what you've been doing." Scolding herself might have been futile since the more she felt these sexual thoughts were forbidden the stronger they were in her mind. "Nothing, really. I haven't been doing anything. You know, I applied for a job..." she heard her voice trail off, fading from the time she started talking. Then this very vaguely familiar sensation between her legs—she was wet, aroused. Despite her total inexperience she understood what was happening. Her fantasizing about doing sexual acts with Benjamin had caused her vagina to prepare for easier, less painful penetration. No matter how wet she became she knew the sex would still hurt, being her first time, depending upon how large Benjamin's penis was and *STOP! Stop this now! think about something else. Benjamin has a girlfriend! He has a girlfriend so he won't want to have sex with me, besides I don't want to have sex with him!* I became friends with him to - why had she become friends with him? Suddenly, even with knowing her initial intention, how pure it had been – wanting to introduce Benjamin to Christianity, wanting him to accept Jesus as his personal Lord and Savior so his soul would be saved – a new motive came to her mind. How she wanted Benjamin all to herself! Wanted to date him, be in a committed relationship with him, maybe even lose her virginity to him (only if they got married of course!) Any of the affection she felt for Karen was gone now, all of her feelings focused solely on Benjamin.

The silence they were sharing did not intimidate her. She refrained from talking, not feeling the need to speak as she normally did when silence prevailed for any extended amount of time.

She would wait for him to speak, wait for him to initiate conversation. That didn't mean she would wait for him to engage her in physical touch. No, she boldly decided to touch him, starting off with a very demure subtle touch, moving her hand inside of his, interlacing her fingers with his. Karen crossed her mind for an instant but Clara didn't care since Benjamin clearly didn't. Why else did he grin and squeeze her hand ever so slightly? A signal he was excited by her touch?

221

Benjamin's other hand disappeared to his side, moving into his pocket and digging around for a moment before pulling out three pills he had found in his car. He had been desperate for drugs, wanting, *needing* to get high badly craving that euphoria and not having the money to buy more. If he wanted more he would have to either steal from his mom (not that the nasty dick licking bitch had much money to begin with, or material possessions he could take and sell), find a job to earn money himself (that was out of the question, Benjamin would not be caught dead flipping burgers, stocking the shelves at Target, or even being a cashier at a convenient store, he would tell anyone he was simply too smart for those sorts of jobs) or (finally, he had to acknowledge, the best option) purchase drugs to sell with an IOU. The dealer he had in mind had accepted IOU's before, at least from Benjamin, knowing him for over four years.

The options of how to obtain drugs had been sifting through his mind when he went out to his car to look for a CD, this rarely happened: a song on repeat in his mind, three lines from the chorus playing over and again until he gave in, thinking he had listened to the CD last in his car. Searching for the CD that was neon orange, believing it might be easy to find because of the bright color, he leaned over the driver's side seat, scanning the messy floor below the passenger's side seat seeing three rather large white pills in the center console. Right away he knew what they were, what he didn't know, or didn't remember, is how they had gotten there. How could he have possibly left these treasures behind? Derived from opiates, obviously opiates were natural, Benjamin concluding God didn't want man to experience pain, at least not too much pain. *So God blessed us with these gems,* Benjamin thought for a moment, almost in a trance quickly thinking: *that's bullshit, there is no God and if there is I sure as fuck don't believe in Him.* He massaged the three pills in his hand, noting the dosage, a number printed on one side. The dosage was high, these pills, if he took all three, would kick his ass, especially since he hadn't done any Oxycontin in a few months.

Setting the pills on the damaged coffee table, nonchalantly at first, he assessed Clara's reaction, watching her see the pills then look at him like *oh, you have a headache and you're taking some aspirin, is that it?*

He chuckled, as he considered what she might be thinking. Benjamin grew in his pants, his penis almost completely stiff now, seeing Clara's sweet innocent face, imagining himself inside her mouth. Then seeing his semen on her face, her reaction if she swallowed, closing her eyes as he ejaculated into her mouth. She would keep her eyes closed as she swallowed, opening her eyes then looking up at him quizzically, possibly pointing to his penis - "Is that all of it now or do you have a little bit more?" she might ask. Too, Benjamin saw the pills, anticipating the euphoria, the intense rush he would experience as a result of crushing and blowing the pills. He did not understand why they created so many narcotics that were crushable, did they want to turn unsuspecting users of the drugs into addicts? Of course, Benjamin was not an unsuspecting user, he knew full well how addictive Oxycontin was, along with all the other prescription drugs he had used and abused: Ritalin, Adderall, Percocet, Vicodin, Fentanyl, Methadone.

"What are those?" Clara asked finally, having wanted to ask him to identify the pills the instant she saw them, touching Benjamin on the thigh, her hand off his body the moment she had touched him. She had no idea her touch excited him further, no clue he was already stiff, that she had in fact caused this visceral reaction within him. Nor did she think she was even capable of causing such a response.

He looked at her, pensive. Fighting the urge to just be honest and tell her the pills in front of her were an addictive potent substance that produced a high similar to heroin. He imagined she was familiar with heroin, might even know it was one of the strongest opiates known to man. Possibly, she had extracted a very cursory knowledge of the drug during the obligatory drug awareness course everyone had to take in sixth grade and then again freshman year. "Tylenol," he said, studying her face as she believed him, gazing at the pills closely as though she hadn't ever seen Tylenol before.

"Why do you have three?"

"Three?" he repeated her question because he didn't know where he wanted to go with his lie.

"Well, what can I say?" Then allowing the rhetorical question to hang in the air.

"Say it!" Clara exclaimed boldly, Benjamin surprised with her demand, almost impressed, appreciating how she had suddenly summoned a certain degree of chutzpah, if only for a moment.

"I must have been anticipating a very large headache." Benjamin couldn't control the smile that appeared on his face.

"Must have!" Giggling now, completely unaware how flirtatious her body language was, Clara moved her hand back onto his thigh. The purpose of this gesture, Benjamin believed, was to steady herself, as in the midst of giggling she had almost lost her balance. Her legs were crossed as she sat on the very edge of the couch, looking as if she didn't want to become too comfortable. For a moment she nearly slid off: grabbing his thigh with one hand, holding her chest with the other. Her laughter dissipated as he stared at her tits. *They're really small,* Benjamin thought, *maybe she's got nice nipples I could chew on to make up for the size.*

The silence they shared was comfortable once again, though Clara still had many questions to ask as she felt his gaze, his eyes upon her. A feeling of discomfort had resulted from her thinking he was judging her, in all his insouciant silence, seeing right through her. Not that there was much to see through: the wall she had put up when she first interacted with him had crumbled quickly.

She had been herself for the majority of the time she had spent with him. Nonetheless, she obsessed over what he was thinking about her, wanting to talk but fearing his criticism. So she stayed silent, concluding that whatever she had to say was insignificant now since she was here with him. At last, as she sat beside him, an invasive sense of serenity overcame her, and she wanted to hug him, kiss him, sit on his lap, take a nap with him.

Feeling a little tired now, perhaps as a result of thinking about the nap and barely having slept the last two nights, she considered falling asleep here on this couch with Benjamin beside her. What might Karen say? If Benjamin was OK with her sleeping here, if he approved, she thought she didn't care about Karen, not what she thought or said or did. And then her head was in his lap, Clara not thinking, only feeling the intense energy of this moment. As she looked up at him she was very docile, unafraid of his gaze. His eyes appeared different now, losing the hardness they typically possessed, the anger gone. His gaze gentle and tranquil, his eyes almost closed now. Clara did not care about Karen. Knowing she was in the next room, that she might even be watching, that if she wasn't watching she would likely find out, Clara did not care. She had no fear because she felt like she had Benjamin's love.

Drifting off now, her head still in his lap as she faintly felt his fingers run through her hair, feeling relaxed as she hadn't been in weeks, not since she had taken the last of the Valium, then nothing. Was he trying to sleep now too? Then his hand between her legs, unzipping her shorts, moving down underneath her white panties, Clara feeling herself shocked back into wakefulness.

She pulled her head away from his lap, pushing his hand away, staring at him not knowing what to say. "What are you doing?" she asked with no vocal inflection, Benjamin unable to tell what she was thinking, or feeling, in this moment, not knowing if Clara was offended, excited, afraid, all of the above, none of the above? She had no facial expression. Sliding further away from him on the couch she said, "I think I should go."

"What, why?" Benjamin was shocked, looking at her as though he didn't quite understand, acknowledging to himself that one of the last things he had anticipated was her taking the initiative to leave after he had shown her such attention, after he had been so gentle and loving toward her.

"No reason," Clara said, giving no thought to the question, opening the front door when, wait, how would she get home? Karen had driven her here. "I - I don't feel well," Clara said, immediately thinking that was a weak excuse. "May I u–use your phone?" Clara feeling very anxious now, not liking the feeling that she was dependent upon Meem for a ride home, imagining Meem might say no, yelling at her awhile first before saying no, or might not even answer, or might answer and hang up.

"Karen can give you a ride home."

"No."

"Why?"

"Well . . ."

"She doesn't care," Benjamin then said he messed around with other girls all the time. "Just so long as she knows I'm not emotionally involved."

225

Clara couldn't deny she felt hurt by the implications of this statement, which were that Benjamin had no feelings for her. Of course, she also felt confused, since they had not done anything sexual, had not even kissed, not yet. Had Benjamin meant what he said to be a slight? Had he intended to hurt her feelings? Did he really not have any feelings for her or had she misinterpreted his statement?

Benjamin called for Karen and the way she materialized almost immediately Clara found strange: it was as if she had been waiting, eavesdropping, perhaps. She looked nonchalant, almost happy, smiling. Clara found that strange too.

"You ready to go?" Karen asked.

Clara nodded, looking unsure, honestly feeling a little anxious over accepting a ride from Karen, what if she decided to not take her home? Where might she take her instead? Clara worried over these two questions, thinking of different scenarios, all the possibilities, like if she drove her out into a vast empty isolated place, forced her out of the car and then drove off. Clara had no cell phone, what would she do in such a situation? Clara weighed a lot less than Karen, so fighting back would not be an option. Regardless of weight, Karen was much stronger than her.

"Earth to Clara!"

"Yes," Clara then said finally she would accept the ride home, feeling reluctant but feeling she had no other choice, not wanting to call Meem, knowing Meem's reaction would be harsh, that is if she picked up the phone at all, since it was after midnight, knowing too if Meem decided to pick her up she would scold her the whole ride home—"SEE *what happens when* YOU *don't listen!*"

Hearing Meem's voice tell her that she had better talk to the Lord and set things straight with Him, as clearly she was *way* out of line, headed to hell too, if she didn't soon repent.

On the ride home, Clara had to resist the urge to talk, as she did not feel comfortable sharing silence with Karen. Her efforts were successful until she didn't have to try anymore, Karen spoke up: "I know you gave him head."

"Head?" Clara asked, though she knew exactly what Karen was referring to, simply too shocked over how she had made this assertion so plainly out of nowhere, like saying she knew what Clara had for dinner, Clara's response little more than a reflex.

"Don't play dumb - you sucked his dick, I'm not mad, Clara, just tell me - did you swallow?"

"I - I don't -"

"I - I..." Karen mocked her stuttering in addition to her rather high breathless tone of voice, laughing now making sure Clara knew she was ridiculing her.

"I did not!" Clara exclaimed, very serious, facing forward out the windshield with her hands solemnly on her lap one on top of the other.

"I know you did," Karen said accusingly. "You have some on your lips."

"Some what?"

Clara spun her head toward Karen, very worried, genuinely having no idea what she meant.

"Come."

"Come? You, you mean sperm?"

Karen had to laugh at that, Clara using such a technical formal word to describe come.

Suppressing her laughter, not wanting to alienate Clara entirely, knowing if she did so Benjamin would be angry, for truly he did like this bitch. "Semen," Karen said finally. "Yes. *Ejaculate.*"

Suddenly, Karen stopped the car, stopping right in the middle of the road not even bothering to pull alongside the curb. Clara didn't understand, clearly had no idea Karen wanted her to get out, as Karen faked a yawn, proud of herself for being so evil, knowing this was quite mild compared to what she wanted to do to this little twat: pull her hair, hard, and then slap her across the face, tell her to stay the fuck away from her man. Knowing if she did so this warning would reach Benjamin, inevitably then he would punish her. This would be unavoidable, she knew, as he always found a way to punish her, even sometimes if she had been good, or felt she had been good, still he was never so creative as when concocting a punishment.

"Well..." Karen stared at her, enjoying her confusion, for a good long while until her enjoyment started to subside. Pointing to the passenger's side door, very sternly she said: "Get out."

"You want me to, to get –"

"– out of my car, yes, go..."

"It's pitch black!"

"So?"

"I –"

"You have legs. You can walk."

"It's after midnight."

"Get out." Karen looked gravely ahead, a simple signal that her decision was final. Clara did not move. Frozen she seemed in her seat.

"I SAID GET OUT!"

Startled by Karen's shouting, Clara quickly opened the door and stepped out. Recognizing the nearby sign that indicated what road she was on, Clara knew she was about a mile from her house.

Feeling no fear over walking in the dark, even with the hour late, even with being all alone, Clara was too focused on recovering from what she perceived to be Karen's cruelty. What had she done wrong? She knew, of course, she knew exactly. She was a potential threat to Karen, even if Karen did believe most of what Benjamin said – that he was playing with her, wanted to have sex with her *"fuck her until I get tired of her"*, wanted to secure her attachment to him then tell her he was finished with her, Benjamin predicting she would not give up that easily. Since he would be her first, *aimed* to be her first, she would get that forever feeling that the majority of girls, especially sweet-natured girls like Clara, experienced, she would beg him to spend time with him, not to have sex although Benjamin anticipated she would have sex with him again if that meant she could see him again – she still felt insecure over the possibility that she could lose Benjamin to this idiot orphan cunt.

Turning off her headlights, Karen watched Clara closely as she blanketed herself with her arms and picked up her pace. She made sure to stay far enough behind so that Clara wouldn't know she was there. No matter, she was likely too worried to care. Karen knew she was the type who worried, obviously dealt with that worry through incessant prayer. Would she attempt to save their souls again? Karen wondered, thinking of how she might react so as to take advantage of Clara's caring, considerate nature.

Karen turned on her headlights, seeing Clara glance over her shoulder, squinting as the lights shone in her face. Her first instinct was to quicken her pace, but she was walking as fast as she could, and did not want to run. Pressing the gas pedal all the way down to the floor now, Karen sped off, watching Clara in the rearview mirror, anxious to see her disappear in the distance.

Meem was waiting, not knitting, just sitting, in her rocker, not rocking, the quilt in her lap nearly complete. All the lights were off, including the lamp above her she usually used while knitting. Her eyes were closed and she was almost asleep when she heard the front door open and close, quietly.

Quickly, Clara moved across a tiny tiled section of floor, tip-toeing over a small space of carpet that separated the entranceway from the stairway. She had no idea Meem was sitting in the living room watching her silently squinting to see her, clicking on the lamp after Clara had ascended several stairs not knowing exactly why she had waited so long, thinking perhaps she could've turned it on the moment Clara had opened the door, supposing she had been too preoccupied surreptitiously watching her.

Almost at the top of the first flight of stairs Clara stopped, not knowing Meem would want to know where she had been, demand other things of her too, yell at her for a good long while, most likely, then, in an effort to raise sympathy, say something like, "Clara you know I'm old, obviously, *very* old, I won't be here much longer, you know that? You know *I'll* be dead soon? You might want to keep that in mind the next time, I hope there won't be a next time, though, you know, I *really* hope we can just get along until I die..." On and on she would go until they would reach some reconciliation. Moving begrudgingly down the stairs, Clara sighed, feeling tired now really not wanting to deal with this! Wanting to go to bed, wanting nothing more than to sleep and forget everything: how Benjamin did not love her, apparently felt nothing for her, also how Karen hated her, clearly wished bad things would happen to her, finally how Meem would forever find a reason to reprimand her, no matter how good she was Meem would *always* have some reason to disapprove.

"Yes?" Clara asked, standing on the landing, the small tiled space where there was a doormat and coat rack.

"Tell me where you've been." Meem's tone did not reflect the frustration her face contained.

"What do *you* want? I'm 17! I don't need to tell you everything, I don't even need to tell you most things, a lot of things I can do on my own and keep to myself!"

"See where that takes you." Meem looked down at her quilt as though to dismiss Clara and allow her subtle warning to achieve full affect.

As Clara walked up the stairs, Meem's words echoed in her ears: *see where that takes you, see where that takes you, see where...*and still, as Clara drifted off to sleep that night, she heard Meem, heard a manic rush of words, most of which chastised Clara for something inevitably quite small and petty, also heard advice Meem had given her over the years, much of it seeming utterly irrelevant now. As usual, the more Clara attempted to dismiss Meem's voice the louder it became, so she forced herself to think of something else - Jeremy, if only because he felt very safe and familiar to her.

Jeremy did not want her, however, she knew that. He had a girlfriend. Besides, he would be leaving for college very soon and Clara believed not too much more time would have to pass before he wouldn't want to see her anymore. Oh, sure, he might offer to see her when he came home, but that would only be for a couple hours. She knew he had no real desire to spend time with her anymore. If he did see her again Clara imagined she would have to initiate it, and if he agreed to see her he would likely only be saying yes out of a sense of obligation, his feeling somewhat sorry for her, and Clara didn't want that, not at all. Of course she still wanted to see him, but she understood now that seeing him more would only reawaken the feelings she had already begun to suppress.

Only moderately successful in this endeavor so far, weeks ago she realized what was happening: she was feeling extra strength sad because Jeremy would be graduating soon, leaving for college soon, and also accepting that he would never want her in the same way she wanted him. As much as she wanted to believe she stood a chance with him - if she wore the right outfit or styled her hair a certain way, or dyed it, if she had bigger breasts, maybe if she lost ten pounds—she knew it wasn't true. Jeremy would never want her in the same way she wanted him. That hurt her to realize, but she thought it far better to be realistic than to continue fantasizing about what would never happen: dating him, kissing him, taking long walks with him while holding his hand, marrying him, eventually, having his children. She would miss him, that much was true. In her heart, though, she realized she had let him go almost entirely.

As her thoughts were fading, becoming incoherent - a sure sign she was nearly asleep - she stopped seeing Jeremy, his face gone now, Benjamin replacing him altogether. Despite his severe exterior, she truly believed he had the capacity to be gentle, the capacity to open his hardened heart to her, and God.

When Clara awoke she was quite confused, disoriented, realizing fully now how alone she was in her life, feeling she had no one on her side, no one who wanted to see her succeed. Worse, she felt other people were out to sabotage her, wanting to see her fail. She didn't feel safe either, that was the main thing. She knew it was only a matter of time before Meem tore into her again, and how much more could she take, honestly, how long until her already volatile strength abandoned her, left her unable to stand her ground when Meem confronted her? Surely, Meem would try to regain the authority she had once firmly possessed over Clara. It was true Meem still held a great deal of control over Clara. It was a control so deeply rooted in Clara, she was unsure whether she would ever be able to fully recover. Very often still she considered Meem when she made a decision, however small, even when she interacted with someone, even total strangers. She censored her mood and tone (for instance, if she was angry or aggravated, not wanting to come across as discourteous or disagreeable), also the words she used when she spoke, carefully selecting them to make sure others knew she was a woman of God. She never allowed herself to speak ill of someone else, never allowed herself to speak negatively about anything in her life, for surely that would not reflect well on her being a Christian. Christians were supposed to concentrate solely on their blessings, weren't they? Christians were to remain grateful for their lives, no matter if their lives were not very good or if they had experienced innumerable hardships. They were always to maintain a positive attitude, right? Clara thought so, believing it absolutely, forcing herself not to doubt her view of Christianity or her idea of what it meant to be a born again Christian.

What might she do today? There weren't many options. Go downtown to look for another job? After all, she had only applied to one place, surely there were other applicants turned down. Her having no prior job experience she thought the likely reason for not even being offered an interview. But, weren't there places that hired high school students in her same predicament?

Naturally, some students who had just turned 16 would have no job experience, no professional references, and Clara was sure some students who fell into this category secured jobs. Already having been turned down once, the truth was she just didn't have the motivation or confidence to put herself out there again with the chance she would be turned away. On a whim, she had applied to *Christy's Cakes*. Now she possessed none of the energy associated with the good mood she had been in. Besides, Meem didn't care about her getting a job. Either way, Meem would find something to criticize Clara for, something to cast her strong disapproval over. So what was the point? Clara began to wonder. Even if she found a job, it was likely to pay minimum wage, or not much more than minimum wage. It was also possible she might only be able to find a part-time position. Besides, Clara had overheard Meem telling her mom on the phone that if Clara did happen to be hired to work somewhere, she would require a quarter (perhaps half, she hadn't decided how "generous" she wanted to be) of all her earnings, just to teach her a lesson: "how important it is to give back to those who have given so much to you over the years."

Clara's focus now was more on finding a man, thinking maybe she could move in with him (she tried her hardest to block out the part of her mind that said this was pure fantasy). She could live with him her senior year, if his parents approved, and surely they would approve after meeting her! After discovering she was a sweet, hopeful child of Christ! And she was a good Christian in her heart and she thought she always would be, always remembering Jesus was her personal Lord and Savior, always remembering His sacrifice for her. Sure, she occasionally had doubts. It was true she had strayed from God lately, turned her back on Him. Truly, she believed anyone who had walked a good deal of time in their faith would have doubts.

Clara closed her eyes, wanting to fall back asleep, but after what felt like half an hour, she gave up, frustrated. What might she do today?

Jeremy was done with that bitch, feeling very strongly he should terminate his relationship with Stephanie before she took the initiative herself. They were clearly finished, if not now, then certainly very soon. Jeremy did love her, he couldn't deny that, but he was still so young, knowing in his heart at his age he shouldn't commit to any one girl, if only for her sake, since he wanted to date around, "play the field". He didn't want to give any one girl the wrong impression, not during his undergraduate years. Jeremy aimed to wait until graduate school to begin his search in earnest for 'the one'. He did believe in 'the one', didn't he? He supposed so. It was true he doubted this belief at times, thinking it more plausible that there were numerous people out there for everyone. Perhaps 'the one' was a romantic notion after all, romantic and therefore fanciful, not real. He tried not to be cynical, if only because he wanted so badly to believe there was only *one* girl who could be thoroughly right for him, *one* girl who could complete him.

He had to admit he was pissed. By suppressing her feelings over the last few months, or at least not revealing them, hadn't Stephanie already taken the initiative, however subtle, to break up with him? Maybe she wanted him to take her hints, to break up with her first, feeling if he dumped her, she wouldn't feel as bad. She felt a certain sense of guilt, however misplaced, and nostalgia, realizing that she would not be ending up with her high school sweetheart after all, the boy she had lost her virginity to, her "first true love" as she had sweetly proclaimed him to be after only two months of dating. "I think it was love at first sight," she could remember saying this, a hackneyed sentiment she never imagined she would express. "And not lust at first sight?" Jeremy had asked. Firmly she had said, "Lust and love can be experienced at the same time you know." "Can they?" He enjoyed challenging her, particularly when she made declarative statements that, however smart they sounded, were essentially opinions with nothing concrete, nothing objective offered as support.

"*Ohh* Jeremy..." she would respond most of the time, concluding that convincing him of what she felt to be true was ultimately not too important, at least not worth arguing over.

Goddamn, though, Jeremy had to concede he was angry, more than a little. *He* wanted to be the one who pulled away. *He* wanted to be the one who told her he would be leaving for college soon, that he simply didn't think he would have the time or energy to maintain anything more than a friendship now that they would be separated by several hundred miles. It was obvious to him now that she was detached from him emotionally, and that she had placed this distance between them on purpose. She was much smarter than Jeremy would ever want to acknowledge. She could be calculating, since she was never in the moment, or at least not usually. Stephanie was always thinking ahead or, if not ahead, then obsessing over the past. Suffering from a rather severe case of low self-esteem, for a reason unbeknownst to Jeremy, for she was prettier and projected an *as-if* confidence that put most every other girl in their high school to shame. One night she had confided in him that frequently she felt far from beautiful, the majority of her self-worth, Jeremy learned, tied into her physical appearance. Initially, Jeremy assured her she was beautiful, didn't she see all the guys who gawked at her when she walked down the hallway? "Well, sometimes I guess," she had said. Jeremy didn't understand her, why did she reveal these sorts of things if she paid no mind to his response, did she not want to feel better? Didn't she believe him? Or did she simply want to solve her issues on her own? Later, when Jeremy detected a pattern in her tendency to hold back her feelings for weeks at a time then open up to him all at once, for over an hour, sometimes nearly two, he ceased offering her encouragement. Obviously she didn't appreciate his positivity. If she did wouldn't she accept what he said, or at least part of what he said? Oftentimes, when Jeremy listened to her for a good long while he would interrupt her, unable to deal with what he grew to feel was her irrational rambling. Also, he learned after some time that the less guidance he offered, the less he tried to placate her, the more she wanted him, in every way - wanting to spend more time with him, talk to him more, have sex with him more.

So, he would just not call her, not accept her calls. If she called requesting closure, wanting to say goodbye, would he grant her that satisfaction? Wanting to be in control of the situation, Jeremy wanted to tell her it was over. He was going to college so didn't she see there could be no future for them? Even if a part of him realized he would miss certain things about her, the way she sometimes laughed, if she was in one of her cheerful moods, over things that were somewhat just plain goofy. He would miss her smile, because she did have perfect teeth and, more importantly, when she smiled a lot of the time he smiled too. She could have that effect on anyone: her moods were so powerful and contagious that if she was happy whoever she was with felt happy too.

Lately, though, whenever he was around her, she had not smiled at all, had appeared quite melancholy, pensive. Several times recently when Jeremy had said something funny, she did smile and laugh, but he could tell her good humor was forced, not at all genuine. Finally, he would miss (oh, how he would miss!) the way she lost herself during sex, becoming so immersed in the act that she said his name over and over, a clear indication to Jeremy she didn't know who she was, not quite, at least had no firm fixed identity, which was fine. Jeremy didn't fault her for that, in fact he found her kaleidoscopic nature attractive. Besides, lots of other kids their age were similar in this way. Jeremy suspected if everyone was honest that in high school one is still testing out different identities, experimenting to find out who one is.

Not wanting to make a rapid decision, he decided he would think, though not too much, about what he wanted to do. At least until tomorrow, at which point he would let Stephanie know. His dick was hard, he realized suddenly: he had been thinking about Stephanie. But, his thoughts had not been at all sexual. Wait, yes they were: *Jeremy JERemy JERemy,* hearing her as she moaned his name repeatedly during sex. All right, he was going to jerk off, he decided, jerk off then call Stephanie to inform her that their relationship was over. Yes they could still remain friends if she wished (he sincerely hoped she would be too hurt to desire friendship; besides, that had the potential to become a hassle, not to mention awkward) otherwise, they were done.

Chapter 47

Karen had her back arched, gazing up at the ceiling, moaning, closing her eyes and then opening them as Benjamin grabbed her body, thrusting himself further inside of her as he squeezed her hips. This required too much effort, he decided soon: wanting to see her do the work, he motioned for her to move on top of him. Realizing, if he chose, he could still be the aggressor. Since he was the one inflicting the pain, he could still maintain the same level of control. His arms were relaxed behind his head, draped off the edge of the bed when Karen started to ride him again.

"Harder, K. Now. *Harder...*" Karen listened then, always seeming so desperate to please him, even if it was at her expense. She bit down on her lip, in pain since she was no longer aroused, her vagina no longer wet. His pre-come did not offer enough lubrication, evidently, since she felt as if he was tearing into her, even with her on top. "Faster." For a second, she considered asking if he had any Vaseline, or lotion. "Are you close?" she asked instead.

"Almost," he said. "Get off." The incidental pun did not register. Thinking he wanted her to touch herself, as he very often enjoyed watching her come as a result of her own fingers, or a dildo, which he had purchased for her not too long ago. Karen slowly continued moving on top of him as she put two, three fingers inside of herself. "*No,*" he said, "Climb off me."

"Oh!" Karen did so, sitting there staring at him for a moment as he stared back at her, seeing the anxiety in her eyes, the anticipation, as she had no idea what might come next. "On your stomach, face the wall."

"Can't I look out the window?" Karen asked, half-seriously, smiling.

"You think you're funny?" Benjamin asked, a question not to be answered, Karen determined, as the smile faded from her face. The rather large window that hung above the Rob Zombie poster would be impossible for her to look out of: it was too high. What she had said she meant as a joke – perhaps his hard-on had depleted his capacity for humor? No, this correlation couldn't be made. He never appreciated the jokes of others much to begin with, much preferring his own, laughing so loudly especially when he pulled one of his juvenile pranks. Karen had grown to find him annoying in this way, wanting to tell him whatever he had done was not that funny, *wanting* to tell him sometimes to shut the fuck up. "I don't have all fucking day," Benjamin said, seeing Karen sitting there not listening to his instruction. Resigning herself to do as he wanted, if only because then this would all be over sooner, she got on her stomach and faced the wall, waited.

This would hurt, that much he knew: he had not had anal sex with her in over a month. In the past, whenever he did her this way, he lubricated her asshole with a combination of Vaseline and lotion. Now, he wanted to surprise her, anxious to see the look on her face, so excited in this moment he didn't consider that he wouldn't be able to see her face, not with her facing the wall.

Benjamin predicted he would have to shove her face in the pillow, if she didn't take the initiative herself. His mother could walk in the door anytime, working part-time as an office temp. The shifts she worked were erratic, though she nearly always came home for lunch. Wait, why should this concern him? Let her come home while he was fucking K. She was fully aware they had sex, in her home no less, sometimes even when she was in her bedroom sleeping, or watching TV in the living room, all she ever asked of him is that he, "keep that bitch quiet, I can*not* function hearing h*er!*"

Chapter 28

Mrs. Henderson wanted to let go of Clara, if only because she couldn't continue worrying about her. Clearly, Clara did not want help, no longer even desired Mrs. Henderson's company. This is the natural course of mother/daughter relationships. Mrs. Henderson understood how the daughter will want to pull away from her mother, just as any child ultimately wants to pull away from their parents, wanting to share everything with their friends instead. Mrs. Henderson just couldn't be happy for her though, feeling too concerned she was in trouble. If not there now, then headed there soon. Clara was spending time with her new 'friends' outside of school, that much Mrs. Henderson knew. Not concerned with Karen so much as with Benjamin, Mrs. Henderson truly believed he had a solid future in crime, having heard that by the time he was a sophomore he had a significant rap sheet already. Always when he was nearby she sensed how far away he seemed, disconnected from everyone, everything, also lacking a certain vital component that most of his classmates possessed.

Mrs. Henderson disliked judging others, if only because the Christian principle stipulated she shouldn't judge others or God would judge her, which she didn't quite understand, because wasn't it written that God judges everyone when they die, anyway? Mrs. Henderson concluded the purpose of this verse is to let Christians know that it's God's job to judge, not theirs. No matter, Mrs. Henderson still judged Benjamin to be trouble, big trouble, believing his motives for spending time with Clara were devious. She didn't believe for a second Benjamin had ever been serious about becoming a Christian when he had attended the Genesis club meetings.

Of course she knew how cynical it was to suspect the worst in him, or in anyone really. But, thinking the best about everyone wasn't too healthy either, was it? That, she imagined, could even be dangerous. Clara saw the best in people, Mrs. Henderson was aware, seeing how she didn't care about the gossip she had heard about Benjamin. Well, she wouldn't be hanging out with him if it bothered her, would she?

A certain part of Mrs. Henderson admired Clara for reaching out to Benjamin and Karen. Whether she fully realized it or not, Clara's excitement to make new friends exemplified how a born-again Christian should act: doing what they think Jesus might do in any given situation. That being said, Mrs. Henderson's concern outweighed most of the admiration she felt. Clara's naiveté broke her heart. The way she still saw good, or the potential for good, in everyone, despite all she had been through herself, seeming to always maintain a bright cheery face. Such was the façade she put on in school since her freshman year right up until a couple months ago. It was true a Christian was supposed to be a light to others, to project a joyful carefree confidence so that others around him might sense there's something different about him. Once this difference is identified, then what? Herein lies the problem. In today's largely secular world, how will anyone know that a person who appears very happy and nonchalant is not just naturally that way, or say, perhaps, simply enjoying what has turned out to be a good day for them? How would anyone know that the cashier at Starbucks is a Christian, or the man with two dogs jogging down the sidewalk is saved? In either instance, it would not be appropriate, or even feasible, to just stop and start talking aloud about God, Jesus, and how one might be born again.

So, she did admire Clara, to an extent, or at least what her initial intent had been. Mrs. Henderson was only a bit skeptical now how much Clara's focus had shifted from saving Benjamin to dating Benjamin. If Clara's intention proved to be more than mere lip-service, and if she followed through and actually facilitated Benjamin and Karen being saved, Mrs. Henderson would be delighted that her cynicism had been absolutely unwarranted. She remembered from childhood her Sunday school teacher saying something from Matthew (or was it Mark?) about how adults needed to become like children in their pursuit of God and in receiving the Holy Spirit to enter the Kingdom of Heaven. Certainly, Mrs. Henderson had to concede Clara had that going for her! One might assess her as 11 or 12 years old based on her understanding of God and the way she interacted with Him.

Mrs. Henderson did have Dorothy's number stored on her cell phone. Ignoring her own ego, pushing aside the distinct possibility that Clara would reject her idea that they might meet sometime soon to share devotions with each other, Mrs. Henderson reached for her cell phone, trying to disregard her cerebral side that informed her that this was all very healthy, basic psychology in fact: the daughter, usually while on the verge of puberty, attempts to slowly distance herself from her mother.

In her heart, though, Mrs. Henderson wanted to call, as she dialed thinking of that silly *mother knows best* saying. I'm not a mother though, Mrs. Henderson thought, when someone picked up on the other end. "Hello?"

"Could I speak with Clara please?" Mrs. Henderson repeated her question since Meem had not responded the first time.

"Who is this?"

"Mrs. Henderson." Then, thinking Meem might not remember her: "One of Clara's teachers from school."

"Oh, yes, I know you," Meem said. "Only it's been awhile since Clara's spoken about you. Well, hold on here a second, she's -"

Mrs. Henderson thought the abrupt silence indicated Meem had hung up. She hadn't though, she simply hadn't finished her statement. "CLARA! PHONE!" Meem yelled. The receiver must have been covered because Meem's voice was muffled, the line filled with static.

"Hello?"

"Hi, Clara. It's Mrs. Henderson."

"Oh!" Clara exclaimed, and Mrs. Henderson immediately interpreted the excitement in her voice as happiness to hear randomly from her favorite teacher. In reality, Clara felt uneasy, if only because she now felt cornered by a woman who she had once so admired, a woman she had detached from emotionally, slowly, starting several months ago. The line was still not entirely clear, so Mrs. Henderson identified herself again.

A long pause before Clara said in a voice so firm and decisive Mrs. Henderson swore someone had grabbed the phone from her: "I'm busy, don't call here again!"

Mrs. Henderson heard herself say Clara's name a couple times, and then stammer, "I...I...," not continuing only because she was shocked over this response, having no idea how to proceed. Still considering what she might say she heard the receiver click, the line dead.

The phone trembled in her hand. Mrs. Henderson resisted the urge to call back, unsure how Clara might react, also not quite knowing what she intended to say. She did have Jeremy's number from the Genesis Club phone list. Wondering if maybe Clara would benefit from a call from him? Their friendship had been deteriorating, she knew that much, suspecting Clara was the one responsible. Mrs. Henderson understood Clara had been infatuated with Jeremy, wondering whether she should remind Clara that Jeremy had a girlfriend. Ultimately, she believed Clara had enough sense to finally see the reality of the situation. Jeremy would never see Clara as more than a friend, most likely even if Stephanie was out of the picture and he was single again. He'd told Mrs. Henderson as much one day at the beginning of his sophomore year shortly after he had joined Genesis club - "She's such a sweet girl, so into Jesus and her faith, I think she could easily become a good friend. I'm just not attracted to her though, I don't know...I don't see her in a romantic way." Mrs. Henderson was not surprised, at the time, saying that was fine, so long as Jeremy made the parameters of his relationship with Clara clear and not lead her on, which he assured her he would not do.

Finally, she decided against calling him, if only because soon he would be away at college. Reestablishing the bond they once had would not be healthy for Clara. Feeling hopeless, Mrs. Henderson decided to pray, a simple vital action she relied on when faced with issues beyond her control. She prayed that God would protect Clara, watch over her and lead her in the right direction. Prayed that He would rescue Clara's heart from being hardened to Him, restore her heart to feeling love for Him. After she was done praying, she felt none of the relief she normally experienced, feeling very strongly that Clara was headed for trouble and there was nothing she could do to help her.

Chapter 49

Jeremy stared at his cell phone and thought of Stephanie - would she call him later, text him? If she did, should he respond? How should he respond? The truth was he had no idea what to do. All he knew was that their relationship was over, how to officially end everything in the best possible way? Most of him wanted to take control and end it himself, on his terms and on his watch.

Another part of him wanted to allow things to unravel as they would, sure the issue would resolve itself if not sooner than later. The problem was he possessed little patience, and also, even if he did force himself to be patient, wouldn't he feel better if he simply took control of the situation? Leaving his relationship with Stephanie behind him? Only he understood it wasn't so simple - even if he formally ended their relationship first, even if he was the one to say goodbye, that wouldn't diminish how much he loved and cared for her, how much he would miss her.

Chapter 50

She had no plans to call Jeremy. Stephanie had already resigned herself to what she believed the inevitable fate of their relationship. High school sweethearts they were, and most likely that's all they would ever be. She had accepted that fully - well, to a degree, actually. High school sweethearts sometimes got married, having children together and living happily ever after. The whole idea sounded very sweet, Stephanie thought. But, they would be attending colleges several states apart, so even if they planned for a future together, planned to – no, Stephanie thought, no, no, they were just kids really. They were still only having fun really. Even if their love had been as true and real as any high school love could possibly be, that didn't mean they were serious enough to plan to end up together, especially in these days when people tended to get married much later, if at all. Besides, about half of marriages do not last, Stephanie knew.

As much as she wanted to claim she was proud of herself for having already pulled her heart away from Jeremy, she felt more sad than proud, sad over how easily, how successfully she had accomplished her emotional detachment. Although, if she had been so successful, then why did she feel so sad? Of course she still loved him, always she would love him. But, why? Was losing her virginity to him the primary reason, the part she had been denying that wanted to be with him always? Yes, she had to admit that in her heart she wanted Jeremy to remain her boyfriend because he had been her first. Unfortunately, she knew the first is generally not 'the one,' the first generally does not last. Maybe half a century ago the possibility was a lot more distinct that a woman's first would be 'the one' she would marry, if only because society had stipulated chaste behavior among women. Women were taught they should wait until marriage to even have sex, and if they're going to have sex before marriage, well, then, that's the man they had better stay with! The here and now wasn't a half century ago. Stephanie understood that. Did that make her feel any better? No. Did that ease her pain? Not one bit.

So, she would not call him. As she turned on the TV, seeing some entertainment news show, she still felt a potent urge to call him, talk to him, hear his voice one last time, say goodbye so she could have closure. If she said goodbye, and felt it fully in her heart and mind, then she might at least experience peace. She'd still carry the *'what-ifs'* - if they both would have been more compromising in their college choice, for instance, and less self-centered with the way they both put so much emphasis on their extracurricular activities instead of spending time together, their relationship may have prevailed. She would never know.

If she felt compelled to find closure, why didn't she simply pick up the phone? She was obsessed with anticipating how the conversation would go that by the time the entertainment show was over she had exhausted herself with this dress rehearsal. She had become so tired that she could not summon the strength or energy to carry through with her plan. How about tomorrow? No, she decided, no, not then, not ever. No matter, she intuitively knew what she must do if she was to stop thinking about him so much. She'd call Kelly, her closest girlfriend who she had not spoken to for any length of time in weeks. Months had gone by since they had hung out together. Now that summer was here, now that Jeremy was unofficially out of her life, loneliness might come.

Kelly didn't pick up so she called her other girlfriend. "Hello?" Lisa picked up after the first ring. "Hey!" Stephanie had planned on asking her to hang out right away. Instead, she waited, wondering if she genuinely wanted to spend time with Lisa or if she only wanted to see her to alleviate her negative feelings – this anxiety she felt surfacing now, mostly because she had finally resigned herself to being finished with him. "Stephanie! I never heard from you after -"

"Oh I know! Finals, you know, I got so busy!"

"I understand."

Silence. To Stephanie's surprise, Lisa was not about to initiate a time and date they might get together. Lisa was going to Vanderbilt University, Stephanie knew they might discuss keeping in touch, though such talk would not be genuine: the universities they were attending were a great distance apart, not to mention how they had barely hung out during their senior year, despite both being on the cheerleading squad and field hockey team since freshman year. Outside of school they had never spent much time together, and if they hadn't then, why would either one of them pretend they were going to once they left for college?

Finally: "Did you need something Stephanie? Are you okay? How's Jeremy?"

Silence. "Shit, my mom is calling for me." A complete lie. "We'll talk soon, OK?"

The question Stephanie asked required no answer, as her tone was curt, suggesting her indifference over whether they might talk again or not. Jeremy on her mind the moment she hung up. Should she call him? She wanted to call him, but she knew that didn't mean she should. She needed to say goodbye, though, so why not call and say what she felt? Was she afraid of her true feelings? That they might compel her to stay with him? She would not call, she decided suddenly, at least not tonight. Tomorrow she might.

Chapter 51

Clara was curious when she might see Benjamin next. No doubt her first problem was she didn't have his phone number. Several times she had thought to ask and then stopped herself for a reason she couldn't immediately identify. She knew he had a girlfriend, was that it? As much as she wanted to get to know him, a part of her feared him, specifically feared becoming too emotionally involved with someone who was taken. Clara could love him, easily she could love him, she feared fully falling for him, though, feared he would not return her affection.

She thought of Jeremy then, who she knew was only a phone call away and who would no doubt agree to meet with her one last time before he left for college. Why had she walked away from him at the party? That had been her choice. Hadn't he offered to get her another beer, or asked if she wanted another beer? Then Clara remembered walking away, and he had said her name, he had called out after her. She had continued walking, all the while resisting the impulse to turn back, to not ignore him, to return to his side, to spend more time with him.

Pick up the phone pick up the phone. The phone: pick it up and dial seven numbers and he will answer Clara, you know he will answer! This impulse she refused like déjà vu. Ignoring what in her heart she knew she should do wasn't anything new. Although not until relatively recently had her resistance been rather consistently successful. What did this mean? *Oh, who cares, stop this! Stop this now! Just call him, call him now and tell him, tell him everything and you know he will listen, he will listen to everything you have to say and then what will he say? Don't call him!* Another part of her insisted she shouldn't call since he would be leaving soon, gone, for God knows how long. She could so easily become attached to him again, effortlessly she could feel such strong love for him, and for what? Any love he might have felt for Clara was strictly in terms of how a friend loves a friend. Any love he might have felt for her was not the romantic kind, any love he might have felt...?

Of course, the idea that surfaced in Clara's mind could not have been feasible, no way. Asking Benjamin and Karen over for dinner some night, how nice she thought that would be! If she told Benjamin to not wear any makeup, if she told Benjamin and Karen to wear normal clothes, if she told them to at least attempt to conceal their tattoos, then Meem might allow her to spend more time with them without so much interference, without the objections or so many questions. If Clara helped to prepare the meal, if the food she selected to serve was not expensive, if she assured Meem these friends of hers were good people who were interested in Genesis club...? When she had invited friends over before Meem had expressed no objection so long as they left by 8:30, if it was a school night, or by 9:45, if it was the weekend.

Clara regretted how she had allowed fear to control her actions. Anticipating Benjamin's potential rejection to her request for his phone number had prevented her from actually asking. Being patient and waiting for him to call was about all she could do now. Benjamin liked her, obviously was attracted to her, wanted to be with her, or so it seemed. Feeling quite enamored with his interest, his attention, Clara failed to consider the consequences of offering herself up to him in the way the desires of her flesh encouraged her to do. When she thought about him for any length of time, she felt her heart beat faster, felt herself start to sweat, also felt that intense mostly foreign very startling sensation between her thighs in her private area. How excited she felt! Thinking about the next time she would see Benjamin, so exhilarated, so full of anticipation! Forgetting about Karen entirely, forgetting how Karen would muddy her joy by her very presence. But first, call Jeremy, talk to him, she knew that would make her feel better to open up to him again. Tell him everything you've been holding in and how badly you want to see him before he leaves. Tell him how much you love him, how much you want to be with him, tell him...

Clara did not want to think of him anymore. How easily he occupied her thoughts, though. How swiftly he crept into her mind, into her heart, soul, making her believe in God again, making her feel calm, happy, alive, *here*. In this moment, thinking about Jeremy, she did not think about the past or experience anxiety about the future. In this moment, thinking about Jeremy, she would gladly forego seeing

Benjamin again. Regardless of her intentions, she knew intuitively that continuing to see him would result in nothing good or positive and would likely pull her away from Christ's light. In this moment, she became keenly aware of that tight, supposedly sacred space between her legs, that small hole that she never dared to touch, at least not in an effort to give herself pleasure. Masturbating: she knew a little bit about that, understood how other girls put two or three fingers inside of themselves, most of them who were sexually active claiming they could "get off" just as good if not better by themselves.

Lying on her bed feeling calm and serene with Jeremy on her mind, for the first time she did not attempt to avoid where her mind led her. She imagined Jeremy putting his penis inside of her, feeling a little fear mixed with excitement, her heart racing feeling nervous as she slid her hand down her body. Closing her eyes as she slipped her hand underneath her white cotton underwear, vowing to get rid of all these pairs of white panties as she pushed a finger slowly inside of herself, thinking them too prudish and bulky like they didn't fit her right, like they were designed for an old heavy woman like Meem, Meem who had purchased these underwear for her in a large quantity as though she was stocking up in case of an emergency, Meem who had informed her that she must (!) wear white underwear if she wanted to be pure in the eyes of the Lord, if she wanted to go to heaven, pushing a second finger inside of herself this time with much greater speed and force. Clara opened her eyes, surprised at how relaxed she still felt even as she pushed two fingers deep inside of herself. Seeing Meem's face wrinkly and bloated, frowning then scowling severely at her, Clara opened her eyes surprised at how relaxed she still felt even as she pushed two fingers deep inside of herself. Then shoving a third finger inside of herself just to spite Meem, to show her how she no longer cared what she thought, to show her how she just didn't give a *fuck* - Ow, she moaned now, three fingers vanishing inside of her now more pain than pleasure now still she pushed harder, further - thinking of Karen then, Karen who had taught her it was perfectly fine to use this expletive to express herself, Karen who she detested, Karen who she presently imagined dead immediately thinking of Benjamin. Feeling nervous suddenly, feeling her vagina tighten clench like a fist around her fingers thinking of Jeremy then, Jeremy inside of her, her fear gone as she pulled her fingers out now relaxing a bit thinking of Christ, Christ's Spirit, His Holy Spirit inside of her as she continued fingering herself, moving her fingers in, out, in, out faster now, harder. Closing her eyes as she moaned loudly not caring if Meem heard her in fact wanting Meem to hear her wanting Meem to know exactly what she was doing seeing Jeremy on top of her now trying to focus only on him: his body that was almost perfect, very muscular and athletic, his voice that was deep and soothing, his strong handsome face, his eyes that captivated her even as they penetrated her, seeming to see into her no matter how thick and shielding she felt the wall she had erected was, Jeremy scaling that wall easily demolishing that wall. Finally after she had imagined him fucking her gently she pictured him pounding away at her, his penis deep inside of her, his thrusts very firm and deliberate - *Ow!* Trying to block out the pain, to focus only on Christ, only on Jeremy and the potential pleasure his penis could provide her.

Soon she felt a strange strong utterly unfamiliar sensation surging to the surface inside her. It felt like a pent-up energy she desperately wanted to release, like she had no other choice, like she might die if she didn't allow this to flow out of her. Fingering herself harder, faster, more forcefully - *"Ohhhh!"* Clara cried out her eyes widening, rocking her hips upward, her fingers inside of her as far as they would go, feeling like she was experiencing a rapid series of convulsions as she stared up at the ceiling, the stars becoming luminous even in the daylight. Looking down hesitantly at her vagina to see what had just happened. She was soaked by a faintly milky white liquid that had seeped out of her onto her thighs, the sheets, and the comforter a little bit, too. Feeling tingly and elated, relieved, she stood up smiling as she walked to the bathroom, thinking she had better take a shower, or at least grab a wet towel to clean herself up.

Chapter 52

He wanted to get rid of her once and for all. Karen - why did he choose to keep her around after all this time? Quite obviously, he could find someone new, and quite easily too. Did he relish the authority he had over her, the control? Well, of course, although establishing this same level of dominance over another female wouldn't take much at all, if he took his time picking his prey. Not imperative to make a close careful selection, as Benjamin had honed his ability to seduce another into submission, destruction even, if he wished that upon her. The line between seducing and his intimidating very easily, teasingly blurred. A young woman might be smiling even as she signed her own death warrant. When he co-signed, a vital act of authorization, she would not even notice, he imagined, she would still be smiling and staring into his eyes pretending not to appear bewitched.

It was true he loved Karen, in a way. He wanted to believe the love he felt for her was special and unique and couldn't be applied to any girl in the same way. He thought of his love as a dark blessing, bestowed upon the worthy, distinct in each instance and perfectly suited to each girl's needs. The love he had for Karen would always be hers and no others. In many ways, he loved her just as much now as he had soon after they had first met.

She slept in his bed. Waking her up would be a chore, he was sure, if only because she was snoring, a signal that her sleep was deep. Such noises she made while she slept! He detested the commotion, the way she sometimes thrashed her body around underneath the covers throwing the covers off her, at times even talking in her sleep. Gibberish that he had tried to decode several times because he was bored and also thought that whatever she was saying might be, like a dream, a key to her unconscious, a key that, if acquired, he could use to fuck with her mind. Never did he make out more than three words, at least not in a row. Why would he anticipate anything else, though? He had recognized Karen's sleep-talk was gibberish from the start, a series of sounds a toddler might make with no real words. When she did this, he felt compelled to slap her, if only to wake her up to see her disoriented, pissed off reaction. He wanted to slap her now, if only to wake her up, imagining she wouldn't even know what had hit her, and if she did, oh well. Perhaps, he could put a dildo in her mouth, using a dirty sock would be unoriginal, he thought. If putting the dildo in her mouth did not rouse her then pressing the dildo's 'on' switch would surely do the trick - Benjamin was quiet as he chuckled, picturing the vibrating dildo in her mouth, choking the bitch with it, choking her until she woke up, maybe for added affect pinching her nostrils together, too. Quickly then, he thought of Clara, as if wanting to dissociate himself from his innate meanness. She helped him distance himself from the unsavory places his thoughts naturally led when he was around Karen for any real length of time. Clara seemed to eclipse his awareness that he was not a good person. So what? Who the fuck cares? Certainly not Benjamin. *At least I am willing to face, embrace even, the fact I am not kind, generous, or thoughtful.* If those were the traits most required for a person to be considered 'good'? He knew he didn't qualify. Furthermore, to be considered 'good', one must be law-abiding. He knew he would most definitely not qualify as 'good', given this criteria, since it was his practice to break whatever laws he thought he could get away with or felt compelled to break. The drug trade aside, vandalism and petty arson were nearly a way of life for him. He snickered under his breath as the memories washed over him. Good times. Damn fine times!

He wanted that fun again. First he'd have to get rid of this drooling, snoring fat cunt currently stinking up his bed. God, he needed to get rid of her once and for all. Clearly, they had no future together. He had no wish to marry, no wish to pretend he could ever commit himself to one woman for the rest of his life. What was marriage anyway but putting on a big show and having a party so you could live in prison the rest of your life? For richer or poorer - what a fucking joke! In sickness and in health - downright silly! If he was to even consider marriage, he would surely select a woman who had money. If that hypothetical rich bitch was to lose her fortune, for whatever reason, he would say bye to her. Well, it was likely he wouldn't even extend her that courtesy. He would simply wake up one morning, having packed his belongings the night before, then leave in the morning while she was still sleeping. Let that bitch whimper and panic when she awoke, wondering wherever he had gone? If he was to even consider marriage, never would he marry a woman who had any sort of illness. Say the woman should become seriously sick while they were married - if she got a brain tumor, for instance, or cancer - there was no way he would stick around, he would pull the same shit with her as with the rich woman who went broke. Unless it was a sure thing she'd kick the bucket quickly. That way he'd have the money. How cruel his thoughts were. He smiled at how casually evil he could be. Did he have the capacity to be compassionate, kind? *Who fucking cares? It makes no difference. And yeah I could be a good person if I wanted,* he concluded finally. Considering what it would take for him to become a 'good' person, even if he knew what that was, he still thought it subjective. Very stupid! Like who gives a fuck? If he wanted to change later, he would, and if not, he'd do something else he wanted.

There were no drugs left. This was on his mind. No random wads of money were stuffed in his back jeans pocket or in the center console of his car. He'd checked this several times. A full year of school remained, time he would have to spend in an institution that he despised, this was on his mind as well. He had no plans for the summer, realizing now how much he valued his freedom, the ability to be spontaneous. "A J-O-B," he could hear his mother's voice nagging him, egging him on as though she wanted nothing more than to see him explode, "You know...a *JOB!* Whyyy don't you find one?" Benjamin would typically leave the room when she would tear into him, regardless of the subject, though not before she could get in a final dig, "You'll turn out lazy! A goddamn inmate just like your father!" Truth be told, he thought he wouldn't mind having a job, most of him thinking he only rejected the idea of finding one to defy his mother. If he had a job he would just spend the money on drugs, he knew. He might also spend some of the money on a hooker, or hookers, the primary problem being he would have to travel a ways to find some fine-assed hoes suitable to his purposes. If he was going to pay good money, straightforward sex wasn't his thing. Craigslist might be the most efficient method to find what he was looking for, although he imagined most of their services would be difficult to find. He imagined the service would be disguised, or at least described discreetly or in code. Why waste money on a hooker though, he wondered? He had trained Karen to let him treat her like a hooker, like she wasn't worth anything more than a common whore. Perhaps she wasn't, since he didn't pay her. If he wished, he could tell her to dress up like a hooker. He hadn't done that before. Was this something to try?

No. He wanted to get rid of her once and for all. Karen still slept soundly, the snoring had stopped, though. Did he really want her to go? He figured she still had a few miles left in her. Everyone had a breaking point, he was aware. If he continuously abused her, wouldn't she eventually work up the strength to end her relationship with him? He felt fairly sure of that, if only because she was a good-looking girl with a bright future. College was something her parents strongly expected of her, or so she said, and since she liked learning and knew a college degree increased the chances of obtaining a good job, she had expressed her enthusiasm about attending. When she went to college, then what? Would she not want to continue seeing him? Soon, sometime during next school year even, would she outgrow him, realize she deserved to be treated well? Then who would he take his anger out on, his hate, aggression? Finding another girl would not take long, but training her would take some time and would be an annoying hassle. However repeatedly he told himself this he still understood how convenient Karen was. He cringed to admit he even…loved her? Yes, he loved her, if only because she was an ultra-compliant puppy requiring his constant affection and direction. At times he was a cruel master, though she didn't deserve his punishment. The times she didn't obey were rare.

Bored with her! On a merry-go-round ride that had no end. Knowing he could get off if he wanted, but he didn't. Addicted to the adrenaline and the drama their relationship thrust into his life - the fights that he inevitably started, the obligatory make-up talks that Karen initiated, rehashing the same words they believed might create some peace between them. Then the sex, which was Benjamin's favorite part of the make-up cycle. Make-up sex was so very fresh and honest, as if they were lovers who had just met for the first time. He remembered their first time had been her first time, the start of their sophomore year.

She had been quite nervous, and he savored the vulnerable, delicate look in her eye, staring up at him as he gently pushed himself inside her. Karen had grabbed onto his shoulders, squeezing the pale flesh on his shoulder blades, wrapping her legs so tightly around him Benjamin remembered thinking at the time that she was attempting to melt into him. *"Benjamin..."* she had whispered his name only once as he penetrated her, closing her eyes as he slid his entire length inside of her. He felt such pleasure, knowing he had been her first, such pride, although he had been disappointed then, even confused. After the sex she had not behaved the way he had expected. Before Karen he had taken the virginity of two girls, and both of them had become extremely attached to him, calling him five or six times a day, texting him constantly, wanting to see him constantly. Perhaps a part of him had been flattered. A greater part of him had been annoyed, though, if only because he felt suffocated by this attention, not wanting the emotional commitment. He had relieved himself of any potential responsibility by extending these girls the courtesy of letting them know up front he had no interest in a dating relationship. Fucking, yes. Attachment, no.

Then he thought of Clara. Was his interest in her only sexual? No, he wanted to use her for leverage with Karen, a way to make her jealous. A way to make her want him that much more when he informed her he might break up with her because he had fallen in love with Clara. He would tell her soon too, not apologizing either, wanting to make her feel unworthy, like she had to earn his love back. He would have a spectacular time with that one. How effortlessly he could manipulate her once he declared his love for Clara. The ways he could fuck with her mind were endless. Smiling, he decided he wouldn't wake Karen up, let her sleep. Let her sleep as long as she wanted, when she woke up there would be hell to pay.

Chapter 53

When the phone rang Clara still lay naked in bed. The fluid that had been secreted from her awed her, alarmed her, paralyzed her. She had not moved for close to an hour, although she had no awareness of how much time had passed. For about half this time she had slept, exhausted. When the phone rang she had been awake, staring so blankly up at the stars on her ceiling that now glowed brightly as night had come. They soothed her even as they sometimes agitated her. The latter when her mind would race ceaselessly, which happened just about every night. Who had called? The phone stopped after two rings, an obvious signal Meem had answered, unless the caller had decided to hang up, which Clara thought unlikely.

Clara did not hear Meem talking in the other room. Meem talked loud almost always so Clara thought either she had hung up or the call was for her. She waited. But nothing. Then she heard those heavy, familiar footsteps. Meem had gotten out of bed, the floorboards creaking under her bulk. Clara got out of bed now too, tip-toeing as a reflex, this being the way she walked when she didn't want Meem to know she was up. Before Clara could open her door, Meem banged on it, only once, Clara being surprised she had even knocked, typically she never knocked. The door swung open, Meem standing there smoking a cigarette, pushing the phone toward Clara's face. Feeling anxious, and a little embarrassed at being naked, Clara wondered who might be calling her at this hour. Perhaps she was in trouble?

Not wanting to stutter, she took a long moment before she said anything. Slowly Meem closed the door, Clara surprised she had not slammed it, thinking she had likely not been asleep otherwise she would be angry for sure, especially since the phone wasn't for her. There was a chance Meem was simply standing outside the door, waiting to hear the conversation. Many times Clara had caught her eavesdropping, if she had a friend over, which wasn't often, or whenever she received a call or made one, which wasn't that often either. Finally: "Hello?"

"Hey." Jeremy! Clara knew at once. There was no denying the connection she immediately felt with him. Wanting to say so much, she said nothing, waiting instead for him to say something. He was quiet a moment, then, "Hello? Clara?"

"What?" She thought her tone conveyed more distress than she felt.

"How are you?"

"I'm fine," she snapped, giving no thought to the question. "I thought you left." That wasn't true, she knew at least a few days remained before that would happen.

"On Thursday."

"What do you want?"

"I don't *want* anything," Jeremy then said he just wondered how she was doing since he hadn't heard from her in awhile.

"I told you," Clara sighed, "I'm OK."

"Yeah?"

"Yes." Clara could feel how much she wanted to continue this conversation. "Now, I have to go."

"Where are you going?"

"To sleep! I - " Clara had to stop herself from saying more. Already she had offered him an explanation, however brief, he in no way needed. "Before you leave I want to see you." There, she said it. "I want to kiss you, Jeremy. I love you! I'm...in love with you." Not aiming to be honest about any of these desires, or feelings, she had expressed them at the last second, thinking this might be her only chance before he left.

A deep long sigh. "I have a girlfriend, we're still...you know I have a girlfriend, Clara, and I don't think I –"

Click! Just like that, she hung up, staring at the receiver as if she couldn't decide whether she felt pride over what she had just done, or regret.

That night she could not sleep. Despite feeling wholly exhausted, she couldn't stop thinking about Jeremy. Her decision to discontinue communication with him had been in the works for over a month, culminating tonight. It would be clear to him now she had no wish to maintain a friendship with him, since she knew the strong feelings she had for him were unrequited. Deep down she believed Jeremy loved her as a friend. That wasn't enough for her, though, not anymore.

257

She wanted him as a lover, a boyfriend. Oh, how badly she wanted to see him!

There was time, she understood, she could call him back, there was plenty of time to change her mind, to call and tell him everything she had been keeping from him for what felt like a very long time now. She could let him know how sorry she was for being rude. She had been preoccupied, lots of things on her mind, most of which would feel inconsequential now that she was opening up to him again, feeling connected to him again, loving him again. *Yes I know we will only ever be friends, that is fine, although that is something I will have to work on accepting, because I want to have you as more than a friend, you know? I want - yes, you understand, you know how much I love you, Jeremy, you know in a lot of ways you were my first true love, the first guy I pictured myself being with forever, the first guy who made me unafraid of forever, the first guy who -* there was too much! Too much she wanted to tell him, knowing if she started talking to him in this way again she would likely end up just feeling awful about herself again. So, she would not call him. She would go to sleep, or attempt to go to sleep. Tomorrow was a new day, anything might happen.

Although he was a little surprised Clara had hung up on him, he was no longer puzzled over her recent behavior. He understood this, mostly, understood what was happening, what had in fact been happening for months now. He wanted to call her back. That would change nothing, though, might even make things worse. But he wanted to see her again! Even if she didn't want to see him, he found himself feeling a little sad, suddenly, knowing she didn't want to see him, thinking the friendship they had once shared irretrievable now. Should he attempt to recover their relationship, if only for her benefit? Or would that be detrimental to her well-being? Jeremy found himself thinking about her drinking. She had consumed a significant amount at the party, and he had wanted to say something but was pretty buzzed himself. He had found himself concluding that a little beer wouldn't hurt Clara, might even help her loosen up a little, relax, especially on this very special festive night. What else was going on in her life? He wondered what she would be doing this summer, how often she might be hanging out with Benjamin and Karen? What were they doing when they hung out and why had she begun spending time with them in the first place?

Soon, he would be leaving. Very strongly he felt there were things he should do before he went away. Nothing specifically came to mind, though. At the graduation party he had seen the three baseball teammates he was closest with. He had gone out to dinner with his parents one last time. His athletic equipment had all been turned in, the last varsity letter of his high school career received. Clara claimed she was well. Jeremy's belongings were almost all packed. His relationship with Stephanie had been left ambiguous. Officially, they were still together, though he no longer wanted to call her. Allow her to make the first move. Sooner or later Jeremy thought she would, no matter what her feelings were she would want some level of closure. Did he require closure? To a degree, since he knew he would feel at least somewhat guilty when he started college if he happened to hook-up with a girl at a party, or even if he flirted in one of his classes. He desired the freedom to act as he wished around girls, and ending his relationship with Stephanie would offer this freedom. Why didn't he call her then? He still loved her, that's why, a part of him wanting badly to continue their relationship while also understanding how unrealistic that would be. He grabbed the phone, thinking he would call her, call her and tell her...?

Nothing, he had nothing to tell her, nothing to say really. Everything had been said, really. They both understood what was happening, what was perhaps finished. Having one last conversation created the illusion that their relationship might be terminated neatly, words like a delicate crisp pretty bow on a package, finalizing it without serving any real purpose as the feelings they had for one another would still be present. He wanted to know exactly how she felt toward him, wondering if she wanted to know the same. What if they discovered they both still felt strongly toward one another, that they had the same concerns, the same reservations about continuing their relationship?

Pick up the phone! Why did he fight what felt so right? Why did he resist doing what he knew might potentially resolve the issue? She should call him, that's why. He wanted her to initiate the entire conversation, her to be the one who felt compelled to open up to him again. So, he would wait. If she never called, then he wouldn't call her either. That was stubborn, he understood, that was perhaps immature, yes. Less than two days remained before he left for college.

Chapter 54

Benjamin did not remember falling asleep in bed with Karen. He felt almost sure he had been on the couch watching TV when he fell asleep. Had he sleepwalked? In the past he had been a chronic sleepwalker, although over the years this mysterious rather persistent condition had subsided. He glanced at the clock. A little past 1 A.M. Going back to bed was not an option. The energy he felt inside himself surfaced randomly, most of the time, very often in the middle of the night when there was nothing much he could do with it. He had nothing to do now. He wanted to do something. What? First he'd wake Karen up. He yanked the pillow out from under her head.

"*What*," she murmured, her eyes still closed, opening her eyes then, looking around finally focusing her gaze toward Benjamin. "What?" The usual warmth absent from her voice. She did not sound or look at all happy or pleased to see him.

"Let's go see Clara."

"What?"

"Say what again, K, I fuckin' dare you."

"Well, you woke me up, what the fuck I –"

"Get your clothes on. I want to see her."

"Now?"

Benjamin nodded.

She tore the covers off her, naked and furious. For a moment, Benjamin wanted to climb on top of her. When she was angry, sex with her was so much better, if only because she just didn't give a fuck and went at it much more intensely, like there was no tomorrow.

Benjamin was not sure what he intended to do once he arrived at Clara's. Obviously, she would be asleep. He did have her home phone number He hadn't been surprised when he learned that she did not own a cell phone. Benjamin was a little surprised that she had not asked for his phone number, though. They had been hanging out for a decent amount of time, what was she afraid of? That he might not give it to her? Was she afraid if she had his number she would call all the time? Afraid that by talking to him on the phone she might become even more attached to him? Benjamin knew she was afraid of him, to a degree. He liked to see the fear in her eyes when she saw him, the fear she tried to suppress. He knew her so well already. He could read her. He understood her and appreciated the fact that she did understand him, appreciated how she had no problem allowing him to take the lead, unlike Karen, who he felt periodically protested his authority. How absurd he found the degree to which Clara seemed to trust him, almost since the moment she met him, staring up at him with that look of blank longing in her eyes. Didn't women who had a strong faith have less trust in men? Benjamin always thought that was the case, now this belief was being tested. No matter, he knew if he wanted to have sex with her, he would have to earn her trust even more, feeling pretty confident that if he attempted anything now she would resist him.

"Are you sure this is a good idea?" Karen asked.

"No," Benjamin said. "It's not a good idea. We might scare her, her fucking grandmother might call the police, then she might not want to see us again."

"Would you care if she didn't want to see you again?"

"I'm not going to answer that."

"What?"

"You already know the answer, K."

"Why are we doing this if it's not a good idea?"

"No more questions." The slight rage that rose in his voice made that final. On their ride to Clara's, she didn't ask another question. Despite having several more, she didn't say another word.

Clara heard something outside her window. She woke up confused, then again heard a noise outside her window, someone tapping, or something thrown…?

Feeling herself become more vigilant as she spent more time awake, experiencing an increased sense of fear as she climbed out of bed and walked toward the window, wishing for a moment there was a man in the house, thinking possibly this fear she felt, often out of nowhere and for no apparent reason, might be diminished somewhat if there were a man present. Clara stood a couple feet from the window now, listening very carefully: again, a single tap, a little louder this time. Standing even closer to the window then, Clara heard nothing, complete silence, then –

"Clara." A man's voice, a whispered shout Clara heard very clearly as her name was called once more. She recognized that voice. Leaning against the windowsill, gazing down into the dark yard she saw Benjamin, and Karen right beside him, a bit behind him. The alarm she had felt was gone the moment she saw him. "Hey!" She thought her greeting had been much louder than necessary. Also her tone had been much cheerier than she had intended. What if Meem woke up? Meem might call the police. Clara would be in serious trouble then, although she found herself unafraid of the consequences, for what punishment might Meem create that she hadn't imposed already?

Benjamin motioned for Clara to come down. He looked calm, and she found herself focusing only on how gentle he seemed, how calm. She was so enamored with him she didn't realize how disarming he was. She should be upset, at least a little, that he had shown up at her house unannounced at such a late hour.

Racing out of her bedroom, rushing down the stairs as quietly as she could, she felt ecstatic to see him, so happy, like how she used to feel when she first had a crush on Jeremy.

Once outside she greeted him with her arms, extending them, having to restrain her desire to run right up to him. "What are you doing?" she asked, unable to control the abrupt joy in her voice.

"You were sleeping, that's what you were doing."

"Yes, but I asked you –"

"What I was doing? Sleeping too, then I thought of you, I had to come over to see you."

263

"Really, Benjamin, *really?*" Clara asked him as though his being here to see her couldn't quite be true, as though it was too good to be true. When Benjamin didn't respond right away, Clara considered her tone. She thought she was being too loud, sounding much cheerier than she really felt, but she was truly happy to see him, so happy she forgot all of her pain and problems. All of her self-doubt and worry were gone, in this moment, as she stood at his side, trying to ignore Karen. The more she attempted to dismiss her the more she noted her presence. Karen had been blatantly rude to her the last time she saw her, how could she forget? Resisting her urge to say hello to her, she waited for Benjamin to say something, to offer some direction, like what they were going to do, where they were going to go. He said nothing. He looked into her eyes, and Clara could not resist his penetrating gaze, his blue eyes that were so serene and in charge, inviting her to continue losing herself in them.

"What would you like to do, Clara?" he asked finally, his tone very upbeat and cordial, sounding so unlike him, his entire face radiating a warmth that had been entirely absent up to this point.

"I don't know, I-I'm not sure, what do you? Want to do?"

"It's up to you, babe."

Did he just call me babe? Her face lit up, and she did not care that she couldn't hide the surprise in her eyes. No boy had ever called her this. She looked at Karen without meaning to. Karen did not react to Benjamin, who was quite clearly flirting with Clara. Instead Karen reached into her pocket and extracted a package of cigarettes. "Would you like one?" Karen's tone was relaxed, even almost friendly. Clara stared at her for a second before quickly averting her eyes, she couldn't risk starting to wonder what she was thinking. That's what always happened whenever she looked into someone's eyes for too long. "Sure," Clara said, surprised she responded this way, finding the cigarette in her extended hand, then in her mouth. Karen quickly lit it and Clara found herself feeling so grateful for what she perceived to be a peace offering. Had she turned down this offer Karen might think she was rude. Why did she care what Karen thought of her? For a moment, she wondered. Karen, who had been rude to her numerous times. Clara thought Karen was quite obviously not a nice girl. Clara turned toward

Benjamin, not bothering to thank Karen for the cigarette, which she recognized was a Newport 100, the same cigarette she had smoked at the amusement park.

Clara smiled widely, utterly unable to suppress her happiness. She knew this joy she was experiencing was the direct result of Benjamin's sudden presence. If he was not here she would not feel happy, would likely feel the direct opposite.

"I don't know what I want to do," Clara said finally, still flattered over Benjamin's attention, his calling her babe and allowing her to decide what they were going to do.

"Well, decide," Benjamin said finally, though not unkindly.

Clara had not coughed so far, as she puffed away at her cigarette, feeling a little proud of herself - *wow I really got the hang of this now!* Then she inhaled deeply, experiencing a slight sense of bravado and thinking how she could not only smoke capably now, but she also had two friends who had come to visit her at such an inconvenient hour. *They must really like me! How could they not, coming over to see me when they could easily be sleeping!*

"There's a playground a few blocks from here," Clara said suddenly.

Benjamin laughed, and his reaction was natural, not at all forced. "What do you want to do there?" he asked. "Push you on the swings?"

"Maybe," Clara said, very seriously. "I don't see why not."

The trio walked to the playground, Karen silent as Clara gushed at every comment Benjamin made. Karen did not react at all to their flirtations, but inside she was seething, not believing the degree to which Clara had changed Benjamin's mood. The last few days he had been his usual irritable self, now he was the exact opposite. She wanted to punch Clara in the nose. Instead she forced a smile at her and took a long slow drag off her cigarette.

Clara sat on a swing and Benjamin moved behind her, "You know it's so late and if Meem finds out..."

"What's she gonna do? What's the worst she could do?" Clara considered for a moment. Benjamin continued before she could respond. "Kick you out of the house?"

"Oh God I hope not!" Clara's eyes widened.

"That was a hypothetical," Benjamin said. "She wouldn't do that, not after all the time she's invested in you. Besides, you're legally almost an adult."

"She could send me to a foster home."

"Has she ever threatened to do that before?"

Clara gazed upward, focusing on the cold steel of the swing set. "Three times before."

"Was she serious?"

"How should I know? She sounded serious, there's no reason to think she wasn't serious."

Benjamin, who had been pushing her gently all this time while Karen chain-smoked on a bench behind him, gave her a good hard push. Clara gasped, smiling, stretching her legs out as she ascended into the air.

"Again!" Clara, having so much fun in this moment, forgot all about Meem, the possibility of her waking up and the punishment she could potentially enforce. She thought Benjamin was right, what could Meem do that she hadn't done already? She wouldn't dare send her to a foster home. Those had been empty threats, or so Clara believed. Benjamin was right, over the years, Meem had spent so much time and energy on her she wouldn't dare risk throwing that all away. *If she sent me away she'd be risking never hearing from me again.*

The stars were out tonight, very vivid and bright and Clara noted their presence as if she hadn't ever seen them before. Benjamin continued pushing her. His pushes gentle for the most part.

"May I have another cigarette, K?"

Karen tried not to glare at her, feeling so annoyed over how happy she looked, also over how she had called her 'K', as though they were friends. Never had she called Karen by her nickname before.

"Ask Benjamin. He has cigarettes."

"She asked you, K," he said firmly.

Karen sighed, rolling her eyes as she handed Benjamin a cigarette. Grabbing Clara's hips as she stopped the swing, Benjamin put the cigarette in Clara's mouth, quickly lighting it, noting how tightly she closed her eyes. He thought she looked very cute. As she was stopped on the swing, staring rather hesitantly back at him, he wanted to grab her and kiss her on the lips, a long hard kiss, knowing she wouldn't resist him If he used his tongue he thought she might, if only because Karen was present.

Clara took a long drag and smiled. Seeing her look so pleased, Benjamin also smiled, finding himself forgetting about his own sorrows and problems, feeling happy that she appeared so happy. As he began pushing her again, Karen found herself feeling resentful, an anger building up inside of her.

"I wanna get off! Stop me!" Clara's tone was forceful. Benjamin had never heard her sound so convincingly demanding. He grabbed her hips, squeezing her hips, then her feet were on the ground. "The slide," she said quietly.

Karen rolled her eyes, feeling a sudden urge to punch Clara in the face. She imagined how Clara's head would twist slightly to the side, then her choking sobs as blood rushed out of her nose.

"Come on," Clara said, motioning for Benjamin to follow her as she walked over to the long narrow slide. Trudging along after her, thinking that he would do just about anything she said, he felt so incredibly horny. His dick was stiff in his pants, feeling like a branding iron, so hot it made him begin to sweat in spite of the midnight chill. He wanted to cover her body with his on the slide, thrilling her with kisses on her chest, on her neck. He wanted to kiss her all over until she just couldn't stand it, pulling him on top of her. Of course that is not what she would say. She'd say, *'Have sex with me, will you, Benjamin?'* or something along those lines. He imagined her looking nervously into his eyes as she smiled ever so slightly. He could not stand this! He wanted to rip her clothes off, wanted to ram his fingers inside of her to loosen her up some, then tear her legs wide open and press himself against her, dry-humping her until she couldn't take the play any longer.

His fantasy did not allow him to realize Clara had already climbed to the top of the slide, smiling widely as she gripped the cold steel handlebars. "Catch me!" Again, her tone was adamant, so unlike Benjamin had ever heard before, at least before this night. He did not respond. He looked over to see Karen, still sitting on the bench. "Benjamin, come *on*! Did you hear *me?!*" Evidently he did not, still did not, at least didn't appear to, and Clara did not care, so delighted by this moment his demeanor did not influence her own.

Clara sailed down the slide before Benjamin could respond, rushing into his awaiting arms, laughing as she did so, wrapping her arms around him, in this moment forgetting about Karen entirely. Then suddenly Benjamin's hand caressed Clara's cheek, leaning in toward her, his eyes locking with hers as he kissed her on the lips. His kiss was so quick and passionate that Clara had no time to respond. She simply closed her eyes, standing very still as she passively accepted his passion. Did he plan to put his tongue in her mouth? Would she find herself unable to resist him? If she turned away, would she regret her resistance, imagining later in rather extensive detail what her first make-out session might have been like? If Karen was not present, Clara knew giving in to Benjamin would just feel so right, so natural. Even with Karen present, giving in to Benjamin would feel right. Benjamin pulled away, Clara feeling most of the anxiety and fear she had felt when she had first met him vanish. He stared at her, passionately, his eyes wide and alive as they rarely were. His sapphire blue eyes filled with an aggressive love for her, calming her even as they excited her with their intensity. In that moment, she felt eternity.

Benjamin looked away from Clara, staring at the seesaw that was right next to the monkey bars behind the slide. An abrupt urge to piss off Karen overcame him - he thought he might have Clara sit on his lap, instructing Karen to sit on the other side, insinuating that she was overweight by suggesting she would balance them out. On the bench she still sat smoking, appearing quite pleased, which was a mystery to Benjamin. There was no way she had missed the kiss. There was no way she could not feel slighted. She seemed to have shrugged off Benjamin's obvious attempt to hurt her. Clearly, Clara was trusting Benjamin. Karen pointedly acted nonchalant as she noted how Clara no longer appeared at all hesitant around him. She watched Clara watching Benjamin glide across the monkey bars, so strong and agile and masculine Karen lit another cigarette and thought that silly, doe-eyed cunt would pay later for trusting Benjamin and for disrespecting me.

Chapter 55

Back at Clara's house, in the driveway, Benjamin's mood changed suddenly. He was very silent, Karen wasn't saying anything either, not caring that Benjamin had opened the passenger's side door for her, offering her a seat in the front. He'd never done that before. It was an act of pure chivalry and Karen could not have cared less, secure in her belief that Benjamin was playing with this girl. Clara was a novelty and soon, he would tire of her, soon he would throw her away and she would be destroyed. She would feel used, like she had been little more than a sex toy to him.

"So I'll see you," Clara said realizing she had left out a key word. "L-later." Clara forced a smile, feeling so anxious over how cold Benjamin seemed now, expressionless even as she smiled so sweetly at him, averting his eyes to avoid her obvious desire to reestablish the intimate eye contact they had shared at the park. He shrugged.

"Benjamin?"

"What?" Benjamin did not look at her as he cranked the volume up on the stereo.

"Could I have your phone number please?"

"I have yours," Benjamin said, as though this answered her question.

"Would you like to come over for dinner sometime? I was thinking it would be nice to have you over." Then, unable to contain her innate desire to be considerate: "Karen too."

He turned to look at her, blankly. "Real soon."

"Well," Clara said, considering, realizing she should simply accept his response and say nothing more. "OK." Clara opened her car door slowly, starring at Benjamin for a moment and then: "OK," she said. "See ya!"

Clara was still asleep in the morning when Meem began rapping repeatedly on her door. "It's Jeremy, Clara, it's Jeremy!"

Why did she sound exuberant, so anxious to pass the phone off to Clara? She probably wanted to eavesdrop and then drill Clara about the conversation once she had hung up. Despite Clara's best efforts to inform Meem that Jeremy only liked her as a friend and had a girlfriend also, Meem still expressed her adoration for Jeremy and hoped Clara might end up with him. Meem was inconsistent in this, however. Sometimes when he called or when Clara spoke of him, Meem acted indifferent, saying, "Oh, him…" or: "You better learn to keep your mind off those boys, Clara, *all* of them, 'cause you're a child. When push comes to shove you're really just a child!" Other times when Jeremy's name came up Meem would say, "*He* is the one, the one you want to marry. A strong Christian man, Lord knows you can hardly go wrong with one of those." Or she would praise him very loudly as she went on and on about what a wonderful man he was, so kind and smart and "he's an athlete too Clara, a great athlete, you know!" On these occasions Meem would talk of Jeremy so brightly and even proudly, as if she wanted him to be her son-in-law, though technically, he'd be her Grandson-in-law She would often tell Clara to ask him out on a date, "Or no, don't! Wait for him to ask you out on a date. That's what girls are supposed to do!" Initially, Clara had been subtle in telling Meem that that wasn't going to happen. Jeremy was only her friend, and would likely only ever be her friend. When the message seemed to continually evade Meem, or she simply chose to ignore it, Clara told her flat out that in addition to having a girlfriend, Jeremy was a boy who would most likely never want to date her. He was too popular and cool and handsome. After Clara had blatantly informed Meem that the chances of Jeremy ever being her boyfriend, let alone her husband were virtually nonexistent, Meem seemed to talk about Jeremy even more. Clara wondered during these times if Meem was trying to annoy her, or hurt her, by mentioning him so frequently.

Clara briefly deliberated whether or not to accept the call before finally opening the door. She thought talking to him would be fine as long as she kept the conversation brief and didn't open up to him. She thought talking to him would be fine as long as she didn't open up to him. "Hello?"

"Morning gorgeous."

It was Benjamin. How had Meem mistaken him for Jeremy? Their voices were quite different, or so she thought. If Benjamin had only said a few words, though, if he had only said, "Hello, is Clara there?" or possibly just, "Is Clara there?" then Clara could imagine how Meem might think it was Jeremy. After all, he was the only guy who ever called her, and one male voice might not be distinguished from another when so few words were exchanged. Several months ago when Meem had noted how Jeremy's calls to her were dwindling in frequency, she had requested a reason. "*What* is happening Clara? *Why* are you not talking to him like you used to? Are you not friends with him anymore?" Clara had ignored this interrogation, ducking into an adjacent room as Meem had continued shouting questions at her.

"Hi," Clara said finally, smiling very widely.

"Did I wake you up?"

"Yes," Clara said. "Well, Meem did."

"I'm sorry about that."

"Oh!" Clara sat up in bed, propping a pillow up on her headboard and resting her back against it. "That's OK... 'cause Meem woke me up actually, it wasn't you, wasn't your fault."

"I was indirectly responsible."

Clara laughed, still thinking about how he had called her gorgeous. "Yes," she said. Benjamin laughed.

Moments of comfortable silence passed before - "So, I wanted to take you up on your dinner invite."

"Oh!" Clara climbed out of bed, wanting to talk to Meem immediately. Meem might not approve of her idea or her new friends, especially once she met them. She might even forbid Clara from spending time with them if she was determined to be difficult as she had been lately.

"I need to ask Meem first."

"Oh..." Benjamin's voice trailed off, waiting for her to elaborate, or redirect the conversation.

"I mean I don't think she'll care really, but it is her house, so you know…I have to make sure it's OK."

"I understand."

"OK." Clara didn't know what else she wanted to say, tell him to have a good day? That she would talk to him later?

"You have a pen?"

"A pen?"

"So you can write my number down."

"Oh!" Clara then said yes, she had one.

After he gave her his number, Clara said she would call him soon, hanging up the phone and rushing down the stairs. Meem sat in her rocker, knitting a quilt that was large and almost complete. She had been fully prepared for Meem to barrage her with questions regarding the phone call, asking all about Jeremy - how he was, why she hadn't talked about him in so long, and when (not if) they were getting together before he left for college. Meem said nothing, though, didn't even glance up from her quilt to acknowledge Clara.

"You know Benjamin and Karen? My friends I told you about?" Meem nodded nonchalantly as Clara continued. "I want to have them over sometime. For dinner. You think I could have them over sometime for dinner?"

"Soon?"

"Pretty soon."

"You have a date in mind?"

Clara shook her head. "I'll come up with one once you let me know if it's OK."

"It is OK, I don't care, what reason would you have to think I wouldn't want you to have friends over? I have always encouraged you to make friends. You just never seem to have been able to. You were always such a loner. Even in elementary school you had trouble making friends."

Clara had no reason to doubt that this was so, but what was Meem's motive in consistently wanting Clara to feel bad? Throughout most of her life, had she attempted to lower Clara's self-esteem on purpose, or had her attempts been mostly incidental?

"How's tomorrow night, Meem?"

"I don't know! You tell me, they're your guests!" Meem began knitting more rapidly then, a signal she used frequently when she felt finished with a conversation and wanted Clara to go, Clara who felt very eager now, so anxious to call Benjamin and tell him the good news.

"What do you think we should have? How about steak?" Clara's question was rhetorical, as her tone clearly indicated she felt so enthused about this selection that that's what they were going to have regardless of Meem's response.

"Reach into your pocket."

"What?" Clara was confused, not following Meem's direction, only staring at her blankly. Meem looked up, giving her very direct eye contact as she pushed her glasses up on the bridge of her nose. "Oh, you don't listen to a word I say!" Meem then instructed Clara to reach into her pocket again, which she did, despite still feeling rather confused. "Feel any money in there?" Meem asked.

Clara shook her head.

"Well, you better find some," Meem said. "'Cause I'm certainly not buying! I can't even afford to buy steak for myself."

Definitely, Clara thought she had enough money saved from her allowance over the past few weeks to buy steak, maybe not one of the more expensive cuts like Delmonico, but surely she had enough to buy chuck or cube steak, the kind Meem bought on the few occasions she decided to purchase steak. "I'll ask them to come over tomorrow night," Clara said, smiling suddenly as she dashed up the stairs to her room. Filled with anticipation, she grabbed the phone off her bureau and dialed Benjamin. She listened to the phone ring until it reached his voicemail. She would leave a voicemail and then she would wonder for most of the day when he was going to return her call.

Chapter 56

Benjamin's face was almost touching the coffee table when his phone rang. In the middle of blowing a line as the phone shook on the coffee table. He hadn't remembered setting it to vibrate, had he done that inadvertently? On occasion, he became paranoid when under the influence of methamphetamine, and something as simple as his phone ringing could trigger him to flip out in a fit of rage when it was anxiety he actually felt when he was randomly startled. He didn't want Karen to know it was anxiety he felt, wanting to sustain her belief that he was immune to such weakness. "Goddammit, K…" Seeing that it had been Clara, Benjamin asked her why the fuck she hadn't answered.

"Because it was Clara," she said, smiling as she danced to music that Benjamin had forgotten was playing in the background. The CD he had selected was a techno mix, a kind of music he seldom listened to except when he got high. He wanted to slap her, right across the face, Karen looking very high and happy, and he would have done it, except he himself was also feeling high and happy now, lifting the phone off the table and calling Clara back.

On the second ring she picked up, sounding so surprised to hear from Benjamin. Benjamin believed the only reason his call had elicited such a reaction was because Clara thought he might not call her back, or at least might make her wait a couple days until he did call her back. After he had accepted her invitation, Clara asked him what he was up to the rest of the day. "Nothing, getting high," Benjamin said, deciding he had no reason to lie - after all Clara knew they did drugs. "You want to come over and do some drugs with us?"

"Oh, no!" Clara giggled, and Benjamin understood this was how she reacted when something came to her attention that made her uncomfortable. "I don't do stuff like that." Benjamin grinned, laughing a little not only because he was very high, but because he found her word usage amusing. How she had chosen to be so general in describing the drugs as 'stuff'.

"Are you sure?" Benjamin asked, forcing himself to sound very serious so she might be more inclined to take his offer seriously.

"Of course I'm sure." Clara no longer sounded playful. "I'll see you tomorrow night."

She hung up before he could say anything more. Upon hearing about their plans for tomorrow night: "Oh, great!" Karen exclaimed, sounding excited even as her expression contained little enthusiasm, if anything she appeared thoroughly annoyed.

"Her grandmother's going to be there," Benjamin said.

"Yeah, so? Why wouldn't I think she would be there?"

"I'm letting you know so you don't act like the bitch you are."

"What about you?" Karen asked, deflecting his comment, or simply choosing to not take it as an insult. "The way you dress...she'll kick you out of the house - no actually she won't even allow you in the door."

Benjamin flipped her off, and Karen ripped her shirt off, as though his giving her a derogatory gesture aroused her. She wore no bra underneath, and as she started rubbing her breasts, Benjamin felt disgusted, not knowing why, exactly. Typically, meth enhanced his libido. Karen bent down in front of him, starting to unzip his jeans. He pushed her away, telling her he didn't want this, he didn't want her.

Softly, Karen protested, "Please," down on her knees in front of the sofa staring at the two haphazardly cut lines that remained on the coffee table.

"Are you that pathetic?"

"Fine," she said, "Fuck you too."

"Didn't you hear me? I said no thank you."

This pissed off Karen even more, and she felt so angry. There was nothing she could do. She didn't have the courage to leave him, and that would be the only real way to avenge herself upon him. She couldn't even manage an adequate retort. Watching him move back to his bedroom, she stayed silent, watching him shut the door partway, then hearing him as he began playing the drums. That fucking asshole would be sorry. She was sure she would figure out a way to make him pay, someday soon too.

Chapter 57

Jeremy was ready to leave. All his things were packed, and he was anxious to be on his way, finding himself feeling unexpectedly happy about his departure, if only because he was excited to explore college, everything about college, with the possible exception of his classes, which he understood was the most crucial component of any college experience. He was most excited about the prospect of going to parties and meeting girls. Already he had decided he would miss Clara as much as Stephanie, although most of him realized how ready he was to move on, much of this realization resulting from his concluding that they were equally ready to continue their lives without him, obviously this was the case otherwise Stephanie would have called wanting and needing to see him before he left, and Clara would have done the same. He had informed them both when he would be leaving, although he guessed they may have forgotten the exact date. Still, they knew he was leaving this week for sure.

He understood Clara was upset, and he understood the general reason for her being so. The crush she had on him had likely developed long ago. It was not at all his intention to make her fall for him, he simply wanted her to know she had a friend in him, that she had someone she could count on, someone to call, to spend time with if she needed someone to spend time with, although he realized how unavailable he had been lately, so busy with baseball, busy studying for finals, busy with Stephanie, who had finally informed him she wasn't OK with his seeing Clara unless she was present. Strange, Jeremy thought, not knowing why Stephanie had changed her mind, for he had been spending time alone with Clara out of school every so often for the entire time he had been dating Stephanie, and she hadn't expressed an objection to this until a few weeks ago, Jeremy wondering now why he hadn't requested a reason for her objection, if she would've offered one had he asked? Had she been jealous of the friendship? Jeremy imagined that was possible, even if she didn't feel at all threatened by Clara she still might be irritated that he felt a certain amount of affection toward her, wanting to look out for her, be there if she needed someone to listen, or offer her support, guidance. Surely, he understood he was in the position to help Clara - the bottom line was she didn't want his help, not anymore, she had shut him out of her life, had in fact been shutting him out of her life over the last few months. It had been a process, and now Jeremy realized she had been successful in ending her friendship with him, at least for the time being. Jeremy believed she might rekindle their relationship, if not real soon, then eventually, eventually she would call him and want to talk and see him again. If she didn't, would he call her? Would he initiate a time to see her? He didn't know, he would allow a few weeks to pass and then decide.

"Bye mom!" Jeremy knew his mom would want a hug, a kiss too, probably, if only on the cheek. Did he not want to give her what she wanted? No, he thought, I am just in a hurry, she can come out here to say goodbye if she wants to. She was out on the back patio, watering plants with her sunhat on.

"Oh, you're leaving already, honey?"

"Yes, you know I have to go mom."

She set the watering can down and walked toward him. "Your father is at work."

"I know." Jeremy closed the trunk, all of his bags were packed and he felt very eager to leave.

"Call me when you're there." His mom extended her arms as she approached him.

Jeremy hugged her. "I love you," she said.

"Love you too." His mom did not kiss him on the cheek, as he had anticipated she would do, so he leaned forward and kissed her on the cheek, very quickly. His mom smiled. Jeremy himself smiled, only briefly, moving toward the driver's side seat, opening the door and watching his mom as she stood there staring at him, as though she wanted to say so much more, and suddenly then she began to cry. "I'll be fine," she then said she would be fine again.

"Oh, mom," Jeremy said, forcing himself not to become involved with her emotion. "I'll call you, all right."

"Yes." She wiped at her eyes with her gloved hand and then waved him away. "Drive safe." She put her hand to her mouth and blew him a kiss.

Chapter 58

Mrs. Henderson wanted something to happen, but what? Some days she found herself on Pinterest, scrolling through pages for hours discovering exotic hobbies she wanted to explore, like scuba-diving or riding motorcycles through mountains. Portions of entire evenings she spent viewing Facebook profiles of ex-boyfriends from high school or college or discreetly checking on her ex-husband. Did he ever think of her? She found herself fascinated that he had an entirely new life, complete with a younger wife who she had already deduced said *'Yes, dear'* or something along those lines to each and every sexual request. *'You want to come on my tits? No? Oh, my face. OK, yeah. I always enjoy a good facial.'* Sometimes she would go shopping to escape. These tended to be the days that weren't bad. Other days she found herself feeling stuck in her home, roaming the halls looking at photos of when she used to be happy with Frank. Her deep desire to have children inevitably interrupted her dwelling upon the past. Only once had they shared a serious conversation about it. The dialogue she had initiated by simply expressing her wish, to which Frank reiterated his total disinterest.

"But don't you want to have a boy to pass your wisdom onto, your business savvy?" Mrs. Henderson had tried not to be pleading, tried to be casual, as if his response didn't matter much either way. Despite her best attempts, she remembered her tone had been urgent, somewhat desperate.

"Don't forget my shrewd stock market knowledge," Frank had said, a bit tongue-and-cheek before reaffirming his opposition to the topic at hand.

"Well, don't you want to have someone to nurture and look after?" she had asked, wanting to prolong the discussion. "You know, have someone to love?"

"You have me," he had said. "You love me. You nurture me. And I do the same for you."

And it was true, she did have him, although that was different, for Frank didn't need to be nurtured, barely ever had the time to be loved, besides when they were having sex, which didn't count in Mrs. Henderson's mind. Clara needed to be nurtured, Clara needed to be loved, but Clara no longer wanted Mrs. Henderson to be there for her. Clara wanted to be free of her, that much was clear. They might reconnect when school started again. Possibly, she'd call her again in a few weeks, to see how she was doing and if she had changed her mind at all regarding their relationship. If Clara still acted as if she didn't know her, Mrs. Henderson would wait until school started again, even though she wouldn't be having her in class anymore, Mrs. Henderson thought Clara would still want to be involved in Genesis Club. She would not turn her back on that, or so Mrs. Henderson believed. She had plans to make Clara vice president, even if Clara resisted, Mrs. Henderson would encourage her, telling her after all it was her senior year, she deserved this position, and besides - *Don't be afraid of anything, Clara, don't be afraid of talking in front of the class, don't be afraid of the responsibility. Serving as vice president will increase your self-confidence!* It seemed likely that no matter what Mrs. Henderson might say, Clara would remain hesitant, and might still turn down the position.

Over the last three years, she had grown more attached to Clara than she cared to admit. From the start she had seemed excited that Mrs. Henderson had showed her such interest, such courtesy and attention. Mrs. Henderson had been equally excited that the girl trusted her right away, opening up to her after knowing her only two weeks. Was her interest in Clara selfish? A manifestation of her own loneliness, her own desire to have a daughter? In a position to help this girl in need, Mrs. Henderson would feel terrible if she hadn't reached out to her, hadn't at least made herself available, transcending the formal dynamic of the student/teacher relationship.

Should she call her right now? Push aside her own pride, call Clara again to check up on her, see if she was OK and make sure she was not continuing to hang out with Benjamin and Karen? They were trouble, Mrs. Henderson knew, didn't Clara see that too? She could not tell her what to do, she understood Clara had reached the point in her life where she didn't want someone watching her every move, wanted to make her own decisions, perhaps didn't even desire guidance or direction like she used to. So what to do? Mrs. Henderson would have to decide soon.

Chapter 59

Karen wanted to see Benjamin die, yes she wanted to witness him suffer a terrible, excruciating death. Get hit by a very large truck, perhaps, or be beat to death with a baseball bat by a drug dealer. She would want photos too, would want to see the agony in his face as he was beat into oblivion. Framing the photos might be a good option. She would place at least one photo at her bedside table so she could see his battered, bloody face every night before she went to bed. She would thank Jesus every night before she went to bed, thanking Him that He had given Benjamin the terrible death he deserved. And he did deserve that destiny. Karen didn't believe in such an ambiguous and elusive thing as fate, but if she did she would thank Jesus for the pain and suffering He had bestowed upon Benjamin.

Impulsively Karen had bought Cinderella peel and stick wall decals, there were at least two dozen of them, varying in size and shape. About half this amount Karen had stuck all over her bedroom walls. Now she regretted that decision, to a degree, feeling like she had put too many on her walls, feeling rather suffocated by Cinderella's perfect pretty face and her sparkly cerulean dress. Right now she wanted to rip her dress off and stick a large object up her vagina, a very large object like a baseball bat, just to see Cinderella's reaction as her chaste hole was stretched beyond belief. She had come to despise that renowned Disney princess. No, despise was too weak of a word. She hated Cinderella, wanted to be more wicked to her than her stepsisters, wanting to see her lose her virginity by being repeatedly raped, just as Karen herself had lost her virginity by being raped at a party when she was 15, held hostage in a room for almost two hours before the man had finally let her go. No, Cinderella did nothing to deserve the fate Karen wanted to see her receive, but what had Karen done wrong to have been robbed of her virginity? Had God punished her? If He was punishing her, what was He punishing her for? Well, fuck God, there was no God then as far as Karen was concerned. If there was He was a total asshole and

280

she wanted nothing to do with Him. For a moment, Karen considered Jesus, the fate He had suffered. Why would God have done that to Him, His only Son? That's right, there was no God. There was no way God could exist, for God was supposed to be merciful and loving, and there was nothing merciful or loving about Jesus being beaten and nailed to the cross, absolutely nothing at all. Yes, God was a prick, and Karen saw no benefit in believing. Jesus had believed in God the Father and look what fucking happened to Him. Gross.

Would Karen miss Benjamin if he died? Most likely a huge wave of relief would wash over her, and she would feel alive again. But, damn it, she so desperately wanted to fuck him one last time, and not gently either. She would want him to fuck her very hard, very aggressively. What an arrogant dick he was! How highly he regarded himself she could not comprehend. Yes, she could comprehend, and it disgusted her even as it had steadfastly attracted her to him.

Karen wanted to die sometimes too. She spent a fair amount of time thinking about death and what a release it would be, a release from the hell that was her life. Did she believe in heaven? Hell no. If there was a heaven certainly she would not be granted entry. Besides, who would want to live forever? No, to die Karen thought would give her eternal serenity, dying would end all her problems, all the turmoil she had experienced and was continuing to experience. Was she afraid to actually die? No. Yes, she was, since she was afraid of the unknown and what was death if not an absolute unknown in every possible way? So, she would live, for the time being, she'd continue to live. Still, she thought, someday she would make Benjamin pay for the hurt he had caused her. She wasn't sure how, but she would figure out a way.

Chapter 60

Is your package safe to mail? You could be mailing hazardous materials and not even know it. Did you know that many common household items are dangerous?

Meem read this sign as she stood in a long line at the post office, noting a few of the items that were not to be mailed. In no particular order she saw perfume, nail polish, glue, fuel, and fireworks. That's something Clara might do – being such a foolish child Meem thought she might just read the sign and dismiss it, or forget it, being lackadaisical. Maybe she'd ignore it entirely, Clara being so disobedient and stubborn, like her drunk mother. Her mother was the entire reason her father left. Her craziness and instability, her neediness, had driven him away. At least he had the fortitude to leave her, Clara possessed none of her father's internal strength, none whatsoever. She was so indecisive, like a piece of clay waiting to be molded and shaped. No wonder her father didn't want to keep in contact with her, didn't want to speak or see her! By simply being her mother's child, she had brought it on herself. She had no one to blame but herself! God was making Clara pay for the sins of her mother. She had to understand that. Her mother who had started gallivanting around town with so many different men, cheating on her husband, under his nose, at first, being so surreptitious Clara's father not realizing how long she had been fucking around on him, having cheated on him for nearly two years before he had received an anonymous call from some gruff-sounding man - "Your wife, I own her, she's mine, not yours anymore. Mine," and then he hung up. When Richard had confronted Debbie about the call she had denied it entirely, simply turning her back on him and putting her feet up on some old dusty leather ottoman. He had followed her into the adjacent room, continuing to confront her, the rage rising inside him until at last she broke down, saying much more than he required. Richard had only wanted an admission of her guilt. Instead, she made the whole situation worse, by describing in explicit detail all the men she had fucked, even giving their names, their occupation, if they had an occupation (a few of them didn't) and then telling him how long they had seen each other, where they had met, the circumstances of their meeting, where they had gone to screw, et cetera.

Since Richard felt anger was far more productive than being visibly hurt, he thought keeping his anger inside would be more beneficial, that it might give her satisfaction to see him breakdown. Debbie might even start laughing, to increase his fury. So he had not said a word. Calmly he had informed her she must be out of the house by midnight. That gave her two and a half hours, which was more than enough time for her to pack all of her belongings.

"Where will I go?" she had wailed, though she hadn't actually been crying.

"Call one of your man-toys." He had walked out onto the back porch to smoke a cigarette as Debbie had hurled the most vicious curses at him. Richard had shrugged off her anger, her anger pleasing him, to a degree. Even with the porch door closed he could hear everything. The door was glass and before her screaming had ceased nearly ten minutes had passed.

In a hurry, she had gathered all her things. Richard not knowing why she appeared anxious rather than angry. Did she not have anywhere to go? No doubt Richard thought she had at least several numbers stored in her phone of men she had seen, or was seeing. Did she not trust those men? She had never trusted Richard, even after he had done numerous things to earn her trust, to prove he was someone to be counted on. For instance, whenever she had an anxiety attack, he was there for her right away, leaving work a number of times to come home to be with her. When she'd received her three DUIs, he was the one who paid the fine each time, bailing her out of jail. He had also bailed her out of jail when she had been caught shoplifting a leather jacket that cost $725, a designer purse that cost $200, and designer espadrilles worth over $400. Sure he slapped her around sometimes, to discipline her bad behavior, show her who was boss. Then too, he sometimes became very rough with her during sex, being aggressive even after she told him to be gentle, slow down. He would push himself inside her even harder then, faster even when she begged him to finally stop. He didn't understand that at all! Richard had been married three times before, leaving all of his wives. He'd gone through a formal divorce twice, and third having been annulled after only three months. He had gotten bored one time, or so he claimed. The second wife was such a prude in the bedroom, wanting him to pray with him before and after they had sex each time! That was enough to make his dick limp. The third didn't know how to cook, not that he required her to cook every night, but damn, a couple times a week? Surely, that wasn't too much to ask. That was enough. He couldn't stand her bullshit anymore, her constant excuses, annoying passive nature, wanting him to do all the work, wanting him to be the man of the house while she refused to do any household chores.

Debbie had told Meem everything that had happened, almost immediately after she had moved out, throwing a tantrum on the phone, starting to cry for a bit, then becoming furious when Meem refused to express any amount of sympathy for her and had hung up. "Thanks a lot, Mom," she had said. Meem had not called her back, not caring at all that their conversation had ended prematurely. In fact, she didn't care much whether or not she talked to her again. As soon as she had learned Debbie had become involved with drugs, specifically cocaine and prescription painkillers, Meem disowned her entirely. Meem, now nearing the front of the line, wondered how Debbie had gotten her slutty little hands on the drugs she spoke of. Did she know a pharmacist, had she seduced a pharmacist, or a friend of a pharmacist? God knew there were such things that happened. What people would do for sex with no strings nowadays, Meem shuddered to imagine! Such corruption there was in the world, such filth! Surely, one day, very soon Meem hoped, God would come back to destroy everything.

"Anything hazardous, liquid or perishable?"

"Huh?" Meem gazed up at the clerk standing so seriously behind the counter stamping the package she was mailing to Debbie. It was a plastic bag full of photos, all the photos she had ever had of her daughter. She had gathered them from her bedroom, the living room, and snatching several that Clara had hidden in her bureau. Meem had rummaged through the girl's entire bedroom, not knowing that Clara had any photos of her mother, shocked when she discovered four inside one of her old diaries from her freshmen year in high school.

Meem had briefly violated her trust by leafing through the pages, though everything she read bored her. She found Clara's ramblings so monotonous and unintelligible. Meem wanted to knock Clara upside the head for every time she read, "Praise Jesus!" or "I can feel the Holy Spirit inside me!" Meem wondered whether Clara would even notice the photos were gone, if she ever still looked at them. Rarely did she mention her mother The only time she spoke of her being when she was provided the pretext of just having talked to her on the phone. "No," Meem said, digging into her purse and pulling out a five dollar bill. "What, are you new? This is an envelope! They're photos! Can you write 'do not bend' on the envelope?"

"Yes, ma'am."

"Do not call me ma'am! *Miss*," Meem said, sliding the five across the counter, having no idea why she didn't like to be called ma'am, no idea why she never corrected anyone else before when they called her ma'am.

The cashier dismissed Meem's comment and started punching buttons on the register. Meem thought about the note she had slid inside the photo sleeve she had put inside a folder. In so many words, the note read, "Dear Debra, here are all the memories I have left of you. Since you no longer remain in my heart, not in Clara's either. All that remains are some photos. So, here, I want you to take them all back. That way you will be out of our lives forever." How would she react to that? Meem anticipated she might be nonchalant, at first, attempting to shrug off this blatant instigation, this obvious attempt to hurt her, then she might be furious and smash a lamp, or a vase, this being how Debbie typically expressed herself when she was hurt, throwing a fit full of rage. Tilting her head back slightly, Meem chuckled to herself as she imagined Debbie hurling a vase half-filled with water against the television cabinet or, better yet, the window, shattering the window too in the process. "Keep the change," Meem said to the clerk, seeing the total and noting how she would only receive a few pennies anyway. As she neared the exit, the only unfortunate part of all this was she wouldn't be able to see Debbie when she received the photos, wouldn't know for sure how she would react. Might she not even care that Meem had expressed herself so bluntly to extricate herself from Debbie's life? No, Meem told herself, definitely not. She will care. How deeply would this impact her life? Meem had no thoughts on that, but she did question if she actually meant to end her already nonexistent relationship with her daughter, or was this merely an attempt to start drama? Meem did not want to think about that last question.

Chapter 61

Benjamin didn't know why Karen had not called him in two days. In the past two days all he had done was drugs, a lot of them, not only methamphetamine, some LSD too. If his mother noticed she didn't say a word to him. If his stepfather noticed he didn't say a word to him either. Not that Benjamin would care if he tried to scold him for his drug use, which he had to know about. He would tell him off as he had done before. Benjamin had no fear about this, knowing he could most likely take that low-life in a fight. At the very least, it would be a good fight, not that Benjamin would fight fair, but if it came to blows, Benjamin saw no reason why he should be fair. Grabbing a steak knife from the kitchen would not be out of the question. Grabbing a glass pitcher out of the refrigerator would not be out of the question. Burying the knife into his heart, and not wanting to waste his time watching that fucking bum die, he would beat his face in with the pitcher, smashing his skull with the pitcher until the pitcher shattered, burying pieces of glass into his face, having to no doubt bend down since his stepfather would be nearly unconscious on the floor, his breathing so labored as Benjamin hoped he would be begging for his life, sobbing, Benjamin liked to imagine the tears running down his face. Seeing his hands trying to shield his face, seeing him as he crawled toward the door, trying to move to his feet until Benjamin grabbed a large piece of glass from the pitcher and slit his throat. The blood he could see, spilling onto the floor, running onto that bastard's shirt. A variation of the murder might be Benjamin stabbing his eyes with a piece from the pitcher, blinding him and then having some fun watching him suffer as he yelled, squirming around on the floor, no doubt continuing to yell so shocked as the realization sunk in that his sight was gone. This would be the more brutal method to kill him, torturing him first, then allowing his death to be very slow, enjoying the fact that he would have no idea what Benjamin was going to do to finish him. Would he plead for his life? For sure Benjamin thought he would, that pussy was so much weaker than Benjamin's own mother, so passive was his nature, so subordinate to his wife. No wonder she had married him, he obeyed her every request. She could say jump and he would say how high. She had also married him for his stability, not that he had much money, living in a trailer, but his employment working in a warehouse was full-time and provided them with insurance, food, shelter.

Such rage inside him! Had Karen finally decided that she had put up with his shit long enough? Perhaps, she was ready to get on with her own life now without him. No, he did not believe that was possible, not a chance. If that were the case, she would have at least hinted at it, dropped a subtle clue that she had become tired of all his bullshit. Never once did she express how much she hated him, how she wanted to move on or she deserved better. She'd never mentioned he had no right to treat her like he treated her. Certainly, she was afraid to move on - her emotions so wrapped up in him that she saw no way out, or so Benjamin believed. For one thing she liked the drugs, without wanting to admit how much she liked the drugs, even to herself. Secondly, the drugs were free, this was a winning combination. Benjamin knew she had no idea whether she had become hooked on the drugs, on him, or both. Karen would not stay away for long, he was sure of that, if only because he could anticipate her pattern. It was always the same. First, she'd become extremely attached to him and then act like she was independent and fine without him. Then, she'd come crawling back. He knew what she would do next, or would not do next. Give her another day or so, he thought, and she will call or drop by, or even more likely just show up on his front door and want to have sex without acting at all like she wanted to have sex. She would feel like she wanted to make things up to him, and he would allow her to feel that way. Oh, Benjamin could be cruel, absolutely wicked, and she grudgingly respected that he made no effort to deny he possessed either one of these attributes. With relative ease, Benjamin could give her what she wanted and end this cycle of dysfunction. Truly she was a good girl, worthy of happiness, but he couldn't help resist doing the right thing by her, giving her what might cure her, or at least make her feel better for the time being. He fully understood how cruel this was, and he wondered if she did as well. Later, he would call her. Now was not the time for impulse. For the first time in recent memory he allowed himself to be much more methodical with his emotions, what little of them remained.

He picked up the phone to call Clara.

After talking to Benjamin, after hearing him say he was coming over tomorrow night and that Karen may or may not be joining them, Clara rushed out the door to buy the steak, so excited that she had a real true friend who wanted to spend time with her! The anticipation overwhelmed her, and she could not control her joy. "What are you all smiles about?" Meem had asked her and Clara, still smiling, had very boldly said, "That's for me to know and you to find out." She felt like the possibilities were endless. Before Meem could say anything, or ask where she was going, Clara was outside, slamming the front door, not meaning to shut it that forcefully. The tattered flowery summer wreath rattled against the rusted door knocker as she climbed into the car. She didn't bother to ask Meem's permission since she knew Meem would say yes. Knowing she wouldn't have a problem with her driving, since she knew where she was going, since she approved of the objective of the trip.

She was only buying steak, though. She was only having a couple friends over. *Oh, this is the start of a great friendship,* Clara thought to herself as she pulled out of the driveway. *This is going to be the best summer of my life.*

Pulling back the blinds, Meem watched Clara disapprovingly as she vanished down the road. Surely she was going at least 15 miles over the speed limit. "Bitch," Meem whispered, clucking her tongue and then lighting a cigarette.

Clara moved down the aisle at the grocery store, taking no notice of anyone. For the first time ever, she did not feel at all self-conscious even though she wore lipstick (!) and a sporty outfit of short white shorts and a cerulean shirt with sleeves accented by sparkly stars, so short it could almost be classified as a tank top. She thought she looked very good: *yes, I look real good, so nothing else matters!* In this moment all she cared about was finding the appropriate kind of steak, knowing that she would likely have little choice, knowing whatever particular kind she purchased would likely be determined by how much money she had. Money she had been saving from her allowance for weeks. A rather small amount of money that would nonetheless be more than enough to buy the items she had selected to serve for dinner: onion rings, salad, salad dressing, and soda pop (in addition to Pepsi, if she had enough money, Clara would buy some Mountain Dew).

Was she forgetting something? Doing a little math in her head after grabbing a two-liter bottle of Pepsi, she decided on a medium-sized bag of barbeque potato chips rather than a second bottle of soda pop. She still had four dollars left. Dessert! Nearing the self-checkout line, Clara passed the bakery, spotting fresh pies and cakes, which she knew she couldn't afford, then seeing the display of donuts, chocolate éclairs and apple fritters. Clara picked out the two largest éclairs, both with excess custard oozing out of the end of each one, then selected the two largest apple fritters. She felt very happy now, knowing she had all the ingredients for a very nice dinner party! Clara was so excited and eager, wanting the whole world to know she had two good close friends coming over to her house, two friends who wanted to spend time with her, in this moment entirely forgetting that Karen had been a real bitch to her. For the most part dismissing the fact that, all things considered, likely didn't give a fuck about her, likely detested her and wanted to see her suffer under Benjamin's strict rude command. Not fully understanding the dynamic of the tryst, Clara could only feel joy, and love, forgetting Karen, focusing only on Benjamin, believing the only way to reach him was to feign friendship with his girlfriend. Did Benjamin really care for her? Clara couldn't imagine that he did, not after the way he treated her! *Kissing me right in front of her! He must love me, or at least like me, have a crush on me!* The question surfaced suddenly in Clara's mind, a question she had ruminated over before: how to get Benjamin all to herself? How to get rid of Karen for good?

Clara was no longer concerned with fulfilling her initial intention of introducing Christ into their lives. In this moment not thinking at all about saving their souls, right now thinking only about Benjamin, how much she wanted what was in his pants. Wanting to explore what was between his legs: his penis, his cock, dick, whatever he wanted to call it. Wanting to see it hard. Wanting to touch it hard, knowing she was responsible for making him hard. For a moment feeling it was wrong, or at least not right, to be thinking about him this way. Unable then to stop herself from imagining him inside of her, making her moan in ecstasy or pain (both?) as she spread her legs and he made love to her.

How badly would the sex hurt? For virgins, Clara had heard that pain and pleasure were interchangeable, the line blurred between the two, often the virgin saying, "Oww!" and "Ohh, don't stop!" in the same breath, or so Meem had claimed in one of the rare instances she had determined discussing sex would not be inappropriate. When Meem talked about doing the "deed", which she rarely did, she brought it up out of nowhere. One time Clara was in the middle of doing the dishes and Meem's hand was suddenly on her shoulder. Leaning in close to Clara, Meem had lowered her voice, whispering for no apparent reason, "When boys get a stiff one - as they sometimes do when sexually excited by a woman - well, they can't think. Yes, Clara, it's quite true, if you don't believe me ask Mrs. Henderson. It's common knowledge, Clara - a boy cannot use his noggin when he has a stiff one because he is only thinking with his dick."

At the time, Clara had not responded. Feeling more than a little uncomfortable and awkward over this sudden sex talk, she had continued washing the dishes, moving a bit faster as though she might more effectively drop or change the subject. "Oh, OK Meem," she had said, slightly smiling, not wanting to offend Meem with her absolute lack of interest on this topic. And then one other time Meem had barged in her room while she was in the middle of doing her geometry homework. "Make sure he wears a condom, Clara, insist on it, you understand? See, I know it's gonna happen, OK, no matter how many times I've told you to wait, I know it's gonna happen, only a matter of time before it happens. But I don't want any grandbabies - not yet! I'm too young, and so are you. We can't afford that so really insist on it, understand? Clara are you hearing me?" Slowly Clara had raised her head and reluctantly nodded. "Come to me and I'll even buy you some!" With that, Meem had gently closed the door, leaving Clara to stare at the door, completely baffled. Presumably, Meem was referring to sex when she had said 'it'. Doing the deed had certain consequences that Clara was quite aware of and Meem had picked that moment to verify that Clara was, in fact, aware of them. Clara didn't understand it, not altogether, especially with Meem sending her mixed messages on whether or not she should wait until marriage to have sex. By saying she would purchase the condoms herself, wasn't she essentially encouraging Clara to have sex? "No, she's promoting safe sex," Mrs. Henderson had informed her. "She's only saying if you find yourself in a situation where sex presents itself as a real option, then at least make sure you use protection."

Clara had felt confused, so uncertain over whether saving herself until she was married was the right thing to do. But now, as she carried the groceries for her dinner party to the car, she was sure remaining a virgin until marriage was the wrong thing for her to do. Oh God, yes.

Karen hated herself for giving in and calling him. Karen thought it was inevitable. The power he held over her was unbelievable, so utterly complete. She was beginning to admit to herself that there was no escaping him. God knew she had tried, repeatedly, and it wasn't a case of her not putting forth the necessary effort.

"When are we going to Clara's?" she asked him over the phone, not bothering to say hi, ask what he was up to, or even mention the argument they had had followed by the almost three-day silence between them. Really, Karen was annoyed that Benjamin seemed to not even notice, certainly didn't even care about the silent treatment she had bestowed upon him.

"Tomorrow evening. At 6:00." Benjamin then asked how she even knew about going to Clara's. He had purposefully not mentioned it to her, thinking he might go to Clara's alone, since he knew that's what Clara wanted even though she'd been coy on the issue, not wanting to divide.

"Clara," Karen said, immediately wondering whether Benjamin would care if she died. She believed he probably would. Not that she was gone forever, he would care only because he would no longer have someone to continually control and hurt.

"Are you gonna pick me up?"

"Do you want me to pick you up?"

"Sure."

"You say that like you don't really care."

"I don't. Well I mean I know where she lives –"

"Jesus, K, what's so hard about making up your fuckin' mind? You want me to pick you up or not?"

"Well, no."

"Well, no?"

"I'll drive."

"Fine."

"Do you want to see me now?"

"Do you want to see me?"

"Tomorrow, I'll see you tomorrow!"

Click! Just like that he hung up, oh how it aggravated Karen that he never bothered to formally end the conversation, never bothered to say 'bye', 'later', or even 'see you later', 'see you soon'. Whatever, Karen thought, I'll deal with that asshole later.

Clara could not sleep that night, feeling so excited that she had friends, friends coming over tomorrow night! She was willing to forget all about Karen's poor treatment of her, wanting only to focus on how they might become better friends. Karen obviously detested her, she had sensed that from the beginning, but there must be some way Clara could make Karen like her. She found Karen attractive, her personality appealing most of the time, except when she looked down upon her, likely thinking she was still such a girl with girlish ideas. Or was that only in her mind? No, she had mocked Clara, not very subtly, either. Karen had been very open in her disdain for religion. Then, in spite of everything else she had been thinking lately, the thought washed over her, *Maybe I still can save her, have her accept Christ into her heart as Lord and Savior!*

Clara sat upright in bed, a certain selfless energy flooding through her. Might she talk to Karen about Jesus tomorrow? *I can't care about her reaction, I have to do what is so heavy on my heart. If I reach her first, then maybe I have a chance with getting Benjamin to believe, or should I do it the other way around?* So full of the energy of the moment, Clara did not feel at all nervous over the possibility that they might dress in that outlandish gothic way of theirs, sensing how Meem would react - "A bunch of heathens that I want *out* of *my* house!"

Climbing out of bed, Clara opened her drawer and pulled out her bible that she had not read in over a month. Two of her diaries were underneath, one was full, the other almost full. Would Clara start writing her prayers to God again? So much time had passed since she had done so she wondered what she might have to say to Him, or if He would even want to listen. Benjamin needed God in his life more than anyone, she was sure she could transform him into the man she imagined he could be, the man she felt God was calling him to be and who Meem might one day be proud to call her son-in-law. Opening the bible randomly, flipping the pages remembering how in the past when she read the bible at least once a day she would sometimes feel she was experiencing what she called a 'God moment'. Feeling as if some higher benevolent loving force had guided her toward the page she had arbitrarily arrived at. On these occasions, finding a bible verse that seemed to be related to almost exactly what she was going through in her own life.

1 Peter 5:6-7 Humble yourselves therefore under the mighty hand of God that He may exalt you in due time; casting all your care upon Him; for He cares for you.

How did that relate to her life? She thought about this for almost a half hour before she closed the bible, thinking about Jeremy – she knew he was away at college now. Even if it was so late at night, she thought she might call him. Then thinking about her father, wondering where that photo of him had gotten to, having no proof that Meem had taken the photo, only suspecting she had. The image of him had nearly faded in her mind. He had a goatee in the photo, she knew that much, and also a very slight grin. Opening the bible then, Benjamin and Karen surfaced in her mind as she furiously flipped the pages. She stopped when her hands came to where two of the pages were stuck together. Licking her thumb to separate the pages, she was immediately drawn to this verse:

Ephesians 2:8 For it is by grace you have been saved, through faith - and this is not from yourselves, it is the gift from God

Clara smiled, thinking about how she was saved, believed she was still saved despite having taken what felt to her like a very long hiatus from her faith, doing a few things she knew God might not approve of. Like not praying at all, fighting with Meem, kissing and flirting with Benjamin, when she knew he had a girlfriend no less, and sometimes forgetting about Benjamin's soul and how he needed to be saved. Not to mention not even caring about Karen's soul, how she needed to be saved, and also how lately she had been thinking a few thoughts that were not at all good or pure. Once a person is saved by Jesus Christ, they are saved forever. The way Clara understood His gift of salvation is that once it is received it cannot be taken back. Still, Clara knew that once a person is saved, if they genuinely believe that Christ died for their sins, they would have no wish of returning to their old way of living. When she finally fell asleep, she imagined Benjamin without the outlandish clothes or the make-up or dyed jet-black hair. She imagined him wearing regular guy clothes, just jeans or khakis and a tee-shirt, and thought what he might be like once she touched his heart with the good news of Jesus Christ. Might they attend church together, she wondered? If so, would Meem go with them, Karen too?

Chapter 62

Jeremy had turned down three invitations to attend parties the first night he arrived at college. After he unpacked his clothes, he focused on hooking up his flat-screen television, then downloaded and installed several university-affiliated shareware programs onto his laptop including two music freeware applications and antivirus software. His roommate had gone out earlier to buy groceries, asking Jeremy to join him but Jeremy had told him he had brought enough food from home to last him at least a week. As an afterthought, he gave him a ten dollar bill and asked if he could buy him some Cocoa Puffs, a half-gallon of two percent milk, and a two liter bottle of Mountain Dew.

His work for the night finished, Jeremy felt a little tired though not at all ready to sleep. He was somewhat stimulated from the newness of the atmosphere, the freedom, and finally the women, the women who were all dressed to impress. While one of the programs had been uploading on his computer, he had gone down to the cafeteria to grab a couple slices of pizza to-go. On his walk back to his dorm, his attention had been drawn to four giggling girls. Ostensibly on their way out to a party, one of the girls wore short white shorts that Jeremy thought he could nearly see through and the other three wore mini-skirts. Now, laying back on his futon, flipping channels until he found ESPN, Jeremy briefly recalled one of the women's bright red lipstick, this one so lucid in his mind since she had stared at him when he had passed by her, his eyes meeting hers, then slipping south to admire her ample cleavage.

Turning the television off, Jeremy knew there was still time to change his mind about going out. Not even midnight yet, the parties he was asked to would all still be in full swing, and although he had no need to drink really (perhaps he would drink some beer, certainly no more than four or five, knowing that once he pushed much past this number a certain threshold was crossed where he became so uninhibited that drunken oblivion seemed almost inevitable) he had a sudden almost paralyzing desire to get laid. Thinking about Stephanie then, how they had not formally ended their relationship, he believed it was only a matter of time before she called him. If not to request some sort of closure then to ask if she might see him, immediately, if this were the case her tone would be urgent. Jeremy had no clue how he might respond since two days ago he had decided she was gone to him. She wasn't who she used to be, he realized, she wasn't the one: so they were done, where they had been there could be no return to.

Should he go out tonight? It was true he did want to have sex, but did that offer him enough motivation to put on some jeans and a tee-shirt, walk half a mile to the university parking lot, and get in his car to drive down the road where the parties were being held? Jerking off would be easier, he was aware of that. A few minutes with his right hand sounded better. After all, this was Jeremy's first night away at college, so God knew an almost infinite number of future opportunities remained to party and have sex. Slipping off his shorts and boxers, he was hard before he had even begun to touch himself, suddenly thinking about Stephanie, unable to think about anyone besides Stephanie. He tried to focus on one of those girls he had spotted on his way down to the cafeteria, but he was unable to see any of them, still seeing only Stephanie, her long blonde hair and how it looked so shiny and felt so soft when he ran his fingers through it, or gently pulled it, as he was fucking her. Jeremy pictured her almost too-white teeth, how they looked so perfect when she smiled, or when she had his dick in her mouth, at times gagging, then grimacing as she gazed up at him, her eyes meeting his as she bobbed up and down on him. Fuck, that turned him on! Jeremy imagined seeing her then with her legs spread, always looking slightly hesitant when Jeremy first slid himself inside of her, then enthusiastically wrapping her legs around him as he pumped himself inside of her. He loved the way she moaned, then he heard himself moan, gazing up at the ceiling as he came, shooting his hot, sticky load all over his stomach. He closed his eyes then, wanting to sleep.

Chapter 63

When Clara woke up Benjamin was the first thing on her mind and no one else, nothing else, not even the fact that she had gone to bed with her bible beside her without fully remembering how she had read for over an hour before she had slipped off to sleep. Then: "Clara, the goddamn vacuum! NOW!"

The smile on Clara's face was not disrupted by Meem shouting from the bottom of the stairs. Clara wondered if Benjamin was awake yet, and if so what was he doing? A few nights ago Clara had vacuumed her room, at Meem's request, Clara telling Meem such a chore was unnecessary, after all the floor was spotless, didn't she see that? "So long as you live under this roof, you will –"

"Where's the vacuum?" Clara had asked her, seeing that this battle was not one worth having, especially since less than five minutes of Clara's time would be required to appease Meem. Sometimes, though, when Clara gave in like this Meem would simply start in on her again, asking her to do something else, and then a third task, very often each subsequent chore more futile than the one before.

Challenging Meem with silence, Clara thought how she would just have to learn she can't speak to me that way anymore, if she does she will be ignored. Clara climbed out of bed and moved over to her bureau, briefly gazing into the mirror before opening the middle drawer and pulling out a pair of shorts and a tee-shirt. Later, before her company arrived, she would change, not having decided yet what she wanted to wear, imagining an outfit that was formal and casual at the same time would be most appropriate. Later, before her company arrived, she would wash her hair with a special shampoo she had purchased from CVS, this shampoo indicated for dry, coarse hair, Clara had been using it for over a week now. Later, before her company arrived, Clara would also apply a minimal amount of makeup which included eyeliner and foundation. Last week Meem had called Clara out on the makeup. Surprisingly, she had not condemned Clara for the stuff, nor had she at all suggested Clara stop wearing it. Instead she asked Clara why she was wearing makeup on a Saturday when she wouldn't be doing anything besides hanging out around the house all day. "I'm practicing for when I do wear makeup out of the house," Clara had said confidently, thinking Meem might not argue with her as much over this matter if she sounded resolute. For what Clara knew to be well over a minute, Meem had glared at her and then - "If you really want, do *you* think I - " then she threw up her arms, grunting in disgust and storming out of the kitchen up the stairs to her bedroom. Clara had fully anticipated the sound of her door slamming shut so was not at all alarmed when that happened.

"Clara - " Meem's voice was almost a whisper. Standing outside her door now, sounding quite tired and winded, she knocked several times, which pleased Clara, since up until about a month ago she rarely ever knocked.

"Come in." As the door opened, Clara wondered if Meem would have walked right in had she not informed her to do so. "I put it in the kitchen closet," Clara said calmly. "Isn't that where you usually keep it?"

"No."

Clara did not respond, again an argument Meem wanted to start that was not at all worth having. Looking away from her Clara gazed at herself in the mirror. "What time are your friends coming?" Meem surveyed Clara closely, pushing her glasses up on the bridge of her nose and then taking a step closer toward her.

"Around six."

"Do they know where we live?"

Hesitating, wanting to tell Meem well, yes, they came over not too long ago in the middle of the night, finally Clara said: "Yes."

"What are their names?"

"Karen and -"

"Benjamin. That's right."

"Excuse me." Thinking of Benjamin again, who had faded from her mind since Meem had obnoxiously interrupted her morning reverie, Clara pushed past Meem who stood at the doorway blocking her, Clara unsure whether she was doing so purposefully or not.

"I like that name. *Benjamin,*" Meem then said Benjamin's name again.

Reaching the bottom of the stairs, not knowing what she might do now, Clara thought about his name, not thinking Benjamin was anything special, at least not his name, it was pretty plain and ordinary, or so she thought.

The drugs were gone. That was the first fact that surfaced in Benjamin's mind when he awoke. The second was that he had no money left. His mother hid all of her money, Benjamin was sure the little bit she had from working as a waitress at a local dive of a diner she kept stashed away somewhere, not only to keep it away from Benjamin but also her own husband, Benjamin's stepfather having taken two rather large sums of money from his mom on two different occasions while they were dating, and then once after they were married. Benjamin didn't know why she didn't open a bank account, which would be a lot easier. "Mind your business and I'll mind mine!" Benjamin could hear her saying this, her voice flat and dead as she offered her standard response when any question even moderately personal was posed.

Climbing out of bed Benjamin thought about Clara then, for a moment wondering if she was awake yet. If so, had he been on her mind at all thus far? What did she genuinely think of him? It was quite clear to him she was enamored with him, but once that infatuation faded, once her Christian values resurfaced and she remembered her initial intention in befriending him, then what? Would her devotion to her faith reemerge, taking priority over the romantic feelings that had developed?

Benjamin would not allow himself to linger on these questions that had such uncertain outcomes. Besides, wouldn't it be more fun to simply sit back and observe Clara, watching her in utter objectivity as she continued to fall for him? He felt no concern or responsibility for what was happening, what could potentially happen. It was Clara who had reached out to him, gotten involved with him. In no way did he feel uncomfortable or guilty when his dick hardened upon considering how vulnerable Clara was and how he might exploit her insecurities to meet his own sexual needs. He realized how stale Karen felt to him, knowing he only kept her around because he relished his control over her, how it had become so complete and final, how she had attempted to end her relationship with him time after time but was always unable to do so.

He pitied both girls, in a way, since both had self-esteem that was obviously low, Karen's having been bolstered a significant amount since she had met him. Karen could easily have gone after a different sort of guy, why didn't she? She came from a good family, even in full gothic attire she was nice looking, and her personality could be pleasing as all hell. Benjamin imagined, though didn't fear, she might tire of him soon, leaving him behind when she left for college. Already she had told him how she would be attending college, informing him of three different colleges she would be applying to. Benjamin himself wasn't sure about college. Really, he didn't know what he might do after graduation - that is if he decided to finish his senior year.

Chapter 64

Clara said she would prepare the dinner herself. Even when Meem offered to help, Clara said no, they were her friends that were coming over and, "besides, Meem, one day I will be out on my own, and I'll have to know how to cook meals on my own."

"Don't you think it's a little early to start cooking?"

"No," Clara then reminded her they were coming at six and it was already almost quarter past four.

As if disappointed or discontent about something, Meem shook her head slowly, standing there stoically for a moment before walking away. Clara heard her labor up the stairs, her breathing very heavy. Normally, little audible effort was evident when she ascended the stairs – Clara wondered if she was feeling all right. Of course, if she did feel out of sorts, Clara would have heard *all* about it by now. Meem was never one to be at all reticent about letting Clara know when she wasn't feeling well, and what exactly should be done to improve her condition. It might have been the cigarettes she smoked. Many times Clara had reminded her how awful they were for her health and each time Meem had scoffed, dismissing her with either silence or some snide tactless comment - "We all have to die sometime. So let me enjoy these last years," or: "Since when do the young feel they have the right to give their elders advice? Just tell me when Clara?"

Presently Clara wondered if Meem would join them for dinner. If prior experiences were any indication, she would not only sit down at the kitchen table to eat with them, she would also insist on grilling the guests, prying into their personal lives with question after question and then hanging around even after the impromptu interview had ended, not allowing Clara to have much, if any, alone time with her friends. This had happened when she had invited Christina and Tammy over her sophomore year. Twice they had come to Clara's house with the intention of discussing Genesis club, mostly fundraisers, and how they might increase awareness and interest in the club. Gradually

Meem had initiated the interview, walking into the living room ten or fifteen minutes after the girls had arrived, saying hi with a slight smile before sitting down on her rocker to start a new quilt. Clara had not seen anything wrong with her presence until Tammy had mentioned something about wanting a little privacy. "Yeah," Christina had agreed, not even bothering to whisper, "Can't we go up to your bedroom?"

"Oh." Clara had been clueless, appearing sad and also a little pensive over their request. "You don't want Meem to be here?" Either Meem had not heard what was being said or was pretending not to hear because she did not look up from the quilt. Christina had stood, then Tammy, answering Clara's question with action. "Well, where's your bedroom?" Tammy asked. "Yeah, that's OK, I guess we can go up to my room," Clara said, as though the girls had asked her permission on whether they could or opinion on whether they should move their meeting up to her bedroom. When the girls had followed her up the stairs, Meem had finally looked up from her quilt. "Where are you going?"

"We just want a little space Meem, that's all."

"You might've said something!" Meem gasped in exasperation and stood up from her rocker. "*I* would have gone up to *my* room."

Then an hour after the girls had left: "Those girls are not nice." When Clara had asked Meem what she meant she said, "Oh, I can just sense it, there's something about them. You know they might not even be Christians."

"Of course they are Christians, Meem!" Clara was bewildered. Raising her eyebrows, she frowned and watched as Meem hurried out of the room. What would prevent this same routine from happening again? If she suspected Christina and Tammy weren't Christians, she was definitely going to know that Benjamin and Karen were not Christians, that they detested religion, in fact. The way they dressed was a mockery of religion in itself. Would she then forbid Clara from hanging out with them? Clara could call Benjamin, it was not too late to call and ask if he wouldn't mind dressing like a normal high school guy, asking if he would let Karen know too, to dress like a normal high school girl, Clara imagining he might ask her what the hell normal meant, Clara not knowing exactly how she might respond, thinking she might just say, "Like a prep, just dress like a prep." But was dressing preppy considered normal? She didn't know, not for sure. All she knew is that preppy attire would be acceptable to Meem, for the most part, so asking if they would dress that way might ensure she didn't have a problem with them, or not as much of a problem with them. What if Meem forbade her to spend any more time with them? That was possible, even very likely. No way would Clara listen. No matter what happened, she would just have to explain to her that she was doing what Christ would have done - reaching out to outcasts who seemed to be seriously in need of His love and salvation. Let them dress however they want, Clara thought. So long as they are respectful toward Meem I will defend whatever they want to wear.

When there was a knock at the door Clara had to concede she did feel nervous, wondering just how outlandish they would be dressed tonight and how Meem would react. Immediately telling them that they weren't welcome here was not out of the realm of possibility, then afterward grounding Clara from spending time with such freaks. Clara moved confidently to the door, not saying a word to Meem as she walked by her. Meem was slumped over napping in her rocker, a quilt spread over her lap that appeared finished. Clara was surprised Meem hadn't been awakened by the knocking. Clara opened the door quickly. She showed none of the apprehension she felt, and was immediately stunned at the sight of her guests.

"Hey, Clara." Benjamin was virtually unrecognizable, wearing plain khaki cargo shorts and a long-sleeved thermal shirt, all the tattoos on his arms covered up. He did not wear any makeup. Karen nodded hello, smiling a little as Clara motioned for them to come inside. Karen wore a pink tee-shirt and a long navy skirt that Clara thought looked like something an Amish woman might wear. Most of her tattoos were on her legs so hers, like Benjamin's, were mostly concealed. She wore very little makeup, only a touch of eyeliner and Clara thought some foundation on her face.

"Well, Clara, aren't you going to introduce the guests?"

"If you gave me enough time maybe I..." Clara stopped herself, forcing a small smile, wanting to keep things as pleasant as possible. "This is Benjamin." Benjamin extended his hand, and Meem stared at him, a little suspiciously, for a moment, and then warmly, accepting his hand and shaking it. "My pleasure, ma'am," Benjamin said. "Dorothy! Please call me Dorothy," Meem said, smiling, sliding her hand over to Karen, "And you must be Karen."

"That's me," Karen said, shaking her hand, reluctantly, not really smiling, which Clara tended to think rather honest of her rather than rude. Meem had sort of bombarded them, forcing a greeting out of them when they were barely inside the house. "I'll help you set the table," Meem said suddenly. When Clara informed her that she was fine and didn't need any help, Meem insisted – "Well, I'm not just going to stay here and eat with you without at least lending a hand." Meem smiled very widely at Benjamin. "*That* would be rude." Benjamin returned her smile. "So what's on the menu this evening?"

"You'll find out soon enough, it's almost finished. I told you I didn't start dinner too early."

Meem dismissed Clara's comment with a smile as she set silverware and a napkin beside each plate. Feeling a little uncomfortable with how quiet it had become, Clara thought perhaps she should start a conversation. What to say, though? She knew one could rarely go wrong with asking a question. Rarely did that fail to initiate a conversation, however brief. Before she could think of one, the oven timer went off.

"Do you need any help getting the food around?" Benjamin asked, and Clara looked at him slightly askance, thinking he was being so unusually polite. She shook her head. "Are you sure?"

"Everything's taken care of. Thanks, though."

"No problem."

Five minutes later, they were all at the table eating and Benjamin had managed to fully engage Meem in a conversation, asking her questions about her upbringing, where she had gone to high school, when she had met her husband, how long they had been married. He'd managed an, "I'm so sorry," when he found out Clara's grandfather had passed away, putting his hand on Meem's wrist very briefly as she spoke, appearing close to tears as she talked about him for what seemed to Clara like quite a long while. Clara wanted to change the subject but didn't have the slightest idea what she might say.

"So he was living when Clara moved in with you?"

"For a few years he was, yes," Meem then said that Clara was very blessed to have known him, even if it was only for a relatively short time.

"I wish I remembered him better," Clara then said she was only eight when he died.

"Things were a little rough around here for awhile after he went to be with the Lord," Meem said. "Clara helped me pick up the slack, though. Even so young, I made sure she was doing chores. At that time in her life, I knew she needed some structure and discipline if she wanted to make something of herself, if she wanted to turn out differently than her mother." Meem leaned forward a bit at the table, looking at Benjamin and putting a hand to the side of her mouth as if what she was about to say was highly confidential. "My daughter." Benjamin nodded his head, raising his eyebrows slightly encouraging her to continue. "Oh I won't discuss her, not here, I don't want to disgrace this dinner table by speaking of such a person, I won't even begin to –"

"Please, Meem –"

"I think it's important he knows what she was like. If *he's* going to steer you in the right direction, if *he's* going to guide you in your walk with the Lord, making sure you grow closer to Him, well, then he needs to know just how much of a harlot she was. An alcoholic on top of that, oh God's sure she did drugs too, I know she did plenty of speed for starters."

Karen appeared shocked and Benjamin delighted. "That's a shame," Benjamin said. "Where is your mother living now?"

"Nebraska," Clara said reluctantly. "Last I heard. She could be in California by now, though. A few months ago she said she was planning to move with her partner to –"

"Her partner?" Meem asked loudly. "What the hell kind of business is she in now?"

"Her significant other." Clara looked at Meem coldly. "She said she was moving with her to San Diego, I don't know if she got there yet."

Meem just looked confused. "What's for dessert?" she asked, looking at Clara, paying no mind to the fact that she was the only one who was finished with her meal, everyone else at the table was still eating.

"Chocolate éclairs and apple fritters."

"Oh, you got éclairs, Clara?" Meem stood up and then leaned in close toward Benjamin, again putting a hand to the side of her mouth like what she was about to say was top secret. "She knows they're my favorite. I like to warm mine up in the microwave."

"You like to do that too?" Benjamin asked, smiling. "I thought I was the only one."

"You want me to put one in for you? You're still eating though…"

"I'm nearly finished, Dorothy," Benjamin then said sure, she could warm one up for him too.

"Oh, he even remembered my name!" Meem giggled a little, moving a hand over her heart.

Clara felt disgusted, and curious, wondering just what in the hell was happening here. Karen appeared as though she might be wondering the same thing, Benjamin being the absolute last person Clara ever anticipated Meem would warm up to. Not only had he changed his gothic attire, he had also changed his demeanor, his personality engaging and pleasing now. The only logical conclusion Clara could come to was that Benjamin wanted to ensure she would still be able to spend time with him and Karen after their visit. For the most part, he was familiar with her strict authoritarian nature, Clara having told him just enough about her that he was entirely convinced she was a lunatic who had used religion to manipulate her granddaughter from a very young age.

"I guess we'll have to have apple fritters then, huh Karen?"

"Not me," Karen said. "I want an éclair."

"Oh, I only got two of each."

"I'm good then."

"You don't want an apple fritter?"

Karen shook her head.

"So are you in one of Clara's classes?" Meem asked, lifting the two plates from the microwave and setting Benjamin's éclair in front of him as she sat back down at the table. "Or how did you two meet?" Meem looked at Benjamin as though both questions were intended for him only.

"I don't have any classes with her. We met through Genesis club."

"Oh, isn't that lovely! Clara didn't tell me her two new friends were also members of that nice Christian club. You know I'm the one who encouraged her to get involved with that club in the first place, since as I'm sure you've discovered, Clara is sort of a loner. She's always been a loner really, just like she's always been a Christian."

"Meem, I haven't always been a Christian. I wasn't saved until I was 11. And it was my idea to get involved in the club."

"Oh, you must not remember then, dear, because I know for a fact I suggested it to you."

Clara rolled her eyes, deciding to allow this one to slide as she started to eat her apple fritter.

"What a wonderful thing," Benjamin said. "That you passed your faith along to Clara, I mean."

"Yes," Meem said as she devoured her éclair, which was already nearly gone. "I think so too."

"Were you always a Christian?" Benjamin asked.

"No," Meem said. "But I always knew Jesus was Lord and Savior."

"I don't understand," Benjamin said. "Doesn't a belief that Jesus is Lord and Savior make you a Christian?"

"Not exactly," Meem said. "You see, I disagree with calling myself a Christian on the grounds that it's more or less a label. Like Presbyterian, Baptist, Methodist –"

"Those are denominations, Meem."

"My point! Denominations *are* labels dear! Just one more way to separate people who more or less believe the exact same thing. You see, I don't believe in creating feuds over something so silly and arbitrary as denominations, which are manmade, you understand? Unlike Christ, who is God-made. If someone asks me what my religion is I just tell him, well, first I tell him it's none of his business, since I believe a person's faith is a strictly personal matter of the heart. Then, I tell him I believe in Jesus Christ. I don't need anyone to give me some asinine label to know I am saved, that His sacrifice for me on the cross is what saved me, is what washed all my sins away and gave me eternal life."

"I tend to agree with that," Benjamin said.

"Which part?" Meem asked.

"Well, I believe Jesus Christ is Lord and Savior. I accepted Him into my heart when I was 14, not too long after Clara as I understand it." He took a slow deliberate breath, looking at Clara for a moment before continuing. "I don't attend church though, and I don't consider myself someone who can be classified under a certain denomination."

"Would you say you're a Christian?"

"Yes, of course. I don't go around telling people I am a Christian though, as I also believe a person's faith is very personal, something that doesn't need to be announced. That being said, if I sense someone is really in trouble, going through some sort of crisis like getting bullied, losing a family member or getting involved with the wrong crowd, start taking drugs, whatever, then I will share the good news of Jesus Christ, you know, to try to spread some light where there is darkness, to try to spread some joy where there's sorrow."

Clara looked at Benjamin blankly, so stunned by his words that they elicited no reaction.

"That's what He would have wanted us to do," Meem said.

"Absolutely," Benjamin said. "As believers, Christ would have wanted us to reach out to those who haven't yet discovered the eternal miraculous gift that is salvation."

Could Meem really be so naïve as to believe Benjamin? Clara wondered, quickly seeing no reason why she should doubt him. She knew nothing of the real Benjamin. She only saw the Benjamin he had chosen to present today, a Benjamin who wasn't too different, based on appearance and apparel and deportment, from most of the prep guys Clara knew, or was acquainted with. Should Clara even be grateful toward him? What she had feared and worried about most - that Meem would forbid her to spend time with them after their visit - had not happened, and likely wasn't going to happen. Based on the way the conversation was going, Karen would stay quiet mostly and Benjamin wouldn't say a word to offend Meem. On the contrary, everything he said sounded designed to please, to cast him in the best most desirable light - a kind God-fearing young man who is very gracious and polite to his elders. Clara felt very unsure, a part of her, also feeling delighted, imagining that the Benjamin he was presenting tonight was possibly the Benjamin she might mold him into being.

Meem stared at him, her eyes warm and welcoming, inspiring him to continue talking about the gift of salvation. He said nothing more as he took a final bite of his éclair. "It's been so nice meeting you, Dorothy," he said as he stood up from the table.

"Aw, you're sweet," Meem said, moving past his extended hand and wrapping her arms around him. He hugged her in return, and their hug lasted entirely too long, making Clara feel uncomfortable, like something bad was going to happen. That was ridiculous, of course. If anything was going to happen, it would be something good, since Meem so obviously approved of her new 'friend' and would have no problem with Clara spending lots of time with him.

Soon after they had left, shortly before it was around the time when she normally went to sleep, Meem knocked on Clara's door. Without waiting for a response, Meem walked right in, Clara thinking the entire purpose of knocking was defeated since Meem had opened the door before Clara had given her permission to come in.

"I just wanted to tell you..." Meem was breathless, as though she was very excited about something, or had just run up the stairs.

On her bed Clara sat reading her bible. "Yes?" Clara asked, since Meem did not continue.

"I think that Benjamin, well, he's an absolute *godsend*!"

Clara looked up at her. "Are you kidding me?"

"No," Meem said. "Why?"

Immediately Clara realized that was perhaps the wrong question to ask. Rather impulsively she had presented the question. No matter, Meem would never interpret it the way Clara for a moment worried she might.

"Nothing, I...you just barely know him, that's all."

"I can tell he's a superior young man," Meem said. "I can tell he'd be, dare I say, excellent for you."

This made Clara smile, a little. Still, she rolled her eyes, imagining how Meem might react if she only knew the real Benjamin, or even a small amount of the real Benjamin.

"Do you think you'd want to date sometime soon?"

"Of course!" Clara sounded a bit defensive as she looked up from her bible. "I'm just waiting for the right time, you know, for the right one to come along."

"Don't you think he's the one?" Meem put two fingers up on each hand, bending her fingers a few times symbolizing quotation marks the best she could, as though putting 'the one' in quotes.

"I don't know, Meem, it's...too early to tell."

"He reminds me of, what's that boy's name, the boy you used to date?"

Clara stared at her blankly. "I never –"

"Jeremy!"

"I never dated him Meem."

"Oh, well, you could have fooled this old lady!" Meem exclaimed. "All the times you talked to him on the phone, all the times he came over to the house..."

"He didn't come over that often." Clara remembered Jeremy, for a moment, with some amount of fondness, even missing him, to a certain extent. Still, she considered how every time he came over it was school related. "We had one of the same classes, and he used to come over so we could study together."

"What class was that?"

Not wanting to prolong the conversation, Clara began reading her bible again, hoping that would be effective in getting Meem to leave her room and hopefully go to bed, which was where she was no doubt headed soon anyway. "He used to come over to mow the grass too, remember?" Meem asked, and the question must have been rhetorical, so quickly did she continue, "A couple weeks ago I found a boy down the street that can do it now, since Jeremy's gone. Not that you care..." Slowly, then, Meem shut the door.

Closing her bible, Clara thought about Jeremy, remembering how he came over for several years beginning freshmen year when she had first met him in high school to mow a rather small piece of their back lawn where it was very steep (Clara always mowed the rest of the lawn). Her heart would invariably race when he came over, the anticipation of him coming to her house and then seeing him out back shirtless wearing his baggy athletic shorts as he went up and down the hill. The first few times she had fantasized about him she had felt guilty, immediately moving away from the window, feeling she had little to no control over Jeremy appearing so suddenly in her mind entirely naked. It had been freshmen year and never had she seen a man in such a clearly sexual way before. Then, as a little time passed, she had begun to fantasize about him again, not feeling bad at all anymore since her fantasies were no longer sexual. No longer did she undress him with her eyes, for instance. Instead, she had begun to imagine how her life would change if she started dating him, how she might be treated differently in school if everyone knew she was dating one of the most popular boys around and if she suddenly became popular herself. She imagined him taking her out for dinner, thinking about how happy she would be, what they might talk about, what sort of restaurant they might go to, and how he would kiss her at the end of the night. Would he kiss her on the cheek or on the lips?

Lying in bed the next morning, Clara wondered what the hell had happened the night before. Of course, she knew why it had happened. Knowing that now she would have no trouble seeing Benjamin in the future, none at all, that much was assured. She could not comprehend how complete his transformation had been - everything designed to gain Meem's approval, and he had done far more than that. Meem had already inquired about Benjamin at length, asking if he was secretly Clara's boyfriend.

No, well do you already have a boyfriend? Is that the reason why he's not?
No, Meem.
Do you think he could potentially be your boyfriend?
No.

Do you have any interest in him as a boyfriend?

No, Clara had said, though really she had a major interest in him as a boyfriend, not wanting Meem to know just how enormous her crush on him had become. Now, sitting in bed alone, she couldn't help hearing Meem's questions again, knowing the answers she had given were lies, offered only to get Meem to leave her alone. Although Clara didn't have a boyfriend, it was untrue to say she didn't think Benjamin could potentially be her boyfriend. Then again, Clara thought, didn't most things have the capacity to be 'potential?'

Had Meem known Karen and Benjamin were together, better questions might have been asked like what does he want with you? If he has a girlfriend, why is he interested in spending time with you? Of course, Clara thought those would be very valid questions, ones she wouldn't know quite how to answer. The truth certainly would not work. Benjamin had claimed he was saved, the truth being that initially her intention in befriending him had been so she could introduce them to Christ. Based on the way Benjamin interacted with Karen, it would've been hard for Meem to have deduced they were an item. Based on the way Benjamin interacted with Meem it would have been impossible to deduce Benjamin's interest in Clara was mostly sexual, although Clara herself had an idea Benjamin did have a certain degree of sexual interest in her, based on the way they had interacted, she thought he might also have a certain degree of romantic interest in her. Suddenly, her door swung open.

"I don't have time for this!" Clara gathered the comforter furiously and covered herself with it, since she was naked, not wanting Meem to see her naked, acting like Meem had never seen her naked before.

"What dear?" Meem asked, hearing her perfectly well only ignoring her as she took a few steps closer to her bed.

"Look, you have to start knocking, do you understand?"

"Do *you*?" Meem asked.

Clara looked at her, slightly confused: was this a challenge?

"Do you understand?" Meem asked again.

Or was there really something Clara had missed? Something Clara did not understand or something she had not done that needed done now?

"What are you talking about?" Clara asked.

"Do you understand?" Meem asked. Clara's face was blank as she stared at her. "The gravity of the situation…" Meem said.

"No I guess I don't," Clara said, dismissing her, not bothering to try and figure out what she was talking about, thinking possibly she was going a little senile, although it was true Meem frequently made comments that were rather cryptic. "I'll come down to talk once I get dressed, OK?"

"Christina's dead," Meem said, still standing at the foot of Clara's bed.

"What?" Clara dropped the covers in shock, exposing her breasts. "She's…she passed away?"

"No," Meem said. "She didn't pass away - it's not like whoops, where'd she go, she drifted away somewhere. No, she *died*! Didn't you hear the phone ring? Well, it was Mrs. Henderson. She wanted to tell you, but I told her you were sleeping."

Clara sat stunned staring rather stoically at Meem then suddenly tears filling up in her eyes as she began to sob.

"The funeral's tomorrow night at 7:00, St. Andrews Church. Mrs. Henderson told me to tell you she'd be there, OK?"

Clara said nothing as she continued to cry.

"OK?!" Meem asked loudly.

Quickly wiping at her wet face with the comforter, Clara finally said, "Yes."

Meem nodded as though all she had wanted from Clara was confirmation she had heard her, Meem not wanting to be responsible for something so serious as Clara missing out on the funeral of one of her good close friends, even though Clara had not been close with Christina really in almost two years. Christina had dismissed Clara as soon as Tammy had moved from Washington state near the very end of their freshman year.

Before Meem could move out the door - "What happened?" Clara asked.

"Car accident," Meem said. "Drunk driver hit her head on. All I have to say is what in the world was she doing out on the roads at quarter past three? No one's up to any good at that time, you know that, don't you?" She stared intensely at Clara who avoided her gaze. Though she had calmed down a fair amount, Clara was still crying. "I don't care if it is summer and a Friday night. *No one* is up to any good out on the roads at quarter past three!"

Meem slammed the door, Clara immediately wondering why she had shut it so hard, if it was an accident, or if she had slammed it in the intensity of the moment, carried away by emotion with what she was saying.

Chapter 65

Where had the idea come from? Benjamin had no idea. Transforming himself so completely had required little time. Changing his personality and acting like he was a born again Christian had been rather simple. The general concept of being one of the preps he understood fully. The general concept of being a born again Christian he understood just as well. What he did not understand much at all is how effortless it had been making Clara's grandmother believe him. Without questioning him much, she had accepted his faith, his conviction. Without questioning him much, she had believed his motivation in befriending Clara was not anything if not pure and good. From this point forward he believed seeing Clara whenever he wanted for as long as he wanted would not be a problem. Whenever he wanted to see her from now on he thought he could simply stop by her house, Meem wouldn't have a problem with his being there. Clara might have a problem with his being there. If Clara knew she had no chance in reaching his heart for Jesus, he thought it possible she might not want to see him at all anymore. Any interest she might have in him as a potential boyfriend might disappear, and along with it any chance of having sex with her.

Benjamin was beginning to see there might just be something to this Christian thing. Who was he to be so cynical? If anything, Benjamin thought of himself as extremely open-minded, so who was he to deny the existence of God? Clara was a good person, he saw that, she was so pure and genuine he had to acknowledge he already liked her more than Karen. Clara would be thrilled if she knew. Karen would fall apart, that was true. By taking a chance on Clara, he had nothing to lose, with the exception of Karen, a loss he viewed as unimportant. He knew he was in the position of playing with Clara, but what fun would that be? She was such an easy target. Benjamin thought he had already demonstrated time and again how cruel and evil he could be. Students at Turner High certainly thought of him that way He even thought of himself that way and although he liked to think he was a person who didn't give a shit what other people thought of him, he viewed changing their perception as a challenge. Rarely did he back down from a challenge. Besides, he did want to attend college. Certainly there were some colleges out there that would accept him despite his mediocre grades. He thought given his background, he would qualify for a decent amount of money toward college. He didn't want to be stuck in this trailer for the rest of his life. Lately, he had been thinking he wanted to make something of himself. He knew he wouldn't have much of a chance to improve his future if he didn't attend college, and he certainly didn't want to spend his days in prison, which he thought was his destination if he didn't stop selling drugs. One day, he thought he might even make the decision to be drug-free.

Benjamin thought about how much he wanted to make love to Clara, in this moment. Wanted to change his ways and be saved as Clara insisted he could be if only he would accept Christ's love for him. This would be a difficult task, he understood that, for how could he possibly allow anyone, especially a dead man who professed to be the Messiah, the Son of God, love him when he didn't even love himself? What would Clara look like naked? He thought she would look hot. What would she look like as she was losing her virginity to him? He thought she would look desperately sexy.

What was Karen up to? He thought he might give her a call, if only because he was a little horny and having sex with her would be better than masturbating. If he pictured Clara when he was having sex with her, he would come in a very short time. He wasn't trying to impress Karen with his sexual prowess. She came only rarely when she was with him, and this didn't bother him, for he put very little effort into it. All he cared about was getting off himself. Last night they had had sex after Clara's, and he lasted a couple minutes, unable to get Clara off his mind. This had happened several times before. Karen had left soon after the sex. How discontent she'd appeared afterward as Benjamin listened to music, Benjamin on the verge of sleeping not acknowledging she was there in bed with him at all. Unable to recall when she had left, Benjamin thought he must have been asleep when she took off. She must have been livid to have made such a decision, for Karen liked sharing a bed with someone. Benjamin thought one of the reasons she put up with him was so she had someone to share a bed with, Karen telling him once her parents argued quite often and she surmised a divorce was imminent. She might have been making this up, though. Many times Benjamin had met her parents and never had there seemed to be any friction or strife between them. Always they had seemed pleasant and happy around each other. In an effort to gain his mercy and compassion, he knew making a story up was something she would do, had in fact done a couple times before. She had told him once she was molested by a priest when she was 10 and how she felt she had PTSD now. Another time she'd told him how she had nightmares and could seldom sleep when she wasn't with him. How weak she was, Benjamin thought, for all her bravado. Clara was likely stronger, or had the potential to be stronger, if only because of her faith. How infuriated Karen would be if she knew he held Clara in higher regard. If Benjamin said most of the thoughts that went through his mind when he was around Karen, she would be devastated. He already hurt her on a regular basis, sometimes purposefully, other times incidentally, but she stayed with him, the stupid girl. Most of her thoughts were put there by him. She scoffed at Christianity and made such a show of her disdain for religion only because he himself repeatedly expressed such a disdain. If left alone with her own thoughts, Benjamin didn't know what she would believe and didn't think she would know either. She emulated his gothic style very closely. It was only months after she had met him that she began dressing that way, though not very well, Benjamin thought. She had a poor fashion sense. She also started doing drugs after she met him, skipping class, changing the way she talked. Once, she had expressed her belief that the world would soon be destroyed from a nuclear bomb, with no evidence to back up her statement, making the statement out of nowhere, then saying that's all the more reason they should "live and let live, 'cause you never know when the end will be here." He wouldn't have been so annoyed with her if a month prior he hadn't expressed a similar belief, telling her he was sure an asteroid would obliterate the earth very soon, for he had seen a program on the Discovery Channel about a panel of extreme nihilistic meteorologists and psychics who claimed to have proof for the existence of an asteroid hovering not too far above earth. With special equipment they had invented themselves, which neither NASA or the United States government had access to, they said they had photos of this enormous asteroid showing its directional orbit bringing it on a collision course with the Earth within two years, "the asteroid could be only months away, and we have proof!" At the time, Karen had shrugged her shoulders, Benjamin thinking it was likely she hadn't even been listening to him as he had been speaking, had simply been looking out the window on the way to school smoking her cigarette. This is another quality of hers that irritated him. When she spoke, she acted like it was of the utmost importance, that one would be foolish not to listen. When he spoke, unless he was angry at her and she wanted to be on good terms again with him, she acted like she was listening a lot of the time only she wasn't. The reason he knew she wasn't was because later on in the conversation when he would ask her a question or say something else, she would say, "I'm sorry, what?" or, "I wasn't listening, can you go back a little bit?"

Realizing now he had spent more time hate-fucking her than he had actually making love to her, Benjamin thought maybe he would call her. Why not a few more hate-fucks before he decided to make it official he liked Clara and wanted to be free of her?

Chapter 66

Debbie had received the photos, initially not knowing how to interpret the package, inspecting it, at first, no clue why her mother would be sending her anything in the mail. With the exception of sending cards on Christmas and Easter, Meem never sent her anything. Meem didn't acknowledge her birthday, telling her when she was still in high school, "Debra, it's another year of life, *that* is the gift God has given you and if God has given you a gift, *I* certainly don't need to be giving you one, nor should you expect one from anyone else. Besides, presents on your birthday? Come on, that's kid's stuff."

Afraid to open the package, she had allowed it to sit on the kitchen counter for three days. Finally, curiosity got the best of her, nearly cancelling out the impending sense of dread she felt. Once the package was opened, she didn't know exactly what to make of it. Dozens of photos of her from the time she was a baby all the way up to her high school graduation? Soon she understood though, thinking what a vindictive bitch her mother was. She'd sent her a subtle message that she wanted no memory of her, wanted to do all she possibly could to take a first step in removing the memory of Debbie from her life.

What to send in return? Nothing was required, of course. Nothing would be preferable, but Debbie was one who appreciated humor in all its forms. Sending her mother a note that said, "GOODBYE MOTHER" would sound nonchalant and her mother would have little choice but to believe Debbie really didn't care about her, didn't care that her mother wanted to terminate their relationship, which was nonexistent. Some years, if Debbie was feeling guilty about something, she would send her mother a birthday card. Some years when she felt monstrously guilty, she might even send Dorothy a Christmas or Easter card. Never did she send all three cards in one year. Seldom did she send two cards in one year. Typically one per year, Christmas being her favorite time to send cards, as that holiday she associated with drinking a lot, merriment, partying. On occasion, they talked on the phone, their calls normally very short, Dorothy asking her a litany of questions before passing the phone to Clara in a desperate effort to gather as much information on her daughter as possible without engaging in an actual conversation. She did this because she was nosy, Debbie knew. She had done that to her in high school, harassing her with questions the moment she got in the door.

Debbie had no interest in calling Clara, or in trying to establish any real relationship with her beyond the perfunctory kind. Sufficient to call her once every other month, right? Besides, couldn't Clara call her once in awhile? The last few months she had not called at all. Usually, she called her mother once every other week, at the very least, sustaining, or at least attempting to sustain, a conversation with her. Even when she had nothing to say, she would talk, asking Debbie questions that kind of reminded her of Dorothy, the way she asked question after question, seeming desperate to know what was going on with her. Besides, Clara was out of her life, Debbie understood soon she would graduate (was she going to be a senior or a junior?) and then maybe going on to college or, if not, be married and have kids. Debbie had not been there for Clara since she was taken out of her home by Children and Youth, an organization in Pennsylvania that investigates all allegations of child abuse or an unstable home life, like parents using drugs in the home, which was what happened in Debbie's case. Over the years, even after Clara learned what had happened with her, she didn't seem to be bitter regarding why she wasn't with her mother from such a young age. Since Meem did not support her visiting Debbie until she was "well-developed" and "not so impressionable", Clara did not make the trip to visit her mother until she was fourteen. This first visit Clara had sobbed for a good long while, wanting to cry on her mother's shoulder, which irritated Debbie immensely. Debbie wanted to push Clara off, this girl she did not know or recognize, and had no real interest in seeing, at least at the time. She was revolted by Clara's profound religious beliefs, which Debbie believed was nothing more than Meem, who she believed was batty to start with, indoctrinating her, pounding this idea into her of being saved by Jesus Christ. "Don't you want to be saved, mom?" Clara had asked her at least three times because her mom had said no each time, Clara being so persistent had asked her again and again before finally giving up. "I have my own idea of God, everyone does, at least a little. I don't need anyone to save me. I believe in God and that's all that counts," Dorothy had said.

"Do you believe in Jesus?" Clara had asked.

When Debbie had said yes, Clara had asked her if she understood the extent of his sacrifice for her. "Let's stop talking about this," Debbie had said firmly, then walked away telling Clara the visit was over. After that, Clara wrote her several cards wanting to discuss Jesus and her faith. When Debbie didn't respond to the first card, Clara had written another, and another. Finally, she had stopped. "She's not a good person, Clara," Meem had said. "I told you how many times, she is a promiscuous drunk."

Clara had started to cry when Meem referred to her mother this way, storming out of the room but not before Meem said, "Well, what, dear? Don't you want me to tell you the *truth*? Why you would want to associate with such a person is beyond me!" Then later when Clara took a glass of iced tea up to Meem to take her pills with, Meem had said, "I suggest you stop seeing her." With only one small lamp in the room, Meem could tell Clara had been crying. She felt no sympathy for the girl. After all she was just doing what was in Clara's best interest, trying to save her from her mother, from becoming like her mother. *If she only knew all the heartache and trouble I am saving her from she'd thank me,* Meem thought. At last Clara discovered for herself that her mother really wanted nothing to do with her. After visiting her four or five times, trying to establish a connection, however small, Clara stopped seeing her, calling her one day informing her she wouldn't be coming anymore, Meem in the background whispering, "You're doing the right thing, Clara, you're doing the right thing." When Debbie confronted her daughter, saying, "I know that old woman put you up to this, I know she did," Clara said nothing, told her mother she had to go and maybe she'd call her some other time. "Maybe?" Debbie had asked. "Maybe!" Sensing her mother was becoming angry, Clara had hung up and then two weeks later when she had called her mother there had been dead silence on the other end. *If she doesn't want to see me,* Debbie thought, *then I don't want to really talk with her and our relationship, no matter how shitty, should be over.* After the phone call, occurring when Clara was 16, she never visited her mother again. Now, Debbie somewhat regretted not having been a better mother, for now that she had broken up with her partner, who had lived with her for nearly two years, she was somewhat lonely, being unemployed and trying to get sober with little to no success. It was the alcohol that had such a grip on her, marijuana too, though she would tell anyone marijuana was not addictive and should be legalized, so in her mind it didn't count as a drug. Sometimes, she did want to have a relationship with Clara. What use was it, though? She lived so far away and was getting older now so Debbie didn't think it was worth the trouble. Clara didn't need her and most of Debbie wanted to just forget she ever had a daughter.

Deciding at last she wouldn't send the note that said 'GOODBYE MOTHER' after thinking about it, Debbie didn't know what she would do today. She had no desire to work, and no desire to date men again. When she had applied for disability a few years ago, she had been approved, to her surprise. Her numerous hospitalizations for mental health issues accounted for the approval. So, why would she want to work? Between the money she received for food and housing and the money for social security, she was able to get by.

The photos were scattered across the kitchen counter. As Debbie looked at each one, each photo, besides the ones that were taken when she was a baby and a small girl, a certain specific memory was evoked, and she wondered what had happened to her, why she had gone down the wrong path in her life, thinking about how she might veer back onto the straight and narrow. This would take too much effort, she thought. Drinking was her favorite pastime, and if it made her die when she was still relatively young, she figured her life hadn't been too bad. There were parts of her life that were very good when she had been very happy. For years Debbie blamed her mother, calling her drunk sometimes in the middle of the night when she had received one of her five DUIs and yelling at her, starting a long heated argument about how Dorothy had been too strict and conservative, trying to control Debbie and not allowing her to date guys until she was out of the house, making her go to church all those years, even though her father never went to church, her brother never made to go to church either, and all those reasons accounted for why she had decided to rebel when she went to college. Two months into the first semester she had dropped out, thinking all she wanted to do in college was party. She had been failing most of her classes, and since she was paying for college on her own, having taken out a substantial loan she wouldn't have the money to pay back, not since she didn't plan to graduate, thinking she had the brains but not the focus or concentration. Also, she told Dorothy how her father had molested her from the time she was eight until she was 12, doing everything with her besides raping her, telling Dorothy how she believed she had known almost from the beginning, and all she had ever done was turn her head the other way, not wanting to get her husband in trouble, thinking her husband might beat her or something worse if he found out she had talked to the police, found out she had betrayed him. Dorothy relied on him for money, and that was reason enough for her to keep quiet, believing she could never survive without him. All this was true. Debbie had been molested and Dorothy had let it go on for years, too afraid to say anything, too subservient to confront her husband. Finally Dorothy had apologized on the phone. Debbie couldn't tell if she was on the verge of crying, "Apology not accepted," Debbie had said and hung up, knowing afterward how she should forgive her mother, if only for her own sake, knowing that bitterness and anger would poison her if she didn't forgive. Most of her feelings she numbed with drugs and alcohol, any feelings that remained she numbed with men. Her relationships typically lasted only a short while, Debbie tiring of one man very quickly, then feeling she had to move on to a new man. She couldn't get past feeling so disgusted after she had sex with the majority of them, thinking of her father most of the time, thinking she had likely only been able to have sex with all the men she did because she was high or drunk.

After looking at the photos a second time, going through them more quickly, she realized she didn't have any good memories. Any memory she had that made her smile or almost smile was soured by what her father had done to her and how she perceived Dorothy was still responsible for the way she had turned out. She began cutting each of the photos, then, with scissors. After a while, she thought this would take too long, so she set them all into a garbage bag, tying the bag and throwing it outside into the garbage can. The man who collected trash would come tomorrow. An hour or so after she had gotten rid of the photos, she wanted to dig them out of the trash, thinking about how her entire life up until age 19 was essentially in the trash bag. Thinking about how she was, in a way, getting rid of her life. Tomorrow couldn't come fast enough.

Chapter 67

No longer could Clara keep her feelings for Benjamin to herself. She had to tell someone. She would tell Meem since she could tell Meem. The old woman approved of him, that much was certain. What was unclear to Clara is Benjamin's sincerity in most of what he had said at the dinner table. Certainly, he had been disingenuous, that much Clara knew. The question was to what degree? No doubt Benjamin had a thorough understanding of Christ and salvation and Christianity in general, the question was how much did he believe?

Wanting to see him right now, Clara reached for the phone. No, wait, this was the impulsive Clara, the new Clara thought things through, did not make rash decisions. Benjamin liked her too, had feelings for her, she believed that. It wasn't long ago when she didn't believe that, wondering what Benjamin wanted with her, why he seemed to have an interest in her, in spending time with her, getting to know her. Not long ago she thought she should give up on Benjamin, thought he was only out to mock her faith and ridicule her in the process. She had processed the possibility that Benjamin was being manipulative, playing along and pretending he was a Christian, or wanted to be a Christian, in hopes that she would sleep with him. Some boys were like that, Clara knew, and she didn't put it past Benjamin that he might be like that. As much as she didn't want to be cynical, as much as she wanted to believe that Benjamin had no ulterior motive in wanting to spend more time with her, she knew he might just be using her for sex and to make Karen jealous. From the beginning, she sensed he had a sexual interest in her, and soon that suspicion was confirmed. From the time she had first met them she had also seen how much he liked hurting Karen, although she still couldn't understand why he behaved this way. Perhaps he liked the power, feeling like he could control Karen, her emotions.

She reached for the phone, immediately sensing this might be the wrong thing to do. In this moment, she didn't care if he was taken.

326

Her feelings for him overwhelmed her, and she didn't care about the possible repercussions.

On the first ring he answered.

"Hey."

"It's Clara."

"I know."

Pause.

"What's up?"

"Oh," Benjamin then said nothing and asked Clara how she was.

"I want to see you," she said, skipping his question. "When can I see you?"

"Tonight?"

"Tonight," Clara confirmed.

Pause.

"You want me to come over to your place?" Benjamin asked.

"Yes."

"What time?"

"Whenever. Well, how about after dinner? No, wait, how about we go out for dinner?"

Benjamin said that was fine and then again asked her what time.

"Pick me up at 6:00. No," Clara then said 6:30 and asked him if he had heard about Christina.

"Christina who?"

"Boyer."

"Who's Christina Boyer?"

"You don't know her?" Clara fell silent, not knowing why she had even brought this up. "She's...this girl I knew. She was in Genesis Club. I guess I wasn't really friends with her. I used to be though."

"Oh," Benjamin said. "So, I'll see you at 6:30?"

"Yeah," Clara said, reluctant for a reason she couldn't immediately identify. "See ya."

Hanging up the phone, she considered Christina's funeral – would she attend and would she ask anyone to accompany her? She disliked going places alone almost as much as she disliked funerals, having gone to a number of them throughout her life, starting with her grandfather's when she was a small girl. The more she thought about it the more she debated whether or not she would attend. Christina and Clara had not been close throughout her entire junior year, had not even really been friends, maintaining a relationship that was perfunctory, preserved only through their association with Genesis Club.

Clara opened her closet to begin searching for what she would wear on her date tonight - wait, was this a date? She smiled to think she was even in the position to contemplate this question. No, she decided, she wouldn't go to Christina's funeral. And yes, she decided, this was a date, quite clearly this was a date.

Chapter 68

Benjamin had no plans to tell Karen. She wasn't the boss of him, if anything the dynamic of the relationship was the other way around. He could do as he pleased and didn't need to tell her he was going out with Clara. What would they do afterward? Would they do anything afterward? Was there any chance he might get her worked up to the point that she would want to have sex with him tonight? Afterward, he planned to take Clara back to his place. No doubt Karen would call sometime over the course of the night, if only because she hadn't so far today. Playing one of her pathetic childish games, Benjamin imagined, thinking she was waiting for him to call her, since lately she had been the one always calling him. When she did call he wouldn't answer. Let her leave a voicemail, he decided. *No, let her leave several voicemails before I call her back.* Then there was the chance she would get so worried about where he was that she would stop by, as she had done this many times before when Benjamin didn't pick up his phone. Doing this even after being fully aware how much this aggravated him. Doing this even after he had scolded her and punished her for her unwelcomed visits.

Should he just tell her the truth, if only to see her reaction? He wasn't afraid of losing her, so he didn't care if she found out about his date with Clara, or the unlikely possibility that she would summon the courage to break up with him for good. So many times before she had threatened to break up with him, but only once had she followed through. After three days of being single she had called him crying begging to come over so they could talk about the break-up. "What's there to say," Benjamin remembered saying to her, "We're through. I don't want to be with you." After he had hung up on her, she had called back and there was no answer. Four voicemails she had left him before he had finally picked up, "What the fuck do you want? Stop fuckin' callin' or I'm gonna –"

"Let me come over and I'll give you the best make-up sex of your life." Feeling slightly horny and so a little weak, Benjamin had acquiesced to her offer. He thought he would fuck her and then afterward tell her to leave, that he only had wanted the sex, that he didn't want to be her boyfriend again. Then something happened that he felt was impossible to predict. Once she came over he realized he had missed her, a little. Once he started having sex with her he realized he had missed her a lot. Then afterward as she started crying telling him how much she wanted to be with him, how much of a mess she had been being single and alone, even though they had only been broken up a short while, he had acquiesced to her request they go out again.

Wait, he wondered why he didn't take this into his own hands and dump her first, offer a succinct explanation that he just didn't like her anymore and then if she persisted in knowing more he would simply tell her he had fallen in love with Clara. Even if he hadn't fallen in love with her he would tell her this to make it clear there was no chance of getting back together.

What would Benjamin wear? The clothes he had worn to Clara's house he had bought his freshman year in high school, a time in his life when he had not yet begun dressing gothic. In his closet were lots of other clothes he wore throughout junior high, most of these still fit. For a moment, he analyzed his intention, thinking about why he had worn a preppy outfit in the first place, wondering if he had changed his way of dressing for one day as a way to manipulate or because he really wanted to change? Likely, at the time, he had worn the clothes and talked like he was a born-again Christian mainly to manipulate Meem, knowing she would allow Clara much more freedom in spending time with him if she liked him and thought he was a kind respectful Christian. Now, a certain side of him did want to change, fully aware that dating a nice sweet Christian girl like Clara would be a good start to changing his entire life.

Benjamin quickly changed into a short sleeved polo shirt and the same khaki cargo pants he had worn to Clara's. It was true that with this shirt on his tattoos were exposed. That was irrelevant, he thought, since he wouldn't be spending any time at Clara's, planned to call or text her when he was in the driveway. There would be no time for Meem to see and inspect him. For a moment he considered wearing his regular gothic clothes, if only because he knew Clara liked him for him. From the beginning, she had seen him for who he was, someone who was the complete opposite of her, essentially, someone who dressed weird and did drugs and got into trouble with the law and didn't go to church or even believe in God. Still, from the beginning, she had liked him. Why change now? Unable to say exactly why he felt the urge to start wearing these clothes he hadn't worn on a regular basis since December of his freshman year, all he knew is that he wanted to do everything in his power to make Clara trust him and enhance the feelings of affection he knew she so clearly had for him. Never would she lose her virginity to a man she didn't love and trust and care for deeply. Too, there was a certain side of Benjamin that wanted to make her happy, knowing that underneath that constant manufactured *I'm a light for Christ* smile a definite sadness lurked.

And then, as he put on his shoes and grabbed his keys, walking toward the front door, *Maybe I do want to change, not be such a badass motherfucker anymore, I don't know, I don't know what I believe, I don't even know what I want, if I want a relationship with her or if I just want to fuck her?*

Already it was 6:15, hadn't she said to be there by 6:30? No matter, she lived nearby. Suddenly, Benjamin wondered why he cared, never had he been the kind of person who felt compelled to be on time for someone else, most of the time he made sure it was the other way around. *Clara's much different from Karen though, if I don't treat her right from the beginning, I might scare her away, and if I scare her away I'll never get to have sex with her.* Then, starting the car and pulling out onto the street: *I wonder what she thinks of my tattoos, if she likes any of them?*

Chapter 69

All night it seemed they had been arguing over the skirt Clara had picked out to wear and the make-up she already wore. The skirt was rather short, at least three inches above the knee, but the make-up had been very modestly applied. Finally, Meem had acquiesced, if only because she was exhausted from yelling, exhausted from being yelled at, sitting down in her rocker as Clara went back upstairs to finish reviewing herself in the mirror. When Clara had received the text from Benjamin that he had arrived and was outside in the driveway, she had quickly descended the stairs and said bye to Meem, not looking at her as she walked out the front door but not before Meem got a few words in, "See where all this takes you…"

"What do you mean?!" Clara was upset by Meem's subtle warning, turning around in the doorway and staring at her, demanding some explanation. At first she had told herself to ignore the old woman, but she didn't understand! Meem had met Benjamin and had approved of him, so what was the problem?

"Mostly it's *that* skirt," Meem said. "Don't act like you don't *know!*"

Clara acknowledged the skirt was a little on the short side. "This is the way girls dress at my age! Girls going out on a date want to look their best. Besides you met him, you like Benjamin."

"This has nothing to do with that nice young man," Meem snapped, and then: "When girls dress that way they're asking for it."

Clara stood in the doorway, not knowing quite how to respond when Benjamin beeped, twice. "This conversation's not over," Clara said. "I'll be back when I feel like it."

"I said 9:30."

"No, when I feel like it," Clara said and then shut the door.

Benjamin thought she looked stunning. As she climbed into the car, he couldn't avoid noticing the length of her skirt. It was so short that when she relaxed into her seat she self-consciously pulled at the front and sides of it. Also, her makeup was so perfectly applied. Knowing a bit about makeup himself, Benjamin could decipher that she had put on a moderate amount, not too much, not too little. She wore sandals and her hair looked so soft and lustrous he wanted to reach over to run his fingers through it.

"Where are we going?" she asked suddenly.

"Where do you want to go?"

Clara didn't know. She wanted to ask if this was a date. "I'm not too hungry," she said.

"I thought you said you wanted to go out for dinner."

"I changed my mind. I had a big lunch." She fastened her seatbelt as he began to drive.

"Well we can drive around until you decide."

"Let's go back to your place!"

The plan wasn't to have sex with him, Clara would tell anyone it was just something that happened. When she suggested they go back to Benjamin's, she didn't know what her intention was, she just knew she didn't want anything to eat and wanted to be alone with him. On the ride to his place she talked nonstop, as though she was anxious, like she knew what was going to happen once they got to his trailer and wanted to get her nerves out now while she still had the chance.

Pulling into the trailer court driveway Clara was silent. Benjamin put his hand on her thigh, caressing her leg for a moment and then keeping his hand still. She looked over at him, smiling hesitantly. Pulling the keys out of the ignition, he leaned over to kiss her. She felt his tongue inside her mouth and then pulled away.

"Let's go inside," she said.

"Well, I want to kiss you," he said. "Isn't it all right if I kiss you first?"

The question must have been rhetorical because he gave her no time to answer it, as he began kissing her again, first only on the lips, as he had begun kissing her, and then with his tongue, moving inside her mouth and probing her with his tongue. Already Clara was wet. As she felt his hand move across her, rubbing her breasts and then moving down in between her legs she was aware she was wet. She reached down to unclick her seatbelt, feeling like she could take no more of this. "Let's go in," she said, breathless, pushing his hand out from underneath her skirt.

He took her hand and led her inside to his bedroom. When he climbed on top of her she could feel his hard penis pressing against her thigh. She lay there still gazing up into his eyes trying to decipher how he felt, trying to decipher how she felt, not knowing exactly what was going to happen, only knowing that she wasn't going to stop it.

Gradually he moved on top of her, running his hand up her leg as he did so. He began removing her clothes, slowly, motioning for her to lift her body up so he could undress her more easily. Clara surprised herself and Benjamin too as she reached down to unzip his pants, breathing heavily as she arched her back, closing her eyes as she gazed up at the ceiling, feeling herself grow wetter as Benjamin began massaging her vagina through her black panties. "I want you," he whispered in her ear as he slipped his tongue inside her mouth, feeling her respond immediately with her own tongue, moving it against his and then sliding it around inside his mouth.

Then her panties were off, she kicked them onto the floor as Benjamin pushed two fingers inside of her. Opening her eyes for a moment to stare sightlessly at the ceiling, Clara found herself putting her hand on top of Benjamin's head, feeling more pressure inside her vagina as she spread her legs, imagining he had three or even four fingers inside of her now. Moving his fingers in and out of her, Clara ran her fingers through his hair, moaning and tilting her head to the side as she closed her eyes and pushed Benjamin's head down, down, down between her legs wanting him to use his tongue on her. Removing his fingers, Benjamin began licking her vagina, moving his tongue around the hole, then flicker-licking her clit as he abruptly plunged three fingers back inside of her, and rotated their entire length around the barrel of her vagina.

An animal growl wrenched from her throat. "I want you too," she said suddenly, playing with his hair and moaning as he continued licking her, "I think I want it," she said, opening her eyes, staring down at Benjamin for a moment, her green eyes meeting his blue ones as he began working his tongue over her clit faster and harder.

"You think?"

"Now!" She moaned loudly. "Oh, God, I want it *now*..." Closing her eyes, she realized he had four fingers inside of her as she tilted her head back, arching her back further as she pushed her hips up into his face.

Benjamin didn't need her to say anything more. He reached into his pocket and pulled out a condom, ripping the plastic off and quickly wrapped his throbbing penis with it.

"Go slow," Clara said. "At first."

"All right." Benjamin looked into her eyes and grinned, feeling very eager as Clara spread her legs further apart. He entered her gently, inch by inch disappearing inside of her and Clara was surprised: this did not hurt nearly as much as she had anticipated. In fact, it felt rather good, although Clara understood the sex had not really started yet, since Benjamin was only inside of her and not moving in and out of her.

"You OK?"

Clara nodded, wrapping her arms around his neck as she felt his body cover hers so completely, all of the fear and anxiety she felt gone now.

Slowly, Benjamin's thrusts became faster, and harder, as he pumped himself inside of her she moaned, squeezing his shoulder blades and then wrapping her legs around him, interlacing them at the ankles, wanting to be, in a way, a part of him, wanting to be even closer to him, wanting him to never ever stop.

"Oh God," she said, her head lolling to the side as though she had lost all muscle control. "Oh God God *God!*" She began kissing him then, small quick passionate kisses, on the chest, as he moved over her body, on the neck, as he moved inside her, on the chin, as they moved as one.

Then he spread her legs further, lifting them up into the air and pulling her body into his, pumping himself inside of her, faster, and harder. "Clara," he said, his chest hovering above her face, moving in and out against her face. "*Clara*..."

She moaned, opening her eyes wanting to establish eye contact for a moment, gazing down seeing his penis moving in and out of her, in and out, in, out. Looking back into his eyes, she tried to block out the pain and feel only the pleasure.

Her head was draped off the side of the bed as Benjamin fucked her, thinking he was going very hard now and wondering why this wasn't hurting her more. Grabbing her legs, Benjamin pulled her even closer toward him, and her head was back onto the bed, resting on a pillow. For a moment Benjamin wanted to grab this pillow and suffocate her, have her die right here on his bed, have her die during sex, while he was inside her, on her first time no less. How beautiful that would be! What would he do with the body?

He grabbed her body, suddenly, turning her around so she faced the wall for a second thinking of Karen, wondering what she was up to, why she hadn't called him yet today. That was unusual. She generally called him first thing in the morning. Was she angry at him? There were a number of things he had done recently that she could be angry about. So what? What the fuck else is new? She'll get over it, by tomorrow she'll call me and if she doesn't I don't fucking care, I have Clara now.

Although, was that true? Did he have Clara now? Just because she had agreed to have sex with him, what did that mean? There had been no talk between them about a relationship, and she still knew Karen was his girlfriend, so what would she think the sex meant?

From behind, he started pumping himself inside of her, faster, and harder, feeling no love for her as he had felt initially, when he had first entered her. He stared closely at this rather delicate, vulnerable, trusting girl who was giving herself up to him. "Stop!" she cried.

Benjamin didn't listen to her request. Continuing to pump himself inside of her, he pretended not to hear her.

"Please stop!"

"Why?" Benjamin asked, not listening to her request, continuing to pump himself inside of her.

"That...hurts." He relented, finally. "I want...to do it...the other way."

"Like we started?"

She nodded and he turned her around aggressively, climbing on top of her body as he looked into her eyes. One glance and he quickly averted his gaze, her eyes were so warm and inviting and kind.

"Benjamin."

He was hesitant as he looked at her again, looking deeply into her eyes. The apprehension on her face had faded.

"Yes?"

"I love you," she said and smiled. It was a sweet, unpretentious smile that gave everything and demanded nothing. She was stating the simple truth, and the pure honesty of it melted Benjamin's cold heart.

Then he began making love to her. For the first time, perhaps in his life, he made love to a woman, feeling love for her. "I love you," he said, suddenly. Wait, had he said that? Did he love her? "I love you," again he said this, grabbing her legs and raising them up into the air wrapping them around his neck so he could go further inside of her, deeper inside of her. His thrusts were firmer now yet still so gentle. Tears filled his eyes, and he wondered if Clara noticed. In this moment, he thought about how much he loved her, how he wanted to love her always, for the rest of his life.

"You know I'm ready," Clara said quietly. "I'm ready to live now."

Benjamin had heard her, although didn't understand at all what she meant. The look he gave her was inquisitive and inspired her to continue.

"Now that I found you, someone who really loves me," Clara said, lost in the moment, her voice louder now and more insistent. "Someone I *know* who loves me, I'm ready to live."

Benjamin leaned down to kiss her on the forehead.

337

Chapter 70

'I fucked her brains out' - Karen received the text message as she was getting ready to go to sleep. Since she had been high the majority of the day, she had not called or even really thought of Benjamin. Right away, she knew who he was referring to. There was little doubt in her mind. The question was what would happen now that he had accomplished his goal? Would he continue fucking her? He had put so much work into gaining Clara's trust that Karen thought it unlikely he would get rid of her now. It still pissed her off. Even having known from the beginning his objective in befriending her, she thought what an asshole Benjamin was to throw it in her face like this. Why couldn't he do it with a little class? She didn't require knowledge of the event, although she wondered if Clara had enjoyed herself, even a little bit. Had the pain she experienced losing her virginity canceled out any pleasure she might have experienced? Karen hoped so. She hoped she'd been a weeping, bloody mess.

I'm going to kill her. The thought came to her so suddenly. *Just put my hands around her throat and strangle her to death.* It wouldn't be hard. She could easily kill Clara with her bare hands. Karen wondered how much Clara would fight back if she attacked her while it was just the two of them. How much of a struggle would there be? Certainly, Clara would fight for her life, fully understanding as Karen squeezed the life out of her that Jesus wasn't going to pull himself off that cross to intervene and save her now. It was ridiculous, of course. Karen knew she didn't have it in her to kill another person. Nonetheless, she found it amusing to consider the expression on Clara's face as she was dying, her expression so innocent and wide-eyed, begging Karen to stop. *Please, don't kill me, I'm a good girl really, you see I-I just made a mistake! I know premarital sex is a sin and I know Benjamin is your boyfriend and I'm s-sorry, I'm really sorry!*

Karen laughed thinking about what her last thought might be. Would she picture Jesus welcoming her into His loving arms? Would she utter one final prayer before she lost consciousness and died? Would her face change color as she was pushed toward the threshold of death? Blue, Karen thought her face would turn some subtle shade of blue. How hot it would be, Karen suddenly thought, to slip my tongue into her mouth and kiss her right as she was dying. How romantic, Karen thought, that my face would be the last thing she would see. What to do with her body though? And where would be the perfect place to kill her?

Expressionless, she looked again at the text message Benjamin had sent her. Why did he send this to her now? Why not wait to tell her in person? Of course, she knew how he thought she would respond. With a passionately livid text message, that's how. Karen understood that her anger would please him, that her becoming emotionally upset satisfied him to no end. Well, the fucker could die and rot, she wasn't going to give him what he wanted! She was done with his mind games. She didn't need him nor did she want him. As she drifted off to sleep that night she couldn't stop thinking about Benjamin and Clara, about how she wouldn't be sorry if they both died.

Chapter 71

Clara had not planned on spending the night. She had gone to sleep in his arms and by the time she awoke, it was dawn, the sun's early, feeble rays starting to shine through the window. At first, she felt disoriented, not knowing quite where she was, or how she had ended up here. Then she felt nervous, knowing Meem had expected her home last night. Had she stayed up all night waiting for her? That was possible, Clara thought, though not likely, since Meem knew she was with Benjamin and Meem liked and trusted and approved of Benjamin. Clara knew she would be in trouble, though. Certainly, Meem would punish her, but Clara didn't care about any of that now that she had Benjamin. She was unafraid now, unafraid of anything, anyone. He was still sleeping, his breath slow and even. Should she wake him up before she left? He looked very peaceful beside her. She didn't want to go home and be apart from him for any length of time. Whispering his name, she watched as he continued sleeping. "Benjamin," she said, louder this time.

"Hmm?" He turned over on his side, facing her with his eyes barely open. Thinking he might close them and go back to sleep quickly she said, "I fell asleep here. Did you know I fell asleep here?"

"Well, I know now." He smiled which made Clara immediately smile.

"We fell asleep together," she said, as if this was a revelation.

"Yeah." He sat up in bed and lit a cigarette.

Clara stared at him. "Aren't you going to give me one?"

"I didn't know you smoked." Benjamin handed her a cigarette and a lighter.

"Well, I heard from this girl in gym class that a cigarette right after sex is the best cigarette you can smoke in your whole life."

"That's right after you have sex, though." Benjamin laughed. "We haven't had sex in hours."

Clara kissed him on the lips before pulling away, or trying to pull away. He held her, touching her breast and then moving his hands between her legs.

"Benjamin..."

"What?"

"I have to go home! Meem's going to –"

"I wanna make love to you again."

Make love. Clara thought it sounded so sweet coming out of Benjamin's mouth. As he slipped his tongue into her mouth she forgot about Meem, unable to resist him now.

Chapter 72

Meem had not waited up for Clara. She knew she was in good hands and found herself unconcerned with the fact that she had severely violated her curfew. She had always thought Clara a rather sad, lonely girl. A little company wouldn't do her any harm. One of the questions she had, though, is what had they done all night? Had they stayed out somewhere all night or had they gone back to his house to sleep? Certainly, they had not slept together. Meem knew a good Christian boy like Benjamin wouldn't dare share a bed with Clara, knowing that was an act sacred and therefore saved for marriage. In any case, Meem would ask her the important questions when she got home, which she hoped might be very soon since there were dishes to be done and toilets to be scrubbed, plants watered.

When Meem heard the door open she rushed toward it to confront Clara. "Where have you been?" she asked in an even, calm tone.

"Hi Meem," she said, moving past her. "I've been with Benjamin, you know that."

"You were supposed to come home last night dear."

"Well, what can I say?" Clara began to climb the stairs. "We were having a really good time and I didn't want to leave."

Meem inspected her closely, as if she might be able to decipher answers by Clara's expression, or lack thereof. "What did you do all night? Did you sleep?"

"Not at all," Clara lied. "We went to a party."

"A party?" Meem asked suspiciously. "What kind of party?"

"Just some get-together in the woods. It was hosted by Genesis Club. I forgot all about it until Benjamin reminded me."

Meem looked suspicious still. "What did you do there?"

"What did we do? Played volleyball and talked mostly."

"All night?"

"Well they had a bonfire. Um, so we toasted marshmallows to make smores."

"Why didn't you call me then?"

"Oh, I guess I forgot, Meem! I was having so much fun and they didn't plan on the party lasting all night, that's just the way it played out."

"Oh," Meem said, nodding her head. "OK, well, there's chores that need done."

"What? I already cleaned the bathroom, I already did the laundry."

"You didn't clean the toilets, dear. And there are dishes in the sink. You never cleaned those up from the other night when you had your guests over."

"Oh, I'll get it done Meem," Clara said. "I'll get it done today. I just have to take a shower and make a phone call first." In fact it was Benjamin she wanted to call - she missed him already, wanting to talk to him, wondering what he was up to.

Meem said nothing as she stared at Clara for a good long while. "Very well," she said finally, dismissing Clara as she walked out into the kitchen.

Quickening her pace, Clara moved upstairs to her bedroom. Seeing the phone was not on the bureau where she had left it, she moved over to Meem's room. The phone was on her bed. Clara wondered who she had been talking to since she rarely spoke on the phone. In fact Meem had been on the phone with Debbie. Having received the package with the goodbye note, Meem had been more confused than angry. Only after speaking with Debbie for several long heated minutes had Meem become infuriated, understanding what the note had meant as Debbie briefly explained it. Well, Meem had hung up on her, feeling pleased with herself thinking she had gotten the last word in.

When Clara called Benjamin there was no answer. Hanging up she immediately called again. When there was still no answer she left a voicemail, feeling very anxious. Minutes later, taking her clothes off preparing for a shower, Clara called him again. Still no answer so she left another voicemail. "P.S.," she said. "I forgot to say I love you."

Taking off the rest of her clothes, she turned the water on in the shower and felt it until it was warm. She stepped in, then, feeling the water run all over her body, slowly falling into a daze, soon replaying the sex in her mind. Thinking about Benjamin on top of her as he moved inside her. Thinking about Benjamin closing his eyes in pleasure even as she closed hers in a delicious pain, biting her lip trying not to allow him know how much it hurt her. Running the bar of soap between her legs, wanting to make sure that moist secret place was as clean as possible, Clara thought about Benjamin. Thinking about his penis, how he had gently stuck it inside her. How she had moaned as he had pushed himself all the way into her, Clara remembered glancing down and seeing that his penis had disappeared entirely inside her. How confused she had been, not knowing how to feel as she experienced both pain and pleasure, far more pleasure than she had expected as he had pumped that huge cock of his inside her so forcefully.

Had he meant it? That was the question she had. When he said he loved her, were those words genuine? Clara wanted to think so, but she couldn't know for sure. As she squirted shampoo out onto her hand and started rubbing it into her hair, she had no idea, for how could she know whether Benjamin really loved her or if he had simply said those words out of pleasure, caught up in the passion of the moment?

Surely, he loves me, Clara thought, why else would he have sex with me? Of course, Clara wasn't so naïve as to believe that men only had sex with women they loved. She knew there were men who only had sex with women to get off. Players, they were called. She wanted to think this was different. Why else would he waste so much time getting to know me, she wondered. Why would he hang out with me so much if all he wanted was to have sex with me? *Besides, I am the one who wanted to have sex with him in the first place!* It was true Clara had been the one who suggested they go back to his place. She had not initiated it, but had let Benjamin take her inside to his bedroom. Benjamin had wanted to take her out to dinner. Why had she changed the plan? That hadn't been her intention, when she had been carefully selecting her outfit, nor had that been her intention when she had applied her makeup and done her hair. The suggestion of skipping dinner had been sudden and spontaneous. Something about the soft gentle look in his eyes, something about the way he had dressed so preppy that reminded her of Jeremy, something about wanting to so desperately escape Meem. Clara would tell anyone that it was a combination of these three things that had made her so suddenly want to have sex with him. Never before had he had time alone with her, so when she had said she wanted to return to his house there had been little doubt in her mind that he would take the opportunity to have sex with her. She had been right with her prediction. There had been a moment when she had experienced some hesitation, sitting in his driveway feeling herself lose control as she grew wet with him kissing her. Quickly, though, that had passed as she had considered how much she liked Benjamin, in that moment thinking too how much he liked her, feeling so much passion in the way he kissed her, thinking how handsome he was, how she wanted to be with him forever.

What about Karen? That was a problem Benjamin would have to solve later, but Clara did feel somewhat guilty for sleeping with him. After all, he was Karen's boyfriend. She had already had sex with him, though. The deed was done and there was nothing she could do now, so why worry? Worrying was a sin, or so the bible said, but she didn't believe that. She suddenly found herself not believing a lot of what was in the bible. Like how it said that all sin is equal in the eyes of the Lord. How could this be so? That would mean worrying was just as bad as stealing, that premarital sex was just as bad as murder.

Getting out of the shower, Clara found herself feeling confused and somewhat alarmed. She had never acknowledged fully to herself how silly some of the things in the bible sounded to her. It was true she had realized that certain things just didn't seem acceptable to her, like how it said homosexuality was a sin. Clara had a first cousin who was gay, or so she'd heard. She had been close to him as a child and always believed gay people were born that way, that homosexuality was determined by biology. How could it be right, then, to oppress and marginalize gay people? Besides, Clara thought now, the bible is a document that was written so long ago, how can it still be relevant now? A sudden sense of panic rose within her. Christianity had always been her foundation, and now she found herself lost in doubt, filled with questions. Certainly, there were other Christians that had found themselves in a similar predicament. What had they done in this situation? Had her Valium prescription been filled?

Hurrying to her bedroom, she pulled open the bottom drawer of her bureau. The bottle was gone. She then remembered throwing the bottle out since there had been no refills left, having used the pills up prematurely. It would be weeks before the doctor would call in another prescription. She could call Benjamin! She had already called him though. Why hadn't he answered? Again the image of him inside her, making love to her, his penis inside of her. She sat down on the bed then sprawled herself across it, unable to erase him from her mind. It made her anxious that she could not reach him now and she wondered what he was doing, if she would see him again soon. Should she call again maybe? Or wait for him to call her? Of course she thought it possible he hadn't listened to her voicemails yet, that he wasn't even near his phone. *No, that can't be, he always has his phone with him!* Clara picked up the phone to call him again.

Benjamin found himself getting hard again. Thinking about Clara, seeing that she had called and wanting to call her back as soon as possible. The first time she had called he couldn't answer. He had left his phone in his bedroom when he had stepped outside for a moment to buy some drugs from his regular dealer. By the time he noticed she had left him two voicemails, he was already high in his bedroom playing around on his drum set. Wanting to have sex with her again badly, he reached for the phone.

"H-hello?"

"What's up?" He decided not to inquire why she sounded hesitant.

"Benjamin! Well, nothing much..." The excitement in her voice she could not conceal. "What are you doing?"

"Getting high." Benjamin decided not to lie. As he crushed another line of Percocet with his driver's license, he considered asking Clara if she wanted to try some.

"Oh." Sounding like she wanted to say more, for a moment Benjamin waited. She said nothing.

"Wanna come over?"

"Sure! Well I mean yes. I'd like to see you again."

"Come over then," he said. "Do you need a ride?"

"No, well I don't think Meem will mind bringing me over."

"See you soon then."

The line went dead before she could say anything else.

When Benjamin hung up, he thought about how much he liked her. There was no question in his mind. What did that mean, though? There were many girls he liked, so many he was capable of liking, what made her any different from the rest of them? But there was something, he was sure of that, something about her that made her different, something that made her stand apart from almost every girl he had ever known. What was it? The fact she had a faith, that she had such a strong belief in Jesus Christ as Lord and Savior? To be fair, Benjamin thought he couldn't dismiss that as the reason, not wanting to think Clara's Christian beliefs could be responsible for making her more attractive to him than perhaps any girl he had ever met. And different from the rest yes very different. He liked that a lot.

Reaching for his phone, surprised to see Karen had not texted or called, he considered calling her, feeling very fucking irritated that she hadn't responded with anger, or hurt – how he had imagined she would respond. He wanted to call her, suddenly found himself calling her, planning to tell her that they were done, their relationship over because he liked Clara too much. Certainly this information would produce the response he hoped for.

"What do you want a prize or something?" Karen asked. "You fucked her so now what?"

"Well, it's more than that. So much more than that. And I didn't realize it until last night."

Silence.

"Karen?"

"What?"

"Did you hear me?"

"I was waiting for you to elaborate."

"I don't have much more to say, I –"

"What the fuck does that mean?" Karen asked. "You say *it's more than that*, I –"

"I'm breaking up with you," Benjamin said. "I don't want to prolong the suspense…that would be cruel."

Karen started to sob, suddenly overcome by what she had dreaded would happen.

"This morning I asked Clara to be my girlfriend, and –"

"What? I thought you only wanted to have sex with her, I thought you were –"

"Karen, listen to me, I'm not going to repeat myself. Clara said yes, Clara's my girlfriend now, so look, I wanted to let you know as soon as possible, I thought that's only fair."

Karen sniffled several times, rather successful in her attempt to repress her sobs. "How did, how did this happen?"

"It evolved, what can I say? I didn't know I'd fall in love. I like you, Karen, but we're done, you see, we're the past, we already happened."

Then Karen began crying uncontrollably, her sobs loud and unabashed. "What the fuck Benjamin, what do you mean? You don't mean that!"

Click! Benjamin hung up on her. Moments later, when she called back, Benjamin did not answer.

Chapter 73

Numerous times today Clara had asked God for forgiveness. Premarital sex was a sin, she had been aware of that when she had made the sudden decision to have sex. She had simply not been thinking about what was right and good in the eyes of the Lord. Now that she had been alone awhile and apart from him she seemed to be thinking about God more, remembering how it said in the bible that a woman should wait until marriage to have sex. Now that she was no longer a virgin Clara wondered if God was angry, or at least disappointed, with her. No, she determined, He couldn't be, for God was supposed to be merciful, and already she had prayed for forgiveness. So now that she knew God forgave her, did that mean she would have sex with Benjamin again? That was a question in her mind for which she had no immediate answer.

Benjamin still wasn't saved – the thought came to her very suddenly. All this time she had spent with him and still she had not confronted him on his faith. On her way out the door she grabbed her bible, praying that today would be the day Benjamin's soul would be saved.

Chapter 74

Had she heard him right? Karen didn't know if it could be true, didn't want to believe it could be true. In a panic she had called him back, thinking he might change his mind, thinking that if they talked this over surely he would rethink things. Over and over she called him and he had not answered. Now, left alone in her bedroom with her parents both at work, her first impulse was to buy an enormous amount of drugs. By the time she had stopped crying she realized she had no money. Besides, getting high would solve nothing, would likely make matters worse. Then she remembered the three Xanax in the rear pocket of her shorts, the ones she had worn two nights ago. Not wanting to think about this situation anymore, she grabbed her shorts from the dirty clothes basket and quickly crushed the pills into several thick messy lines. With a rolled-up five dollar bill, she blew the lines in a matter of seconds, immediately relaxed by the strong familiar sense of euphoria.

For a moment feeling like she didn't care about anything Benjamin had just said, Karen grabbed her car keys off the bureau. She would drive over to Benjamin's house. She would drive over to his house right now to talk to him. She had to talk to him right now, had to make him see he was making a bad decision. He was picking the wrong girl, didn't he understand? *We're soul mates, you must know by now Benjamin. I'm the one you want. Me!*

Chapter 75

Sex was one of the furthest things from her mind that afternoon when she arrived at Benjamin's. Holding her bible close to her chest as she stepped out of the car, Clara waved goodbye to Meem as she drove away, shouting out the window that she would be back in time to pick Clara up for dinner and she had better get those chores done tonight. Clara had every intention of initiating a conversation about Jesus Christ and how Benjamin could be saved through Him. She hadn't even reached the front door when it opened suddenly, Benjamin standing there wearing only shorts and a big grin on his face. He couldn't wait to take off her clothes.

"What are you smiling about?" Clara asked.

"Maybe that's just my natural reaction when I see you."

Clara started to blush, could this be true?

"What do you have there?" he asked.

"My bible. It's the new international version and –"

He grabbed her by the hand, pulling her in close to him, kissing her on the lips, slipping his tongue inside her mouth. "I love you," he said.

The bible fell out of her hand, landing on the front stoop as Benjamin led her inside to his bedroom. Stunned by his sudden passion, Clara had no time to tell him she loved him too. Surely, though, he understood she must have loved him, for she disregarded her bible and did not protest when he began removing her clothes. Seconds later he was inside her, holding her hand at first as he penetrated her. Closing her eyes, she tilted her head to the side. Gently then he began to make love to her.

Chapter 76

When Karen arrived at Benjamin's the first thing she noticed is that he was home - his car in the driveway in its usual spot. Perfect. She pulled her keys out of the ignition and crept toward the trailer. Neither of his parents were home, his mom and stepfather's cars were both gone. Karen knocked on the door and waited.

When no one came to the door, Karen prepared to knock again. Then she heard something. A series of quiet very definite sounds that denoted motion, movement of some sort. So, Karen knew he was home. What was he doing?

Moving to the side of the trailer, where his bedroom was, where the sounds were coming from, Karen continued hearing the same sounds, they were still soft though growing louder now.

Karen grabbed a milk crate that was sitting on the ground next to the garbage cans. Standing up on that, the crate provided her enough extra height so she could peer inside the window.

Benjamin and Clara!

They were both naked on his bed having sex. For a moment Karen could only watch, frozen in the window, eyes widening, watching the bed shake and the headboard slightly bang against the wall as Benjamin fucked her. *I hope he's hurting that ridiculous little cunt.* It was the only thought in her mind at this time. Then all she could feel was rage and hate pumping through her veins, her heart pounding as she approached the front door.

Neither Benjamin nor Clara had heard her knocking the first time. Positive that someone was at the front door, Benjamin pulled out of

Clara even as she tried to hold onto him tighter. "Where are you going?" she asked.

Still on top of her, Benjamin turned his head, listening. "Someone's at the door."

"Well I don't hear anything." And indeed, the knocking had ceased. Benjamin heard the front door squeak, slowly opening.

Entering the trailer on her own would infuriate Benjamin, she knew, realizing now she just didn't fucking care. She could see him still in his bedroom, in the process of throwing on some clothes as though she hadn't seen him naked before. "What are you doing here?" He was surprisingly calm, though Karen could see as he stared at her that his eyes were filled with hate.

"I wanted to talk...about us. What you said on the phone, you didn't mean that, I know you didn't mean that."

"I did mean it," Benjamin said. "You are history to me. Don't you understand that, Karen? You don't exist."

Wanting to get at Clara, knowing that the silly bitch was in there, although also knowing that Benjamin didn't know that she knew, Karen tried to push past him. Benjamin stood there firmly, a barrier. "I know she's in there," Karen then started to yell, "I know that stupid cunt is in there -"

Benjamin grasped her shoulders, attempting to move her toward the door so she would leave.

"LET GO OF ME!"

The knives were in the kitchen in a butcher block right next to the toaster. Only three knives were there today. Benjamin stepped toward her as Karen grabbed all three knives - two butcher knives and one smaller knife that she thrust into her back pocket. Without thinking, she spun around and sunk one of the butcher knives into Benjamin's throat. He fell to the floor, grabbing at his throat as blood poured out of him and onto the white linoleum.

Clara screamed, grabbing Benjamin's cell phone and dialing 911.

Karen burst into the bedroom, right as Clara slammed the door shut and tried to lock it.

Covering her naked body with a white sheet, she screamed as Karen lunged toward her, stabbing her in the stomach and dropping the other butcher knife in the process.

Collapsing onto the floor, Clara held her stomach as blood seeped onto the carpet. Without even thinking now Clara reached out, seeing the butcher knife that Karen had dropped. Her hand was on the handle when Karen stabbed her again, sinking the knife into her heart. Clara gasped for breath, throwing one of her hands up in an attempt to defend herself as Karen grabbed the knife she had been trying to retrieve.

"*P-please...*" Clara wheezed briefly, her body shaking as blood spilled out onto her naked chest.

Karen raised the knife, about to stab her again when Clara's head rolled to the side, her body wholly still.

Rushing to her feet, thinking she should somehow clean up the crime scene, Karen saw Benjamin dead on the kitchen floor and then heard the sirens outside. The police were here, and she knew now she could not escape without being arrested.

Printed in the United States
By Bookmasters